Totally Bound Publishing books by Ellen Mint

Happily Ever Austen
Pride and Pancakes
Rash and Rationality
Madeline's Park

Coven of Desire
Retail Hell
Claw
Snow Print
Fang
Whisper
Badge
Wings
Scales

Collections
Some Like it Haunted: Ink
My Bloody Valentine: Love's Curse

Coven of Desire

SCALES

ELLEN MINT

Scales
ISBN # 978-1-80250-521-4
©Copyright Ellen Mint 2023
Cover Art by Kelly Martin ©Copyright March 2023
Interior text design by Claire Siemaszkiewicz
Totally Bound Publishing

Published in 2023 by Totally Bound Publishing, United Kingdom.

Totally Bound Publishing is an imprint of Totally Entwined Group Limited.

SCALES

Dedication

To those thirsting for some demon peen,
this book is for you.

Prologue

Twenty years ago…

Death drifted on the wind. The well-to-do Parisians and their *au pairs* couldn't sense it. The sun was warm and the air fragrant with roses. Children dashed about in the park, caring nothing for skinned knees as they raced each other down the slides. I clutched my bag closer to my side, hoping my spell book would soothe my nerves. It too radiated a warning that I couldn't place. Everything was wrong except to my eyes and ears.

I scanned the entire park with my peripheral vision, dragging my nails along the blue leather of my book. *There!* Among the bushes stood a shadow darker than night itself. Could it be —

"Mama!"

"Holy…!" I slapped my chest and pulled in a breath. "Laylee." All I saw were her big brown eyes gleaming with a dangerous combination of mischief and joy.

"Shouldn't you be playing?" I gazed back at the other children clustered around a patch of snails.

"I did, but…" In her tiny hands, she lifted up a fallen ribbon of neon purple. Her mouth was turned down in disappointment, as if she'd failed. I took the strip of satin and she obediently turned around, only for me to stare in confusion at the two puffs on her head. One was perfectly formed, with the ribbon tied into a bow. The other had been smooshed by whatever had torn the second ribbon free.

"Let me." Didi reached over and took the ribbon.

Layla gave a little chuckle, as if she knew who the real talent in our awkward family was. Then she shifted to the side and waited. Didi reformed the puff she'd put in Layla's hair in a split second, then tied in the ribbon. "There." She patted Layla's shoulders and turned her around. "Now don't you go losing that. Purple's special."

"M'kay," she said, then launched onto her toes to kiss Didi's cheek. Layla always kissed her over the scarring, and I winced each time.

But Didi only patted her cheek as if sealing in the kiss, then waved her back to her new friends. With her hair secured, Layla approached one of the larger boys, who wore far too nice clothing to be roughhousing on the playground. At least they seemed to be getting along. The boy handed her one of the larger balls. She bounced it on the ground and laughed.

"This is good for her," Didi said.

I sighed at the unspoken argument.

"She needs to figure out how to make friends."

"Why? She has us, and when she comes of age, she'll have a coven."

Didi stared at me like I was mad, but it was how I'd been raised. How she'd tried to raise me, anyway.

Pulling her purse into her lap, Didi said, "There's more to life than just the craft."

"Like what?"

My oldest friend nodded to Layla bouncing the ball with the boy. "Like that."

I scoffed at the idea. "Laylee's only —"

"Five. And in another twenty years..."

She'd have to continue the line, by any means necessary. Old memories churned inside my heart. I shuddered to find my palm pressed to the heart locket dangling from my neck. I wasn't foolish enough to put a picture in there, but the memory itself was a danger to me and to her. *I should throw it away.*

"You've got that look in your eye," Didi said.

"The air's wrong."

"Great. First nice day in a month, and the air's gone bad." She stretched her arms and fell back against the bench. "What is it? Monster? Demon?"

I dragged the locket back and forth on the chain, listening to the wind. "I'm not sure. It tastes of...fear, but also pride." I smacked my tongue, the metallic twang of iron sliding down my throat.

"Damn it!" The English curse rang out amongst the French from behind. I glanced over my shoulder as Layla's ball skittered off the clay ground and into the bushes. It struck something near them, something so black I couldn't make it out. Then, it bent over.

"Oh, no."

Layla dashed after her ball at hyper speed. A hand and a bright white sleeve protruded from the darkness.

"Didi..." I fought to keep my tone level as my daughter stopped before the smiling face of Conquest.

"Fucking hell." Didi tore through her purse, tossing her book out. I leaped to my feet, chasing after Layla, who'd frozen before the man in white.

"*Bonjour*," he said, every syllable like chewing tinfoil. I rolled my hand, cracking through the shield of realms and overloading myself with power. The man in white picked up her ball and held it above her head. "You're supposed to say '*bonjour*' back."

"Bun-jur," she muttered, her eyes on the grass.

A shield, that'll stop him. Unless he punctures through it just like...

He reached a hand out and I raised my palm, prepared to launch the first spell I could think of, even in public. The man in white bounced a finger against Layla's ribbon and she sneered.

Whipping her head back, she clasped her hands over her hair. "No."

All he did was laugh. "As obstinate as your..." He raised his gaze and leveled it at me. Memories of the dark corridors, the screams and stench of burning flesh, tried to boil in my brain. I clenched my fingers, willing the flush of magic to chase it away.

"Here." He held out the ball. Layla stared at it a moment, then she lashed out her hands to snatch it away and took a step back. "Be careful with your toys or you might lose them."

She nodded, her ribbons shaking in the dead air. Layla glanced over her shoulder and cried out, "Mama."

I held my hand out to her, willing her to run to me. The man in white stood close enough he could whisk her away...or do the unthinkable. The wind shifted and I cast my shield. Layla shrieked and dashed for me. He didn't grab her, but slowly stood as I caught my daughter by the shoulders and pinned her safe against my legs. She held me so tight I feared I'd fall, but I wouldn't look away from him.

Didi ran up beside me. She hefted Layla into her arms and cast a protection around them.

The man in white laughed. "Seems you still have one toy remaining, witch." He tipped his hat at us. "Until we meet again."

I wrenched my arm back, ready to rip the entire park apart with hurricane winds, but Conquest vanished into the shadows. The birdsong returned and the air lightened without the crushing weight of the Horseman.

Tears streamed down Layla's cheeks, but she didn't make a sound. Didi tended to her as I shored up the tatters I'd made in the barrier. After wiping Layla's face, Didi looked to me. "Izzy, what do we do?"

"We keep moving."

With Layla safe in Didi's arms, the three of us dashed to the small apartment we'd need to abandon yet again. We were in such a hurry that we never noticed the ball that fell from Layla's hands. There wasn't time for her tears.

Chapter One

Layla

"Mom?"

Fifteen years. For fifteen years, I'd stumbled alone in the dark. No mother to teach me how to drive, to show me what tampons to buy, to coo over my prom dress or embarrass me at graduation. I had faced every harsh sunrise alone, my family...my whole world ripped from me bit by bit.

"Hello, Layl—"

I ran to her and buried my face in my lost mother. Instead of her soft belly cushioning my tears, it was her shoulder that caught me. Uncertain hands patted my back, and as I crushed tighter against her, she returned the hug. I'd never thought I'd feel those arms again.

Never imagined I'd hear her voice calling to me.

The scents of jasmine and burnt wiring plunged a rosy spear of nostalgia through my heart and I sobbed. I'd broken her bottle of perfume my first week in the foster home. It'd shattered on the sink. Even with glass shards slicing up my fingers, I'd tried desperately to mop it up so I wouldn't lose it. So I wouldn't lose her.

Nimble fingers tugged through my hair, parting the twists as she cupped the nape of my neck. A tingle I'd always thought came from my imagination pulsed at her touch. Now I knew it to be magic, my mother casting a spell to calm me as if I were a child in a panic after a nightmare.

"You..."

My arms fell away from her. She'd left. She hadn't just left—she had made certain I wouldn't follow. That I couldn't follow. I staggered back, punch drunk from the emotions roiling in my heart. Wrinkles had built near her eyes and her cheeks sagged, but it was my mom. Looking at her, the years I'd spent building over the scar of her death ripped away.

"You left."

She smiled dolefully. "I know. I didn't have a choice, but that's in the past. What matters is what happens next."

"In the past?" In the fifteen years of mourning her, my grief callous had hardened over a node of rage. Seeing her broke it open.

"Do you have any idea what I've been through because I didn't have a...?" My lips wobbled, tears spilling over at the word 'mom.'

"Laylee." She sighed with my old pet name. I shivered, both in anger and...relief to hear it again. "What matters is you've done it, gained your powers and your..." She jerked her head to my purse. On instinct, I slapped a hand over it to protect my spell book, but that only made my mother smile with pride.

"Though, I'm concerned."

So am I.

"It was quick thinking of you to amplify the realm creature, but you should have been much stronger fighting against the man in white."

What? "You! You were there. You were there at the house, the monster ball. And you didn't say anything!"

My mom shrugged, and her blonde braid slipped off her shoulder. The woman, the face behind the mask in the crowd—it had been her and I'd walked on past. I hadn't even once looked back to her. She could have been killed because of me, and I'd never have known.

"Lucky for you, I was. I saved your life. If you'd been hit by that abomination's spell, it'd have cast you through every realm into depths I can't even imagine." She crossed her arms as if she expected gratitude—like she'd brought my lunch to school after I'd left it on the table.

I clenched my fist, rolling the power inside of me down my forearm, over the back of my hand and into my palm. It ebbed with each pulse as I sank my nails deeper and fought to keep from screaming. "You left. You left me alone for fifteen years."

"Layla, now is not the time."

"You abandoned me!" I shrieked and opened my fist. Fire sprang forth, dousing the green-tan grass in flames. My mother pursed her lips and raised her hand.

Even though I knew she had to be a witch, seeing wind erupt from her movements floored me. She had magic, same as me. She was the only person who'd known what I'd face, and she had left me in the dark instead.

"Honestly, this is not the place to be—"

"How long have you watched me? How long have you stood by the sidelines refusing to help me?" I gripped my temples, my body shaking. I rewound through my past. Every time I'd feared for my life, had my mother been there? Even back before my powers, before Ink and the book? When I'd been kicked out of the system with nothing to my name but the clothes in my backpack, where had she been? When I'd slept in a rat-infested apartment because it was all I could afford, had my mother known?

"There's a lot you don't understand yet. Look…" My mother reached out to wrap her arm around my shoulders, but I ducked away.

"I understand perfectly well. I know you faked your death, that you killed an innocent woman—"

"She was going to die anyway," my mother interrupted.

It sure as hell hadn't looked that way in my vision, but I clenched my jaw and kept going. "And you left me. You left me alone."

"Layla. That isn't what—"

I dodged her again, both of my palms up. Power crackled between us, the air tasting like lightning right before the strike. "And the second you find me, when you come back into my life, it's just to tell me I'm not good enough?"

"It's not that you aren't…" She groaned and pinched her nose. "Didi's better at this."

I gulped at the mention of my dead auntie. Just when I'd accepted my mom was never coming back, Death had snatched Didi away, too. Had my mother known that as well and still refused to come back?

"Please, let me explain why I—"

"No. No, I'm not… I can't deal with… Ink!" I closed my eyes tight, picturing my incubus, from his jet-black waves to his come-hither smirk and down his sinful body. I zeroed in on the new tattoo on his chest of a heart made of chains. As I pictured it, hands swept across my waist and my cheek pressed against a pec.

"You rang?" Ink asked.

I clasped my hands around the back of his neck. Ink jerked as if surprised, then he tenderly swept his arms around me. "My bond, are you suffering yet from the angel's malady?"

"Who's this?" my mother demanded, her hands raised to cast a spell at the man holding me safe.

"I was about to inquire the same. An enthusiastic grave robber perhaps?"

I turned a single eye back to my mother, the other buried in the darkness of Ink's chest. "She's no one," I said. "Take me home."

Ink wasn't stupid. He stared at the woman with my face but paler and less voluptuous features. Still, he caressed his palm over my back as he said, "While I am not one to call a lie a lie, perhaps it would be in —"

I turned tighter in his grip and gasped out, "Please."

He bent closer, his lips almost caressing my forehead. "Of course." Ink swept me up in his arms and the realms parted. My skin tingled in a way it never had before as Ink took a step out of the cemetery and back to our home.

Just before he did, my mother cried out, "Layla," one last time.

Chapter Two

Garavel

It was wrong of me to enjoy this. Sunlight cut through the clouds to warm my skin. I flattened my wings to let the thermal winds lift me higher into the sky. Far below, a tiny version of myself skipped across a tiny pond where a little deer was drinking.

The world was at peace, and it was all my fault.

What'd the lady witch call it? A lazy Sunday, not to be confused with the sundae that came with nuts and hot fudge. If those were lazy, they'd become sundae soup. My stomach rumbled, a strange sensation that had begun when I'd done the unthinkable. Hunger, exhaustion, pain—what'd once been abated by the overflowing love of my creator were now my constant reminder of how I'd failed him.

Holding my arms outstretched, I let the hot winds take me where they wanted and closed my eyes. The last time I'd traveled these lands, the skies had been dark as pitch for months. Fire had tumbled from the clouds in place of rain. And impenetrable towers had formed out of the bones of the Earth, jutting from the broken terrain.

Still, we had celebrated, all of us around the ring of angel fire. It kept us warm without casting any light to warn the enemy. Though we'd laughed so much that night, passing the last bottle of nectar between us, it was a wonder the mages didn't hear. As the demi-angels slumbered on the ground, our assigned witch had drifted away.

Staring across the blackened and charred remains of creation, she'd listened to the howls of the mages' twisted experiment and asked, "What happens now?"

Almost everyone in my company had died that day, including the witch I'd sworn to protect. But I didn't want to remember that—their bodies broken and faces shattered. Wherever a demi-angel died, their blood created a paradise. The blood of creation never ended, it only changed for the next life.

"What happens now?" Her soft plea rang in my ears, the woman eons dead.

I'd wanted to tell her something wonderful. That one day we'd win, the mages would lose and all would be right with the realms, thanks to the Accord. But I couldn't, because the wolves attacked and I never spoke to her again.

"What happens now?" I repeated, opening my eyes. I'd flown out of the forest formed from the bones and blood of my friend. Instead of the serenity of the garden, my wings took me back to where I'd run to after I'd collapsed my whole world. I didn't deserve what she had given me, but I couldn't turn it down either. Where else was a murderous angel to go?

A soft pair of whiskers brushed against the back of my head. I reached behind with a finger and the tiny kitten emerged from my wings. She'd been tucked up in a nap, nestled on top of my sword in the ether, and I hadn't had the heart to wake her. Even high in the sky, little Fiona had no fear. She walked onto the nape of my neck with steady legs, her claws scratching down my ebony skin.

"Are you hungry?" I asked, dangling my finger for the sharp jaws. She strolled out onto my shoulder, peering over to the long fall below. Fiona gave a single sharp meow. I didn't speak cat, but I'd guess she either wanted a treat, to be placed down, or was about to sharpen all ten of her claws on my back. It was usually one of those three.

I tucked a wing in, rolling onto my back so the kitten would walk onto my chest. As I went, a great rumbling rose from my stomach and I slapped a hand over it. "I think I might be hungry, too." A scent rose in the air, one of fire and ash. It should have read as death, but my mouth began to water. "Something smells…"

Cupping Fiona close, I turned. Smoke belched from the back of my lady witch's castle. *No!* Conquest must have found her. I flew with all haste around the neighborhood, circling lower. The large metal beasts roaming the roads bleated at the sight of me, but I didn't care. I had to protect her. I had to save her after everything that —

Instead of a great fire, only a hint of smoke rose from a black rectangle in the back garden. And the machine was tended by the mage's pet. They gave beasts a bad name. Tucking my wings in, I dove for the monster cruelly skewering something into the smoking machine. He had no idea I was there, my descent as quiet as the owl's until Fiona meowed.

The werewolf stared up and slammed the lid on his torture device. I flung my wings open wide and the wind pulled me back until I nearly hovered above his head.

"You about gave me a heart attack," he said, wiping a hand through his white-yellow hair. It left a black handprint as he did, which made me grimace. The beasts would often mark themselves so crudely to keep track of who belonged to whom.

He returned to whatever he was murdering, only glancing up to me once. "Are you going to land before my neighbors call the cops? Or put you on TikTok?"

I didn't know what this Tok Tik was, but it sounded deadly. Dropping to the ground, I placed Fiona on my shoulder and squared off against the werewolf. He paid me no mind, which had been his constant state since I had taken to sleeping in the attic. "What are you killing in there?"

"What?"

"Fire, smoke, ash and..." I pointed to his torture device. He'd laid another set of them on a table beside the machine. One had a flat head with holes in the middle, no doubt to amplify the speed with which it could damage flesh.

"You mean this spatula?" He lifted the flat one, then laughed. "I'm not killing anything. I'm making dinner. You know, food, that thing you keep eating. And the demon. At least I don't have to feed Dan. Yet." The werewolf closed the lid just as I began to peek.

I reared back at the clang, my hand reaching back for my sword before I thought to. The wolf stared long at me. "You really think I'm killing something in here?"

"It wouldn't surprise me. Werewolves would often kick smaller, helpless creatures into their master's fire."

"For fuck..." He slammed the tool to the table and stalked closer. "I don't have a moon-damn master. Or a mage. Or anyone telling me what to do. Here, look. It's burgers. That thing you ate a whole bag of when Layla got takeout." He yanked the hood up, revealing small patties of meat sizzling on the fire.

My stomach rumbled at the heavenly smells and pops of fat. Even Fiona peered out from my wings to breathe deep.

"No dead fairies, or imps or tiny rabbits. Satisfied?"

He sounded as if he'd won, the noise grating on my nerves. "There's nothing stopping you from doing it later."

The wolf scoffed once, shaking his head and turning away from me. Fiona tried to leap off my shoulder for him, but I caught her mid-flight. She grumbled as I returned her to the safety of my feathers. While hunger rolled in me, I would have preferred to harvest berries from the forests than eat with him. I took a step to leap into the air, when the wolf sighed.

"Is this how it's always gonna be?"

"What?"

He raised his hands, then dropped them to his sides. "I saved your life. Doesn't that mean something?"

Your brethren murdered all of my friends. It means nothing.

Rather than respond, I turned my back on him. A dangerous move to a wild animal, but I knew I could take him in a fight...and Fiona would warn me. When he did not attack with his small pitchfork, I jumped, taking flight.

If I hadn't killed my creator to protect the accords, to save...everything they had died for, I'd be underground. I'd be asleep in the alcove, waiting for the next turn of the Celestial wheel. Instead, I had nowhere to go save a firm nest of sheets atop the house's beams. I deserved worse for my betrayal.

My little passenger meowed and brushed her chin against my cheek. Her gentle rumbling made me smile and I flapped into the sky.

"Hey, would it kill you to not take off from my backyard? The FAA is going to shoot you down."

I paid no heed to the werewolf's baying and took off for the sun. But as I went, I dropped a few feathers straight onto his flames and meat.

Chapter Three

Ink

When we arrived at the house, I anticipated my bond pushing out of my arms. Instead, she lingered, her face pressed to my chest. No sobs erupted from her lips, yet the whole of her being shuddered in anticipation of tears—like the air before a storm's rumble.

I cupped my hand to the back of her head, gifting her the time she needed until she slipped out, her feet striking the front porch. She dabbed at her eyes and focused on a package left before the door. "Thanks," was all she said as she picked up the box. "Even more books for Daniel?"

"The dead are not known for wise fiduciary decisions," I said. Layla stared at me and I shrugged. "As long as they retain two pennies, their afterlife is secure."

She snickered nowhere save her lips and I, in turn, frowned. Waving her hands, she parted the protection spell that did little beyond masking the house from obvious magic. Just as she was about to cross the threshold, I caught her hand.

"Shall we discuss the woman—?"

"She's no one!"

"My bond." I stared her dead in the eye. Even were I a simple mortal, the resemblance and gap in age were obvious. As I was greater, I could see the tendrils of parentage connecting the two.

Layla shrank in place. I swept her into my embrace and plucked the ghost's spending spree from her hands. She needn't concern herself with his mess when her own grew exponentially. "I don't want to talk about it," she said.

"While I myself am a renowned proponent of secrecy, are you not concerned about how the wolf will react when the truth is revealed?"

It seemed they'd only just repaired matters after their last rift—though both had borne the same brunt of obscuring truths. Now, the lie would rest squarely on her shoulders. And with a Horseman prowling the city, it wouldn't do well for the wolf to run into the forest in a snit.

"I'm not lying to him, I just...I can't deal with it right now. You know?"

"No," I said, shaking my head. "The more painful a subject, the more readily a sin embraces it."

"Must be nice," she muttered. "Everything's a mess. White's coming, the angel's dead, the entire universe could get torn to shreds at any second and my mom shows up? She left me and she just... No. I can't. I'm sorry." Her heart slowed and her desires slipped from a panicked sunburst to a desolate gray. She wanted nothing more than to receive nothing, a fate worse than death for the sin bound to her. My being shivered, wanting to push away.

Leave her for the wolf to tend to. Or the damn ghost. No doubt he has a litany of poetry on how to soothe maternal wounds. There is nothing for a being created only to take to find here.

I brushed the hair behind her ear, her style from the ball still as springy as the night a week prior. "You may take all the time you require," I said. Layla lifted her fallen gaze, her eyes brimming with unspent tears and surprise.

"Really?" For a moment, she smiled, but it faltered into a piercing frown. "I didn't think you liked to wait?"

I chortled at her request. "I've lived for two thousand and some years. An hour spent idle here and there means nothing."

She's noticing.

There was nothing to notice, only a sin keeping his meal healthy and protected before the next feast.

Liar.

"Besides, keeping secrets from Calvin can be delightful fun."

"Ink..." Layla rolled her eyes, but she laughed as well.

"He gets this furrow on his brow when he's concentrating with all of his brains. It's rather delightful, particularly when he's completely wrong."

Layla smacked her palm to my chest in a more playful than scolding manner. I felt no pain, as I couldn't, outside of my brief stint as a mortal. Instead, I cupped the back of her hand, holding her palm above where my heart might linger. No one had ever ripped open a sin to see what was inside.

She flexed her fingers, pressing them deeper into my shirt and the muscle below. A tingle ran against my skin, deepening the tattoo she'd wanted below. It seemed to grow darker at my bond's whims each day.

Layla stared deeply into my eyes. "Are you okay?"

"Ignoring the great Celestial battle about to commence and rip apart everything in this realm? Perfectly content."

She bit her lip and breathed slowly. "Are you sure?"

What sort of a question is that? I was myself, as I had been since a Grecian scholar had birthed me from his shame. A sin was unchanging, incapable of being anything other than what they were meant to feed on.

Right?

"Thank the moon you're home."

I turned from my bond to find the wolf standing at the front door. "Speaking of the mutt."

He cast an exhausted look my way, then wiped his hands on a towel strategically placed on his belt. As if I didn't know he wore it to draw attention to his prodigious feature. Calvin dashed down the stairs and swept his hands around Layla. She collapsed into him, though her palm remained on my chest until the last second.

"What is it?" Layla asked. "What happened?"

"I'm going to barbecue that damn winged chicken," he growled, his wild side shining through.

"As he is made of ebony, that would be quite educational to watch."

"What'd Garavel do?" Layla focused on the business of keeping her coven of men in order. With the addition of the not-angel, it'd become a twenty-four-hour job.

Calvin muttered under his breath of feathers and ruined meat. I rather doubted the demi-angel attempted to throttle the werewolf's beefy todger with his wings, so my attention waned considerably. Layla tended to him, as was her wont. I'd been leaving the two to their sentimental lovemaking more and more, hoping it'd smooth other the lingering hurts. Shame there was another lie added to the pile.

"I'm sorry about Garavel, he's not..."

"I know. I get it. Killed his father, no idea what to do with it. Been there, done that."

"At least he refrained from vanishing into the woods for weeks to lick his wounds."

The werewolf glared at me as he draped a protective and possessive arm over Layla. "I'm guessing Ink brought you back from the cemetery."

"Oh shit, my car!" Layla smacked her forehead and groaned. "I should go back and get it." She took a step, then paused and shuddered. I knew, as she did, that there was a good chance the problem she refused to face had remained.

Only the mutt was left unaware and forced to guess. "Leave it. I'll get it later. For now, dinner's ready. You just have to pick off the burned feather bits."

Layla rested her head on his shoulder, Calvin holding her by the waist. "I love you," she said so freely. He returned the sentiment, the two sharing a simple kiss on the stoop of their home.

I'd watched the same scene play out millions of times with only the characters changing. It'd been nothing more than a minor inconvenience, for my hunt was impotent against unflinching love. But the way he brushed his thumb across her cheek, how she leaned her hips ever closer and blinked... I couldn't turn away, and I didn't know why.

"Ink?"

Layla's voice startled me. I found my hand clamped over my heart, directly above the tattoo, and stuffed it in my back pocket.

"Are you coming?"

I chuckled and swept to her side. "I didn't realize it'd be dinner and a show. Olive oil is a delicious lubricant for both eggs and cocks."

* * * *

Daniel

She was singing. Not the old Chinese lullabies she'd tortured me and my sisters with. No, it was a song from the sixties that'd come in over the radio in every elder's home we'd visited. The same one that my mom would take me by the hands for and dance to until I had hit puberty and walked ten steps behind her.

The cemetery was nice if not small. There was no headstone yet for the fresh grave, just a little sign with a number marking where my bones had ended up.

A trio of old women solemnly marched past, handbags at the ready, and my mother stopped singing. I used to cringe and hide under my hat whenever she'd sing. Now, I wished she'd start again. She nodded to the women watching their neighbor trying to keep stoic at the graveside of her son.

"Bet I'm the talk at the Mahjong tables. Again."

Disappointment was an understatement from that crowd. Not a doctor, not a lawyer, not even a low-level pencil pusher. No, Mrs. Lu's only son, her youngest child became a...rock musician.

"Funny thing, Mom, now that I'm dead, you got your wish. No more music for me. All I can do is research to try to save the world from… That part probably wasn't included in your speeches."

Her head lowered and the dreaded sound began. She'd always start silently, giving no hint except for a tremble of her shoulders. Then there'd be a snort, and the tears would fall without reprieve. She stood in the graveyard alone, no one there to comfort the woman whose son had died from drugs, or gangs, or drugged-up gangs.

"Mom. Please, don't… Why are you even doing this? You had to know I was dead. Or did you really think I'd vanished for thirty years and was out there somewhere?"

Fuck. Did she?

Memories flitted through my mind, as crisp as the day they had been formed. My mother had been hunched over in her favorite chair. The one she'd said her parents had brought over from China. She'd loved that chair with all her heart and she'd sat in it, bawling. No polite tearing up out of pride or regret. A waterfall of tears had stained her cheeks as she had cried out. I'd approached her, terrified of her reaction, certain that the world was ending.

"*Mom.*" I had reached a hand to her, to wipe off her tears.

That day, she'd sat up, her face red and soul raw. Rather than let me comfort her, or her comforting her startled son, she'd ordered me to my room. It wasn't until my father had come home that I would learn my grandma had died suddenly overnight. And I never saw that chair again.

My fingers sank through her cheek and she shivered, clenching her shawl tighter. There was no dawning recognition, no eyes lighting up as she sensed

I was beside her. The emotional tap shut off. My mother wiped at her eyes with a hankie.

I couldn't keep doing this. I needed to be back with Layla, studying up on the Horseman and preparing for the apocalypse. *My mother never wanted comforting anyway. Why should I bother now that I'm dead?*

Closing my eyes, I thought of the piece of my bone sitting in a change purse in a junk drawer. I'd taken a step when my mother called out, "Jin!"

My birth name froze me in place. She had only used that when she was very angry, or—in theory—very impressed, but I had never heard that one. That honor was only reserved for my sisters.

Dashing, I stepped in front of her. "Mom? Can you see me? Feel me? I'm here. I've been here ever since..."

She walked through me, barely even shivering, in order to bend closer to the sign. "How could you?"

"How could I what? Die from a gunshot wound? Guns are made for exactly that end, Mom."

She held her hand out above the grave where my skull rested. "We sacrificed everything for you."

"Oh, here it comes. 'Why can't you be the dutiful son all the neighbors have?' 'Your cousin's in med school'." I blew on my hair, expecting the fringe she despised to fly up. "Well, I'm sorry if I don't want to spend my whole life living up to your expectations, Mother."

"If you'd just...gone to college before—"

"Always with the damn college." She wouldn't let me have a cent of the money they'd socked away for college. No, if I was going to be a 'rock musician' I had to go it alone. So I did. We played shit venues, split free bread and sugar packets for food, slept in the fume-spitting van and made it on our own.

We were going to make it on our own. They did. Tiger Whisper got an album…a real one, not some cassette tape we recorded in Fingers' den. And I got—

"If you hadn't run around with those hooligans."

"They're my friends, Mom. Not that you'd understand. You never understood. I don't even know why I'm talking to you." I stuffed my hands under my jacket. When did the damn bus come through here so I could get as far from her as possible?

"If you'd…if you would have…"

"What, Mom? What do you want from me?"

She crumpled to her knees and pounded a fist into the wet dirt. "I miss you so much."

"Mom? What do you…?"

Pain burned in my chest. I slammed my hand over the wound and found blood blooming up through my T-shirt and denim jacket. *What's happening?*

"Help," I cried out, but my mother wasn't looking at me. One of his tantrums, she was probably thinking. No, she had to see this and get me to a hospital. "Mom…" My body pitched and I fell to a knee. My whole chest burned and I breathed, hearing my ribs splinter and pierce into the opening wound.

With my last ounce of strength I reached for her. "Mommy." My hand sailed clean through her shoulder.

What am I doing?

I shook my head and glanced to my chest. The blood stain and open wound were gone, erasing any proof that Brian had been the one to kill me. Because I was dead. I knew that. I'd known it for thirty years and counting.

That was just a momentary lapse. Confusion from being with my mother, and her grief overwhelming me. I shouldn't be here. Seeing her again was a mistake. I needed to focus on Layla, on preparing her for what was to come and hoping that...

No. That's too much for me to even wish for.

You can do this. Zero in on the task ahead and ignore all distractions.

Funny how often I used the mantras that had been crammed into me for placement tests. But back then, all that mattered was what college to get into, what class to sit, how to brag to the neighbors. Now, the entire world was at stake.

Bet my doctor cousin never saved the universe.

Layla flitted through my mind. It was her smile that kept me going, that gave me a purpose after all those decades of waiting. If I could touch her just once, taste her, hold her, stroke her hair... That was worth hanging on to.

I checked my chest once more to make certain the blood was gone. My mother too stood up. She wiped her knees free of the wet dirt, looking embarrassed at the outburst. Rather than look to her son standing behind her, she dug into her purse and placed an offering at the grave. To my shock, it wasn't the same candy and treats, but a box of guitar picks.

"I wish I hadn't chased you away."

"I'm sorry, but I can't come back here anymore." I pressed a ghost kiss to her cheek. Her skin broke out in goosebumps. Picturing the house, I took a step. Before vanishing to Layla's side, I said, "Goodbye, Mom."

Chapter Four

Layla

"Who's got the coleslaw?"

"Ah, it has landed by my side. Here, my bond." Ink passed over the bowl, but not before scooping another two spoonfuls into his iced tea.

I ignored his culinary quirks and filled out my plate.

"Anyone need relish?" Cal asked, holding up the jar.

Ink gasped. "That is an abomination that should be put to the fire."

Cal blinked slowly at him and deliberately dumped a pile of pickle relish onto his burger patty. The incubus hissed like an angry cat, stirred his tea and slaw drink, then tossed it back.

It felt normal, not in that I'd grown used to their dinner arguments, but like we weren't a witch, werewolf and demon. Instead, we were just a typical family enjoying summer's first barbecue at the table. I reached for the plate of hot dogs, and Cal's hand bounced into mine. He smiled and debonairly allowed me first choice. They looked impeccable, with perfect grill lines, save two on the side with a burned pattern across the skin.

Before I could choose a hot dog, Ink reached over and scooped up the ones with a feather charred onto them. "You don't have to eat them," Cal insisted, even though he had one of the messed-up burgers on his plate. "I just...didn't want to waste food. Times being, I don't know."

Ink coated his hot dog in chocolate sauce and bit down. "Mmm, this is quite delectable."

"There's a disgusting giant bird feather burned into it," Cal said, slack-jawed.

"I know. I had no idea angels were so tasty. Do you think other Celestials are as delicious?"

Cal groaned and jammed a fork into his slaw. He didn't answer, but loaded the prongs with shredded cabbage. Ink put down his hot dog and turned to me. "My bond?"

"Why do you think I'd know?" I'd actively avoided the feather-burgers.

"Nearly a fortnight has passed and you still haven't sealed the deal?"

Jesus Christ. My face burned hotter than the crisped hot dogs. I actively turned away to glare at the bowl of chips Ink wanted instead. Rather than drop his prodding, Ink gripped my chair and pulled himself closer. "Do you require suggestions? Mood enhancements? Perhaps a perch for our feathered friend?"

"Some friend..." Cal muttered.

I glared at Ink and he at least got enough of the message to return to his meal. After taking another large bite, he placed a finger to his lips and drew it

Ellen Mint

across. Wait? Was he saying all that shit about Garavel so Cal wouldn't ask about...?

"Layla." Daniel ran headlong into the dining room, then paused in the middle of the table. "Oh, you're here too." He stared at Ink, who smiled.

"Enjoying the fruits of the vine, which, alas, are unreachable to the exhaustingly departed."

Shaking his head as if that'd dispel Ink, Daniel focused on me. "The cemetery? You vanished so quickly."

"Your books are here," I interrupted. "They're in the living room."

The distraction worked, Daniel staring as if he could see through the wall. "Good. I hope — pray — they'll shed light on our current predicament."

"Would you mind moving?" Cal asked. "Your..." He waved to Daniel's crotch at table level and his cheeks pinked. "Is on the... You know, I don't need pickles. It's fine."

Even as Cal resumed eating, Daniel moved to sit beside me without pulling out the extra chair. He swept his palm over my bare arm, setting off a chill in his wake. I fought to keep from shivering when Ink cupped his blazing hot hand to my other side. Then he perched his chin on my shoulder.

"Shall we eat off of our beloved from now on?"

"No, we shall not," I declared despite not throwing him off of me. Ink snickered at Daniel, who didn't rise to the bait.

"Seems as good a time as any to have a quick meeting," Daniel said. "A coven meeting, I guess."

"No, thank you." Ink slapped his hands to the table and pushed back his chair. "Demons don't do meetings. Nor do we suffer assemblies, itineraries or conventions, or touch photocopiers unless body parts are involved."

"This is important," Daniel insisted.

"Then send it to me in a scry."

I came between them to say, "Maybe we should wait until Garavel's here."

The incubus slammed his chair back in place and sat bolt upright. "Now you have my attention. Tell me, what are your plans to rupture that ebony purity? And is there life remaining in your camera?"

"Ink..." I couldn't guess why he'd care. He certainly wanted nothing to do with me and Daniel, and only bothered with Cal when our play sessions got spicy. But for some reason he was obsessed with Garavel and the fact we'd only kissed.

"Yeah, babe. What are your plans with the wolf-hating angel?"

My stomach dropped at Cal's comment. I'd been under the delusion that those two would finally start getting along. Garavel had to realize that not all werewolves were bad, and Cal... Well, he'd been trying to play nice, but he seemed to be reaching the end of his rope.

"He doesn't hate you," Ink said. "I'd say it's more loathe. Despise? That marrow-deep abhorrence that only a lifetime of pain can create."

"You're not helping," I said and pushed away from the table, my hunger gone. Cal stared at my half-finished plate, then me, but didn't say anything. "Daniel's right, though. We need to figure out how to stop Conquest." My voice dropped at the real name of Mr. White and I flinched.

Ink chuckled at my reaction and scooped away the other half of my burger.

"Perhaps the books you got in the mail..." I prompted Daniel, who lit up at the reminder.

"Yes. One is a history of the horsemen, though it called the first rider Pestilence, so I'm uncertain if it'll be helpful." He dashed through the wall to the living room. I took the mortal route, placing one hand on the wallpaper still scarred from Cal's brother.

"How do you know if any of them are helpful?"

Daniel managed to open the box despite being a ghost, and extracted two books. I picked up the first, the cover a generic forest with the title in big, blocky letters. "There's a ton of people just making shit up. Maybe it's all lies."

"You'd be surprised how many women would claim themselves to be hedge witches while bearing not a mark of magic on their souls." Ink walked into the living room with the entire bowl of chips. Cal lingered behind, chewing through another four burgers on his plate. The wolf inside of him required a lot of calories.

"Exactly. You can think putting a crystal in your water bottle will give you vitality, but that doesn't make it magic."

"I daresay if quartz were to lodge in one's throat, their vitality would be quite short indeed."

Daniel sighed and opened up the last book. "It's not a problem."

"No? I mean—" Cal took a step forward and placed a hand to my back. "—what if we rely on a spell to protect Layla and it isn't real?"

"That can't happen," Daniel said with a laugh. He flipped another two pages, then stared up at us. "You can see that, right?"

"See what?"

"The books, the real books about magic. It's obvious."

"To whom? These appear to have been printed upon the flesh of dead foliage and not centaurs." Ink twisted a thinner book that looked like it belonged in a school library. Though why kids needed to learn about the apocalypse was beyond me.

"You're serious. You can't... The real ones glow. Not as bright as Layla's book. But I only have to pop open the cover and..." Daniel flipped through the thickest of the books in an old leather binding and sighed. He tossed that book aside and picked the children's story from Ink's fingers. "Ah, here. Look."

He pointed to a simple sentence about Death.

"Yes, Death does ride on a pale horse. How very useful to our conundrum," Ink said.

Daniel shook his head. "It's glowing, it's real knowledge. Magic knowledge. Look, I've been thinking. In all that I've read, there's nothing, no hint on if it's even possible to kill a Horseman."

"He is like Ink, and nothing can get through him," Cal said.

"Please. That man inhabits a white suit that'd make a mint julep shiver in terror. My fashion sense is impeccable compared to that derby atrocity."

"What if we don't have to kill Conquest? Pestilence. Whatever his damn name is. What if we take out his general instead?"

"You wish to kill the red wolf." Ink smirked at the idea but I turned to Cal.

He looked straight at us, but his stare was a hundred miles long. The red wolf was his brother, the eldest and most unwanted of the pack, who'd used that hate to torture his siblings. The same brother that now led the werewolves who had once belonged to his father. It was all a mess.

I reached over to him, uncertain what to say. It had been one thing when he killed his father in the heat of the moment and in self-defense after Eli was murdered. But this? It was too much.

Cal shivered and he stared at Daniel. "How?"

The front door flew open and we all spun. I raised my hands, the fire spell coming first. Ink spread his wings, his human skin crackling away to the demonic. Cal shifted his hands, claws crumpling the paper plate.

Without a care, Garavel strode into the house whistling under his breath. "The world's not broken yet," he declared.

I shook off my spell, chuckling at his happy response to the near-end of the world. Garavel smiled brighter and held his hand out to me. The edge of his feathers ruffled, and a tiny black face poked out. Fiona scampered over his arm and leaped for me. As I caught her, he tucked in his wings, turning from an angel into a normal human. A normal six-foot-seven human with perfect ebony skin that glowed, but human nonetheless.

"Hello, lady witch," Garavel greeted me. From anyone else, the word witch was said with a sneer, but for him it represented trust and companionship. My insides melted at the ever-present gratitude in his eyes as he looked at me.

"Did anyone see you?" Cal asked, breaking me from the angel. I startled to find he'd kept his claws out despite it only being Garavel.

The angel looked at him and raised his wide shoulders. "How am I supposed to know?"

"Typically someone shouts 'It's a bird, it's a plane, it's…a winged man come to herald the apocalypse,'" Daniel answered with a smirk.

"Guys, it's fine. He knows how to be discreet. Right?"

Garavel nodded, then perked up. "Is the evening meal ready?"

"Uh, yeah. Burgers and hot dogs, nothing special." I stepped to the side to let him dash for the dining room. Before he made a break for the food, he placed his wide palm nearly across the entirety of my upper back and let it slip lower.

"I made it," Cal piped up. "Despite your best efforts."

"Well, as Layla has eaten it, I doubt it's been poisoned. Though…" Garavel glared overlong at the burger on Cal's plate and the two looked about to come to blows.

With a sigh, I plopped Fiona onto the back of the couch and walked to the front door. Garavel had yet to get into the habit of closing them. Angel citadels must have been nothing but wide-open archways. "Look, can we all be civil for one night?" I grabbed the door and faced my guys. "We've got important shit to talk about. Conqu—"

A gale-force wind blew the door open. I wrenched it as a force dashed past me. Something zipped through the air and struck Cal's chest. It burst open and a net clamped around him. Ink was spinning in place, when a small disc flew in and stuck to the ceiling above him. His body froze mid-leap, all of his weight perched on the ball of one foot.

"The Horseman has arrived," Garavel thundered, unsheathing the sword from his back. As he twisted it, the edge glowed. I skittered to his side, conjuring a shield spell, when the attacker waltzed in.

"What the hell?" I sputtered. "How did you find me?"

She tipped up her hat brim and stared me down. "The only house in the entire city with a negating magic spell. Sloppy."

"Guh." Cal grunted while fighting with the net. "Who the fuck is this?"

"Watch your mouth around my daughter."

"Your..." He stopped struggling long enough to glare at me. "Daughter?"

I wanted to melt into the floor as the kind of embarrassment only parents can cause reared back from the past. My head fell even as I kept my hand up. I couldn't look at Cal or my mother.

"Werewolf, Sin."

"Ah, she got it right. Interesting," Ink chimed in despite his being a statue.

"A ghost." My mother clucked her tongue and shook her head in a soul-crushing display of disappointment. "Though, the demi-angel is a surprise."

"Who precisely are you, madam?" Garavel asked. "And if you have any relations to the Horseman, you will not leave here today."

My mother didn't answer him, all her consternation focused on me. "Layla, what are you doing with this riffraff?"

"They're not... They're my..." Every word died on my tongue at the judgmental glare in her eye. I hadn't seen it in fifteen years, and all of my defenses were too rusty to be useful.

A snarl broke from behind and I turned as Cal shredded the net. Panting, he rose to his feet and glared down my mother. "This is my house," he said and wrapped a hand around my waist. My mother's eyebrow shot up at the familiar move. "And you're not welcome."

She laughed at him. "Cute. That only works on the fae and bloodthirsty elves, but keep trying, wolf, and you'll see how quick my temper is. I came to speak with my daughter after she so rudely abandoned me mid-conversation."

"Layla?" Cal asked slowly. I cringed, gritting my teeth to keep from screaming incoherently. My heart pounded, fearing that his protective arm would either harden or slip off. To my surprise, he clung tighter to me, pressing my shoulder to his chest.

"Maybe it's because you've been dead for a decade, but the polite thing to do is knock."

My mother stepped closer. Despite being nearly a foot shorter, she stared Cal down. "When my daughter is in danger, I don't bother with niceties."

In danger? She burst into my home, my life, attacked my men without question and she claims I'm in danger? I began to shake in Cal's grip. Not tremble, not quiver, no—it was a quake of pure rage.

"Are you fucking serious?" I snarled at her, stepping forward. "These men are the only reason I'm not dead a dozen times over."

"Most of that was my intervention," Ink piped up.

"And you threaten them? You…you pin my incubus to the floor." I whipped my hand to him and the thrown sigil. "You hurl a net around my boyfriend. And…I don't even know what you were going to do to Daniel."

"Who? Oh, the ghost. He's a ghost. I wasn't going to do anything. They're as harmless as a dandelion puff."

"Ooh, that's a good one. I'm remembering that," Ink said.

Daniel had helped to train me in magic because my mother wouldn't. Ink had helped me fight against the creatures that tried to eat me because my mother ran. And Cal...Cal loved me when no one else wanted to.

Tears burned in my eyes, but as I focused on my mother, they burned into puffs of steam. Fire coursed across my hands and up my arms. The heat burst against my still healing face, but I refused to feel it.

"Get out."

"Layla, I don't know what demented gang you've fallen in with but—"

"Get." I stomped my foot and raised my hand. Flames shot up, nearly taking out my mother's hair. "Out." I added my other hand, the fire licking against my tank top straps.

"You're not listening to reason," she chastised. "Listen to me."

"No!" I shrieked at the top of my lungs. The fire leaped off my tongue and shot for my mother's face. At the last second, she threw her hand up, batting it away. The flames bounced against the wall where they caught on a fake potted plant. Fiona hissed at the fire, her tiny paws scrabbling to get her away.

I quenched the flames, pulling away the magic until only sparks flickered on my fingernails. Garavel reached over to the plant and clamped his hands around it. The plastic leaves crackled and broke, but the fire was out. Everything inside of me ached, like all of my organs had been dumped onto the floor. I clenched my fists to keep from teetering.

"I'm not listening to you, Mother. I'm not talking to you. I need you to leave."

"And then what...? Conquest —"

"Is my problem. I'll find him. I'll stop him with their help." I held my hands out to encompass my guys. "Not yours." With that, I turned my back on her.

"Very well. If you're going to pitch a fit like this."

I heard her shove the front door open and her shoes hit the porch.

"You're not even going to say goodbye...again." My lip wobbled and I bit so hard to keep from crying I tasted blood. If my mom heard me, she didn't respond, only the closing of the door answering for her.

I took one step and my body collapsed. Cal and Garavel both caught me, holding me up. I should have taken control, but all my resolve was gone.

"Layla...?" Cal whispered and I braced myself for another fight.

"Please," I moaned, crying and angry and lost all at the same time.

He brushed back my hair and I winced. The fire had gotten too close to my cheeks. Cal flinched from my pain. "Let me heal you up. Then...when you're ready."

I hurled my arms around the back of his neck and held him close. "I love you." I bawled against him, needing him to know, wishing they all knew.

Cal pressed a hand to the small of my back and buried his nose in my hair. "I love you too."

I didn't deserve him. I didn't deserve any of them.

"Not to ruin this tender moment," Ink said, "but could someone get onto the ceiling and wash that damn ward away? My ass is cramping."

Chapter Five

Layla

"…and the demon was the first one you told?"

I grimaced at Daniel's accusation and did my best to not look at Cal or Garavel. Said demon smiled with his signature smirk and cocked a hip in pride.

"I didn't technically tell him. More he figured it out," I mumbled, my explanation falling to incoherent babble.

Garavel picked a piece of burger off for Fiona, then glanced to me. "She's a witch, too. Aren't you excited to see her again?"

Yes.

And I hated the part that was.

"She may have a deeper pool of knowledge. Not only for spells and wards, but our current clip-clop problem as well." Daniel cupped his palms and mimicked horse hooves to make sure we all got it.

"An excellent point," Ink chimed in, instantly souring Daniel's smile. "With her at our helm, we shall have no use for you."

"Ha. Says the guy that turned into a lawn jockey two minutes ago."

They fell into such familiar bickering it was like white noise to me. It was the burning gaze from the only quiet member that sent me scrolling through my phone. A text from Dana!

I didn't even read it, just dialed her up and pressed my phone to my ear. "Sorry," I announced, walking past the glut of men to the front porch. "Got to take this."

"Layls? Why the shit are you calling me?"

I held my tongue until the door shut, though I heard something shatter and Cal groan about Garavel's wings. Wrapping a hand tighter to my chest, I began to rock on the balls of my feet. "Just saw your text."

"Uh-huh, and a normal, not-crazy person texts back. They don't call."

I saw my dead mother who's very much alive, and I don't know how to deal with it.

"Sorry. Did I...?" *Oh, shit.* I clenched my eyes tight. "I didn't wake Angelo from a nap?"

"Nah. He's coloring. Better not be on the walls, either. Sorry, it's been a long day."

All I wanted was to hear her problems. To nod along and offer useless advice on how to raise a six-year-old. To metaphorically pat her back and tell her she'd got this. To cling to the normal challenges of life instead of apocalyptic ones.

"Anyway, that thing I texted about. You interested?"

"Um..."

"You didn't even read the damn thing, did you, Leeland?"

Another shattering noise broke from inside followed by cursing. Pressing the phone closer, I took off down the sidewalk. Made of cobblestones with animal footprints worked into the concrete, I'd always thought them a cute design and had never put together that all the prints were from a wolf.

"Sorry. I've... I went to get the flowers back from my mom's. Sorry."

Dana sighed at butting into my grief. What was 'the dead person comes back and tries to wreck your life' stage? "Do you need help? I've got like half...a quarter bottle of tequila."

I laughed at her offer. "No. I'm fine. Just curious what your problem is."

"See, here's the thing. I sorta agreed to help out my cousin and his step-dad. They run this little lakeside retreat thing every summer, but the winter did a number on the place. The bastards guilt-trip me into it every damn year regardless of the shit I have going on."

"Except you have Angelo now."

"Yeah. And running around in tick-infested trees chasing after a kid doesn't sound like my idea of fun."

A small resort in the woods sounded wonderful right now. No horsemen, no werewolf pack, no mothers back from the grave. Just a cabin, a lake and quiet serenity for the first time in... I couldn't even hazard a guess.

"Fariah's agreed to pitch in, and she's taking her new girlfriend, too. I haven't met her yet. What about you?"

"No."

"Hm... You don't think she's embarrassed by us?" Dana asked, then she burped on command.

I laughed at the idea of brash Dana meeting Fariah's no doubt soft-spoken girlfriend and wrapping the poor woman in a crushing hug. It was either total affection or complete loathing with Dana, no in-between. A bit like Garavel in that way.

"What do you need from me?"

"Well, I love Fariah and all, but does she strike you as the power tools type?"

Fariah used a knife and fork to eat Cheetos. I grimaced and shook my head even though no one could see me.

"And since you've got Cal with you, not to mention the smug Tattoo..."

She was never going to warm to Ink.

"Just thought adding you three should get it done even faster. At least before Memorial Day, anyway."

Before Memorial Day? That was quick. "When would we head out?"

"This Friday. I can get you a van to fit all your man meat, so that's not a problem."

Friday? I couldn't. I had work. I had my mother issues. I had the potential apocalypse that could launch at any second.

The front door opened and Cal stood framed in the threshold. From behind, I caught a flash of feathers.

I had four other problems on my hands.

"I'd love to help you out..."

"Great. I'll text Fariah like a normal person—"

"But I've got too much—"

"Layls." Dana dropped into her mom voice. "Listen. You've been running ragged. I know you barely passed finals, no doubt thanks to smirky boy. And your manager is a grade-A douchebag on a whole-dick bun."

I chuckled, though she wasn't wrong.

"You sound like you could use a vacation."

"A vacation where we put in back-breaking labor."

"Yeah. Isn't that what all vacations are?"

Lie on Cal's chest under a blanket of stars. Skinny dip into the blue waters with Ink. Snuggle by the bonfire with Daniel. Introduce Garavel to the wonders of s'mores.

"It sounds lovely, but..."

"Think about it, okay? But get back to me soon. The rental place is a bitch."

I nodded to Dana just as Cal unfolded from his wary stance and walked over. "All right. I'll give it a think."

"Bye. And fucking text me next time. I thought you were dead in a ditch when the phone rang."

Laughing at her worry, I ended the call and Cal slipped a hand around the back of my waist. Even though he had to be furious with me, I leaned back so my cheek pressed to his chest.

"It's getting late," he said.

"The sun's up." Children dashed down the street on their scooters and bikes. What would happen to them when all the deadly creatures of the realms returned?

"And we both have a two AM shift."

Damn. I'd forgotten.

Cal rubbed my back as we stared together out of his little garden patch. He'd start up at me. He had to. I'd lied... Okay, for an hour, tops, and it was more a 'not giving the full explanation' kind. But still.

The May wind scattered a rain of cherry blossoms. Cal's chest expanded against me as he breathed in the fruity scent. Then he plucked one of the fallen white blossoms from my hair. It was so damn fragile, it took nothing more than a breeze to tug it free. I'd felt the same facing off against Mr. White—my skin and bones as frail as a petal on the air.

How am I going to stop him?

Cal scattered the flowers on his walkway, where they stuck to the cobbles. He brushed his knuckles against my cheeks and reached back behind my ear. I leaned into his touch even as I closed my eyes tight.

"Just...call me awful. I'm a liar. I didn't tell you about—"

He placed a finger to my lips and I stopped.

"Babe, there's a lot of this witch stuff I don't get. I'm glad you've got Dan to help. And there's a lot of this end of the world, magic returns, humans are mages and made werewolves I don't understand. But you've got...*him* to help with that."

"I should have told you. I just freaked out. One second I was looking at her grave, the next she was... I'm sorry."

Cal winced and he brushed back through my twists, catching one and winding it around his ring finger. He formed a gold and mahogany ring with my hair before letting it go. "I don't know much about the magic world, but I know a lot about...conflicted feelings with an absent parent. I'm not mad. I...I understand. It's hard, to sever that bond. To even think you should. And maybe you don't want to. Maybe you need time. I just want you to know that..."

He entwined our fingers together and smiled as the dappled sunlight landed in his hair. "Whatever you want, whatever you need, I've got you."

I leaped up to hug him, wrapping my arms tight to the back of his neck. For the first time that day, tears of a different sort built in my eyes. I wanted to thank him, to swear I'd come to him no matter what. I said, "I love you."

Cal cupped my chin and smiled. "I love you…"

Another great crash broke from inside and a plate went whizzing through the open door. It shattered at Cal's feet. He dropped his hold, took a deep breath and gazed at the sky. I kicked the broken pieces to the side and wrapped an arm around him. "Let's go to bed."

* * * *

Trying to not look my haggard expression in the eye, I stuffed the last of my twists into my bonnet and walked into the bedroom. Cal had already stripped down to his boxers, the ones with the tiny moons all over them. He finished tugging back the blanket to look over at me. Slowly, a cheesy smile rose as he stared up at my hair.

Self-consciousness ran through me and I almost yanked the bonnet off. "This, um…do you think it's stupid?"

"What? Garavel flying Ink around Superman style? It's fine as long as they don't get sucked into a jet engine."

I laughed, then felt horrible for laughing. "No, my…" I pointed to my bonnet, then smacked the top as if that'd make it look less Red Riding Hood grandmother like. It even had lace on the edge that I hadn't cared about when I was single. Now I felt stupider each second one of them saw me.

"Your night cap?" Cal asked and he walked away from the bed.

"It's just, you're not my first white boyfriend."

He swept his arms around me, resting the heels of his hands at the top of my ass. "But I am your first werewolf boyfriend," Cal said with a grin. Then he blinked. "Least I think so."

First boyfriend to have a collar fetish, that much was certain.

Cal ran a finger against my throat, setting off a chain of goosebumps. "I like when you've got your bonnet on." He traced up to nearly my hairline while staring down at me. "It makes you look like you belong here."

I hadn't considered...

"And, if you're wearing it, that means I can do—" He clamped his hands over my ass and in one fell swoop, hefted me into the air and tossed me onto the bed. I landed with a mighty squeak, shocked and impressed at his move.

Cal stalked around the bed, his head dipped so the light only struck his gleaming eyes. I felt like the grandma about to be devoured by the big bad wolf, and it made me shiver.

"My, my, what a big..." I looked to his cock, the thick flesh already straining against its confines. "Personality you have," I finished with a smile.

He didn't play along. Instead, Cal jerked as if he'd been under a spell and raked his fingers through his hair. "Ha, funny. Let me get the light."

Oh. I scooted back and turned on the little bedside lamp just before the main room one fell. Cal took his time adjusting his laid-out clothing for the next day. By the time he got in bed, I was already under the covers. Normally, we'd both be so exhausted, we'd pass out instantly—threats of near death and dismemberment will do that—but I sat up against the pillows, trying to calm my mind, and Cal mimicked me. For a time, only the still creaks of the old house and the flap of giant wings filled the air.

"Do you want — ?"

"I've been — "

We both laughed, and I thundered on first, suspecting he was going to try to get me to talk about my mother. "I'm not sure if you heard my call..."

"Accusing me of eavesdropping?"

"No, just... It was Dana. She's got this old cabin up north."

"Ah. That would explain the text I got from her about getting you to say yes. I didn't know what for."

"She texts you?" I mean, we were in the same class, sure, but...

Cal leaned over the bed to pick up something in the box by his nightstand. "Sent me this, too." He dropped a plain white T-shirt on the bed, but as I turned it over the blocky text of "Team Cal" leaped out at me.

"You have to be kidding me. You're, uh...not gonna wear it, right?"

His shadowed smirk did not assure me. The guys were on shaky ground already. Chest beating and machismo contests would not help save the world. Unless the answer to defeating Conquest was to challenge him to an arm wrestling and hot wing competition.

"I mean, I don't see any Team Ink shirts."

"Please don't give him any ideas. He'd come home with a jacket decked out in rhinestones spelling out his name and favorite sexual positions."

Cal slipped his finger under my bonnet, raising the edge so it slipped behind my ear. He scooted closer and brushed his lips against it. "Want to tell me yours?"

"My bond, do you have need of me?"

Jesus! We both jumped at Ink's face plastered against the window. He waved a hand in greeting. Garavel somehow hovered while dangling Ink from his arms.

"No. I'm good. Going to bed."

"You are aware what that piece of furniture is best employed for, yes?" Ink asked. At my glare, he reached up to the angel. "Onward to scope out the neighborhood to the west where the tiny monster of ankle destruction resides."

I bit my lip, waiting for them to vanish. Cal had gone quiet. "I'm sorry, it was the rhinestones. I couldn't stop picturing him as a disco demon."

He laughed, thank god, and worried a hand over my thigh. "Fair enough. I don't think I can get that image from my head either."

Slipping to his pillows, Cal turned to play the big spoon while I kept sitting up. "I think I'm gonna do it."

"Convince Ink to roller skate to ABBA?"

"No."

"If you ask, he'll do anything," Cal said with a shrug.

No, he wouldn't. Ink answered to himself and no one else. I shook off thoughts of the incubus and plowed on ahead. "Dana's cabin retreat repair vacation. Or whatever it is."

Cal sat back up. "Is this about your…"

"Some of it's that. But, you know, it feels like we've been running and running since last year. I just, I want a break. Get out of town, leave, leave the Horseman behind, leave the pack, leave all of it. For a week. Right?"

He stared through space, which was happening regularly whenever the werewolf pack or Eric were mentioned. Cal snapped out of it and he smiled down at me. "You know, it's not a bad idea. Dan can do his research. Garavel can learn more about human society without other humans around. Ink can boogie down to the Bee Gees under the disco ball."

"Oh my god, stop!" I slapped his chest, and the hard muscles stung my palm.

Cal cinched his arms around me, pulling both of us to the bed. He kissed me sweetly and curled a finger over my cheek. "I'm game if you are. Though, do you think you'll be able to get time off?"

I'd already been out on sick leave, unpaid of course, for a couple of days after the angel torched my skin. An entire week for a vacation... "Yeah. I've got it saved up. Why wouldn't they?"

"Well." Cal sank back into his pillow, his eyes closing. "We can always send Ink in his bellbottoms and fringe cowboy vest to 'convince' the manager."

"It's okay. I've got it." A vacation, a real one. No crazy witch hunters kidnapping me. No demented Celestial trying to start a war. No werewolf cult threatening to kill me to get to Cal. An honest vacation full of blisters and splinters in the mosquito-filled woods sounded heavenly in comparison.

The hungry wolf lay beside me, his eyes shut and mouth slack. I reached up to turn off the light, when a thought struck me.

"Cal?"

"Sleeping. Honk shoo."

I flicked off the light as I asked, "Don't you need to shift?"

His hand latched around my stomach, pulling me tight to his body. "No," he whispered in my ear. Teeth clamped down against the thin skin, and I shivered to my toes. "I did it last night."

"You did? When?" It'd been a long night of listening to Daniel's theories, then listening to Ink ridiculing them.

Cal didn't answer, letting his hand do the talking. He curled his palm over my top breast, kneading it. "You were asleep. I didn't want to wake you."

He pinched my nipple and I squeaked in surprise. His wandering hand canvassed down my waist, over my hip and landed at my thigh.

"I wouldn't mind," I said. If he didn't shift, he'd... "Oh, fuck." Cal reached under my panties to part through my untamed cleft. He crooked a finger inside, beckoning me to come.

"Don't worry about it, Layla." Ducking under the covers, Cal slipped down my body. He kissed my belly, then bit hard. I squealed and he thrust two fingers deeper inside. "I've got this under control."

Cal squirmed deeper under the covers until his feet popped out on the other side. The lone blue light in the room caught on his pale skin. I started to giggle at the sight when Cal bit down on my hip. *Holy shit*. I jerked in shock and he got a full handful of my ass.

"I know you need at least an hour to..."

Using just his teeth, Cal tugged my panties down. They caught on my upper thighs, the round flesh not giving in to the elastic's demands. But that didn't stop Cal, who planted his chin firmly between my legs and began to lick. Vulva, clit, inner thigh, crease—he went everywhere with his tongue.

"Are you trying to distract me?" I moaned, reaching for his hair.

He formed a seal around my clit and sucked. The sensations were almost too much, my brain spinning out in flames. Cal backed off, gently licking as I struggled to breathe. *Fuck, that was amazing.* Time stilled until all I knew was my chest struggling to funnel air in, my heart pounding like a hummingbird's, and Cal's wet, worshipping tongue all over me.

I needed more. I started to stretch my legs to give him room when a hand clamped down. Cal pressed tighter, trapping me, and he roughed his stubble over my sensitive inner thighs.

"Fuck. Me." I bit down on my own hand, trying to balance the seething pain with the cascading pleasure.

A low growl rumbled from between my legs. He licked harder, both of his hands pressing on my thighs. In that tight spot, his tongue hit everywhere at once and his nose pushed against my pubic bone. Fuck, that was a good pain. Cal began to grunt, increasing the speed of his tongue.

How did I forget how amazing he is at this?

Why do I let him leave the bed?

I reached for the mess of blond hair brushing against my skin when he clamped down again over my clit. This time, he sucked just right and there was no stopping the inevitable.

"Cal. Fu-uuuuck." The orgasm shuddered down my legs first, both my thighs flailing and kicking him off. I could barely register what happened before it rushed up my chest. All the panting struck at once, my head lightening to fluff, and I arched back into the bed.

A knowing, solitary laugh of pure machismo punctuated Cal's giving head. He climbed back to me. Even helped to slip my panties on, though they were soaked beyond reckoning now. I reached for him, my hand heading for that thick cock. Instead, Cal flipped me over.

"It's late," he breathed in my ear. Despite his assertions, he pressed his cock to my ass and it felt ready for a ride. Cal swept his palm just under my breasts, using the tops of his thumbs to toy with them.

"Don't you think you deserve a reward for that performance?"

He chuckled slowly and kissed the nape of my neck. "Tomorrow. In the basement?"

"Before or after you shift?"

"Before," he cried out with a groan. "I'm patient, Layla, but not that patient." Slowly, his hand stopped rubbing me and fell to the bed. After a few moments, his erratic panting steadied to a slumbering rhythm.

Snuggling closer, I picked up his hand and kissed the knuckles. "Good things come to those who wait," I said.

Cal gave a single laugh in response.

Chapter Six

Layla

I half expected to find a unicorn leaping over a psychedelic rainbow on the side of the van as it pulled into the driveway. An ominous cloud of smoke blew around it, hiding the two occupants in the front seat.

"Pretty sure we rented that same van to tour Illinois," Daniel mused beside me. The hot summer sun bounced off everything but him, making him stick out to any who could see the ghost. Lucky for me, the two humans joining us on this trip couldn't.

The driver's door opened and Fariah popped her head out. She'd tugged up her high neckline to cover her nose, only a sliver of her eyes and forehead visible. "This thing stinks like dead fish."

"Yep, that was the one. Never could figure out where the fish came from."

"I've got some air fresheners in the house..." I said with a wave.

"Allow me, my bond." Before I could answer, Ink popped off to hopefully get the good ones and not a bag of cloves or burning sage.

"Morning, Layla." Fariah slipped out of the van and breathed in the blooming lilacs. "I wish I could take that plant with." She pointed to the soft purple petals, and I feared just what we'd gotten ourselves into.

"Are you going to introduce us to...?"

Fariah glanced to the shadow in the front seat showing no signs of moving into the light. "Maram's a bit shy. I told her about you and Calvin, but..." Fariah stared up into the grinning face of the demi-angel. "He seems new."

"Hi, I'm Gar—"

"Gary," I leaped in, trying to act cool as I said the first normal name I thought of. *No angels here, just regular old Garys.*

"Yes, I am Gar-ee." He extended his hand, which was when the kitten decided to burrow out from the hood on his jacket and leap down his arm.

Snapping her hand to her side and stepping back, Fariah said, "Charmed to meet you. Layla, is he...?"

"He's a friend of my family. We go way back. Homeschooled though, so, you know. He can be a bit intense without meaning to."

Fariah smiled patiently at him and nodded.

"But he's cool," I kept explaining. I didn't know why I didn't think to tell them that Garavel would be coming along. Maybe because I hadn't been certain he'd agree. Though he'd damn near run to the front door once I said we were heading into the forest. He really liked trees. "Right?" I tried to slug Garavel on his massive biceps, but my knuckles hit a mountain and I had to hide the pain.

"Yes. Cool as a cucumber," he said and bounced the sunglasses barely clinging to his nose.

Fariah turned to wave to her girlfriend and coax her out, which was when Ink didn't bother to use the door and appeared next to me. "I have procured a scent called 'falling rain' and another dubbed 'coconut bliss.' I assume this mimics the post-orgy when one uses coconut oil to soothe any throbbing flesh."

Pausing inside the passenger seat, Maram gulped, her eyes widening as she stared at the incubus calmly handing me every air freshener in the house.

I jostled the scents and smiled. "One of these has to work against the fish smell. Right?"

Maram waved Fariah over and the two whispered in what I had to guess was Arabic. Fariah shook her head and cupped her girlfriend's shoulder. "It's okay. I knew about that one. Dana calls him Tattoo."

The quiet one only snorted once and gazed out at us. "Hello," she said, sounding like a tiny wren greeting an elephant, then she slipped back into the fish van.

"The app said it'll take us six hours to get there. Without stops."

"If you'd like, I could drive," Cal offered, but Fariah shrugged him off.

"The rental, and insurance, is in my name."

"She means she wants to have the front seat all to herself and her new GF," I whispered loudly to Cal. "First road trip is a biggie."

He gulped and took my hand. For ours, we had met a desert nymph, who was then kidnapped by witch hunters, that Cal and Ink had to save. Then I'd met his mother. I'd much rather have had a six-hour drive in a fish-scented van with four strangers over that one.

I was leaning down to pick up my bag when Cal beat me to it. He gave a playful wink and slung it, then two others on his back. "Show off," I shouted with a giggle as he dropped our luggage into the trunk. Ink wandered beside him, shoving air fresheners everywhere while Garavel dangled his hood string for the kitten. Daniel bent over the wheels and stared at the tread, then swung his foot at them. Lucky thing he was a ghost, as his leg went sailing past.

"Layla, can I speak with you?" Fariah jerked her head and we trailed to the garden.

Rather than speak, she watched the guys get into a minor argument about how best to stack two carry-on bags and a suitcase crammed with Daniel's books. Daniel kept insisting the books be on the back seat so he could research. Garavel told Cal to put them on the side, and Ink kept trying to sneak the box away and toss them into the trash. Poor Cal was struggling to find any compromise as he flung the heavy box around.

"Is this…okay?"

Shit. I gulped, realizing I hadn't technically told Fariah about my complicated relationships. Dana gave me enough shit for the both of them, but Fariah would have to deal with it for a week.

"If you need to stay behind for work, I can tell Dana. She's more likely to listen to me."

Oh. My cheeks burned at how fast I leaped to the wrong conclusion. "No. It's fine. It's all good. Got the vacation time for the vacation."

"Even Cal?"

There was no way he'd let me go without coming along. And there was no way I'd let him stay here alone knowing the pack was out there. "I believe he used the bro-code on the manager."

"Ah. Must be nice."

Cal snarled at the two men arguing, grabbed the trunk and slammed it hard. Garavel and Ink both moved just before it'd have struck them.

"And you're sleeping with all of them, which they know about?"

Fariah had a way of cutting right to the bone. At least Dana had cussed me out a bit before asking. I gulped and looked over at her. Her face was neutral, not even her perfect eyebrow arched in amusement or horror to give me a sign.

Technically, I'm only sleeping with two of them. One's more of a mutual masturbation situation that's complicated. And Garavel...we're figuring that out.

I couldn't say any of that to the poised lady at my side. Instead, I jerked my head wildly hoping it came off as an enthusiastic nod. Yes, I'd slept with all three and there was a high chance of that happening on this trip like some complicated puzzle of pegs and holes. *What if that's too much for her?*

"Should make sleeping arrangements easier, at least. Shall we?" Fariah shouted to the guys.

This was going to be great. The sun was rising, lifting the dreary skies out of cold spring into a sparkling summer. I could leave all the witch shit behind and spend one week by the lake with four hot guys. What could go wrong?

Cal opened the door and Ink held his hand out. I took it even though it was just one step inside. The fish smell hit me first, then the overpowering ozone of the air freshener. I slid to the first seat by the window, looked to the four men standing outside and smiled.

As one, they all surged for the van.

"I'm sitting by Layla," Cal said.

"Like the bottomless pits of Tartarus you are," Garavel thundered.

"She could sit on me instead?" Ink offered.

"Can the demon turn it off for two seconds? I'll sit by our beloved," Daniel said.

Ink yanked a bottle of table salt out of his pocket and poured the contents on the seat. Daniel shivered and reached his hands out for the demon. "You goddamn..."

I slipped on my earbuds and turned to face the window as the dick fight continued. *No problems at all.*

* * * *

Ink

We stopped at the edge of civilization. While I was excited at being able to move my legs once again, the stained and weathered building gave me pause. Dried dirt gusted across the empty gathering for vehicles where none save the lone pumps of liquid tar stood.

"Oh god!" The wolf slammed open the sliding door and plummeted to the ground. He threw his arms wide and breathed in deep. "No more fish and whatever the hell Ink was eating."

"A delightful egg and sardine sandwich with extra marshmallow fluff. I did offer you a bite."

He turned an entertaining hue of mottled gray at the mention of my packed lunch. I'd made enough for the entire group, but only the demi-angel had shown interest. He poked his head through the door to the outside world and blinked against the falling sun. "Wow."

I'd had the unfortunate luck of being pinned beside his girth—an outcome I'd normally find no fault in had it not been for seven hours and counting. There were a few 'accidents' as well when the man forgot himself and his wings erupted. I would be finding feathers hiding in crevices of my body for many a day.

Garavel hopped out and stared around the desolate pustule on the ass of society. "This is amazing!" he shouted and dashed after a rug that turned out to be someone's dog.

"That guy's always at eleven," Calvin muttered while wringing the back of his neck.

With the others well distracted, I returned to the metal box of fish and flatulence to extend my hand. "My bond?"

Layla removed her electronic symphony and stared at me. Slowly, her cheeks blushed as the situation struck her. After bundling her belongings into her purse, she slid across the seat with as much grace as one could manage. "Ink, you don't have to…"

I caught her not by the hand, but the waist. She giggled while I placed her on the earth, making certain her feet were stable, her hips flush and her nipples glancing against my chest. That sensation teased down her spine and Layla momentarily bit her lip before she shook her head.

"What are you doing?"

"Helping you out of the carriage. You could have tripped and struck your head or broken your delicate wrist. There may have been a serpent lurking below that'd sink its fangs deep. I dare say any true gentlemen would do no less."

"Oh for the love of…" Calvin groaned and he stomped for the pump, fiddling with the buttons until it beeped sufficiently.

To my surprise, my bond wasn't smiling. "Is it gonna be this dick-measuring contest the whole trip?"

"They have those in these parts of the world? We should both enter, mutt!"

"Can't hear you over the sound of my wallet draining to zero," he said then stuck the nozzle rather suggestively into the van's secret hole. I opened my mouth to comment on it, but the other women we were to behave around exited. The one in an ever-changing array of hair scarves was of little interest to me. Though, the woman that made her entire being blush pink gave me a wide berth. Interesting.

I wanted to learn more of this Maram and approached her as she huddled with the other women.

"Why don't you ladies head on inside? I can watch the pump."

"It's okay, Cal." My bond stared askance at the doomsday station. "We can wait with you."

He pulled her closer and placed his forehead against hers. "I'll be fine. Besides, I know how long it takes you to go pee."

Wrong declaration. Layla slammed a fist to her hip and glared at him. "Watch it or I'll make you sleep with Ink."

She gathered up the others and led the pack inside. I leaned to the left and called out, "Was that always an option or is it only available while we are on sabbatical?"

My bond responded with a raised middle finger from behind her friends as they vanished into the filth-encrusted glass building. I kept an eye on them for as long as possible.

"Thank god you've stopped."

I had enough control of my body to not even twitch at the ghost's voice booming beside my ear. With a wry smile, I turned to face the worthless wretch. "Here I'd hoped you had finally ascended to wherever scraps of human souls go."

"Ha. Ha ha. So damn funny. Why don't you stay here and I'll sit in the van the rest of the way? You can teleport too."

The bitter spirit grumbled and folded his arms, as if the height of attractiveness for a woman was a man pitching a tantrum. I shifted my weight and eyed him up. Were he not such an infuriating braggart as helpful as a bladeless knife, he would be handsome. Less the traditional lantern jaw and strong nose of the werewolf. More the enticing and rarer to find androgynous features that could set ablaze an entire new world inside mortal's hearts.

Sadly, he was a thorn in my backside and his face being fair only made me want to wish him a second death.

"Are we close? Please tell me we're close. I had to wait in the dark house for the last two hours trying to not go mad."

"How do you know you succeeded?" I asked. "Perhaps your mind is fragmented beyond reproach and you're dreaming all of this."

"Ink. Knock it off." Calvin returned the nozzle to its preferred hole and accepted a scrap of paper. Humans and their paper.

I folded my arms. "Are you to act as the dick wrangler when she is not around?"

"That..." He waggled a finger at me and I grinned. "No. We're almost there. Can we keep it chill until then?"

"Hm." I ran a palm down my toned and sleek body—the mountainous pecs, the multitudinous abs. "I'm afraid I am only capable of being scorching."

The ghost, who—thanks to his ectoplasmic predicament—was eternally chill, gawped at me. "I don't know how you weren't banished to hell ten days into existence."

"With this ass—" I slapped said accoutrement in his direction. "—who could hate me?"

"Witch hunters," Calvin said.

I growled at the reminder. I'd expected such a childish taunt from the ghost, but not him. Not unless it was his time of the month. "One time out of two thousand years hardly—"

"No!" He slammed a hand to my chest then pointed to a vehicle in the distant parking lot. "Witch hunters."

The plain white van bore a single mark declaring it to be animal control. Two people shadowed by the harsh sunlight slipped from it and walked to the demi-angel happily playing with his kitten.

"Oh, shit."

I nearly ripped through the realms to confront both, but Calvin clamped a hand to my shoulder. "They may not be. Let's…let's walk over there like normal."

"And if they are as we feared?"

As he turned to me, his eye gleamed. Exactly as it should be. "Ghost?"

He jerked at his mention. Perhaps he was losing his control on the mortal coil. That'd be nice.

"If you wish to be helpful, find our beloved and tell her what could be transpiring."

"Is that smart?" Calvin asked.

"Would you rather we leave her in the dark?"

He winced and shook his head. The ghost vanished with his sad little fade. No doubt he'd make it sound more dire in her ear. He ached for the drama of the living. But—I cracked my neck and flexed my claws— we could handle two solitary hunters.

Garavel rose from his dusty play and patted off his jeans. It unnerved me to see an angel, even a demi one, dressed in such peasant garb. He should have been coated in real gold.

"Hi," he boomed and held a hand out to the first potential hunter.

To my surprise, there were no pretentious black suits. Instead, they wore canvas body suits that hung in all the wrong ways. My body curled inward at the horrors before me. Garavel showed no such fears as he waved to the second hunter after the first refused his handshake.

"Hey, are you guys with animal control?" Calvin asked. I had to give him points—he was a professional at keeping his voice level in the most trying of times. A small gain from his years fearing retribution at the hands of his abusive father.

"Yeah. Where'd you get the kitten?" The first one barely looked to Cal, his pig-eyed sights set on Garavel.

"I found her. She was playing in a dumpster."

That apparently was not the right answer. "You got any ID?"

Garavel shifted the precocious kitten higher where she sat on his shoulder like a watchful companion. "What's an ID? Is it like ice cream, because I think we all need some. It is hot out here. Ink? Don't tell me, rocky road with those cheese pretzels mixed in?"

The indestructible giant had no idea what tightrope he was walking. I shifted closer, attempting to put myself between the hunters and the demi-angel who had yet to meet this monster. They didn't tear their eyes away from Garavel for a second, even as I shifted to reveal the reds of my eyes. If they were hunters, they were awful at it.

"We're gonna need to see some ID and proof you own the kitten."

"How can anyone own a living being?" Garavel asked with such sincerity even I cringed…internally. I did have some standards.

Calvin glanced my way and slowly shook his head. I was in agreement. They were not witch hunters, but simple-minded assholes with more bravado than brains. "Hey, Gary, why don't you go with, uh…Inky here."

"Inky? I should flay you alive for that."

"The girls are finishing up and I think there might be some ice cream in the store." Calvin played his part beautifully, except there was one small catch. Garavel despised the one giving him orders.

He folded his giant arms across his impassive chest and held his ground.

"You know him?" one of the hunters put to the wolf.

"Oh, yeah. Gary and I go way back. He's my…girlfriend's cousin."

Calvin's fragile house of cards was collapsing quickly. The not-hunter had enough sense to realize something didn't add up. "He needs to have his ID on him. And that cat should have a collar with updated tags. I'm gonna have to call this in."

This was not working.

Taking the lead, I guided Calvin and Garavel behind me. "No, you shall not."

"Sir. Please. No reason to make this worse than it needs to be."

I chuckled slowly, letting the rumble of my baritone dip to the depths of hell. "Oh...you have no idea how worse I can make it." I shook away my human visage, revealing the crackling red and black skin below, horns piercing from my forehead. For a final stab, I unfurled my midnight wings, the shadows dripping off my back.

Both sad, pathetic men turned white as a sheet.

"Fuck! What is that?"

"I don't fucking know. Get out of here!" They scrambled for their noxious van, both leaping to get inside. Though one failed to account for the door and slammed his genitals upon it. Red faced and cursing a storm, they reversed their vehicle as I cocked my hip and waved.

"Those goddamn monster reports were right!" they shouted to the road as they hit it and continued on.

"Cal...? Ink?"

At the voice of my bond, I slipped back on my handsome face and turned to her. She was out of breath and clinging to a bag of treats purchased from inside. "What... Daniel said..."

"Do not concern yourself, my bond." I wrapped a hand around the back of her waist. "A minor misunderstanding."

"But he said—"

"It's all good," Calvin continued, distracting her as I peered into the bag. "We were just talking."

Ah, the cheese cleverly disguised inside a pretzel anus. My favorite. I fished the treat out and popped open the bag.

The wolf turned back to look at Garavel. I waved him over. The immoveable statue broke into a wide grin and loping run.

"Are you sure you handled it without any problems?"

To my knowledge, no one save those rotten-brained scalawags had seen my true form. And I rather doubted anyone would believe their mad ramblings. "Yes." I popped the first of the cheese pretzels into my mouth, savoring the unholy texture of dried bean cheese and stale dough. "I'd say we saved the day with no consequences whatsoever. Huzzah for us. Go team!"

"Okay. Fariah and Maram are waiting at the van, so we should get going. Almost there."

Calvin wrapped an arm around Layla and pulled her close. He whispered in her ear and she giggled while burning red across both her skin and in her desires. This close to a full moon should make for a very entertaining vacation.

Only Garavel paused and stared in the direction of the long-vanished van. All they'd left behind were their panicky tire tracks. "What do you think they wanted?"

"That, my long-slumbered friend, is a long conversation. Come, I believe I saw a fudge bar in Layla's sack of goodies."

He dashed to her side as I stared out across the wilds of the northern forests. I hadn't been so stripped from civilization's delights since my descent to hell.

At least this time I have Layla.

Chapter Seven

Layla

We almost missed the sign overrun with bushes along with the turn down a winding dirt road. As the van took the last of a series of sharp rights, the pressing forest cleared. Small green cabins poked out from the woodlands. A handful of pine and birch trees were allowed to grow in the middle of the grass area.

Fariah kept driving toward the longer white building. We passed a sandlot with two poles up and I pointed. "I think they have volleyball."

"Is that the game where humans fire cannons at each other?" Ink asked.

"I'm pretty sure you're thinking of piracy," I responded. He'd sat beside me for this leg of the trip and had my legs draped over his lap. Ink paused in caressing down my calves to shrug.

"I shall have to acquire an eyepatch and verdant plumaged bird."

Ignoring him, I dropped my legs and scooted closer to see out of the window. Blue-gray water stretched to the horizon before the van. Small waves crested in soothing patterns until they slopped against a single dock bowing with them. Fariah turned away from driving into the lake and put the van in park.

We all stared around the campsite without opening a door. Rustic was the kind way to say run-down and on its way to collapse. I began to hope this place at least had running water. No five-star glamping for us, that much was certain. As the dust settled, the white building's door opened and a man carrying a stack of wood walked out.

He hurled the wood onto a pile of other ripped-up lumber and held a hand above his eyes. I'd expected a man around Dana's age, at most in his thirties, but this guy had salt in his cornrows and too much cracking on his face. What if we had gone down the wrong path? What if he was a terrifying loner who didn't take too kindly to lost college students on his land?

"Are you Dana's crew?" he shouted, and we all breathed a sigh of relief. Fariah turned off the engine and we began to slide out of the van.

She was the first to walk over to greet him, showing no signs of concern that we thought he might have killed Dana's cousin and was waiting to finish us off. I needed to stop watching those old slasher movies with Cal.

"Are you Dante?" Fariah asked.

"Yep. Let me guess, you're the quiet one and you are the…" He pointed at Fariah, then turned to me. "Wild one."

If a twenty-seven-year-old bartender had called me a wild one, I'd have blushed so hot I'd turn feverish.

But Dante said it like an older teacher eyeing up a potential problem.

"Only at Dana's urging," I said, trying to defend myself. He laughed and nodded as if he'd suffered from some of Dana's ideas.

"Well, glad you're here. We've got to get shit done before…" Dante stopped talking and looked up as the rest of the crew exited the van.

With wide-stretched arms, Ink greeted the falling sun like a yoga instructor. Cal was already hustling back to the trunk to get our stuff and Daniel popped in just in time to tell him to be careful. It was when Garavel eased his way out of the tight fit that Dante full-on choked. He sputtered in shock at the massive man scratching the palm-sized kitten.

"Are they…are you all with them?"

"Wherever my… Wherever Layla comes…so do we," Ink said. Rather than groan at his barely disguised innuendo, I nodded at him for not using the bond stuff. That'd been a long discussion.

"The more the merrier and all. It's just" — Dante pulled out a clipboard he'd had tucked in his back waistband and waved it around — "winter did more of a number than we thought. There's only two working cabins. I guess, if the guys don't mind sharing, and I put you girls — "

A tiny squeak broke from the last and un-introduced of the group. Maram had managed to remain eclipsed by the van and unnoticed until she cried out. Fariah reached for her girlfriend and took her hand. "It's all right, love."

"Wait, what's happening?" Cal dropped the heavy books, then shrugged the two bags off his shoulders.

"He wishes to bed Layla with the other two women," Ink said. At that innuendo, I glared.

Cal took my hand and subtly pulled me closer. "She can stay with us. Figure you two'd want some time alone anyway."

His assumption got a wary nod from Fariah, as if we were all supposed to keep pretending no one was having sex. Dante tapped his pencil against his clipboard. "Here's the thing, each cabin's only got three bed frames. And I think you're gonna need at least two to fit, er…"

Garavel perked up at the attention and smiled. "Gary. I am called Gary now."

"Okay. Gary. So either we split down the boys and girls or…"

Ink chuckled. "It is no bother. I do not require a bed to lie in."

Oh, yeah. He didn't sleep. Most he'd do was cuddle beside me after and go very still until I was out. Then I'd find him on the couch the next morning arguing with QVC.

Dante didn't understand the lack of rest needed by near-demons and he stared down Ink's well-kept and ill-prepared clothing. "You think yourself some kind of extreme camper?"

"You'd be surprised at what I can survive." His charming voice crackled and I nearly rushed for him, when Ink smiled. "All I need is a rock for a pillow and a blanket of leaves. Shall we unpack our belongings?"

Dante kept tapping against his clipboard, then he shook out of it. "Here's the thing, I thought you guys would be in before the sun set. All the mattresses are up in the storage shed. I'll need some of you to move them. Think you three can handle it?" He turned to us girls who couldn't think of any reason.

"As for you guys, Gary, right?"

"Yes. I am Gary." He nodded at the uncertain name, then stared at me. I gave a quick thumb's up, then had to hide it by scratching under my chin.

"It's a mess in the main kitchen. I'm gonna need your help tearing out the water-damaged floor so we can hopefully get the damn stoves hooked back up to the propane."

Garavel nodded as if he understood all of that. A month ago he'd woken from an eon's slumber where people cooked over open flames to a world of microwaves. He really enjoyed making ramen once we taught him the necessity of water. That had been an exciting Saturday.

"What about—" Cal stepped forward and pointed to himself, then Ink. "What about us?"

"Or me? Shall I simply stand here as I have been for hours?" Daniel said, not that anyone but our group could hear him.

"There's a boat ramp we share with the other resorts on this side of the lake. It's just down the road a couple of miles. Think you can drive to it and put my boat in the water?"

Cal nodded even while he kept staring at Dante. With enough of an acceptance, Dante tossed his keys to Cal, but it was Ink who caught them. "I believe I shall best operate this land and sea vessel."

"Like hell you are." Cal wrenched the keys away from Ink. "The last time you drove, you almost slammed her car into a van."

"To be fair, it was my first time. And I didn't kill anyone…sadly."

Both men approached the rusted truck with an aluminum fishing boat on an attached trailer. Ink ran his hand over the boat's hull, then moved to leap in. "I shall ride from the dinghy," he declared, but Cal at least knew to stop him.

"Just down the road, right?"

"Can't miss it," Dante said with a wave, then he focused on us. "The mattresses are in the shed behind the water purifiers. You'll have to walk through the damn cocklebur patch, so I hope you've got boots."

"Layla, are you…?" Cal called to me. I leaned away from Dante's instructions to look to him. He was half inside the man's truck, his face etched with worry.

"She is safe," Ink chided. "Gary is there."

That didn't seem to appease Cal, but he began to lower to the driver's seat. "I love you," he called out before closing the door and starting up the engine. As the truck with boat in tow rattled down the road, I slipped on protective rain boots along with Fariah and Maram. Dante put a steadying arm around Garavel and led him toward the mutilated kitchen.

It might not be the vacation I wanted, or even needed, but it was better than what I'd have gotten at home.

"Mind the sewage puddle," Fariah called.

More or less.

* * * *

Ink

With the wind tugging back my stylish hair, I could understand the appeal of traveling at such fast speeds. Though the bombastic shriek of various dirt clods shattering to their doom put a damper on the fun.

When the third tried to smack me, I abandoned my solitude and rolled up the window.

The wolf was tense. With hunched shoulders, he gripped the steering wheel as if it'd cursed his mother. I'd preferred the company of dirt to this version of Calvin.

"Is she okay?" he grumbled, the first few words spoken outside of asking for directions.

I shrugged and grew curious about the secret compartment before my knees.

"Well?"

"Well, what? This is Layla we are speaking of. I'd say at any moment in time there's a ten-percent chance she's being attacked by previously unknown assailants. That chance doubles on holidays."

The wolf snarled and slammed a hand to the steering wheel. A great screech of tuneless bells erupted and I clamped over my ears. "We shouldn't have left her. This is a bad idea. I'm turning this around…"

The truck and its large cargo slowed, but before he could do something foolish such as tip us over into the ditch, I clung to the wheel. "She can take care of herself."

"Really?" He stared me down.

Sighing, I shook my hair back and leaned into the seat. "At the moment she is content, though slightly nervous."

"It could be that guy! Whoever the hell he was. Dante. What kind of name is that? Dante. Ooh, look at me, I went through hell."

Interesting. I released the wheel. Calvin did not whip it around, but guided the truck back onto the empty road.

"Hmm," I mused, tapping my finger to my lip. "Most curious."

"What?" The wolf nearly ripped my throat out in his stewing.

"After all this time, after all the pleasure and numerous beds metaphorically broken, it is now that you suffer jealousy."

"I'm not—" Calvin insisted as if Envy wouldn't have a ten-course meal off him at that moment.

"Is it the moon? Is it rising, or falling or in some retrograde with Mercury or other flighty Etruscan gods?"

He clawed at the back of his head, leaving obvious red marks below the blond hair. It did him no favors. "Maybe I'm worried about her, is all. After the Control guys, and then we find that dude and leave her there at his insistence."

"While I do not share this lightly, you should know that Mr. Dante bore nearly no desire for our beloved."

He blinked, his wide pupils shrinking as he turned to me. "Really? What do you mean by nearly?"

I shrugged it away. Humans always had random flits of desire for those they had no intention to press it upon. I'd learned to tune it out long ago. A green sign declaring the next right to be the boating ramp appeared. "Besides, why even waste such time worrying? She is under the protection of a demi-angel and they are nigh on indestructible."

"Ah yes, Gary. Because this wasn't awkward enough. Thank you so much for the reminder." He grumbled at me while turning down the road. The dirt lot became paved as if by a miracle. Calvin headed straight for the lake where a single dock bobbed, but another boat waited in the way.

With a groan, he threw our vehicle into park and glared out the windshield. Two elderly gentlemen were struggling to get out of their boat and up onto the dock.

"This is going to take forever," Calvin moaned.

"We could play a game to pass the time."

"No."

"Not even..." I offered, but he cranked his glare on me and not the older man shuffling for his smaller truck in a delightful maroon. "I must say, I was surprised at how well you took her little obfuscation of the facts."

"Obfus... Ink, I'm too tired for this."

"Even she seemed certain you'd become a right bear about it. Excusing the pun."

"Was that even a pun? Look, she's dealing with a lot right now. And family shit, parent shit is..." His sentence trailed off and he picked at the peeling leather on the steering wheel. "It's the worst."

"Of course. Here I feared my time in hell had dulled my senses, but you are as mad at her as you are at yourself."

"What? No, I'm not. I'm not angry at anyone except for that goddamn old fogey backing up at one mile an hour! Hurry up!" He pushed on the middle of the steering wheel, but this time no sound emerged.

I waited for his tirade to end, Calvin once again nearly assaulting the harmless vehicle before he slammed his head back into the armrest and sighed. "I'm not talking about it with you."

"Good, because discussing your traumatic feelings and how to move past them would be a fate worse than death. And I've been to hell."

We enjoyed the slapstick comedy of one old man trying to reach for the hitch while the second kept surging the truck just out of his reach. I wished I had a bucket of bouillon cubes to supplement the entertainment.

"He could have killed her," Calvin whispered, dooming me to yet more of this male bonding I'd managed to avoid for two thousand years.

"There is a long list of potentials there. To which he do you refer? The angel? Conquest?"

He clenched his hands tight and dug not his nails but full claws into his flesh.

"Ah, that he." The final brother of clan Werewolf and current thorn in his side. "Yes, I suppose had we not all been there prepared to rip his head off, he might have gotten a swing in."

"You don't know Eric like I do."

"And I'd prefer to keep it that way. Listen, put on your friendly smile, the one you always dole out when not sulking alone. Enjoy my bond in the very skimpy beach suit I slipped into her luggage."

He stared at me as if stunned I'd do such a thing. But his desires shifted from a strangling black to a leg-shaking red lightning quick.

"Once this vacation has ended, we shall return and destroy Conquest's little pet, assuming you don't have some moral objection."

Calvin shook his head hard. He seemed resigned to his eldest brother's fate.

"Then we'll celebrate with an orgy and cake."

He snickered at my summation, as if such an end were impossible. While I would have preferred to not concern myself with the affairs of witches or horsemen, should Conquest accomplish his mission, many would suffer. My greatest fear was that I would be included in that list.

The old men finally achieved their goal and began to pull out of the lake at a speed that would rival a baby turtle. At least Calvin now seemed calm and even laughed at the situation.

"I am curious though. Why is it Dante who flared your jealous side?"

"Ink, it's not..."

"The ghost is a stubborn stain left lingering far past his expiration. Garavel cannot even stand to look at you, yet you let him reside under your roof."

He breathed deep and flexed his fingers, but no claws punctured through.

"As for myself, well, I can bring her to unending bliss with a crook of my finger. And she finds my buttocks quite appealing."

"Maybe it's because you're part of the package deal. Maybe it's because I know some nights she picks me over a sex demon."

I had to tip my hat to that logic. Though he must have been aware that I let him have his time in order to keep the peace for Layla's sake.

"Maybe I just..."

"Hello!" The geriatric gentleman shouted out his drawn window. Cal slowly rolled his down and looked to him. "Young man, you should be careful. It's late."

"I'm just taking the boat to a resort. Don't worry," he said as if the men were about to arrest him for boating at an inopportune time.

"The monster's out and about."

He said it with such certainty even I almost skirted past his comment. "What monster, pray tell?" I asked. Those controllers of animals had said the same.

"See them wakes out there." He pointed a shaking finger to the lake and a series of waves guided by nothing more than the wind.

Ah, he was crazy. Well, that happened too.

Calvin seemed to sense the same as he waved his hand and gave a noncommittal, "Thanks for the warning." With that, the men left and we were free to place the boat in the water.

I assisted by standing on the dock and telling him when to go deeper with the trailer. He leaped out of the truck and approached the side of the boat. "I'm gonna unhook it."

"Understood."

Calvin did as promised and the small sloop careened off its tackle into the water. I watched it carry on past, sailing freely without a care in the world.

"What the shit!" The wolf dashed onto the dock beside me and nearly plunged into the cold lake. I clung to the back of his shirt collar, preventing a freezing dive, but he turned his wrath on me. "What the hell, Ink? You were supposed to catch it."

"You didn't say."

"For fuck... Okay. What now?"

I folded an arm across my chest and placed my elbow there to hold my chin and stare at him. "You are aware I'm a demon."

"More or less," he added before groaning. "Okay, fine. You get to the boat, start the motor. Do you know how to do that?"

"I'm certain I can figure out which buttons make it purr."

"Not even touching that. Can you find the resort off the lake? Right, yes, demon powers. They let you know everything about everyone."

"It is a burden," I said with a weary sigh.

He pointed to the boat continuing its lone journey to nowhere, then turned to the truck. "I'll drive back to Layla…and the rest. Tell them you're coming."

"I'm certain my bond will find the humor in that."

Rather than chuckle at my joke, he stomped off the dock and leaped into the truck. With the door remaining open, he drove the trailer out of the water, streams gushing from every angle on the metal skeleton.

"Calvin!" I called as he reached to close his door. "Do try to hold off on disemboweling Dante until I arrive."

I enjoyed the low grumble before he slammed the door and drove off into the sunset. Speaking of… With barely a flick of my wrist, I stepped into the in-between. It was a desolate, inhospitable place where the Celestials stashed whatever didn't work in creation. They were fantastic rabbit holes for the beings that could walk them. Mortals, however, could not.

I frowned at the memory of the ghost insisting Layla had done such a thing. If so, she'd have been under incredible stress. I was always certain to keep her in the real world even as I carried her elsewhere. But to walk fully inside the in-between would unravel her being bit by bit. No. He didn't know of what he spoke, as was usual for the man pretending to be an intellectual.

With only a moment spent dashing through space, I emerged in the middle of the boat. It rocked at my weight, bobbing to and fro, but I was able to keep steady and look damn fine while doing it. Orange and pink cascaded across the lake ripples like fire riding the waves. For all this world's faults, of which there were an unending many, the set and rise of the sun would forever be beautiful. It deserved another moment as I stood in the boat with none around me save the mournful call of a bird searching for its mate.

"Hm…"

The ripples shifted and, for a moment, the lake before me darkened from a deep indigo to black. I watched the color shift travel farther away in the direction of a solitary island far on the horizon. Yet another of this world's mysteries. I shrugged it off and bent over the black box strapped to the back of the boat.

"This should be simple enough," I declared as I squared off against the motor.

In the distance, the birdsong vanished to only the lapping of the waves.

Chapter Eight

Daniel

"Can someone get the door?" Layla called, her voice muffled by the twin mattress pressed to her chest. Her arms strained as she walked for the swinging shed door where no one stood.

Taking a step, the mattress bounced into the shut door and Layla groaned. "Hello? Fariah? Anyone?"

I'd been unable to do anything but watch as she'd laughed, chipped nails and picked burrs off her jeans with her friends. Even my words were only a distraction for Layla, to the confusion of the other women who couldn't see me. Thirty years of my undeath had been spent screaming into the uncaring void, but I'd never felt so worthless as now.

She tried again, calling for the quiet one. "Maram? Don't tell me you two are off necking."

Straightening my spine, I stepped across the creaking floor. The space was narrow and crammed full of old mattresses, broken bed frames and lawn equipment. Instead of trying to move around them, I walked through and stopped before the door. "Allow me," I said to Layla. *Concentrate.* For months after my death, I hadn't been able to sit, then one day it came to me. I'd been reduced to reading books over people's shoulders, often stuck inventing the ending for myself, until one glorious day I realized I could hold them. If I focused hard enough, there was nothing I couldn't do.

I glared at the handle. All it needed was for the latch to lift and the whole door would swing open. I'd have been able to bend that tiny piece of metal in half when I was human. I could move that. I knew it.

The dead air crackled as I reached for the latch and my hand sailed through. *Damn it. Try again.* Each swipe of my hand failed. Forgetting the handle, I tried for the latch itself, when a warm palm pressed through mine.

With a great whine, the door shuddered open. Layla hefted up the mattress and waddled into the sunset. I stepped out and death-stared at the door. It teetered on its hinges, a soft breeze proving to be more of a nuisance than I was.

Clenching my fists, I reared back to punch the door. "Daniel?"

Her sweet voice stalled my useless attack and I quickly crossed to her side. Layla had her cheek pressed to the stained mattress so only one of her deep brown eyes could stare at me. "Can you tell me where the hell I'm going so I don't walk into the lake?"

"Of course." I nodded, taking my job seriously. As I gazed around the open field with not even a blade of grass in her way, my confidence shriveled. "Just keep heading forward like that."

"Thanks," she said.

There was no need for her pity. I knew I was dead. The wind rustling the trees and never touching my skin reminded me. The sun baking the grass but never warming my bones kept me from forgetting. For as infuriatingly useless as the demon was, at least he could have opened the door for her.

"I've been thinking…" I jogged to her side, paying no attention to where she walked. "What if destroying the champion doesn't stop Conquest? What if he picks a new one?"

Layla shrugged. "We kill that one, too. Did you find anything about witches taking on a Horseman?"

Only a very short fairytale about an old hag in the woods who'd once captured Death. It didn't end well for the hag. I shook my head, not wanting to put that dark tale in her mind. The others wouldn't say it, but she still bore a red flush from the angel's burns. I wondered if it would ever fade away to her natural light brown. The circles under her eyes grew more haggard with each day, and her shoulders bowed from the unending amount of weight heaped on them.

"I wish I could help." I sighed, slowing to a standstill.

Layla stopped and dropped the mattress on her feet. "You are. There's no way I could have read a quarter of the books you have on all this magic shit."

I knew why I did it, and it wasn't from a love of knowledge.

Warm fingers brushed through my cheek. I held my palm against the back of her hand, wishing just once I could feel the softness of her skin. Layla gazed at me, her eyes brimming with a mass of feelings. "I'm glad I have you to talk to."

"Just what every guy wants to hear." I tried to laugh it off, but even the one outlet we shared was in jeopardy out here. She could shrug off the others catching her talking to herself once, maybe twice, but a full-on conversation? *I don't even know why I came.*

"Oh…" Layla hauled up the mattress and resumed her blind waddle for the cabin. "I love playing with you."

I smiled at her satisfied grin. Even if I couldn't touch her with my fingers, I could guide hers to impossible highs. And she'd let me in on secrets I doubted the damn demon knew.

Layla made it up the stairs without tripping and banged the bottom of the mattress against the door. "Everyone decent in here?" she shouted before the door opened to her friend, who didn't look out of breath.

"Layla?" The lilt in Fariah's voice told a different tale and Layla smirked at catching them. "The last frame is back there." The two women vanished into the cabin, the door slamming behind. I floated through to watch Layla drop the mattress on the squeaky bedsprings. It skidded from the fall. Rather than adjusting it, she rubbed her shoulders and groaned.

She glanced over at Maram, who'd taken to fixing the sheets on the bed. "These things are loud," Layla said, pressing on the mattress and the springs. Together they squealed like a rat in a trap. "Gonna be real hard to hide any hanky-panky from the camp counselor."

Fariah laughed and nodded while Maram blushed and bent lower until her straight black hair fell over her face. "We were thinking, why not take that to your cabin?"

"We don't need three," Maram blurted out.

Ellen Mint

"Do you even need two?" I asked. I'd never had any interest in the shy girls my mother had dropped before me. Fariah held my attention like a soggy bag of milk, and Maram was even worse. But two attractive women alone on a springy mattress... I might have been dead, but I wasn't married.

"Pretty sure if I tried to move it, Dante would make me clean the latrines," Layla said. Her hand slipped off her shoulder as if she'd grown too weary to massage it. Without thinking, I took it. She jerked in surprise at me claiming her fingers. But as I cuddled in behind her, almost nuzzling my chin against her neck, she smiled.

"All this hard work demands a treat. I know of an empty cabin. and if you cause the bedsprings to squeak, you'll quiver at the punishment."

As she bit her lip to keep from answering, I swept her hand across her belly. Instead of feeling her skin on mine, I could sense what she did. It was almost like being alive, except feeling everything through a sleeping bag. The sensations were dulled, yes, but a sip of water to a dying man was better than none at all. I caressed higher, running her thumb over her bra band and casually knocking against the breasts above. With her fingers, I toyed with her shirt, lifting the thin cotton in a tease.

The entire time I played with Layla, the other two had no idea I was there. Fariah plucked another set of sheets from the old box and handed them to Maram. "I think you could take the mattress, at least. For the...camping one."

The reminder that Ink existed nearly threw me off, but Layla was rising on her toes as I dipped her pinkie under her waistband. "I will spread your thighs to near

91

buckling and watch you drip down them in anticipation."

She moaned at my words, but then looked to her friends. "Oh." Layla tried to play it off. "Don't worry about Ink. If he says he's gonna sleep outside in the dirt, he will."

"Think of an excuse to get out of here right now, and I'll only keep you on the edge for five minutes instead of fifteen."

Her breath caught and she squirmed as I drew her hand over the front of her jeans before leaving it on her hip.

"Are you okay?" Fariah asked. "You keep rubbing your stomach."

"Ah. I think I pulled something carrying all those mattresses. I should go and check the van for..."

Layla jerked her head and turned just as the door opened to reveal the werewolf. Her customer smile became a genuine one at his arrival. "Cal! How'd it go?"

"No trees were struck and the boat is in the water. Looks like you three were successful."

She reached her hand to him, and I slipped free from my hold.

"More or less, though Layla wrenched a muscle."

She slapped a hand over her shoulder and grinned. "It's nothing."

"Well, can't have that. Here." The blond-haired, blue-eyed, V-shaped, all-American Boy Scout wrapped his wide hands around her shoulders and dug in. The moan I'd hoped to draw from her instead came from his deep massage.

Layla's eyes rolled back and she gulped. "That's amazing. Yes. Right there." He leaned closer and whispered in her ear, which only caused her to giggle.

Awkwardness stampeded through the air, Fariah and Maram trying to not stare at the couple I knew were flirting and wanting more. She smiled at Cal, and he in turn at her, both warm bodies capable of touching, licking and thrusting together. I slunk back, my skin prickling even in this dead air.

I knew she wanted me. I knew she'd sometimes choose me. But they were easier. They were available. They could hold her and rub her and tend to her in ways I'd only dream of. Turning, I glared at the door. With a lash of my hand, I slammed onto the handle and the latch popped up. The door flung open and I stomped out.

"That was weird," Layla's friend called, no one knowing about the ghost cockblocked by himself.

* * * *

Garavel

"Where should I put this?" I asked, holding up the heating box that was used to cook food.

"Uh…" My new friend flicked his ear and gestured to the recently cleared floor. "There's good. Least until we get the gas lines cleared."

With a smile, I placed the metal box on the floor with one hand. The other was busy holding perfectly still while the kitten slumbered across my forearm.

"You, uh, you got a routine for that?"

"Hm?" I glanced to Fiona who sensed my slight movement and stretched her tiny forelimbs. "Yes. I learned to let her sleep when she wanted, then pick up whatever she chewed on in the morning."

Dante chuckled and wiped off his forehead. "Yeah, fine. Keep your secrets. Whatever they are, have to be worth their weight in gold. You're bigger than the damn fridge."

He pointed to the larger cold box we'd also carried out of the kitchen in order to rip up the flooring. It looked like a fire stalker had walked through, its steps burning half the room down to the stone. Though those weren't in this world any longer. Few of the old creations remained.

Fiona meowed and darted up my arm, digging her claws in for an anchor. She arched her back against my cheek and purred loudly. "I think my kitten is hungry," I said.

"Yeah, sun's going down. Better get something to eat before the riots start."

"Riots? Have you heard any pitchforks sharpening?" I dashed to the window and stared out. There were no signs of torchlight flickering in the distance but I did spy the ghost walking toward the van.

"It's a figure of speech. You know... Never mind. Come on, man. You earned this."

I frowned at the concept. I was created to do as told. If I obeyed, I received nothing more than a satisfactory feeling. If I failed, I deserved to be crushed to rubble. Simple. Easy. Earning implied that some people deserved more for their sweat, regardless of the outcome of their labor. I didn't like the idea.

My steps echoed off the empty halls of the dining area, as Dante had dubbed it. I'd walked in a structure reminiscent of this once, when humans rode on horses instead of motorcycles and kings were as common as quartz rash. Thinking about the old days turned my stomach, which was already looping as the hunger grew.

Dante stepped to the courtyard and called out, "Hey, girls! Let's stop for the night."

The two I'd come to know as Layla's close classmates appeared from a far cabin. I looked to the ghost who was bent over his box of books, gazing at a tome without touching the cover.

"Where's the crazy one? Oh, there she is." Dante pointed to the west and I followed.

A confounding mix of serenity and giggling came over me. My lady witch, silhouetted by the halo of the falling sun, looked to us and smiled. Dante must have caught my unintentional sigh. He raised an eyebrow, staring from me to Layla, then gliding closer.

"Man, no. No, you are not into that."

"Into?" I asked just as a nugget of advice from my good friend Ink pricked in the back of my mind. A blush burned across my cheeks from how matter-of-fact he'd been. "No," I sputtered, trying to not think of the softness of her lips spread across mine. Or the slender curve of her calf as she'd slipped down the hem of her skirt. "I'm not into her...yet."

"What?"

"Hey, babe!"

My sunny day darkened to clouds of fire rain. Bounding from the other cabin came the werewolf. When he reached Layla, he tossed his arm across her as if marking his territory. They were savages through and through.

Layla was kind enough to pat the wolf's paw and entwine her fingers with his as the two of them approached the gathering side by side. Fariah stood by her beloved as well and I felt queasy. No, not exactly queasy. I knew that feeling from when Ink had me try his coconut shrimp cake. This was a queasiness from me being once again surrounded by mortals with beloveds while all I faced was another long nap in the earth.

Except that was gone too. All I had was nothing.

"You're back?" Dante put to the wolf.

"Here's your keys." He underhanded the jangling ring to Dante, who caught them, then turned to stare at the dock.

"Okay, where's the boat?"

The wolf shrugged as if he was incapable of any responsibility. "Ink's bringing it in."

"Does Ink know how to drive a boat?" Layla asked. The wolf once again shook off his duty. She turned away from his smothering and caught my eye. For a moment she smiled, not at the wolf or in amusement, but only for me.

Celestials save me, I can't handle this. I crumpled my shoulders up and almost extended my wings to sweep around me in embarrassment. The sharp cry of "Ahoy!" stilled me from accidentally revealing myself.

Ink stood at the prow with all the pride of a masthead. He grinned, holding his pose even as the boat rode the waves past the dock and into the thick weeds. With a jolly kick, he leaped off and took a bow. "Your watery transportation has arrived and in mint condition." He held up the rope attached to the bow. "Is anyone going to take this?"

"I'll do it," Dante grumbled.

He seemed unexcited for Ink's return, but I was elated. At least I didn't feel so off kilter with my demon friend at my side.

"You know, it's funny," the wolf said, staring down Ink. "I didn't hear a motor."

"Perhaps you should have your ears inspected for mites. I hear they can be a real bother. My bond." Not caring for the protective arm of the wolf, Ink swept Layla up and kissed her on the lips.

Her cheeks shifted strawberry pink, and she glanced over to Fariah and Maram who had to have heard. Ink rolled his eyes. "I call her my bond. Does anyone here have a problem with that? No? Delightful. Problem solved. Now, what were we to do about dinner?" He clasped his hands and rubbed them in anticipation.

Dante showed less excitement. "The stoves are all out of commission."

"Is it to be MREs for the week?" Fariah asked.

"Lucky for you, we've got a grill. You two, you eat meat, right?"

Fariah and Maram looked to each other. "Some of it."

"Yeah, Dana yelled it at me. What about the rest of you? Big guy like you has to eat a whole hog." Dante chuckled and elbowed me in a friendly manner.

"Uh-oh," Ink said. He turned to whisper in Layla's ear.

What is that about? Perhaps something the wolf told him. I nodded to Dante. "Yes. I enjoy all manner of animal. Have you ever had unicorn? It can be quite gamey but with enough spices it stews up well."

Dante laughed. "Yeah, sure. So, who's going to do the cooking?" He extended a metal handle to Fariah and Maram, then Layla. None of the women raised their hands.

It was Ink who took it. "Allow me to dazzle you."

"That's…" The wolf snatched it away. "I'll man the grill. You can assist."

Ink chuckled beside him. "The last time I assisted, the Tsar nearly tore his testicles clean off."

"I do not want to know."

"It is a humorous tale involving copious amounts of beer and a farmer's plow…"

As the two followed Dante to the black metal contraption, I was left alone with Layla. She slipped beside me and scratched Fiona's welcoming cheeks.

Why did I feel shaking in my knees and a quiver in my chest? I'd had no qualms being alone with her before. She'd even watched me undress in the alley, which I hadn't given pause to. But now the idea made my mouth dry—something I hadn't known was possible.

"How are you doing?" she asked. "Is Dante cool?"

"Oh, yes. We moved all the furniture in the room to another side. It was helpful?" I had no idea. I had only done as I was instructed. That was much easier than ordering. I'd commanded great armies, planned battles that lasted for months, executed sieges for centuries—but they were always at the behest of my creator. Now I answered to no one but myself. Any mistake, any slip or harm I caused would rest entirely on my soul. How did humans cope with that pressure?

A cool hand pressed to my forehead and I blinked in surprise. Layla was strained on her tiptoes as she stared up at me in worry. "You looked…I don't know, scared. Sick? Can angel…can you get sick?"

She was concerned for me. I reached for her hand with the intention to remove it respectfully. But as I touched her graceful fingers, mine slipped in between hers. Rather than gently push her away as I had so many other witches, I guided her palm down my cheek and across my jaw until it stopped before my lips. Like the fool I was, I kissed her not on her mouth, or the other more heart-stopping places Ink had told me about. No, I kissed her chastely on her palm while staring into her eyes.

Layla lowered her eyelashes and swayed her hips closer to me. I was about to open my hand to free hers when she touched my chest. Using my pecs to guide her scaling, she stood at the tip of her toes and pivoted her head back.

Does she want me to kiss her?
There's a lot of people around.
What if I do it wrong?
What if I hurt her?

"Who wants a grilled ketchup bun?"

Ink's cry from the cooking station shook Layla from her course. The wolf wrenched the rolls from Ink and chastised him. "No one wants that. Babe, do you mind taking the salads from Mr. Culinary Infusion here?"

"On it," she said with a wave. I anticipated her running to their sides, but she swooped her palm down my chest and tenderly patted once.

Before I could ask what that meant, she returned to the experienced men who each pecked a kiss to her cheek as they slipped an apron over her head. How could I hope to compete with that?

Chapter Nine

Layla

I dropped my plate into the washbasin as the last of the sunlight faded to an indigo glow. Ink slipped in behind me and stared. "I see you enjoyed my slaw of many colors."

"It was…" I tried to not glance at the bush that was the recipient of a rainbow coleslaw. "Very creative."

"Told you," he crowed to Cal, who rolled his eyes before he landed them on me. I wanted to smile, but an all-too-familiar awkwardness arose. What were we supposed to do next?

"Seems as good a time as any to turn in," Dante declared, catching all of us by surprise.

"But what of the gathering of logs? Shall we not ignite them for the trading of spine-tingling tales?" As Ink asked that, he pressed two fingers to the nape of my neck and trailed them down fast to press on my tailbone.

"There's no lighter fluid, so knock yourself out if you want." Dante seemed exhausted by us already. He waved his hands and walked away. "Come morning, the real work begins."

Great. I rotated my shoulder, fighting off a cramp I knew would only get worse in the morning.

"*Carte blanche* to start a fire," Ink declared once Dante was out of range in the main building. He bent over the old wood in the pit and waved his fingers closer.

Fariah sat perched on a lawn chair, her knees tight together to balance her plate. She reached over and took Maram's hand. "Do you want to stay or...?"

Maram blanched and shook her head as if she were terrified of the flames. "No, thank you."

"We're going to turn in. Layla. The rest of you." With their hands clasped, Fariah led Maram back to their cabin.

"Hm, this is not working." Ink sighed.

"Because the wood's wet. You won't get anything without..." Cal tried to explain, but Ink wasn't hearing it.

He extended a hand to Garavel. "Give me a feather."

Without pause, Garavel reached behind to pluck one of his forearm-long feathers off his wings and passed it to the demon. Ink waved a palm over it and flames burst off the spine. They climbed nearly three feet into the air. As the fire danced in Ink's claws, his face warped, the flesh bubbling away to reveal the demon skin below. His eyes shifted from amber to blood-red as he watched me, seeming to wait for me to turn away.

As if I hadn't seen his full demon costume before. I met his stare and he dropped the feather to the wood. The tanned, ridiculously handsome man returned. The flames flickered from the middle of the log pile, struggling to catch, when the light dimmed and a puff of smoke twirled out.

"Like I said —" Cal placed a hand to Ink's shoulder. Fire burst free, the flames shooting across the entire pile. The bottom of the logs blazed a heat so white it almost turned blue, while a great orange haze shifted against the darkening sky.

"Creation magic. It's guaranteed to impress the masses." Ink rubbed his palms and held them closer to the fire. "Who wishes to go first? Or should I tell you the tale of a man who challenged Lucifer to a riddle contest? It did not go as he'd planned."

The buzzing insects zipped away from the smoke and heat, nearly drawing me in for a moment's reprieve. But as I rubbed my shoulder, Cal placed his hand there instead and resumed the massage he'd begun. "You boys have fun. I'm heading to bed."

"Why don't I come with?" Cal offered before anyone else could.

I'd expected nothing less. Squeezing his hand, I took off for the cabin, letting my hips sway as I went. Cal trailed behind like a lost puppy who deserved a reward.

"My bond," Ink shouted for the whole world to hear. "The lubricant is in your medical bag."

"Thanks." I tried to not grumble at him.

When I pushed open the door, the scent of cedar and damp plywood struck me before I was overrun by the intoxicating aroma of musk and pine. Cal wrapped his arms around me, prying at my shirt and reaching for my breasts as he kissed down my neck. I moaned and leaned back, clinging to his hair for support. His thick cock prodded against my tailbone in the same spot Ink had pressed, and a more feral groan slipped out.

Cal was huge, not so much in length but in terms of width. Some days I was amazed he didn't pass out getting an erection. He could feel like splaying myself on a train and that required a lot of long foreplay to get ready.

"You're worried," he said, pulling the hair off the other side of my neck. Cal danced the tips of his fingers down my throat like drops of rain. I pulled in a steadying breath, and he soothed his palm across my collarbone.

"I guess I am. It's stupid."

He slipped his hands away and walked around me. I stared at the squeaky mattress, which was certain to tell everyone out at that bonfire what we were doing. Cal caught my hands that I hadn't realized were trying to pick my nails off and held them safe. "About...? I know there's a lot to choose from right now."

Out of every supernatural mess in my life, it was the most normal worry in the world. The idea made me snicker, causing Cal to frown. "I'm thinking that..." I placed my palm to his chest, his pecs spread wide apart, and traced down to his abs. They'd been fading as of late, along with the rest of his muscles, thanks to not needing the wolf to fight off all manner of monsters. I found the sight of his softer body more enticing because of it. Swaying my fingers over his lower hips, I whispered in his ear, "You won't fit."

I cupped around his huge cock and Cal grunted. He bit my ear and licked the lobe. "That is a very good worry to have. Luckily, we know where the lube is."

I giggled at his reasoning and Cal tugged off my shirt. The cock in my hand thickened even more, reminding me why I was right to be concerned. He swept a hand over my breasts, still hidden beneath my bra. I kissed his moaning lips. Cal pressed a leg between mine and drew his knee. The wetness sweeping over me was a surprise. Maybe it wasn't such a problem after all.

"Layla, you are so fucking beautiful." He spread my legs wider. My rocky balance tipped into tumble territory, when sturdy hands clamped to my ass and raised me off the ground. As he lifted me to his height, his cock trailed from my lower belly down to the top of my thighs.

Cal stared up at me clinging to his shoulders and he smiled. "I fucking love you." He bit the top of my breast.

"Holy!" The simmering in my panties transformed to a hurricane. I fought to cinch my legs around his waist, to feel the proud crown of his cock pressing against me. Except there were two pairs of jeans in the way.

"We have a pants problem," I said, shaking away my fallen hair.

Cal chuckled. "I think I know one way to fix it." He tossed me to the bed. The mattress was harder than a rock and the springs creaked like a screen door in a swamp, but I didn't care. With one hand, Cal wrenched his T-shirt off by the back of the neck. I couldn't make out the veins I'd licked or the muscles I'd bitten in the low lantern light flickering from the table. But the silhouette of him hurling his shirt to the side was enough to fuel a dozen wet dreams.

He marched with unbreakable authority to me and I tried to sit up to meet him. Cal grabbed my pants by the hips and tossed me onto my back. "First yours," he whispered, working the button then the zipper. As he bent over, he placed a soft kiss to the right of my belly button. I wiggled to help, hoping the pants wouldn't catch on my ass or ankles. As Cal pulled them down, he kept kissing me. First at the top of my panties, then directly over them, at the top of my thigh, sweeping his tongue down the inner part and finally at my calf as he worked my jeans off.

"Now mine." He leaped onto the bed, pinning me between his arms. Cal kissed me hard, drawing his tongue across mine. Instead of reaching for his buttons, I gripped the back of his head and sucked on his bottom lip. "Layla," he groaned my name from his chest and picked up my hand. "You're torturing me."

He guided my hand to his jeans and the spartan belt looped in place. I tugged on the strap, tightening it around his thin waist. Cal surged closer, the bed squealing from our every movement. As I let the belt fall open, I reached for the zipper and curled my palm over the cock below.

A loud alarm blared out of nowhere.

We both jerked so fast in surprise our heads bonked. "What the…?" I sat up more carefully and Cal fumbled to his feet to chase down the noise. His hunt led him to my purse where he fished out my phone with a large white circle in the notification bar.

"Damn, I forgot."

It was my full moon warning, a couple of days early. Cal stared at the white orb, his handsome face turned terrifying from the bright blast of light. "I didn't realize it was so close," he whispered. "Maybe I should slip out and transform just to get it over with."

What, now? I sat up in just my underwear, my panties soaked and lips sore, to stare at him. "Are you doing it to avoid me?"

"No."

"Jealousy? Did Ink say something stupid?"

"No. Well, he probably did, but that ain't it." Cal cinched his belt back on even though he'd be putting on his fur.

I tried not to take it personally, but he was willing to run out into the forest rather than fuck me. Hard for that blow to not bludgeon one's ego to death. I folded my arms, trying to look resolute, but they turned into a self-hug instead.

He dropped my phone back into my bag and hunted for his shoes before looking at me. "Layla, it's... Okay, it is you, but." He stared down my body and swallowed. "I need a little time in the cold air to keep from... Fuck, this is embarrassing."

Oh! My body flushed when I recalled how I'd almost brought him to the brink without meaning to. Cal's Adam's apple bobbed in his throat as he clawed at the back of his head. I slipped from the bed and wrapped a hand around his naked waist. "Well...if it means I can enjoy you for even longer, then how can I say no?"

A smile dawned over his worry. He cupped my cheek and kissed me, tenderly at first, but the heat ramped back up. Cal palmed my ass, snapping the elastic of my panties. He pulled back and moaned, "You make this so hard."

I cupped his cock and smirked. "I know."

"One hour, tops. I promise. Fur and back." He dashed for the door, then stopped and stared. "I love you."

"Love you too, you big..."

Before I could finish, he ran out, in a hurry to grow the fur then come back to me. Grinning ear to ear, I picked up my phone and looked for the dirtiest book I had.

* * * *

Garavel

The kitten's purr rumbled across my shoulders as I stared into the fire. "I made so many of these during the war. Though...the witch would hide the flames."

Ink ceased prodding a stick into the cinders and knocked it against the stones. "In all that time, you were left to smolder your affections without any release?"

I pressed my thumb into the sitting log, trying to not think of the few times when I'd sat beside a woman and wondered. "It wasn't...done."

"Which part, the dashing romance with kisses to the hand and whispers at the ball? Or the ravishing behind the curtains while the butler hunted for his lordship's wayward sister?"

I frowned. "Both? I guess."

"Well." Ink clapped his hands, the force scattering sparks from the fire. They blew through the ghost, who barely looked up. "We can't be having any angelic blue balls now, can we? You're made of gemstone. Will they turn to diamonds if left under enough pressure?"

He stared at my lap, which I inspected, fearing I'd spilled food across the pants of sweat Layla had given me. "Will what?"

"Never you mind, my friend." Ink dashed around the bonfire and perched beside me. He draped a confiding arm over my shoulders and pulled me close. "Tell me, in the time I was away with the wolf, did you and our dear witch have a chance to speak?"

"No."

"So it's a virgin field to plow. I can work with this. Loosen up your limbs, angel." He popped back to his feet and shook his arms out. I did the same, feeling silly but enjoying the movement. Fiona had different thoughts. She leaped from her cozy hideaway in the dimension where my wings resided in order to stalk a bug in the grass.

"Why am I doing this?" I asked, flailing my hands until one slammed straight through the ghost's head. "Sorry."

He stared up at me and sighed. We hadn't spoken much, only a few words here and there.

"Because!" Ink tossed back his shoulders as if he wore a cape. His wings of shadow emerged as they folded up behind him. "Tonight I shall train you in the arts of wooing and bedding your dear lady witch."

"I'm done," the ghost said. He slammed the book he'd been reading and rose. If I twisted my head to the side, his ephemeral form vanished so it looked as if the tome was floating all by itself. "Good luck, angel. You're gonna need it."

"I'm not really an angel. They're the creators of all and... Oh, he's already left."

"Ignore the waste of sentience. He's only bitter because he hasn't seen his accoutrements in decades."

"Why? Did someone steal them?"

The incubus barked a laugh and wiped a tear from his eye. "In a manner of speaking. But Daniel does not matter. No, we are here to discuss Layla. Ah, there it is again."

"What?" I wiped at my head, finding it wouldn't stop sweating.

"The mere mention of her name causes your pulse to race and your eyes to widen in anticipation...or fear. Probably fear."

"I..." Instead of the smiling demon, I watched my kitten. Fiona had failed in her hunt and was toying with a tuft of tree bark instead. If it weren't for her safety, I'd never have returned. Never have spoken again to the lady witch. Never tasted her lips of my own accord and heard the trumpets of heaven. "I like her," I admitted aloud.

"Obviously. It doesn't take a lust sin to figure that out. You've had nearly a fortnight to reveal your intentions. What's stopping you?"

I dropped a crumb of the sweet yellow cake to my kitten. What was keeping me from her? "She's busy," I said.

"True. My bond does seem to keep steeping herself in responsibilities. But there have been moments. I've savored them quite readily..." He gleamed at the idea, his demonic body glittering with red light.

"You mean sex."

Ink blinked at me.

"I know what that is. Angels created it."

"Then I owe them my unending gratitude for such a feat. Perhaps a gift as well. Do they like salami? Never mind. Should we ever arrive at the gates of heaven, I'll worry about it then."

I laughed at the ludicrous idea. "That cannot happen."

He hummed as if he expected the realms to dissolve and the Celestials to return from their chosen exile tomorrow. "The return of angels and demons is not the current priority. What have you done with her, your lady witch? Have you sucked upon her breasts?"

"No." I gulped. Her forbidden fruit beckoned and terrified me more than any pomegranate from the garden could.

"Pressed your finger between her guarded cleft?"

"The what?"

He blinked at me and sighed. "Tell me you've at least kissed her."

I nodded. That we'd done. "Twice."

"Well, twice is better than once, and better still than never. Where to begin? Ah, of course, woman on top. Simple for a first timer. After removing her clothing and yours…"

Removing her… Then she'll be naked. And I will be naked with her!

"You shall part her thighs and place your cock against her cleft."

The…what?

"If you have troubles, let her take the lead. She can find it better than most men, save myself. Once she has lowered herself upon you, you will have little time to gird yourself. I've heard mortals speak of thinking about a ball of bases, whatever that means."

"Stop. I don't…" My chest burned. I dropped my head, braided my fingers behind the nape of my neck and fought to breathe. There was a rocky cleft involved but where would I find it without a map? And what did I need a chicken for? Was a sacrifice necessary? Why were we naked the whole time?

It had been easier when my creator had controlled my feelings. If I grew too close to a witch, he'd sense the threat and purge the emotions from me. Now I was a kettle of confounding thoughts and ideas. How could thinking of touching her under her clothes both excite and terrify me? It made no sense.

"Shall we pull it back and go for a more remedial teaching? How to talk to women one-on-one." He reached into his pocket and removed a set of spectacles. After placing the black frames on his nose, he pulled them to the tip and stared at me over them. "You have found a woman that you wish to speak with."

I nodded.

"But when you approach her, you feel light-headed and your body parts spontaneously wet themselves."

I rubbed my sweaty palms over my knees and gulped. "Sometimes my tongue becomes dry, like sand."

"That, my friend, is what we in the business call attraction. Or terror. But seeing as Layla is not a nightmare demon come to drive you mad, I'll lead with attraction."

"How do you know all of this? Do you feel the same when you talk to her?"

He cracked into a wide grin, silently laughing before tossing his head back and casting a guffaw to the skies. Ink wiped his eye and sighed. "No. I feel nothing but control when I whisper in her ear, caress her skin, bite her shoulder and spread her legs. Which is what you need to do."

"I do?"

"Yes. Control, of yourself. Tell your palms to cease sweating, your knees to hold straight, your tongue to whip off witty jokes that make her laugh. If you display your ability to completely command every facet of your body, every woman will swoon as you pass."

He finished by posing, sweeping his hand through his hair and sticking out his backside. I wished I had a notebook to write all this down.

"Your turn. Pretend I'm Layla. Walk up to me as if you were created to bring her unending pleasure." He pushed me into the dark grass where I stumbled, uncertain what he meant.

No sweaty palms. I moved to wipe them off, but stopped and told them to cease being damp. I couldn't tell if it worked as I extended my arms wide to look larger. That always worked during the war. *Pleasure.* How did I bring her pleasure? I pulled in a breath and raised my head. Alas, that caused me to stare above the demon's head. All I could see was a tuft of black hair as I strode over with my most confident self.

"Hello there," Ink said. "You look like you have something you want to say."

"I…" *Breathe. Confident. Control. No sweat. Pleasure.* "I don't know what to say. What do I say?"

"'The gazebo's empty' always worked for me."

What was a gazebo? Was it spicy? Did I have to eat while being in control?

"Here." The demon patted my arm. "Let me give you some advice."

To get her to like me? To want to kiss me again?

To get naked?

Ink wrapped a hand around my shoulder and he stood up taller to whisper in my ear. "Be yourself."

"I've been myself for the past two weeks and all I do is stutter and run away from her. How is that helping?"

He smirked. "I know, it's worthless advice, but humans bandy it about like it's gold. You are stressing yourself over a minor issue. Give it time and…"

Her cabin door opened, and both of us fell silent. Instead of Layla rushing into our arms, a gut-wrenching voice said, "One hour, tops."

I clenched my fist, squeezing tighter as the wolf ran off into the night, no doubt to do despicable things. The veins running through my body popped free of the ebony flesh, lifting off my skin, but I couldn't stop. Had they been doing what Ink described earlier? And he ran out on her right after? *That monster.*

"Here it is."

Ink's words snapped me from the night of howls. I shook away my fist, pulling back the strength that'd toppled towers, and looked at him. "What is?"

"Your opportunity. Get in there and give her your everything." He pushed me toward the cabin. I staggered on a foot, my mind reeling.

Talk to her? Right now? What if she wasn't wearing any clothes?

Oh creators, what if she was naked? What if the skin over her breasts was as soft as her lips?

The insatiable excitement carried me another four steps closer before the terror kicked back in. I couldn't do this. I didn't know what to say. What if I made it worse and somehow took back the kiss?

"Remember, control!" Ink shouted.

Control. Breathe. Stop sweating. Clefts. Chickens. Tell her she looks nice.

Control.

I walked up the first step, then the second.

Breathe.

I can do this.

"Cal, is that you? That was quick."

I couldn't do this. The demon, the ghost, even the cursed werewolf could walk up to her and ask for another kiss. But I was a mess of...

Breathe.

I gripped the handle and pressed on the latch. The door swung open.

Control.

Chapter Ten

Layla

I'd barely found the right chapter when I heard the steps creak. Had something happened? Cal tried to get his shift over as fast as possible, but even he couldn't be that quick.

After he didn't answer, I leaped off the bed, picked up the electric lantern and almost walked into the opening door. The beam of light caught off of nothing but darkness as if night itself had walked into my cabin. I squeezed my eyes tight and focused.

"Oh, Garavel. You scared me."

"I did?" He froze in the cabin's tiny entryway and stared down at me. Then his jaw dropped.

I self-consciously crossed my legs, growing aware of how little I had on as a cool breeze cut through the cabin. Goosebumps rose and I rubbed my stomach to try to warm myself.

"I'm...I'm sorry," he said and jerked his head up.

I laughed it off. "It's not your fault. Just...jitters about sleeping in a new place."

"Jitters?"

I turned away from him to place the lantern back, but stopped and stared over my shoulder. Oh yeah, he was laser focused on my ass. Innocently, I grazed my palm across the panty line barely keeping my cheeks in check. He gulped like a fish on a line, his gaze drifting slightly higher to match my movements until he stared me in the eye. Garavel full-body shuddered and stared at the wall.

"It's a feeling of unease," I said, picking back up the conversation.

"Oh, like when I eat too much of Mr. Ink's cooking."

I laughed at the idea while also partially terrified. "Not exactly. More like goosebumps and the hairs on the back of your neck standing on end."

The hairless angel rubbed the nape of his neck, then shrugged.

"Okay, it's a human thing. Like something's not quite right. I'm sure it's nerves. Anyway, you don't have to keep standing in the door."

He nodded at my suggestion, but didn't move. I walked to my bed to give him ample room to wander about. After sitting down, I less-than-innocently crossed my legs. Still, Garavel remained rooted. "Was there something you wanted? Needed?"

"Yes!" he gasped.

I'd never seen a man look so knotted up. He kept slapping his palms together, then twisting his fingers, while bobbing on his knees like an old black and white cartoon. "I wanted to... I, um, I needed to..."

"Are you feeling okay? You're sweating a lot." Could angels catch fevers? Would my healing magic work on him? I moved to stand up to offer and he leaped a full foot to the right.

"You weren't supposed to... The clothes came later. And there's a chicken I don't have."

What in the hell was he talking about? "Is it a fever? Like a burning through your body? I could ask Daniel, there may be something in one of his books."

"No!" he shouted, crab-walking for the far edge of the cabin. "No need for anyone else here. I'm...I'm fine."

He was anything but fine—none of us were. But I didn't even know where to begin to help him. I was alive because he had killed his creator. Seemed like every day that passed, he grew more nervous around me, and I wondered if that was disguising his resentment. At that rate, it wouldn't be long until he despised me as much as Cal.

"I was just here for..." He launched for the farthest bed and ripped the blanket off. "This. I'm going to sleep with Mr. Ink tonight."

"You mean beside. With implies you're going to... You know, never mind." I wasn't in the mood to have the metaphorical versus literal talk with him yet. "Are you sure you want to do that? It's gonna get chilly and there are a lot of wild animals—"

"Yes. I like animals. And I haven't slumbered under the skies since the stars were born." He tossed the blanket over his shoulders like a cape and walked backwards to the door. Sadly, he was off by a few feet and smashed into the wall. I winced, but Garavel only smiled and side-stepped to the left.

With one last grin, he yanked on the door and dashed out.

"Gary," I called out. His fleeing paused. "Sleep well."

Slowly, Garavel looked over his shoulder at me. "You too, lady witch."

He vanished into the night where hopefully Ink would keep him safe. Good thing the angel and demon had become fast friends or I didn't know what I'd do with him. I wrapped my hands around the back of my neck and pressed my thumbs into the sides. God, the knots were like steel girders. I dug in again, tempted to call up my magic. Did the book have a spell for relaxing muscles in particular?

Slipping off the rickety bed, I reached for my purse sitting on the folding table.

"Layla…"

I jerked my head at the voice. "Ink?" I called out even though I knew it wasn't him. Not even my wayward incubus answered, so I plucked out my spell book and laid it on the table. Why did I think this was a good idea?

Exhaustion plus low light equaled my dyslexia going bonkers. My ancestor witches' awkward handwriting jiggled in place, erasing any hope I had of finding a spa-day spell. Maybe a rejuvenation and relaxation potion? As I flipped the pages, no longer needing to make the request aloud for my book to know what I wanted, I watched more and more of my handwriting mix in with the strangers'. Notes, phonetic spellings, even highlighted sections all flew past. It didn't strike me as strange to treat it like a text book until I remembered the thing could move on its own.

"Layla?"

A presence tugged back my hair. I whipped around, ready to clobber or burn it. But nothing stood in the empty corner. "Fariah?" I called out, more certain the voice was female. "Maram?" She was a little weird, sure, but not 'go invisible and terrify people' weird.

Unless my best friend is dating a creature that can do that. Crap.

"Give me the reveal spell," I commanded, letting whoever was in there know I was on to them. The pages flipped fast, landing on one of the spells Daniel had helped me decipher. I held my palm flat to the wall and recited the syllables he'd written with my hand.

A pale blue light burst from my palm that, much like UV light finding bloodstains, was supposed to illuminate whoever was hiding. I wafted it across the whole corner, discovering a fading bit of graffiti declaring "Robert was here." Another quick check around the whole of the cabin found nothing out of the ordinary.

"You're losing it," I said to myself, snapping my book shut and placing it securely in my purse. At least if any of the humans opened it, they wouldn't be able to read anything. Was that a spell the witches had cast to protect themselves and their progeny? Or were the angels behind that one too?

It didn't matter. I was working myself up into the wrong kind of lather over nothing more than some creaky branches. After taking one last look with the lantern, I returned to my bed and picked up the book.

"Layla..."

My hands fell and I stared at nothing. Warmth bubbled through my veins. It felt like fresh chocolate chip cookies, snuggling under blankets, petting a new puppy and slipping into a hot bath all at once. All the stress on my shoulders slipped off in one go. I oozed out of the bed onto unsteady feet, my head floating and body bouncing in place.

"Come and find me."

"Sounds good," I said to the voice and reached for the door latch. The chill of the metal struck me, ripping a hole in the cozy blanket wrapped around my soul.

Better put clothes on.

Shirt and jeans seemed like too much work, so I dug through Cal's side to find his robe. The smell of his body bounced off the heavy sleeves that hung past my hands and I breathed deep. *Lying in bed with him for hours with my head on his chest. Ink massaging my feet and calves.* In total bliss, I reached for the door handle and opened it.

"Yes. Come find me," the voice taunted.

Numb and smiling I walked into the warm and sparkling air, following after my new friend. *Funny, the magic voice almost sounds like mine.*

* * * *

Ink

Curiosity might kill the cat, but demons were afforded an unlimited set of lives. Besides, some things were worth risking death over.

The wolf was surprisingly agile as he dashed through the woods, caring nothing for the twigs and rocks certain to prod into his feet. I gave him a wide berth, not wanting to reveal myself in undue time. Or until the proper fanfare arrived, perhaps with golden trumpets and a dozen peacocks. My bond had been enjoying his brute force seduction attempts with much vigor. For him to bolt could spell yet more trouble, or a pressing requirement to urinate.

While the trees around our camp site were young and nubile, the deeper we pressed, the more gnarled and cantankerous they became. It was by the fifth branch snagging on my shirt and attempting to remove my pants that I began to wonder why I didn't simply travel between realms instead. How did mortals manage in this cluttered world?

Thankfully, the wolf paused, his back to me as he faced down a pine with its needles splayed out above our heads. *Ah, it must be the urination, after all.*

"Do not stop on my account," I announced.

Calvin's shoulders shot up to bury his neck. He fought to lower them to hide the surprise, then glanced back to me. While the scant starlight whitened his bare chest, he remained in his signature shapeless denim. Strange.

"Ink." He sighed as if I was not a threat to him. "What are you doing here?"

"Here I was wondering the same. You and our beloved appeared to be reaching a fevered pitch when suddenly you ran."

He tossed back his blond hair and stared into the tattered branches faming the night sky. "Is it possible to ask you to not — ?"

"No. I mean, you may ask whatever you wish. Plead for the heavens to rain caramel upon your cheeks. Beg for the seas to turn to wine. It simply will not happen."

"Okay. Fine. Since you're so damn nosy all of a sudden, I came out here to shift."

"With your trousers remaining?" I pointed to the abominable jeans that required serious tailoring to be acceptable.

He pursed his lips in an insolent pout no doubt my bond either found enticing or infuriating. Knowing them, both. "I didn't want to walk back to camp totally naked in case of..."

"Logical, but also a lie."

Surely he knew I could read every half and full truth radiating about his head. It made hunting so much easier to know when the woman who claimed to be recently widowed kept a cuckold at home. Or if one of the solid legs in this four-spoke relationship was seeming to return to his more disconcerting ways.

Calvin didn't question me on it, probably because he was, on the whole, terrible at falsehoods. Instead, he took his time shaking his head then zeroed in on me. "What about you? Layla's all alone back at the cabin and more than ready to..." He shivered, not from a chill, but a heat running down his spine. No doubt the thought of her reclining in the bed waiting for his return toyed with his resolve. "What are you doing here?"

"A most astute question."

The chill of the forest air sharpened to an ice pick. I needn't move as she took no time to saunter into the clearing. The wide-brimmed hat was gone. Instead, her blonde hair was curled into soft ringlets and piled across her bare shoulders. She wore a thin shift in her signature crimson the same color at her lips.

"Who the fuck are you?" Calvin reacted not as most men would upon finding a nearly naked woman in the middle of a forest. As his eyes began to scan down her, I stepped in between, hoping to stop the oncoming disaster.

She chuckled and posed, one hand on her hip, her breasts turned to the side. "Yes, Eros. Who the *fuck* am I?"

I gulped at the force she directed at me, reminding me how long it had been since I'd last dined. While I was nowhere near as weak as a Sin reaching desiccation, I felt as strong as a strip of birch bark compared to her. She'd eaten recently and had her fill. Somewhere in the world were a half-dozen men dead with only smiles on.

"This is Lust," I said to her viper grin.

"Great." Calvin threw his hands up in exasperation. "Another one."

"I put the question to you as well, Lust. What are you doing out here?"

She batted away my accusation with a flick of her wrist. "Perhaps I'm looking for you."

"You never look," I responded. We were all predators in our own way, tigers and lions moving through the foliage hunting for easy prey. Lust was in a league above us—hunting with such prowess we didn't even see her do it.

"Imagine my shock, my very horror to find that my dear Eros is out here in the woods. Where there's insects instead of nubile virgins, mud instead of amphoras of honey and cuddly wildlife..." She pointed to Calvin who snarled. "Instead of bevies of ample flesh."

She was digging for something, and I had a pretty good idea what. "The honey can wait, and I have no use for virgins. As for the flesh...it's quite ample and pleasing to the palate."

I didn't realize I'd leaned closer to her until Lust tapped her long red nail to my cheek.

"This is getting weird, so..." Calvin groaned, unaware of the mental battle before him.

"Then why, dearest Eros, did you let another bumbling fool take your prey when she was practically begging for it?"

I should have known she'd been watching that. Lust punctured her nail deeper through my skin until ichor dripped down my cheek. I felt no pain, but she dragged her finger through my blood, then licked it off with a giggle.

To my growing consternation, the wolf couldn't cease inserting himself into this. "What bumbling fool? Me? Because I was handling Layla just fine on my —"

"Not you." The angry side of Lust snapped through. Rare, not for its existence, but for her using it on mortals. She almost never felt anything for them, the way people never felt rage or concern for their sandwich. "The big one."

It took a moment before it dawned on Calvin that she referred to the angel. "Great. Tonight's going just...frickin' great."

She perked up at his rising emotions, a familiar trick to make feeding easier. I once again stepped between them to focus her ire elsewhere. "If you are here to find me, pray tell the reason so we may all abandon this chilled night."

Lust chuckled. Instead of answering, she removed her compact and turned her back to me. With great care, she inspected her perfect visage and makeup. An eye red as a sunset beamed from the mirror. "What makes you think I'm here for you?" She snapped the compact shut and whipped around to face me. "That was always your downfall, Eros. A cocky swagger can only get you so far before you require the stones to back it up."

Her aura shifted to a ravenous black, tendrils snapping through the air to suck up any errant magic. With it, she grew more forceful, guiding all her strength into a single finger pressed to my sternum. I locked my leg in even as the knee bent. The femur vibrated within the limb, prepared to crack in half from the two immoveable forces.

She wanted me before her, to praise and celebrate her as I once had upon my creation. I'd always run from Lust, crisscrossing the globe in search of a place without her. She'd always followed, happy to tear through an entire village and drag me along with. I hunted beside her, happily, greedily, never looking back until the nights grew as empty as the days.

When I swallowed deep, a scent lingered not only in my nose and on my tongue but wrapped inside my very being—jasmine.

"Why are you here?" I countered. The memory of my bond holding my fading mortal body in her arms gave me the strength to rise. How she'd kissed me with everything she had to bring me back let me turn the pressure back on Lust.

It was little more than a soft poke in comparison but her eyes widened at my attempt. "You really believe you have all the answers, Eros?"

"Depends on the topic."

She chuckled. "Found yourself a little woman to take nibbles from, a home to pretend to settle in. Don't you understand how easily it can all come crashing down?"

I raised my hand to shield myself. But it wasn't to me she directed the full force of her power. An unbreakable shield of erotic hunger radiated around her and she turned it all on the idiotic werewolf still standing there. "Look at me," she commanded, clutching tight to his cheek.

"Calvin, close your ey —"

Lust backhanded me and I slammed into a tree. It would have hurt had I been mortal, but all my concern was on the damn idiot's eyes doing as he'd been told. They didn't skirt across her body, but languidly took her in. If she did this…if she killed him, my bond would never speak to me again.

I struggled to my feet, only for Lust to shake out her wings. Sharp as diamonds, they snapped back to slice through my skin and she enveloped herself and Calvin in them. He was visible beneath her impenetrable shield, about to fall to his doom while all I could do was watch.

She tripled her focus on him, impossible power surging through his body. He groaned at the hardest erection of his life as she mentally pushed him close to climax. Staring him in the eye, Lust reached for his crotch and ordered, "I'm going to fuck you and you're —"

"No."

Her hand froze and she cocked her head in shock. "No? Don't you want me to give you the best sex of your life?"

With a deep groan, Calvin managed to blink. "Not particularly."

How in the twelve realms…?

Lust seemed just as confused as I. Her wings fell and Calvin jerked his head from her tight grip. He took a step back, freeing himself from her pressure, though his trousers remained well tented.

"Seems someone's finally refused you, Lust," I taunted, trying to bury my shock behind an aura of insouciance.

Wild, demonic eyes whipped back to me, then to her unbothered prey as if she'd lost all control. "As if I haven't watched you fail a thousand times before, Eros." She was fighting to gain back her perch, but Calvin had thoroughly obliterated it.

I patted her back in mock sympathy. "Rejection gets easier each time."

With a loud snarl, Lust extended her wings, the diamond sharp edges slicing me again. I didn't let my smile dim for a second. She slipped into the in-between realms and I happily let her go with a wave. "Try to not be such a sore loser. It's quite the turn off."

We both waited, listening for the scream of a vengeful incubus. But without her presence, the low hooting of owls and cry of loons returned instead. "Well..." Calvin adjusted himself, squeezing back the erection she'd caused. "Succubi aren't that hard to combat."

"She is an incubus."

"I thought succubus equaled lady. Incubus was a...you know."

"An incubus is one who pursues sex, a succubus is one who lures in with sex. Gender has nothing to do with it." I'd rather focus on the pedantry than what had occurred. In all my time with her, in all my travels, from nun to king, from monk to empress, I'd never seen anyone refuse Lust until now.

"How...?" I started before squaring my stance. "Perhaps it's because you're a werewolf. Maybe it does not work on your kind, and I'd never noticed before."

Calvin in his nonchalant fashion shrugged. "Could be. All I know is, I'm too moon-damn exhausted to shift. I'm heading back." He took a few steps for the cabin before glancing back to me. "Layla?"

"This does not seem like a topic she needs to hear about. Yet."

"Yeah. That was...not fun." He smiled as if he hadn't just battled with the strongest will I'd ever known. With a quick jog, he ran out of the woods to lie with or even beside our beloved.

A dangerous, volatile thought churned through my mind. While many mortals could be unaffected by us via gender and sexual preferences, there was another deeper reason we were incapable of combating. Lust could overcome any obstacle save one. Calvin could be so deeply in love with my bond that he wanted no one else for life.

I'd be deluded to compare to that.

Chapter Eleven

Layla

The air reverberated with my name. It echoed in waves, each syllable striking quickly before the next. I turned my head around, trying to find the source, but it came from everywhere and nowhere. Light radiated off my palm, not in a cute orb, but a crackling and sometimes hissing simulacrum of fire. Whatever witch had come up with the first magical torch either hadn't gotten it quite right, or had wanted to scare the piss out of villagers.

"This way..."

The voice skipped, darting through the trees in a stream of sound I could see. Blue and purple lines dashed around the forest, traveling deeper into the woods. For a moment, I stopped and stared up at the sky. Harsh moonlight cut through the branches and I shivered.

What am I doing out here?

Warmth bubbled around me, chasing away the momentary cold. Giddy, I followed after the voice luring me away. "Hello?" I called out, trying to be friendly. "Do you need help?"

I walked into a small clearing where a deer could sleep for the night. Instead of a fawn slumbering below the tree, nothing but the damp leaves and mud sat there. *Did I miss them?* I turned over my shoulder, trying to make sense of where I was.

"Oh yes, mistress." The voice laughed and the air crackled. Pain sundered up my hand, my little torch snapping electricity back through my arm. Groaning, I fought to close my palm and cut off the spell, but an invisible pressure forced it open.

The indigo and starry sky snapped to pieces. A blood-red cut apart the jagged blue, and every one of the stars opened its eyelid to stare at me. I clung to my wrist, fighting to get the magic to end. Electricity ran up my whole body, every hair standing as I tumbled to a knee. A chill colder than anything on earth rose behind me.

I knew this place. I'd fallen here when Mr. White had attacked me. This was the in-between and I didn't belong here. If I didn't get out soon, I'd...

"I need your help." The once-sweet voice shifted, shattering to a screech that bashed into my ears. I had to find a way out. The presence behind me grew colder. I wouldn't look at it, knowing that if I did...I couldn't look away.

Get out of here.

Run!

The order didn't come from my mind, but inside of it. I jerked as my mother's old lullaby rolled in my ears.

Where was my chain to Ink? How did I get out of here—?

"You're not going anywhere—"

"Layla?"

Cold pierced my shoulder and I screamed. The entire world jiggled and I blinked, tears tumbling from my eyes. Instead of a blood-red sky covered in eyeballs, the white moon and stars gazed down at me.

"I saw your light and...?"

Even as I turned, my heart pieced together it wasn't the terrifying voice, nor the one giving orders. Still, I pressed a hand over my heart to find Daniel standing behind me. It'd been his cold hand that had touched me and not whatever existed in the in-between.

"You scared the hell out of me," I said, shaking my fingers. Why were they aching so bad? *Must be the chilly night.*

"Sorry. I was calling to you, but...it was as if you couldn't hear me." Deep worry etched across Daniel's impossibly hot face.

"I must have been in another world," I said, reaching over and placing my palm above his heart. It disguised the bloom of blood spreading over his jacket below. "I'm sorry. I can see you and hear you. I swear."

He put on a smile, no doubt for my benefit, and leaned closer. My hand sank into his chest, the cold of him tickling my fingers. Daniel brushed his forehead to mine, setting off goosebumps. "What are you doing out here in a"—his gaze drifted from my eyes down to my chest and he shuddered—"barely tied robe?"

Gulping, I looked to find the knot had come completely undone, revealing my bra and a hint of my panties to the forest. *Sorry, woodland creatures and any passing gnomes.* I moved to cinch it up when Daniel slipped his fingers inside of mine. He stopped me from closing it up and placed my palm to my stomach.

"Hoping for a midnight rendezvous in the forest?" Daniel ran my hand higher, pushing aside the robe so it fell off my shoulder, leaving my right half practically naked.

"Where there's bugs, and poison ivy and…" I tried to list off all the bad things about that idea, but my brain shut down. He'd hooked my fingers around my bra and pulled me closer to him. With my thumb, he traced the curve of my breast spilling over the top.

"And…?" Daniel prompted. He slipped into my other hand to take control. With it, he brushed my numb fingers down my pelvis and ran a finger over my panties.

"You cannot make a grilled cheese in the toaster. I don't care how many videos—"

Daniel yanked himself out from possessing me and turned around just as Cal and Ink…? What the hell was he doing out here?

"Layla?" Cal sputtered. "Are you wearing my robe?" He stared down at me, then growled. "Why don't you do that more often?"

Oh, god. Despite the obvious male approval around me, I pulled the robe closed and double-knotted the tie for extra support.

"While the question goes without saying, I shall attempt it regardless. What brings you into the forest?" Ink asked.

"I was…" Why was I out here? I'd been reading, then Garavel came to talk to me. No, he just came in to get something. Was that why?

Cal punctured through my confusion with a weary sigh. He enveloped my waist with one arm and held me close. "You didn't have to."

Ellen Mint

"Have to what?"

"Come find me. I can't get lost in the woods. My nose is too good. But you could while trying to track me down."

I glanced to my demonic tracking beacon and the ghost hanging around my neck. I had two separate Find-Your-Layla apps thanks to Ink and Daniel. But Cal nuzzled my neck and breathed deep. With a heavy pant, he whispered, "My robe is going to smell like you for days."

"Oops?"

He snickered, letting the moonlight fall on his fang. "As if you didn't do it on purpose." Cal leaned closer, lifting my chin to kiss me, when his entire body pitched to the side. Ink was first to catch him, but I was a close second.

"Sorry, I..." He looked back to Ink who went strangely quiet. "I must have worn myself out with that last shift."

Three hot men who wanted to answer my every fantasy stood around me, but an unquiet feeling sat in my gut. Ignoring it, I focused on Cal. "We should get to bed."

"That is much preferable to a rotting forest floor. Nary a stump for balance in place," Ink said.

"For sleeping," I countered.

"I suppose your dear wolf has run through the gauntlet tonight. You should refrain from draining him dry until he's regained his stamina."

Cal shot him a dirty look for the low blow, but Ink shrugged it off. My incubus scratched his chin and stared past me to Daniel lurking just at the edge. "Or should we return to the cabin of slumber and leave you two to continue whatever druidic worship of the dead you'd intended?"

I blinked and the sky glitched. Only for a second, and no doubt from an errant eyelash, but the sight caused my heart to beat rapidly. Shaking my head, I slipped an arm around Cal's waist and he did the same to me. "I'm tired too. We can have a hedonistic forest foursome tomorrow."

"I shall wear the puckish antlers," Ink declared with pride.

I was too tired to ask if he meant that as a joke. With him, it was impossible to tell.

"Ghost? Will you be joining us or do you intend to zip back to your reading?"

That might have been the nicest thing Ink had ever said to Daniel. Even Daniel looked surprised at his being included, then Ink had to say. "You are the type to bring a novel to an orgy."

"I'm out. I'll see you come daylight, Layla. As for you." He stared hard at Ink and spat out, "βάλλ' εἰς κόρακας." Daniel vanished as Ink laughed.

"They have very little use for me," Ink called to the air.

I hobbled beside Cal, the two of us stupid enough to head into the woods without shoes on. Glancing over at Ink who was staring back into the forest, I asked, "What did he say to you?"

Ink smiled. "It's not for a lady's ears."

I waited for a laugh and the real explanation, but that seemed to be all that was coming. With a shrug, Ink bowed and vanished, leaving me alone with Cal. Clinging to him, I stared back once, making certain the sky was still blue and having no idea why.

* * * *

I spent the night sleeping in Cal's arms. He hadn't said a word, just shoved his bed frame next to mine and scooped me up. Morning came way too fast for my liking and before I knew it, I'd agreed to chase out all the spiders lurking in the outer cabins. What happened to the others I couldn't guess, though it seemed Dante had plans for all of them. But we'd been promised a treat for the afternoon and that kept me going as I plunged through the third massive spiderweb, praying none of them laid eggs in my brain.

My skin prickled, but not from imagined eight-legged creatures scurrying over it. I couldn't say why, but my first thought was that someone was watching me. Which was stupid. If it was any of my teleporting guys, they'd announce themselves, probably along with a snide remark about another. Though they seemed to be on their best behavior for this trip. Maybe this whole bevy of hot men at my beck and call thing could work out.

"You're deluding yourself," I whispered to my reflection in the mop bucket. Wringing out the old head, I slapped it to the ground and began to mop while beats sashayed down my spine. For the first time in ages, I didn't think about magic, or monsters or even IV bags. Instead, I let my mind wander. The cabins were rustic in that summer camp way I'd only ever seen on TV.

I'd asked my mother about them once, curious but also nervous about so many other kids in one place. The only time I'd been around children was on the playground for an hour a week at my auntie's doing. My mom had snuffed the idea out, insisting if I needed to spend a week in the woods, I could do it with her and her new friends. There were always new women in passing. Multiple rings on their fingers, scarves in their hair, tattoos of all shapes and sizes — it wasn't until I got thrown into the American school system that I realized how weird it was. They never stayed around long. Almost as if they both needed something from the other despite not liking my mom.

Only Didi had remained right until the end.

I missed her, but no one celebrated Auntie Day with flowers and brunch. People pitied me for not having a mom, and they didn't even ask about my aunt. I rolled mourning her in with my mother. Didi would put me in front of the television every Sunday and work on my hair. I'd be so excited to pick the barrettes and ribbons. She'd had a purple and ivory butterfly barrette I'd screamed murder over when I lost it.

Didi smelled like apples all the time, even in winter. And she was always singing to her plants. No matter how little time we spent at a place, she'd have it covered in thriving greenery. We'd play jungle cats in them all the time.

I didn't realize I was crying until wetness rained on my shirt. Why wasn't it her? Why couldn't she be the one to come back after faking her death instead of my mother? Didi wouldn't have attacked my guys. She'd have made them a fruit salad and told them to eat it all up.

"Layla?"

Damn it. I dug into my eyes, trying to disguise my tears. Pulling in a cleansing breath, I looked over my shoulder to find Garavel standing in the doorway. "What's up?"

"Are you sad?"

My first instinct was to lie, but he asked with such earnestness my tongue stuck. I nodded a bit, then turned away from him. "I was thinking about my..." Did angels have aunts? Did they have anyone outside of their creators? "My friend who died. It was a long time ago. I shouldn't feel bad about it anymore."

"I watched many of my friends die."

Fuck, of course. He wasn't just the big, goofy marshmallow with a kitten and a heart of gold. He had also been a general in a huge angel war. "That can't have been easy." I glanced over my shoulder.

Garavel stood in the doorway, his head nearly hitting it. He closed his eyes and breathed deep. "I would try to honor them by singing their songs around the fire so others crafted from the earth would know those who'd fallen before."

His voice caught in a ragged breath. Abandoning my mop, I gingerly placed my palm to his arm. For being carved from ebony, his skin was softer than cocoa butter and as warm as a jacuzzi. He didn't flee or curse me out, so I tried running my hand up and down to comfort him.

"They died a long time ago," he said, shutting down the conversation.

I nodded and moved to step away when Garavel placed his palm to my cheek. "But I still think about them."

The tears started in rivers at his kindness, but Garavel gasped. "Oh no, I...I said the wrong thing."

"No, you didn't."

He raced to run away, but by my single palm, I held the great man as if I had all the power. Slowly, I ran my hand down his shoulder to his arm. "I spent a lot of time hiding my grief. It's nice to be allowed to let it out."

Garavel watched me caress him. My brain stuck, only telling my hand to soothe his arm and nothing more. All the while I thought of Didi cooking up a huge pot of rhubarb and asking me to get the sugar. At the same time, I pictured Garavel in his angelic regalia sitting around a fire singing for other demi-angels as tears dripped from his eyes.

"You don't have to hide with me," he said, bending over nearly at his waist. I gazed up into his deep brown eyes. Garavel placed his thumb to my hairline and followed along the edges.

"You don't have to hide with me either," I said, hoping he'd understand. Garavel blinked and slowly smiled with a grin I'd only seen reserved for his kitten. "Everything you've been through, you can talk to me about."

"It was many, many, many years ago. You wouldn't know anyone in it."

"But they live in you."

Garavel laughed once without any sound. He cupped the back of my hand and raised it to his chest to place it over his heart. "We are rock, as unbreakable as the stone of the Earth. Our bodies can be chipped and repaired, sanded back to smooth. But inside, each loss cleaves a piece we can never heal. After the war, I must look like a geode."

How much pain is he carrying? Not only from the war but…?

"I'm sorry," I whispered, guilt swarming through me.

"It was a long time ago, and you would have been on the side of good."

"Not that. About what happened in the underground tunnels."

Garavel's soft features hardened to stone. He didn't drop my hand but he clenched tighter to my fingers. Still, I had to press on. He acted as if nothing had happened, but a storm was coming and we had to all be ready.

"I don't wish to speak of it," he said.

"But he…he was like your father. More than your father, and you…" Maybe I should have felt special that he had picked me over a literal angel, but all I knew was an ever-pressing guilt that I'd caused the destruction of a being that had created everything.

Garavel retracted his hand and shook his head. "No."

"You said it yourself—you can't hide the grief. It's in there."

"I cannot speak to you about him!" he shouted and turned to run. I reached for him, needing to not lose this moment, when another hand caught mine.

Out of habit, I jerked back and conjured a spell. Ink breathed against my ear. "Let him go."

"He's in pain."

"And you will only deepen it."

I shook away the fire even though I had an urge to turn it on him. "Thanks," I snarled.

"You don't understand. You cannot."

"He made the right choice. We're gonna save the world, all the worlds, including wherever the rest of the angels live. That's a good thing."

Ink tipped his head and sighed. "Perhaps, in the future when all is right and we are free to lap honey off of nipples and thighs. But now, does he seem ready to celebrate all he lost for a better world?"

I wanted to argue with him that I could help Garavel, but maybe Ink was right. Maybe just being around me made it worse. Then what? I didn't know how to move past this. "How do you know so much about angels?"

He snickered. "I do not. But when an oath is sworn by bone and sealed in blood, I know all too well the pain of breaking it."

"Ink?"

The human façade faded away. His demonic skin didn't crackle with its usual threats and anger, but dulled to a mournful gray. I ran my fingers across his cheek, for once feeling the craggy bumps of the volcanic visage. At my touch, he threw back on his appearance and smiled at me. "Come. The time of toiling is over. Let the feasting begin."

God, I hope Cal was put in charge of that. I moved to slip my fingers out to head for the food but Ink kept a hold of them. Slowly, he raised my knuckles to his lips. Closing his eyes, he kissed them deeply.

Chapter Twelve

Ink

Rather than return to their toiling after consuming the tubes of meat, the group was given a reprieve to enjoy the afternoon. While I grew suspicious of an offer of generosity, the rest bore no such concern. With little fanfare, we traveled to the shared beach. Layla sat perched on Calvin's lap while I'd offered the same to him. He declined.

"All right, here you go," Dante said, pausing the carriage just long enough for all of us to leap from its confines. The rest of them clung to towels and coolers while staring down a path between two fences. "You'll get a few hours, then I'll swing by to pick you up. Cool?"

Before anyone could answer, he turned the car and sped back in the direction of the camp. Layla stopped beside me and laughed. "I'm surprised he didn't ask if we had our juice boxes and water wings."

"Do we need those?" The quiet one perked up, then her eyes widened in shock. I'd never known another creature so stunned at their own voice before. She was soothed by Layla's friend, and the two walked for the beach.

I strolled next to Garavel, who tended to his feline companion. She sat perched on his shoulder like a king atop his castle. I reached a finger out for her, then extended the claw. Without pause, Fiona scratched her cheek and head against the sharp edge.

After the unforgiving rocks and choppy lake, I expected little more than reeds to give way to chilling water. Coming upon an expanse of sand was a surprise. Now, was it a sand so white as to appear as snow that baked one's feet? No. Was it a fabled sand black as midnight which glittered with a thousand stars in the sun? Also no. But it wasn't rocks. Those were located farther to the west where the land rose to a small cliff.

"What do people do at the beach?" Garavel asked.

"Preen, pounce or parboil. Often in a single day if they're ambitious."

He frowned at my summation which was more trite than useful. "That sounds complicated."

"What do you do at beaches?" Despite my long years and many travels, I'd never known anyone from the before times. Even Lust did not exist until after the realms were sealed away.

"Oh, nothing exciting. We'd dig a hole and put our injured in the sand. Then a witch would zap it and they'd be good as new."

"Yes. Quite dull." My comment sailed around his head as Garavel stopped and stared in the direction of the rest of the group. I rather doubted his attentions were on the sour ghost staring forlornly across the waves to the island. Nor would he have had much interest in the two women dressed head to toe for the water. And if he was inspecting the werewolf pulling off his shirt, I'd have had a few follow-up questions.

I'd guess all of Garavel's rising hunger was for the woman who laid out her towel, unhooked the two straps on her overalls, and tugged them off her hips. Buttery silk fabric in royal purple clung to her bottom half, revealing the curve of her lower belly and hips, as well as the underside of her buttocks. While laughing, she removed the baggy T-shirt from work and the dear angel gurgled at the midnight black bikini lifting her breasts with nothing but a single string against the nape of her neck.

"What is that?" He struggled, pointing to Layla while struggling to not look too hard.

"Modern swimwear." I too was surprised to find such intriguing choices that people would wear outside the home without batting an eyelash. In my time, women had been expected to either drown in their skirts, or skip the whole thing and go in the nude.

"I've never seen anything like that."

"Enjoy it, my good man," I said, slapping Garavel on the back. The poor angel seemed to have his brain crystalized by the curvy flesh, amplified thanks to Layla's swimwear. He was rooted to the spot, his heavy weight dragging him deeper into the sand. I could either stay and guard him, or show him the backup ideas I'd had for Layla's vacation swimwear, but my curiosity beckoned me closer.

The beach was sadly not as empty as I'd hoped. Not many rested on the sands, but in the distance sat a handful of people at the tables and near the controlled fires. A few more gentlemen were resting on beach towels without a care in the world.

"I love your suit," Layla said to the quiet one. She'd removed a coverup to somehow reveal more clothing than before. A red and white striped swimming outfit clung from her wrists to her ankles. "It's so retro."

Maram blushed nearly as bright as her outfit. "Thanks. I got it at a store."

"Do you need a swim cap?" her friend asked Layla. She'd already suctioned her hair safely in place. My bond shook her head.

"I think I'm gonna lie here and soak up the sun."

"There's also a huge bottle of sunscreen in the cooler."

Instead of Layla accepting it, Calvin dove for the offer. "Really? What SPF? Thirty?"

"Your pasty ass needs like a hundred or more." Layla gently prodded at him as he squirted the unerotic white goo into his hands and splattered it over his skin.

Calvin leaned closer and whispered, "You'd be sad if this pasty ass went lobster red." Without a care, Layla leaned back to stare at said backside and she bit her lip.

"Instead of this..." I stared down the wolf who'd turned whiter than a sheet from his slather, then I caught Layla's hands. "...concoction, why don't I drench your body in botanical oils?"

"Oils? Sounds like a good way to burn," the pale one said. He added even more of the goop to his hands and slapped it across his legs. Was he trying to out-white the ghost?

Ignoring his cry for attention, I glided Layla into my arms. She wore the suit more beautifully than any mannequin or model could. The knot on her hip cried for a hand to pluck at it, to pull it taut and reveal her curve before plunging a bite to the bare flesh. The top fit her even better, her cleavage more tempting than the oasis at the heart of the desert. I brushed aside her hair with my chin and placed my palm to her warm back. She leaned closer into me.

"Jasmine-infused oils from the baths of the richest nobles massaged across your arms, legs, over and under your breasts, then your buttocks and…we go from there."

Her breathing slowed as she pictured what I offered. *Abandon this ten-penny beach for a proper relaxation under my maestro hands.* There were a multitude of ways to work off stress, after all.

"Ink." She opened her eyes and stared at me, then down. "Are you going to wear that the whole time?"

Critiquing my wardrobe was not the reaction I'd hoped for, unless it was questioning how well it looked in the sand. "I hadn't considered," I said, feeling eyes falling upon me. They were dressed like dockworkers on a break in tattered linens and distressed denim. I was the only one with enough pride to remain in a sturdy crimson shirt and black trousers.

Alas, the outfit that drew all eyes to me also caused me to stand out at this beach. I reached for a button when Layla beat me to it. My eyebrow rose in surprise, surprising me. How did I not anticipate her wanting me shirtless?

She'd moved to the second by the time I'd formed my thoughts. "If you wished me naked you only need ask."

Layla froze with her unbuttoning, her fingers shaking. "Are you naked under there?" Was she battling with wanting to see while also concerned for the rest of the beach trying to pounce on her incubus?

I guided her fingers lower, placing them to the buttons on my pants. "There is but one way to find out," I said while shrugging off my shirt. The sun parted through the clouds, a ray striking my naked chest. Even though I was nothing more than a sin, I basked in the flush of heat. Layla paused in her unbuttoning to look to my flesh.

"It's gotten darker," she said, brushing her hand over the latest tattoo. They appeared at her whims, my appearance forever shaping itself to her needs. I stared down at the heart of chains to find she was right. What had once been faded to near invisibility was almost black. Well, it could all vanish tomorrow.

Her trembling fingers pinched the zipper pull. She tugged it down a half-inch, then stared me dead in the eye. "There's something under there? Right?"

"Do you trust me?"

Layla bit her lip harder to keep her thoughts to herself, but she also undid the zipper. My trousers fell and she gasped.

"Thank god."

I'd had enough sense to slip on the crimson trunks I'd picked up along with her bikini top. Calvin glanced over and held up a thumb. "Nice. They're kinda short though."

I glared at his extravagantly long trunks that cut past his knee. "Not all of us wish to look like petulant toddlers."

"Boys." Layla placed a hand to both our chests as if we were about to come to blows. "Happy day, please?"

"Believe me, babe, if Ink didn't make fun of my clothing, I'd be worried something was wrong."

"And if the mutt ever dressed like an adult, I would fall straight to hell from shock."

Her hand slipped off of Cal, though she kept a wary eye on him. "I'm glad you're getting on, I think?" She didn't release me but leaned closer. "And thank you for wearing something decent."

I snickered at her tender plea. With my voice barely above a breath, I whispered in her ear, "Perhaps you should look closer." Layla reared back and blinked, then she bent lower to inspect the spread of my thigh where an outline of a couple in soft red were copulating in the downward wolf position. Another beside it was of simple dual oral enjoyment. All across my trunks were bodies enjoying the best parts of having them.

"Ink!"

I caught her chin, her eyes blazing at me for being so bold. "Would you have it any other way?" I asked, and kissed her.

A nibble of desire flowed from her. It'd take nothing more than a touch for me to push it open for a proper feast. I wasn't starving, but I hadn't sampled a full meal in some time thanks to Layla's frazzled attentions. Lust's parting shot trailed through my thoughts. I reached a hand around to cup the back of Layla's head and drive her wild.

She vanished from my grip. Shocked, I hunted around in fear that she'd been whisked off by ne'er-do-wells only to find the wolf holding her hand. "Come on, let's get some swimming in."

"Really? It's probably cold," Layla complained. She crossed her legs as if in annoyance and not to enjoy the rush of pleasure I'd left embedded inside her.

"So? That's why you swim around, get the body pumping!" He waved his arms about in excitement.

"I don't..." Before Layla could argue for sanity, Calvin bent over and picked her up. He slung her on his shoulder and marched for the dock.

"Ha ha. Very funny. Cal? Cal, what are you doing?"

"We. Are. Relaxing." He grunted after each word.

Others sat up watching the arguing couple striding across the wood above the water. Layla wiggled her legs and clung to his back as she tried to peer behind herself. Suddenly, the wolf stopped and stared across the quiet lake.

The mortal adoration of nature and serenity always confounded me. In any mountain view, at least a dozen small mammals were being torn to shreds and another two-dozen busy making more small mammals to be eaten alive. Nature cared little for inner peace.

Layla placed both hands to the wolf's back and raised herself up off his shoulder. At this distance, no one could hear her, but I heard her thoughts in my heart.

It's beautiful.

Oh, shit!

I jerked at the movement my bond felt from her stalwart mate breaking into a run. "Cal? Cal!" Her screams echoed across the still lake. Without a care, the wolf reached the end of the dock and leaped. For a moment, the sun silhouetted their bodies as they floated in the air. Then, it all came crashing down with a great splash. Panic surged through me the second Layla struck the water.

Without thinking, I took to my feet to chase after. He couldn't be foolish enough to harm her. He was more careful than all of us. What if Lust had gotten to him and was using the wolf to torture Layla?

"My..."

I skidded to a halt as two heads popped out of the water. Laughter tumbled in my ears and through my soul. She kept chuckling while swimming over to him and locked her arms around Calvin's neck.

"Told you it wasn't cold," he said.

"You are—" Layla burst up and shoved Calvin back under. "—in so much trouble."

He was only under for a few seconds before rising to take her in his arms and share a kiss that warmed her from her heart to her toes. She seemed content with him, her protector, her mate. I turned from their awkward fondling and swimming. There were other matters to attend to. Garavel no doubt needed instructions on how to man the beach, and the ghost required a dressing down at all times.

With certain steps, I walked back to the crumpled towels and abandoned coolers, only for the wind to shift. Instead of the scent of charred hot dog skins and beer-drenched urine, I smelled pomegranate blossoms, and my heart sank.

I only caught the flick of her blonde hair, but it was enough. Without pause, I cut through the in-between and emerged in front of Lust. She didn't leap back as I'd hoped, but jutted out her hip as if she'd been waiting for me.

"You always let others play with your toys?" she taunted.

"Come now, Lust. Even you know the usefulness of a helping reach-around."

She laughed like the spider flicking her web. "Perhaps, but I don't let anyone take my toys home with them. What has happened to you, Eros? You're so weak, I fear I could knock you over with a kiss."

I patted my chest, the muscles thriving and strong, my skin dewy and fresh. "I'd say I'm as hale as ever. Though what of you, poor Lust? How ever did you survive the humiliation of your prey refusing you?"

That arrow struck deep. Her eternal smile dipped into a momentary snarl. I never saw the demon below, Lust always preferring to maintain her illusion no matter the cost. But as she glared in the direction of her greatest failure, the blonde woman flickered and a hint of blood dripped from her eyes.

"How long you've been away if you think that minor setback will stop me."

What was I doing? Despite how much the wolf could cramp my style, it would do no one any good if she hooked her claws into him. Steadying my shoulders, I prepared for a long discussion. But first, the requisite compliment. "There is none who has existed or will exist that can reject you."

She patted her hair while accepting my bribe, though I feared the praise didn't have the same impact it once did. I'd been able to achieve months of freedom for a simple appraisal of her outfit.

"Tell me, Lust, in the name of our shared history, why are you pursuing me?"

"I'm not," she said.

I blinked at the bald-faced truth before me. There wasn't even an attempt at a white lie. What was happening?

"Honestly, Eros, the realms don't orbit around you. I'm here on business."

I glanced over my shoulder at the human specimens for her choosing. It was like picking between an egg sandwich found in a sewer grate, or a can of mystery meat that squirmed. They were so far beneath her notice, if one were to approach her, Lust would cut them dead for breathing.

"I would very much enjoy watching you hunt them," I said, jerking my head in their direction.

She laughed harder and patted my cheek. "I bet you would."

"Who are you talking to?"

Delightful. The ghost had decided to join us. At least he had nothing to fear from Lust, as he was already dead and lacking the necessary organs.

Ever incapable of knowing when he was punching above his weight class, Daniel staggered up to Lust, looked her square in the eye and asked, "Who are you?"

She had enough class to ignore him. Turning from me, she gave a coquettish wave. "Until I see you again...Ink." Lust sashayed into the forest, not once looking back and only leaving me with questions.

"Well...?"

Questions and a nosy specter who would make my life harder for it. "Ask the wolf," I said.

"Or I could ask Layla. Bet she'd be interested."

I tipped my head to how quickly he used his only weapon. "I suspect she would be, yes. Should you open with how you were jealous of the attractive blonde woman I deigned to speak with? Or perhaps describe to her the mystery woman in lurid details."

He snarled, as all he could do was make noise and wave his hands around. I could not understood why the Celestials allowed ghosts to exist. On the whole they were pointless. Perhaps it was a mistake they never cared enough to fix.

"I'm gonna tell her," Daniel threatened.

"Be my guest." I extended a hand in the direction of the lake and spotted Layla, not toying with the wolf's bone in the water, but dropping to her knees on her towel.

The ghost scowled, another hallmark of his, and stomped his foot. Not even a grain of sand shifted. "I don't get you."

"Nor shall you," I promised.

Daniel no doubt missed the double entendre as he steamrolled ahead. "This whole vacation you've been running around acting like you're taking care of everyone. Why? For her sake? Cause then you're up here talking to strange women you won't tell Layla about. Seems like you're only doing it for your sake."

"Is there a point when I'm supposed to speak, or do you intend to answer all your questions yourself?"

"I hate you."

"So I gathered."

The ghost crumpled his hands into fists and shook them violently in my direction. A rustling sound drew my attention and I watched the branches of two trees above my head clamp together and tremble before breaking. They fell to the ground as Daniel turned to stomp away. His final parting shot was, "I'm going to tell her."

I ignored the curious branches, no doubt caused by tree rats, and waved to him before taking off to speak with Layla first. Whatever the ghost said, whatever he invented, would only make her worry. And she was supposed to be on vacation. A simple explanation of my past, downplaying Lust's attack on her mutt, would be best. No reason to cloud the murky waters of this relationship with the fact Calvin was so devoted to her he couldn't be turned by the world's first incubus.

I was about to call to Layla where she slept on the towel when a man jerked away from her and dashed off. Curious. Leaving my bond to her sun and sand, I pursued the man who held one of the game-playing devices close to his chest. He was unaware of me lurking behind him as he lowered the device. An image of my bond appeared on the screen. Her eyes were closed, her body relaxed, and he zoomed in on her breasts.

The disgusting yellow desire set off a rage in me. "Give me that," I ordered.

He jerked in shock and turned to me. The man was taller than I, but not by much. He was beefier as well, and that was by a half of a cow. The difference seemed to give him a foolish sense of power. "Fuck off!"

The disgusting cretin tried to cram the phone into his pocket, but I refused to reach into such a fetid place. I wrapped my fingers around his arm and wrenched it out. Then I clamped down, pressing my claws in so his hand would open.

"Fucking...what the fuck are you?"

Now that he was subdued, I carefully picked the device out of his hand. It woke to the same image of my beloved on her back, vulnerable and unaware. That he or anyone else would try to take advantage boiled my ichor. I wanted to tear his testicles out through his mouth, then feed them to him.

"W-w-what are you?" he cried out and I realized I'd let my illusion slip.

Tamping it back, I raised up his phone before his face. "You were taking illicit pictures without consent." With no effort, I crushed his phone in half, letting the pieces fall to the sand. "If you do it again, that will be your manhood. Understood?"

He agreed vehemently with me, as all did when their genitals and crushing were involved — whether they enjoyed it or not. I released my hold and let him fall to the sand to mourn his lost Sheep Wars saves. Brimming with righteousness, I raised my head to walk to Layla.

She sat up and laughed as her friends came running to her, all dripping wet. They dug into their cooler for shared snacks and even waved over Calvin, who finished drying off. It was a moment of easy mortal fun that had no need for me.

Wanting to keep the peace, I left her to her friends, hoping the one who loved her with all his heart would protect her best.

Chapter Thirteen

Layla

"I'll be fine," I tried to assure Fariah. She frowned and stared past my shoulder to the men doing their best to look helpful and non-threatening. Aside from Ink, who smirked and waggled his eyebrows. Always a team player, that one.

"How will you get back?" she pressed yet again, when Dante interrupted.

"Look, I've got to meet the gas guy. So either get in the van or don't."

"I'm good, I promise. Don't worry," I said with a wave and shut the door. Through the window I spotted my friend with a single peaked eyebrow, but when her girlfriend caressed her shoulder, Fariah's attention turned elsewhere.

The sun was setting and taking the beachgoers with. The handful of swimmers were called in by their parents and loved ones, while the tanners and barbecuers packed up their coolers and returned up the road. It left me alone with my guys on an empty beach.

"Shall we?" Ink slipped closer and extended his hand. With a laugh, I placed mine atop his. He bowed his head and guided me to the middle. Daniel plucked my book from my bag and laid it on the ground.

"Seems the stance is more important than the words. Lower your hands a touch."

"Like this?"

He stood and took control, holding them just above my shoulders. "Now," Daniel whispered from behind. "Speak the words."

A string of German slipped from my lips, the syllables almost fumbling despite him repeating them in my ear. Even so, the magic bubbled up from my center, widening and stretching to fit my whole body.

"Tip your head up," Daniel said and he slipped from my hands. Instead, he placed his chilled palm to my stomach and lingered. I did as he said, speaking the final phrase.

The bubble shot out, extending over a hundred feet in every direction. For a moment, the air shimmered as if every surface was covered in glitter. It faded but didn't entirely vanish as I dropped my hands and stumbled.

Cal caught me, a protective arm already around my waist before I realized I was falling.

"I think that worked," I said. "The illusion is in place."

"Excellent!" Ink called from the trench he'd dug into the beach. Without care, he tossed dozens of branches into the middle, breaking them in half with his bare hands if they were too big. Once it was enough, Ink scraped his thumbnail down his cheek. Haunting blue fire danced on the tip, which he placed to the logs. They erupted in an instant, hellfire dancing across the dried bark and into the sand. Where the light touched, my illusion shimmered, turning the darkening sand into a reflection of the starry sky.

"Are you okay?" Cal whispered, holding me close. "We can head back still…"

"I'm good. It was a lot of magic," I assured him. "And someone kept throwing me into the water."

"It was only two times."

"Three!" I argued, trying to fight back the urge to laugh and kiss him. Each damn time he'd find a way to trick me into standing, pick me up and run straight for the docks. I was going to have to find a spell to give my hair a chance of not looking like a squirrel's nest for the rest of the vacation. But none of that mattered.

"My lady." Garavel picked Fiona up from investigating the dunes. "Is it safe?"

"No one should see anything aside from the regular old beach for hours."

He smiled and in one swoop extended his massive white wings. Tipping his head back, he raised his arms and breathed deeply. I found myself matching his slow breaths, my chest rising with his, my stomach flattening and filling with air. It was strangely calming. When he finished, Garavel tucked his wings back and leaped into the air, flying through the darkening sky and circling around us. I watched him with his great smile visible even from the ground.

"Shall we commence with the dessert?" Ink asked. He hefted the surprise cooler out from behind his bonfire and raised it to the light.

Cal leaned closer to whisper in my ear, "Does he mean the food or —"

"My dear wolf, if I mean debauchery, I will say as such. Is it too early for that?"

I tried to walk in the sand and found it harder going than I expected. "Yes. Let me at least eat something before you...eat."

He chuckled as if I'd made a pun. Cal guided me over to the fire and let me sit on the only towel. The other guys were left to rough it on the sand itself. While Daniel hunched over my spell book, flipping the pages back and forth and tousling his hair, Ink pulled out packets of food. Hot dogs, sausages, marshmallows — those made sense. Then came the solitary can of spam, a packet of ramen noodles and three hardboiled eggs already peeled. Cal prodded them. "I've learned enough to not ask. Just hand me a couple hot dogs."

After picking up a dual-tipped branch, Cal prodded the first sausage onto the end. Ink paused in prepping his food to stare. "I've found it's best to worry the flesh between your palms as one would a screw into a corked wine."

Cal did just that. "You've done this before?"

"Roasted sausages? Not precisely." Ink smirked and the fire rose, deepening his demonic smile.

Cal full-body shuddered as he jabbed a single hot dog into the flames.

"Do not be such a fusspot. Plenty of men enjoy the press of a tube inside their sausage."

"Nope. Nu-uh. Not gonna happen. It ain't happening, Layla," he told me.

"I'll take it off the list," I said with a laugh. Cal shivered again and hunched closer to the fire. Ink placed a marshmallow loaded onto the stick in my hand.

He brushed back my hair and breathed in my ear. "My sausage is yours for the manhandling, my bond."

To finish, he picked one of the larger hot dogs out of the package and gently worried it onto a branch while staring me in the eye.

I didn't shake in disgust, but I wasn't certain where I stood on the whole idea. *Maybe save the impaling of dicks for much later down the road.*

Ink must have read my mind as he shrugged and turned to the fire. Before he slipped away, I took his hand and pulled him closer. "Thank you." I kissed his cheek. "This was a great idea."

He turned and cupped my jaw in his hand. Slowly Ink traced his thumb over the edge of my lips. "It was, wasn't it."

The ground shook and I found Garavel had landed. Ink's attention shifted to him in an instant. "Have you had the pleasure of a mashed mallow, my good man?"

Garavel slowly shook his head. He gave a wide berth to Cal, who finished roasting his hot dog and leaned back beside me. Instead, Garavel walked to Ink's side and the demon helped the angel hold his marshmallow over the fire. Some days it felt like Ink had adopted him. And to think when they first met, I'd feared it would be all-out war.

Together, all three of us thrust our marshmallows into the flames. Ink had managed to tie together a multitude of ten different branches, giving him a small sapling's worth to roast. The heat of the fire warmed without burning, chasing away the chill of the impending night. "So this is what camping's like," I said.

"You've never been?" Cal asked.

I shrugged. "My mom…" The brick dropped again. Before my thoughts could run back to her, I soldiered on, "She preferred city life. What about you?"

He rammed his second hot dog into the fire and glared at the flames. "We didn't camp, not for fun anyway." For a beat, Cal glanced my way and wariness lurked in his blue eyes. Oh shit, the compound. It didn't have any electricity so every day there had to be like...like this.

I reached over to comfort him, but he suddenly jerked and pointed. "Your marshmallow's on fire!"

"Damn it!" I yanked it out and whipped around the flaming sugar bomb. The outside crusted over in black char as I went.

"Is that what we do?" Garavel asked. He mimicked me, waving his less burnt treat around.

"You eat it." Ink pulled one of his out while it was still flaming, plucked it off the branch, and stuffed it in his mouth. When he smiled, a flicker of fire danced behind his teeth before he swallowed it all down.

Garavel stared at the demon trick as if it all seemed logical. "Got it." With the tenderest of nibbles, he caught the edge of his marshmallow between his teeth and swallowed. Euphoria dawned in an instant. "This is fantastic!"

"Wait." I leaped to my feet and reached into Ink's contraband cooler. After finding the right ingredients, I broke the graham cracker in half and added a sliver of the chocolate bar, which was a fancy dark variety. "Here, you've got to sandwich your marshmallow between the chocolate and crackers."

"I believe I did the same with two widows and a traveling actor once," Ink chimed in. "He played the chocolate role."

Garavel stared in wonder as I squeezed his marshmallow off and handed him the sandwich. When I pressed the s'more together tighter, melted chocolate and marshmallow goo oozed off the sides. Garavel moved to lick it off and his entire being glowed. Literally. Ecstatic, he bit it in half, then swallowed the rest in one go.

"This is the most incredible creation I've ever eaten. What is it called?"

"A s'more. Can't get more American than that," Cal chimed in.

"Did you know the graham crackers were created to curb sexual urges?" Daniel inserted. He looked up and stared directly at Ink. "Is it working?"

Ink picked up one of the lust-banning graham crackers and held it pinched between his claws. "Hm." He licked the edge, tracing the imprint like it was a vulva. Ink groaned and he dragged the side of his tooth against the wet cracker before plunging through the middle with his tongue. It crumbled in half, but Ink only smiled at Daniel. "Have I abandoned my wanton ways?" He glanced to me. "My bond? Shall I devour you as thoroughly?"

I fought to keep from shivering as Ink placed a hand to my waist. The burn in his eyes was hotter than the hellfire and I found my legs wobbling. Ink leaned close, his lips parting as he pressed his cracker-crumb thumb to my mouth and slipped the tip in. He tasted of fire and I struggled to not moan.

Suddenly, he blinked and pulled back. "Do you require another mallow of the marshes?" he asked first to me, then Garavel.

What the hell was that? Ink smiled as if nothing happened while he actively skipped past a chance to do whatever the hell he wanted to me. Instead, he dug into the bag of treats while Garavel watched. *Shake it off. There's plenty of night still.*

I tried to keep my wounded ego in check, when I caught Ink's gaze pointedly darting from me to... Garavel had his hands clenched tight, his eyes wide as he stared at me. Did my incubus just step aside to give the angel a chance?

A chuckle rolled in my throat. "You must really like the s'mores."

Garavel nodded with a smile until I placed my finger to his cheek.

"Because you've got some chocolate right..." Slowly, I swept down his cheek to his lips. "Here." I slipped my chocolate-dotted finger into my mouth and sucked off the tip while staring at Garavel.

I expected a lot of reactions but never anticipated his wings erupting directly into the fire. Flames caught, sparking up the feathers and running from one side to the other in a second. "Get some water!" I shouted to the others who were leaping to their feet.

Garavel glanced back without a care and shrugged. He tucked his wings in and the fire vanished. Plumes of smoke rose from his back and he waved it away from his face. I rushed into the acrid fog, clinging to Garavel's arm to try to help. "Are you okay? Do they hurt? I might be able to heal you with my..."

"Don't worry," he said with a laugh. "Happens all the time." He reappeared his wings, but with more care to keep them out of the flames. They didn't even look singed. How?

"Creation magic," Daniel said with a scoff. "Though, if angels all left after this realm was locked off, how do spells for their feathers exist?"

Garavel looked back at him. "The witches were gifted a hundred feathers to help seal any rifts once the

Celestials fled. I suppose they could have lost some before their work was finished."

He sounded so hopeful but I gritted my teeth and glanced to Daniel who had the same thought. Without angel overlords there to keep them in check, there wasn't much reason to do as told.

"Nearly cause a genocide and get rewarded. Sounds right."

It wasn't a reflection on humanity from Ink, but a bitter growl from Cal. He picked at the sand, not paying attention as we all turned to him. When he felt the eyes, he jerked and stared back at us. "What? Kill werewolves, get an angel feather to do whatever you want with. That's what happened, right, not-angel?"

Garavel folded his arms and stuck out his jaw. "It is not genocide to stop mindless beasts from killing."

Damn it. "Hey, we've still got chocolate…"

Cal rose. He took his time wiping off his knees and calves before he glared at Garavel. "You know, your high horse is looking a little shaky after you killed your own father."

Fuck! I swept my hand in a circle, preparing a shield spell, but uncertain who to protect. Neither Cal nor Garavel moved, but the air crackled. A hand clamped to my stomach and I almost unleashed a spray of lightning, but it was only Ink trying to tug me away from between them.

Garavel sneered, his patient and welcoming face warping to rage. "You know nothing about me, monster."

"No? I'd say we have a shit ton in common. You sleep at my house. Eat my food. Want to fuck my girlfriend. And we're both in the 'killed our psycho daddies to save Layla' club. We should get T-shirts."

Garavel snapped out his wings, igniting both in the fire. Rather than snuff them out, he let the flames lick around his body. "How dare you even speak of my creator? He's the greatest Celestial to ever exist."

"Was. Because of you." Cal smirked as if he'd won some battle while Garavel curled his hands into fists. If he took a swing, could I stop him? What if he killed with one punch?

I ratcheted my arms back, prepared to stop this, when Garavel flapped his wings. Sparks scattered across the sand, fleeing from his feathers, and he shot into the sky. Only a cloud of smoke drifting across the moon revealed his path as he vanished into darkness.

Without the immediate threat, I shook off my magic, but turned on Cal. "Why did you say all of that?"

He'd turned his back to me, his shoulders hunched as he picked up a half empty beer bottle. Even if he was drunk it wasn't right, but at least it'd be an explanation. Except Cal had only had two the whole day. Instead of finishing his third beer, he ran a finger over the lip.

"All that power, all this work just to bring someone back from the dead, and he's the one you pick." Cal jerked the bottle in Daniel's direction, then hurled the beer. It harmlessly sailed through Daniel and was cushioned by the sand, but the ghost glared.

I gritted myself for another fight, but as Daniel looked to me, his head dropped. "I'm going," he spat out fast, before adding, "to the library. I'll see you later." He vanished before I could say a word to stop him.

Cal too shifted away, his arm falling lower as if he intended to plant a hand to the sand. "I'm going to. Got to shift. Always got to shift."

"Cal...?" I wanted to ask him what the hell his problem was, but he looked at me, and my heart clenched.

His eyes that'd been full of laughter all day were red and near tears. "It could have been anyone," he repeated and took off running into the forest.

Damn it.

"That was the worst case of raging FMS I've ever seen," Ink said.

Eli. The brother he killed his father for, the brother he'd lost that had shattered his heart. Why didn't I even think to try to find a way to...?

Hands cupped my shoulders and pulled me lower. I didn't realize I was tumbling until my ass hit the sand. Ink kept tugging, forcing me to rest on his chest. He cinched his hands around my waist and placed his chin on my head.

"FMS, it's Full Moon Syndrome. They can become quite a burr if they haven't worked out all that aggression. Maybe if we give him chocolate?"

"But he's been shifting every night. He did last night before you ran into him?"

Ink went quiet, only gently swaying with me in the sand. I tried to strain my ears to listen for the flap of angel wings or the howl of a werewolf, but save the cry of a loon the world was silent. "What do I do?" Garavel was deep into grief, Daniel was struggling with what being alive again would mean, and Cal... What if I'd pushed him too far with the angel? What if he was fed up with this whole arrangement?

"Nothing," Ink said. I glared up at him. Leaving a boiling pot alone would only set off the smoke detector. He sighed and turned me back to face the fire. "There is naught you can do tonight. Best to let them feebly stew in their emotions for the eve then fight for a solution come morning."

I shook my head, my chest tightening with every wild thought. "What if Garavel's spotted?"

"He will spawn myths of a new cryptid in this area. The man of rock and feather."

"I've never seen Cal like this. He could do something stupid."

"You have, and he has, but only to the detriment of his pants. He will be fine."

"Daniel's been at odds with the spell to bring him to life. I think he fears he's not worthy. Oh shit, I shouldn't have said that."

Ink pulled in a breath, then held me tighter. He bent low to perch his chin on my shoulder. "I swear, I will keep your words in confidence, my bond. Though that the ghost has a shred of humility is earth-shattering."

There was that other problem too. I shifted in Ink's grip, turning to face him. He showed no signs of exhaustion with me, only patience and care. "I'm worried about you, too."

"Me? I seem to be the only one not pitching a tantrum."

"You've been…" *Different.* It had taken a while for me to notice, but he'd been kinder, softer and less like the selfish prick who'd fucked me ten ways from Sunday on Halloween. "You almost died."

"You almost die by the week," Ink said. His tone was light, but I recognized the sharp fear in his eyes. What if it wasn't just because if I died he went back to hell?

"This was different, though. You were mortal. If you'd died, if I hadn't been able to save you from the curse—"

"My bond." He brushed back my hair and I collapsed my hand to his chest. It was the only touchpoint I had left to keep from falling to pieces. "You have nothing to worry about concerning me. I am as nefarious of a not-demon as ever."

What if he didn't fully come back? What if that cursed brooch had changed him?

"What about you?" he asked, confounding me. "The ghost, the angel, the werewolf, even the incubus." Ink snickered at the last part. "You carry all these worries inside your head and heart, yet when do you care for you?"

"I'm...fine."

He closed his eyes and breathed deeply. "How I wish it were that simple. I am not the wolf—I cannot lick your wounds. I am not the angel—I cannot wish the pain away. I wouldn't want to be the ghost even if he were capable of anything. What I am is the selfish sin only here to feast off the fallen and corrupt. So I know that if a person gives, and gives, and gives of herself without taking anything in return, she will crumble to sand."

"Ink..."

The wind tousled his hair and he closed his amber eyes. Shaking his head so more of his brimstone scent filled the air, he sighed. "Be selfish on occasion, if not for your sake, then mine...and those other damnable fools who'd be a stain on the ground without you."

I took his cheek and pulled him to my lips. Every other kiss from him was an express flight to my core—hot and wet, they'd rile me up and flood my panties. This time, when I pressed against his mouth, he tenderly cupped my lips with his, brushing his fingertips against my cheeks and down my neck. That kiss went straight to my heart.

Chapter Fourteen

Ink

The air sang with her desires. A wave of tender caresses and gentle kisses beaded up with bubbles of wanton thrusts and deep bites. I held her cheek, tilting her head so I could kiss her how she wanted.

Beginning with a soft press of my lips, so faint as to be almost a kiss of the breeze, I pulled her closer. Layla parted her mouth, but I didn't press the advantage. Rather than rush to the inevitable conclusion, I savored every touch and taste of her nubile lips. The strength of the bottom one, how it melted as I pressed it between mine and drew my tongue beneath it. The adorable curve of her top lip. I dared to traverse Cupid's bow with my tongue. Its draw slackened as she came undone in my arms.

"Ink," she moaned. It was a sound so normal, not hearing my name cried out in the midst of wanton desire was more of a surprise. But this moment, the stretching of the 'I', the hard 'K' at the finish... My being jumped and pleaded for more.

I brushed my knuckles back from the hollow of her cheek up to the curve. Her lips broke from mine as she smiled and leaned against my meager hand. Starlight danced in her eyes, her brown skin radiated moonlight and the swell of desire filled her soul.

"You're beautiful," I gasped. No Venus demanded greater worship, no Godiva could scandalize hearts, no Helen would turn a head like Layla. I raked my fingers through her twisted hair and folded them at the nape of her neck.

Her eyelids slipped closed and she drew her smile to the side. "If you wanted to sleep with me, you just had to say so."

A laugh fell from me, though a stricken feeling rose—as if I'd been stripped clean of all my armor. "Perhaps..." I swept my palm down her graceful neck, a touch of goosebumps trailing my wake. Straddling higher, I placed my lips to Layla's ear and whispered, "I also find you beautiful."

She turned her dangerous eyes on me. Not for the power they could wield, nor the pain they'd borne witness too, but the bottomless empathy I could scarcely understand. Layla smiled and dove for me. She tasted of my tongue, her desires heating to a proper simmer. I traced across her shoulder, following the slow, delicate swoop until I caught the string of her top and wound it around my fingers.

The gasp was manna from hell. Her teeth pressed to my top lip as she squirmed until nearly in my lap. "I never did thank you for the bikini."

"No." I toyed with the string, tugging the knot against the nape of her neck and letting my fingers glance against her naked skin. "Not that I require such formalities."

"I've never had anything fit so perfect."

I caught her eye and smirked. "Nothing?"

The blush not only on her cheeks but through her desires invigorated me. I held her jaw, savoring in the burn below my fingers as the hunger of what I put in her mind chased across her face. All these times, all these ways I'd had her, and the mere thought of me mounting her was enough to make her blush.

Layla kissed me harder. She struggled to her knees to reach my height. When I slipped my tongue inside her mouth and swept it across her, she widened her legs. Did she even know? Or was it her body and desires pleading for what I kept hidden behind my scandalous bathing suit?

Heat twirled through her desires, once-small plumes growing in veracity with each kiss. I wanted her needs to burst into flames that could rival the sun. But to put a human so close to that...for me to drink of it would be dangerous.

I pulled back from her tempting lips and caressed down to cling to the knot at the back of her neck. "Shall I...?" I asked, taking the two tied strings in hand.

Layla bit her lip and nodded. She stared up at me, her eyes nearly hidden in shadow as I began to tug on the ties. My heart lurched. A strange energy bounded about my body, almost causing my legs to tremble. If I hadn't existed for thousands of years and bedded millions of bodies, I'd almost think it nerves. What did I have to be trepidatious over?

With total certainty, I pulled the knot apart. The strings came undone, but I didn't let her top fall. Instead, I wrapped them around my finger and rested it on the back of her neck. I traced a single fingertip down her back, listening to the rising beat of her heart. The music shivered in my soul as I reached the second tie. I toyed with it, almost reaching for the string before sweeping my palm down her back. When my fingers brushed against the low top of her bottoms, Layla moaned and flexed her thighs.

"You're gonna kill me," she cried out in rapture. No fear, no realization that the charmer she'd brought to her bed was secretly a monster. Her body cried out for me, her mind begged for my touch and her heart…was better in the hands of another.

Shaking off the dour, worthless thoughts, I reached below her bottoms and cupped her buttock. Firm and tight as she used every muscle to keep herself upright, her ass required a deeper flex of my fingers. Kneading into the flesh, I pressed my lips to her neck and licked across her throat. She gulped and I bit down, sucking her jasmine-scented skin between my teeth. The rising groans from her drove me to traverse my fingers from the celebrated swell of her ass deeper into the sacred grove.

Her desires shifted, uncertainty dancing in the cloud. I would not push beyond what she wanted. There were none to compete with tonight and only her pleasure that mattered. Rather than rile up her concerns, I reached for the long-abandoned tie.

Hands were already there.

I expected to find Calvin or even Garavel tugging off her top, but it was my bond who held her strings, her smile widening when she caught my eye. Without a thought, she pulled the bow apart. "You took too long," she said by explanation. I rolled my finger, letting the last of the strings come undone, and her top tumbled free of her beautiful breasts.

My control slipped, the illusion momentarily cracking. Black wings of shadow blanketed the moon, the sharp scent of brimstone filling the air. I shook it away, the red flesh vanishing before it got farther than my chest. Speaking of…

Once the moonlight returned, my being was ensnared by her bounding breasts. I drew my palm to the sides, caressing the buttery-soft skin as Layla closed her eyes. With a touch used for selecting delicate silk, I traced above then below her breasts, avoiding the pointing tips. Layla peeked and tried to sweep her nipples over my wandering palms, but I had better ideas.

Bending, I pressed a kiss to her lips. They flexed to meet mine from slack surprise, except I was already moving. A languid lick down her jawline, a nuzzle of my nose and nip of my teeth to her neck, a kiss and nibble across her collar — at each touch, Layla sighed in ecstasy and she tipped back. Her hands clenched in the sand, digging with every touch while I kissed across then down her bosom.

A simple roll of my tongue around her nipple set off the gasp. Pulling it closer into my mouth, letting the tip of my teeth graze the tender skin, burned her hot. "What has set your mind ablaze?" I asked, each word spoken against her firm skin before I brushed my wet lips and nipped.

Her voice, throaty with hunger, struggled to rise. "When we first met and you…"

I smiled with her nipple between my lips. "It'd taken you quite off guard to be brought to the plateau of pleasure from such a simple touch."

Fingers dug into my hair, sand cascading to my shoulders as she pulled my head back to stare into my eyes. "You're my first incubus."

But you are not my first witch.

With a smile, I tossed aside that disquieting thought and focused on the only creature who mattered. "Your desire is my..."

"Command?" She quirked her head to the side with a smile, rivulets from her hair cascading down her breasts.

I watched them traverse her curves, circling the hills and meeting together below to continue their decent to the middle of her thighs. Water was life to the mortals of this realm, and she was life to me. Her desires cried out for nipple play, for me to bite her shoulder and take her from behind as the wolf rarely did.

I didn't know why I brushed my finger over her cheek, held her jaw and kissed her. Or why I did it again, placed a hand to her bare waist, and pulled her to me. I played supplicant to her. Me. Not because she desired it but because I could lie back in the coarse sand and gaze in wonder at the impossible beauty straddled above me.

Her hair sparkled with beads of stars and her skin glowed like moonlight, the shadows deepening to unexplored mysteries, the highlights gleaming like diamonds. I wanted to kiss her not to desire's end, but my own. I slipped my thumb across her lips, tracing the red and plump flesh. Layla parted her mouth, her chest rising in a sigh as I touched her so innocently. Her eyes sharpened and she darted her tongue out, circling my thumb in a demonstration of her prowess with other organs.

The bubbling desires burst, flooding me with her same ache. I pulled at her bikini bottoms, tugging them past her hips until nearly all of her bush and buttocks were bared. Sitting up, I licked across her belly while roughing my palms around her back, then under her breasts. She cried out as I hefted them, toying with her nipples in a quick burst of erotic frenzy. Tracing down her skin with my tongue, I dipped into her belly button, which caused her to giggle and gasp.

When my chin fell into her spread of coarse black hair and the edge of the silken purple bottoms, I stopped. I enveloped my arms around her waist and kissed her sweetly. Layla dug into my hair, her fingers massaging, then scraping at my scalp as she flexed her thighs. I knew what she wanted — it would take naught more than a moment to please her.

What is stopping me?
What do I want?

I jerked at the alien thought riding in my mind. I always knew what I wanted — being free of shame or humility allowed me instant gratification. Yet...

Layla reached behind to take my hands. She guided them lower, then pressed my palms to her buttocks. As I massaged them, she began to grind against me. I leaned back in the sand, allowing her bottoms, hot and slick from her desires, to sweep over my cock prodding below. A tingle ran through me. I pulled in a breath, expecting for a sensation of strength to ring in my veins. But the tingle grew bolder. It shivered down my thighs and I widened them, opening Layla's legs as well. She plunged deeper against my cock and I nearly gasped.

"God, I want to ride you so bad, but the damn sand..."

I dug into her hips, stopping her thrusting and the strange vibrations in my body. "My bond." Without effort, I rose to my feet and swept her into my arms. I carried her for but a moment and laid her beside the bonfire on the towel for beach sitting.

"I don't think this will stop the sand," she said, looking perturbed.

I laughed and stood above her. Even naked save the purple bottoms barely clinging on, she remained defiant. "I assure you, not a single grain will impure your body."

"How?"

With a grin, I tugged off my trunks and took my hard cock in my hands. "I'm an incubus," I declared.

Layla lifted her foot, brushing it over my calf and up my inner thigh. As she did, the sand fell off her and rolled back to the beach. Her inquisitive toes darted against the crease of my thigh, then tapped against my bollocks. I snatched at her ankle, holding her foot up. Her eyes widened in shock until I ran my palm over her calf, removing more of the sand. I walked closer, dropping to my knees while placing her foot on my shoulder. Layla raised her other, and I did the same, clearing it of the coarse sand and approaching her.

Her bikini bottoms had shifted so a curve of her brown vulva appeared. It glistened from her desires, wet and slick, calling to me. I reached for the last of her clothing to free her from it, when Layla shifted.

"Work around them," she said. The desire to feel my cock pushing aside her bikini piped through her.

The idea set off the tingle stronger than before. It zipped across my whole chest, causing the tattoos to shift and deepen. Lost in her eyes, I drew my nails down her outer thighs while knee-walking closer.

When I reached her thigh crease, I spread her legs wider and Layla's eyes rolled back, which was when I tugged aside her bottoms and thrust my thumb in.

"Yes!" she shouted, grinding back. I had already slipped out, spreading her arousal around her lips and clit for ease. Layla widened her thighs and whimpered.

I want her.

The thought was a blip in the paragraphs of desires radiating in the air. But the moment it touched my mind, I dove for her. I barely pushed her bottoms aside before I thrust my cock inside. Layla cried out in shock at the force, then clamped her hands to my waist, trying to pull me in deeper.

I obeyed, only jerking my hips back an inch to then plunge with all I had inside. She began to pant, her hands wringing the muscles around my waist. This position was causing her pleasure. I should maintain it.

Yet...

I bent over, digging one fist into the towel. Layla's leg slipped from my shoulders, shallowing her. She blinked in surprise, then gazed up into my eyes as I appeared above her.

"You're beautiful," I repeated, tracing her lips with my thumb then kissing her.

She parted her mouth and I thrust hard. The delightful O shape to her lips made me grin and I did it again. Each one, she'd gasp and run her hands through my hair. I bent lower to kiss her, when Layla clung to the back of my head. She pulled me until my nose struck the towel and whispered in my ear, "Take it off."

"I thought you wished to keep your bottoms in place," I said, confused by the change of heart I couldn't hear.

Layla shook her head, refusing to let me rise. Panic and excitement surged through her. "Not that. Take off your illusion."

I jerked in shock and sat back from her.

Her eyes opened and she grinned. "I want to fuck the demon."

Chapter Fifteen

Layla

Ink stared at me like I'd gone mad. I tried to think how to roll back what I'd said, but he took my hands and extended them above my head. "Why do you want that?" he breathed in my ear, not in a sexy way, or as a taunt. He sounded utterly confused.

"Because..." *I don't want it to always be the lie.* He could be the ludicrously hot, charming and sardonic man with other people. I knew him — I needed to know all of him.

I shrugged, incapable of voicing all of that. "Why not? I mean, you've done all this insane shit. Orgies at the Vatican, BDSM in royal courts, other stuff you brag about. Surely someone's desired the demon before."

His eyes grew wary and my resolve crumbled. *Oh. Shit. It's just me. I'm the fucked-up one.* Of course, I wanted to fuck a demon, so...hard to sound sane after that.

Ink closed his eyes and dipped his head down, but he didn't relax his grip. My body tightened, every muscle a wound band as I wanted to spring away and run. Slowly, the Mediterranean tan faded from Ink's face and down his body. The flesh became black as midnight with veins of red lava crackling below. Horns rose from his forehead and curled back like a ram's into sharp points with tips of gold. As the illusion trailed down his body, Ink whipped a tail with a spade-like end. It reached his feet, which clipped into the familiar hooves of the satyr or classic devil.

His delicious and deadly voice plummeted to a thigh-quaking rumble. "Well...?" Ink opened his eyes. The sclera were completely black while his irises burned with fire. They were mesmerizing. "Do you still wish to *fuck* this?"

He released his hold on my wrists and took one of my hands. With almost skittish care, he guided my palm to his chest. Where there'd usually be smooth skin and a hint of ribs were crags. It felt like touching a mountain with the hand of god, tracing century-worn peaks and valleys that dipped into a hot vein of red. I slipped out of his hand and Ink let me go. Instead of pulling away, I continued lower. My pinkie dipped into one of the deepest veins, the heat nearly scaring me off, but I kept traveling.

Ink breathed deep, raising the hills where there'd once been pecs. I passed his stomach, the rocky terrain burning hotter the lower I went. As I stared at his demonic flesh, wondering what it'd feel like to rub across my body, to run over with my tongue, my hand drifted until I glanced against his cock. Dark shadows erupted from Ink. On instinct I clutched to the first thing I had, which was his not-as-rocky, but not-as-smooth cock.

He groaned and spread his demonic wings out. The feathers strained to the sky, black shadows dripping from each tip. Smothered in midnight, I grew bold. His cock was wily, bending and reacting to my touch in a way no human's could. Large ridges circled from the base all the way to the tip. It didn't have the same mushroom-like crown, but came to a more tapered end with small nodes circling just below the tip.

As I swept my palm up to the top, his cock didn't just twitch... It reached for me. Somehow, the end pierced in between my fingers and curled up to my knuckle.

"How...?" I gasped.

"How can an incubus direct himself to every pleasure center inside the body?" Ink almost laughed, not in derision but glee, like he was ecstatic to show off this party trick. He closed his eyes and his cock curled around my finger, then pressed the widening tip to my palm. "That is how."

Ink pulled his hips back, retracting his magical cock. "Layla, I can return the illusion if you'd —"

"No!" I shouted, almost surprising Ink. He blinked, the fire in his eyes momentarily puffing up smoke. I stared anew at his face. If I didn't know it was him, I couldn't have guessed. But the cheekbones were similar, the same swoop to the jawline I'd nibbled so many times. His lips were the only smooth part of his visage. Unlike the rest, they were black with a sprinkling of red, like onyx. Only the hair hadn't changed at all. The medium-length ebony locks curled, nearly touching his shoulders.

It was Ink, my Ink. And I wanted to fuck him.

I clung to his jawline and pulled him to me. Ink's eyes flared in surprise, the flames rising when I kissed him. The heat flushed my face and the scent of brimstone sent me reeling. But as I touched his lips, the hot stone pressed back, and my body melted. I ran my fingers through his hair and felt the dark shadows of his wings on the back of my hand.

Slowly, I began to fall back to the towel. Ink came with. I couldn't stop running my palms over his forehead, his cheeks, needing to recognize him and know him. "I want this. You know I want this."

"And yet it is still difficult to believe."

Wrapping my arms around the nape of his neck, I raised myself off the ground. The heat of his body rumbled down my naked breasts. *God, to feel that inside of me...* I drew my tongue around his ear. With every last ounce of strength in my body, I commanded, "I want you."

All I saw were Ink's flaming eyes homing in on me. They burned from red to white. He reached back and clenched my wrists.

Was that the wrong thing? Did I screw up?

Ink plunged to the ground, pressing my hands into the sand above my head. He deliberately drew his gaze down my body, smoke rising from his lava veins the longer he stared. Something brushed against my leg. It drew higher, toying with my inner thigh like a flat leather flogger. I looked to his cock to find it rigid and ready for duty.

What is...?

"Oh...fuck!" It plunged into me, the small tip flattening fast to a wide spade. His tail — he was fucking me with his tail.

Ink bent over me, his knees pinned astride my waist while he swirled the tip of his tail against my clit. The pin-point, vibrating pressure was ramping through my body. I flexed my hands, trying to keep from coming in ten seconds, and arched my back. Ink kissed my lips and pulled his tail from my clit.

I sighed at the release and began to kiss him back.

He nudged my head to the side with his horn and bit my neck. Before I could even gasp in pleasure-pain, he slapped the flat end of his tail against my whole vagina. The wet sound made me jump far more than the sensation.

Ink twisted his tail, rolling the flat edge up from the top of my taint to my clit. I tried to grind back, whimpering for more. When I caught the tip of his tail on my clit, the pleasure zapped through me. The vise on my wrists tightened, pinning me deeper into the towel.

"Ink." I fought to keep from going mad. My body from the waist down was burning, pleading for his touch to quench it. "Please."

He smiled and bent closer, tracing one of his horns over my cheek. "Please bring you to the heights of pleasure with only my tail?"

I wanted to answer, to scream yes, but I couldn't stop panting, my head buzzing from too much oxygen. "My bond, my pleasure is your..." He swept the edge of his tail against my vulva and, with the tip, vibrated my clit beyond reason.

"Desire," Ink whispered.

I fought with everything I had, my body hanging on the edge by a nail. When he spoke in his low baritone that dripped down my throat like molten honey, I was lost. The orgasm struck so hard I screamed a feral cry of rage from my flesh sack not being able to withstand any longer. Lights sparkled in the darkness, ribbons of whites and blues trailing through the shadows of his wings around me. I hummed and whimpered, swaying with a beat I could see and not hear. All the while, Ink held me. He kissed my cheek, brushed his horn against my hair and caressed my shaking thighs with his tail.

It was anyone's guess how long I was caught in the thrall of my orgasm. I wished the ebbs and flows of it had been for thousands of years, but I doubted my heart could have survived more than two minutes.

By the time I finally gathered myself from the abyss to form a coherent thought, I slithered my hands from Ink's slack grip and smacked him in the chest. "Why the shit didn't you tell me you could do that?"

He laughed and I slapped him again. "You know, I have no idea."

My hands slipped, trailing down his rocky body for the cock I had yet to know in its full glory. Ink stilled, his breathing steady. He bent closer, placing more of himself in my palm. When his forehead landed on mine, he breathed, "My bond..."

I glanced up into his eyes. The fire was gone and in its place was a field of golden honey. Ink's lips parted. "I want you."

"I know you do," I purred and guided him for my drenched vagina.

Ink placed my legs around his waist and he pressed closer to me. Still, he kept his prehensile cock out of reach. I tried to focus on the sensation of his body on mine, how it felt like a hot stone bath. But a heat taunted just outside my fallen bikini bottoms that I couldn't escape.

He caressed my cheek, pulling me close for a kiss just as he entered me. My swimsuit strained at the hip, fighting to accommodate as more and more of him thrust inside. The ridges pressed to every throbbing nerve inside of me, dragging back the tide of orgasm.

And yet, I'd felt the same a hundred times before. On my back, on top, pinned to the wall—the skin was different but the cock hadn't changed. I gulped at the realization that I'd been fucking him, this demon, this near-boiling incubus for six months.

"It's you." I gasped. "It's always been you."

Ink smiled, no doubt confused about my orgasm-induced revelation. He swept a hand over my breasts, toying with my nipples as he began to thrust gently. "It's you as well." Unlike so many times before, Ink didn't go slow.

He grunted, his hips pushing harder and faster. His magical cock bounced against every pleasure center, pounding into the node that was either my G-spot or the source of my power. I clung to his shoulders, fighting to hang on. His body heated, brushing over mine like a bath at the hottest setting. Then it kept going.

I whimpered.

I loved it.

I couldn't stand much more.

I needed it all.

Ink dropped his forehead to mine and he kissed me hard. "I wish it always had been," he whispered as he gave one final thrust. My orgasm didn't surprise me, this one more controlled as it consumed my body to an all-over tingle. But the soft gasp and tremble of Ink's lips shocked me to the core. In all our times together, he'd only been focused on my pleasure to feed him.

Was this what happened when he could feel pleasure from me?

He closed his eyes and the demonic image melted. Soft human skin caressed mine, toes dug into the sand and he pulled out a cock with a perfect ratio of girth to length and pristine skin, but otherwise normal. For a beat, Ink swept his shadow wings around us, keeping us in our private cocoon. But even those faded and he sat up, the moon perched behind his head like a halo. He blinked human eyes and gazed at me.

"Are you...?" Ink began to ask, tracing a hand across my skin that still radiated warmth from his body. He shook it off with a smile as if he was foolish to show concern. "Congratulations, you are the first mortal to experience a sin of lust in the flesh."

Instead of pride, a notch of shame shuddered in my exhausted belly. He'd been around for thousands of years. I couldn't be the only degenerate to ask. "Surely there've been others," I argued.

Ink drew back his hair, the only part of him that hadn't changed as he slipped from demon to human. "Very few are aware of what I truly am...until the hour draws nigh."

I bit my lip in thought and pain from the bruised and burned skin struck back. Instead of wiping it away, I pressed harder, chasing the sting. "So I'm the only one fucked-up enough to ask." I tried to shake it off as a laugh, but when I looked to Ink, a prickle of tears wavered in my eyes.

Ink's mouth parted and he scooped me into his arms until we both sat. He brushed back my hair as I pushed my cheek tighter to his warm and smooth chest. Any hint of the demon was long gone as he cuddled me closer. "You are the only one daring enough to try.

Perhaps this is too raw a question to inquire now, but I wonder why."

I shrugged, trying to cling to the compliment of daring and not warp it into deranged. "I dunno. I guess…we haven't really had time together alone lately."

He pursed his lips, his hands slowing through my hair until he held my shoulders. "You seemed to desire a compilation of cocks and tongues, and I am more than happy to provide."

God, it was good. Ink and Cal, even Daniel joining in when he would—just thinking about them made my toes curl. "I missed being with you, and I wanted to be with you as you are. To see if I could."

Ink fell silent, only the breeze and crack of the burning logs filling the air. "Can you?"

I smiled genuinely and sat up. Ink's usual smirk was gone, his entire face stoic. I grazed my palms over his cheeks and brushed my fingers through his hair. "You can read my desires, right? What do they say?"

He looked around, his lips parting, but before he could tell me what I already knew, I pulled him to me for a kiss. Ink caressed down my back. He ran his palms to the tender sides of my breasts and carried on to the top of my ass before I slipped back. "And I'm still pissed you kept that tail trick from me."

His great smile made me grin back. "I fear you will never cease to amaze me, my…" Ink caught my hand and pressed it tight to his lips. The word bond was muffled and incoherent, but it couldn't have been anything else. "I shall endeavor to dream up even better tantalizing tail tortures for you."

A fear of what he had planned chased through me, but it blossomed into excitement. Except… "Though, it might be best to keep your human look on when with the others."

Ink chuckled. "Concerned the ghost will go mad with fear? Or is it jealousy that weighs upon your brow?"

Oh, I was not answering that. I pressed my lips tight to keep from revealing anything, but Ink laughed and leaned back. "I assure you, I shall keep my mortal visage in place, lest the wolf grow envious of my unending talents."

I rolled my eyes when Ink pulled me across the towel and into his lap. His limber cock pressed against my right asscheek as he nuzzled my neck. "While I refuse to retread maudlin poetry and make comparisons of your luxurious lady parts to flowers, I am heartened to be alone with you." Ink held me tighter as he whispered in my ear, "And I live in anticipation of many more private interludes with you."

Every damn word from him always sounded like either a double entendre or smirking sarcasm. But his voice was stripped to nothing but a genuine hope to be with me as himself one more time. My heart leaped and I held him tighter.

He'd almost died for me. I'd felt him slipping and in that moment I was willing to risk everything for him. That fear, that giddy feeling, hadn't left me. As I embraced him, my body wrapped up and held in his, my heart did the stupidest thing possible.

"I love you."

Oh. Oh, fuck. I knew I had said it aloud even as I tried to tell myself I hadn't. Every other time it'd been in my mind, locked safe away where he wouldn't hear it. And now…

Why isn't he saying anything?
How badly did I destroy everything working?
"Ink...?"

His body tightened like a drawn bowstring. I hung off his taut arms as he turned his chin. "We are being watched," he said.

A likely story, and wonderful distraction to keep from having to confront my confession. I turned to look and the air beside a bush shivered. A shadow lay in the sand without a body to cast it. As I sat up taller, the branches snapped and whatever it was ran.

Ink sprang up, keeping me in his arms. "We cannot let them escape," he said.

"Why?" I hunted for my lost bikini top, struggling to tie the knots back on.

"Because whoever it was knew to look through an illusion spell."

Dread plummeted in my stomach as I stared to the still trembling shrubbery. Only a witch hunter would think to bother, a witch hunter that had just seen Ink in his true form. "I will catch them ahead, you remain here," he ordered and vanished.

Like hell I am. Hefting up my purse, I finished tying on my top and ran into the woods after our peeping tom.

Chapter Sixteen

Ink

The world shuddered, small tears forming in the in-between space and the earth where I'd puncture through, then dive back. Magic leaked from one to the other, chasing a stripe of red over the black sky. The once staid branches shivered and blinked as I leaped out. A head turned from the outline of night and I smiled.

"Found you."

Winds blew in from the tear, buffeting against the watching man's face. His shadowy skin flickered. A shudder danced down the scales, flipping to a shimmery violet and peridot. I took a step, prepared to detain whoever this was, when a scent struck me.

It was not of this Earth, nor the spaces in between the realms. It was nothing — the impossible where all smells from dust, to dander, to the air itself ceased to be. It was the scent of hell.

He is...?

Light burst above me. I rolled my eyes up just as the invisible barbs sank into my flesh and pinned me in place. It would hurt if I were human, though it also wouldn't work. "I'm afraid you missed..." I called to my bond. The unnamed and unknown creature spun into the brush and vanished.

"Wait!" I shouted, but he'd already gone, leaving nothing but a trembling branch in his wake. I heard but could not see a person approaching from behind. "Hurry and release me."

"I don't think so."

My shoulders relaxed, causing the magic threads to drag me closer to the ground. A sigh of exhaustion rattled in my chest, but I fought it off as I turned to face not my witch, but the witch who'd birthed her. She held one hand beneath her splayed book, the other weaving a spell around her fingers.

"If you're hoping for a late-night swim, I'm afraid the beach is closed."

"Cute. Are all demons so infuriating?"

"I wouldn't know, having met very few —"

"Silence!" The very air cracked as if thunder struck without lightning.

I bowed my head. "As you wish, but you were the one to ask."

The woman, Isabel as Layla had called her, paced in a circle around my accidentally tripped trap. She recited gibberish Latin, igniting a rune on the ground before moving on.

"If I may break your rules once, what are you doing?"

"Banishing you, demon."

"Oh, this old nugget. Haven't seen a hell portal in many a year. Though, you drew that one wrong. It should look more like a three-legged dog."

The elder lady glared at my impudence and a sickly sensation wrapped across my flesh. She looked far too much like my bond when she was in a foul mood for my liking. I closed my eyes to keep from thinking on the comparison. While growling, she scraped away her poor rune sketch and tried again.

I nodded at the improvement. "Much better."

"Why are you helping me?"

"Ah, caught on to that. You're quicker than some, I'll give you. I've had entire squadrons of witch hunters in their buckled hats and furrowed brows stomping at perfectly good ground in rage. The bears would usually get them before they'd catch on."

She loomed toward me, not so much above. The materfamilias was shorter than my bond, damn near making her pocket-sized. A fact I was certain would cause her no small amount of wrath should I remark upon it.

"You may wish to read the spell again," I said, pointing to her book. Rather than doing as I said, she snapped it shut and slammed a foot to the ground. Her ring of runes lit up, though that apple with a circle for a hat was wobbling. I folded my arms, waiting, as the sky lit up bright white.

"Ink?"

The mother collapsed her hands, cutting off the magic while I harmlessly looked to the woman running into the clearing. She too had her book out, her body scratched and hair knotted from the foliage. Once Layla spotted me, I waved. Confusion knit on her brow and she turned to the woman holding me captive.

"Mother. What the hell are you doing?"

"Protecting you," the elder woman declared with a sniff.

Layla glanced around the empty clearing. "From what?"

"That," she declared with a toss of her hand my way.

To my surprise, my bond growled. "Get him out of there!"

"I will do no such thing. That is a..."

"He's not a fucking demon." Layla rolled her hand in a familiar counter spell. I raised my chest, prepared to dash forward and scoop her into my arms. Her mother snapped forward, a gush of wind shoving Layla to the side and disrupting the magic.

"It doesn't matter what he is. It's what he's doing to you that does matter."

"Sometimes three times a day," I said.

Layla scowled at me despite it being the truth. She kept her hand out, ready for a spell, but cast nothing. "How are you here? How did you find me?"

With a slow glare, Isabel stared at her daughter. "I gave birth to you. We have the same blood. I can find you anywhere across the world."

Pain sundered through my bond's anger. She clamped around the necklace holding the ghost's bone and held tight. "You...you could...?" Tears sprang into her eyes and she lashed out. "You knew the whole time!"

"Of course I did. You're my lineage. Which is why I'm protecting you...?" Isabel glanced over her shoulder not to her daughter's crying-rage, but the glint of gold above her breasts. "Why are you wearing that?"

"Because it's mine. I got it after my mother fucking died."

"Take it off this instant!" Isabel reached for it. I hoped she'd win that argument and wake to the incessant pedantry of the ghost. But alas, Layla was the younger and more agile of the two. Snarling, the mother crushed her hands to fists. "You're being a brat. I didn't raise you like this."

"You didn't raise me at all!" Tears catching, Layla hugged to the outside of my prison, away from her mother's reach.

Perhaps something in her child's plea reached through to the stubborn woman. Or, most likely, it was because Layla could launch a spell off before the elder witch stopped her. Either way, she paused and in a more soft tone said, "I did it to protect you. Everything I've done is to keep you safe from him."

"Who?"

"And instead of preparing, you're a shell of what you should be. You let this monster feast upon you."

"Ah, we're back to me again. I should tell you, I've only served as a family therapist once, but it was for the Borgias and, well...we all know how that turned out."

The two women ignored me, as seemed to be the motif of the eve. Isabel squared her studious shoulders and hefted her book up for another round of chanting. She failed to account for my bond's impeccable stubborn streak.

"Ink is not a monster." She hurled a massive disenchanting spell through the woods. It wiped away nearly half of her mother's work, and also tugged off a quarter of my illusion. The skin of a monster crackled and hissed in the magic-infused air before remolding to the pleasing human form.

Isabel jerked a hand my way as if that was explanation enough. Evidently she'd missed my little rendezvous with her daughter on the beach. "Stop being so selfish. You're a witch. Act like it."

"You're my mother, act like that!"

Instead of turning to her pleading daughter, Isabel focused her ire on me, as if I played any part in her abandonment. "I'm not trying to be cruel, Laylee."

"Your actions speak otherwise," I said.

Isabel curled her fist and flung a gust of wind at over a hundred miles per hour at my chest. Freed of the prison, I dodged behind Layla, holding her safe in my arms. Though the older witch's attack crumpled the trunk of a tree, twisting it until it splintered in half.

"You should be able to do that," Isabel said. "No, you should be even stronger than that. If it weren't for that thing…" She aimed a finger at my head, but Layla walked closer.

I did not like her acting as a shield, though it did give her mother pause. "Ink is not a thing, he's not a monster. He's my…"

The answer hung in the air, given not a breath of sound. I'd heard her. I wished I hadn't. For mortals, the pleasing of their genitals often led to a delusion of affection. They'd deem it to be love to give themselves an excuse to enjoy more. I'd always laughed it off. But from her lips it rang a different bell.

"I know what he is," Isabel spoke over us with a dismissive wave. "And I can't believe Didi let you summon him. Why? Were you that lonely?"

"Didi?" Layla whispered.

"I knew she could get soft, but she had to teach you better."

"Mom." My bond slipped from my hands as she stepped closer to her agitated mother. But when Isabel looked to her, Layla's head dropped. "Auntie died."

"What?"

"A year after you did, from a heart attack."

"That…" Isabel shook her head. "That's not funny."

"No fucking kidding. The state raised me. 'Raised.' I was sent to foster home after foster home with another half-dozen kids. Dumped out onto the street once I hit eighteen. If it wasn't for Ink, I'd have been eaten by scroungers before knowing shit about witchcraft."

Each word broke through the old witch's armor. Her unassailable lips drooped and her shoulders faltered. "No. Didi was…she was going to watch you. Train you when the time was right. Then we'd… She can't be gone, too."

That most dangerous of emotions, compassion, flooded through Layla. She broke her guarded stance and reached for her crumbling mother. Alas, another joined our little counseling session, altering the dynamic.

"Babe? Please tell me…" Calvin, at least in shorts, leaped into the clearing. He froze at the older woman who'd tried to kill him once before. Slowly, he curled a hand around Layla, trying to put himself in harm's way for her.

"The wolf too?" her mother spat.

"There is also a ghost and a demi-angel somewhere around here," I added.

As if on cue, the loud gust of giant wings cut through the air. Isabel stepped back, quickly losing her high ground. Garavel dropped to his feet, his white feathers glowing even in the darkest of nights. He tucked them back and stood up. "I saw the light and thought it must be… Oh. Hi."

Instead of the vengeful witch, his dour turn was aimed at the wolf holding Layla. Ah yes, that mess.

Ellen Mint

Once he enjoyed the ripe fruits of our beloved, it was certain to fix itself.

"My lady, are you—?"

"What's going on?" Because it wasn't enough of a celibate clusterfuck, the ghost decided to make an appearance. "What's she doing here?" He pointed his ire to Isabel.

"I don't know," Layla said, and turned her back on her mother. "And I don't care."

"Laylee, you're in danger."

"Yeah, because my mother left me to fend for myself. But thanks to these guys, I've survived far worse than you can imagine."

Isabel dropped her head and whispered, "No, you can't. Not as long as he's out there." The winds shifted, gusting through the trees. Calvin clung to Layla to keep her from blowing over.

As they died down, she glanced over her shoulder to find the elder witch gone. "Mom?"

"What was she doing out here?" Calvin asked first. "Babe? You okay?"

"No." Layla wrenched her hand from his. Garavel reached for her, then Daniel, but she kept darting away from all of them. "I need...I need to go back to the cabin. To sleep. You..." She looked to Calvin, who had enough brains to appear regretful for his actions. "I'm mad, believe me."

"I know. I can explain—"

Layla flung her hand up to stop it. She clenched her palms together and began to tremble. I could take no more and scooped her up off the cold ground. Her tear-stained eyes turned to me in shock, but she flung her arms over the back of my neck. "I will take you to your cabin. As for the rest of you, return at your leisure, but do not wake her under penalty of incubus."

With my threat left hanging in the air, I dipped into the in-between. It was a simple enough trick to keep Layla existing in my arms in one end, then zip to the other, so she arrived in a blink of an eye. I guided her to the wooden floor just as she began to pace in a circle.

"I can't goddamn believe that she's... Why did she do that? And to accuse you, to threaten to... What was she doing?"

"Mostly mucking with the barometric pressure," I said. Layla continued to erratically leap across the cabin's living and sleeping room. I lit the lone lantern and raised it to illuminate her.

"Oh, fuck!" she shouted, her face knotting into pain. Concerned, I hunted for danger or obvious injury, but Layla continued. "My mom saw me...with you. And you were... Shit!"

I rather suspected the creature who'd been enjoying our languid interlude was not her mother, but she seemed beyond reproach at the moment. "My bond." I reached out to catch her, but another round of pacing began.

With a sigh, I sat on the small table with a deck of cards.

"And Cal. What is up with him? Just trotting back in like he hadn't been a jackass."

I shuffled the cards, whipping them from one hand to the other, before shuffling again. "He'd worked off his wolfish energy. You know werewolves — it's either howl, bite or...become intimate with the couch leg."

"Not funny."

I fanned the entire pack out and smiled behind it. "I beg to differ. Pick a card."

"Why?"

"You're approaching hysterical and require a distraction."

"I am not fucking... Fine. It's a queen of hearts." She then showed me her card, defeating the entire purpose of my distraction.

I took it from her and added it to the pack. "I'd been hoping for the ace of spades myself."

"All I wanted was one week. Just one goddamn week without any monsters..."

"Present company excluded, I hope." I laid out the cards in a tarot grid, though anyone with actual prophecy could read the future with a pack of bubble gum and string.

Layla snorted and looked to me. "You're not a —"

I broke the illusion, beaming the full force of the demonic skin and wings at her. To my surprise she didn't even blink, but resumed her pacing.

"No creatures I hadn't already fucked."

I tipped my head to her for that one. Hm, my immediate future held a five of clubs. That didn't bode well.

"No goddamn witch hunters..."

"Who you also have never fucked."

Her stillness paused me from revealing my next card. Her face was turned from mine, hiding her expression. I could see no hint of subterfuge in her desires, but a tendril of blue caught me. What could she have to feel shame for?

Aside from being caught on a public beach riding the cock of a demon.

"No dead mom, and just all of you guys getting along. I mean, I quit..." She stopped and heaved her head to her hands.

Abandoning my far future to the next turn of the cards, I rose and wrapped my arms around her. "My bond, fretting so will not help."

She took a deep breath, tugging on the precariously tied bikini top. It would take little more than a kiss for me to unknot it. "I know."

"Your mother has buggered off."

Layla snorted at my mild cursing and I smiled. "Calvin and his current peccadilloes can be confronted come the morn. As for all the monsters and witch hunters you have yet to take to bed... I'll draw up a dance card for you to decide who gets first go. I'd recommend stocks of lubricant and burn ointment."

Her cringing mix of blue and violet desires faded to a more neutral puce. She leaned her head on my shoulder and sighed. "I can't believe out of everyone, you're the responsible one."

"It is a mar on my insouciant reputation."

I brushed back her hair, trying to tame the knots in her twists and remove the debris. Layla rested her cheek on my sternum and her hands drifted lower down my back.

"You should slumber before the others return."

"Or..." She dug her palms into my buttocks and beamed an impish smile at me. "We could have some fun indoors."

Her desires shifted hard, as if she were trying to order them as a distraction. With a regretful sigh, I caught her hands and held them between us. "You require rest," I said and kissed her on the forehead.

Releasing her hands, I turned to leave her to it. A soft voice cried out, "Ink, is this about me saying..."

I love you.

My smile came fast and I rounded on her quicker than she could see. "My bond, your body has been taxed to the brink. Mentally and...strenuously physically. It would do me no good for you to drain yourself to near exhaustion."

She nodded, accepting my excuse. I brushed back one of her curls, her hair an utter disaster after the day of Calvin tossing her into the lake. If she were my queen, he'd have lost both of his hands for such a stunt. Tomorrow, it could be easily fixed.

"Goodnight, my bond." I kissed her lips, sipping from the desire wafting around her. Even in her anger, she still ached for the wolf and hungered for the angel. Where I fit into that mix didn't matter.

Layla wandered to the table and looked down at my unfinished reading. Without a thought, she picked up the next card and sighed. "Was this your trick?" She held up the same queen of hearts.

I bowed deeply as if it had been. "If you will excuse me..."

"Where are you going?"

I did not answer, but slipped into the in-between. Her mother meant nothing to me. The werewolf and angel spat was meaningless. All my concerns were on the creature and the piece of hell he'd brought to Earth.

Chapter Seventeen

Daniel

I shouldn't be looking at it. Without thought, I turned away, and read through another book on the history of dragons. Most of it was rubbish, but a spell had worked its way into the edges. It was also worthless, a potion and incantation combo to help with hemorrhoids. But it kept me from glancing back to...

Damn it, I looked again.

Holding the book in my hands, I rose. After scouring every potential tome claiming to be real magic, I thought I'd found the answer. We had the angel feathers. Layla wore my bone around her neck. The unicorn might be a problem, but the incubus could withstand a goring or two. All that remained was the demon blood, and I'd finally found a way to open a tear to hell and retrieve it.

"Has anyone got a spare trash bag?" Layla shouted, her cheeks spotted with dust.

The only problem was that I could never tell her about it.

"Here," that quiet one said. She'd seemed less reserved the past few days, almost smiling on occasion. After handing it over, Maram turned, not to follow Layla. No, her eyes landed right on me and I froze, dropping the book back to the table. She blinked slowly, then returned to mopping.

What am I thinking? Of course she can't see me. She's human.

Abandoning my books, I watched the only one who could see me stack a pile of milk crates. She wore the same overalls that cut off at her upper thighs, but this time with a crop top with a deep V-neck. Her hair was hidden below a kerchief, completing her mind-numbingly sexy farmer look.

What I wouldn't give to find a hay bale to pull her behind.

"Layla?" I whispered beside her.

She began to hum and put an earbud in to pretend to listen to music.

"Ye-es!" she sang, then looked to me.

I couldn't tell her. If I told her then she'd know and the whole problem would be on her. No. It was best to keep it to myself.

"Is it about a werewolf?" she sang when I didn't respond.

I frowned and stared out through the open door. He'd stripped off his shirt in order to show off every damn muscle while carrying firewood. Instead of begging for forgiveness from me or the angel, or even Layla, he'd just gone back to work as if nothing happened.

"No," I said.

"Or the angel?"

Garavel was busy with his kitten and seemed to have shrugged off the wolf's verbal barrage without a care. I shook my head.

"Then what?" Layla's singing was straining and she glared.

"What's that song?"

We both went wide-eyed and turned to the curious Maram. "What about the angel?" she sang before blanching. "Or was it the werewolf?"

"It's a...a demo. Friend of mine's in a band. He doesn't want anyone else to listen to it until it's done. Sorry."

She nodded to Layla's lie. "Okay. Well, when it's finished."

"I'll be sure to give Fariah a download link," Layla said with a big smile. "I, uh...need to get more crates for crate things. Excuse me." Before Maram could respond, she ran out of the door and into the sunlight.

She collapsed a hand to her face and moaned into her palm. "Why did I think that would work?" I walked next to her and she peered from the edge. "Please tell me whatever you had to say was important."

"It is. I think. I..."

"Layla?"

Wonderful. The damn werewolf waved to her, tossed his logs onto the pile, then jogged over. Her shoulders tightened and she looked away.

"You're mad. I know. I...I fucked up, and I'm sorry...Dan."

Me? He was apologizing to me first and not his girlfriend?

"I get why, and yeah, what happened to you was fucked up. You deserve a second chance at life and all that. So...are we cool?" He held out his hand and I stared at it.

"Daniel."

"Uh, Cal?"

"My name, it's not Dan. It's Daniel."

He winced and raked a hand back through his hair. "Oh. Sorry. I just, growing up with my brothers we'd all get... Doesn't matter. Daniel. Whole thing. No Dan. Got it." He continued to wave his paw around as if I could take it. I chose to focus on Layla and follow her cue, but she kept staring off into the forest.

"Fine. We're cool."

With an, "Okay," he pulled his hand back and reached for Layla. "Babe? I am..."

"I'm sorry!" As she spun around, tears gushed from her eyes. Both Cal and I reacted with utter terror. He was able to hold her while I helplessly watched. "I should have asked you about Eli... I didn't think."

"No. No, I'm the idiot."

"It's just, the spell requires the soul. And without it I don't know what would happen. But we could try. We have two feathers."

His face twisted like his heart was about to shatter. He ran his fingers against Layla's cheek, mopping up her tears. "Eli's gone. He's...he's where he can't be hurt anymore." Cal wrapped her up tight in his arms and placed his chin on her head. "He's at peace."

And just like that, the one who'd caused her pain healed it. Not by groveling, not by pleading for her forgiveness and understanding. Not even by reciting a poem he'd spent hours searching for. No, a simple hug and kiss to the tip of her nose was all it took to heal that rift.

I clenched my hands, feeling them tighten, the bones digging into my palms. But if I tried to do anything, from brushing Layla's cheek to swinging at Cal, it'd be nothing but a cool breeze. The demon loved to call me impotent in his childish way, but watching another man adjust Layla's kerchief and wipe off the dirt I'd noticed hours ago drove the nail in. *What am I to her?*

The researcher didn't get the girl. Best he'd get was being nearly blown up when the bad guy found their lair.

"Layla?"

She turned from her attentive boyfriend to the whisper on the wind. Her brows raised and she parted her lips as if to beckon me closer.

"Lady wi...!" the angel boomed, his arms wide as he walked over. "Lady-la," he said instead, looking at the others who didn't give a shit what he called Layla. The cat perched on his shoulders mewled impishly in her direction, before it spun and hissed at me. A tiny black paw swiped through where my arm would be, but it sailed on past, only angering the kitten more.

"Fiona wished to visit with you," Garavel said for his cat. He plucked the little thing off his shoulder and passed it to Layla, who was already cooing and using baby talk. The angel scratched the top of the kitten's head without a care, before he looked straight into Cal's unwavering eyes.

Was it time for another apology? A pat on the back as all the men put aside their differences for the sake of Layla. All but me, who couldn't put anything to the side.

Cal opened his mouth, but Garavel interceded. "Do not speak to me, wolf."

A flush ran over Cal's face and he shrank back. "Fair enough," he said and coughed.

Layla watched while petting the cat who purred from her touch. Lucky feline. "What about dinner on the beach? We could have more s'mores and sleep under the stars."

"I didn't say it to be a jackass."

For fuck's sake, does he ever learn?

Cal, proving he was the type to shove his hand into an open trap, kept talking. "I was trying to help."

The angel sneered and stood higher, blotting out the sun. It cast Layla in a shadow as she helplessly tended to the cat while stuck in between them. "Maybe we could go out in the boat. Have you ever gone fishing, Garavel?"

"Help? All your kind knows is destruction and chaos."

"See, this shit... It's like talking to a wall. An unbending, impenetrable wall!"

"I've never done it myself." Layla kept going, trying to break them up. "But how hard can it be?"

Cal stood taller, but still a few inches below Garavel. I felt like I was hiding with Layla beneath two sequoias. "I'm not your enemy."

"Your kin is the champion of the man who caused the death of my creator," Garavel thundered.

"I mean, Dante's got to have like a rod. That's a fishing thing. Rods?"

The wolf snorted. "You mean you. You're the one who killed him because he was going to kill Layla. Say it. Admit it. Tell yourself that you stopped your father from murdering the woman you love."

"That is not why I killed him!" Garavel shouted. Every voice died, the birds fell silent, and once curious heads swung back to their work. A blush burned over Garavel's onyx cheeks and he hunched lower until Cal was taller.

"Ha! You've got that line down great!" Layla shouted to cover for him. "Can't wait to see that play. That you're in."

"I despise you, werewolf. I despise your kind. They should have been obliterated from the Earth, their ashes tossed to the pits of creation and the memory of them purged."

Cal tipped his chin in a challenge. "What are you going to do about it? Hm? What are you going to do to take down the big, bad wolf?"

Garavel clenched his fist, Cal dropped a shoulder in anticipation of a shift and Layla...she looked to me to stop this. They were going to hurt her, if not physically, then deeper. I shook, darting my gaze from one to the other, trying to think of a way to end this before they did.

Calvin growled, rippling his lips to show off his set of fangs. Garavel reached behind for the sword that'd cleaved off the head of his creator.

"I know how to get to hell!" I shouted.

Layla slammed her palms to both of their chests. The kitten scampered from her shoulder over to Garavel, knocking another brick out of the tension. Cal was the first to shake away his stance. "Why do you want that? I thought you hated Ink."

"You found a way to get demon blood. Real demon blood?" Layla's eyes glowed with excitement and my heart sank. *What did I do?* How could I tell her that in order to open a portal to hell, a sacrifice was required? The ultimate kind.

Ignoring the two men realizing how foolish they looked and awkwardly pretending to not see the other, Layla ran to my side. Her lips parted, hope rising in her expectant eyes.

"Look what I've discovered!" the damn incubus shouted for all to hear. We all turned to find he held an old acoustic guitar above his head.

Dante tossed a bag of old wood onto the fire and dusted off his hands. "Ah, that thing. We get youth groups up here that do sing-alongs. They must have forgotten it."

The allure of the instrument drew everyone closer. Ink, aware of his growing audience, leaped up onto a lawn chair beside the fire. He held the guitar on to his shoulder like a violin and plucked at a string. The note cried out as his grip slipped. "Hm, I fear this lyre is far too unwieldy for use. Anyone else wish a go?"

He passed it to Fariah, who shook her head and gave it to Maram. The guitar rounded the fire, every person sitting on the logs and benches. A few tried to pluck the strings. Dante did a riff. When it landed in Layla's lap, I stared down at it from behind her. It was in bad shape and needed tuning. The strings were far too slack, the body required oiling, but it was a guitar.

"Do you know how to play?" Dante asked.

"Oh, no." Layla laughed.

I took a knee behind her and reached into her hands. She jerked, sitting bolt upright, and I ran her fingers over the strings so light they didn't make a sound. I hadn't touched a string in over thirty years but at the rush of metal dancing against the tips, it all came back.

Shifting closer, I repositioned the guitar in Layla's lap and played a chord. Too flat. After some minor tuning, I tried again and smiled. With her fingers, I drew forth an old song. Not one we'd written for Tiger Whisper, not even an old rock ballad from the days doing covers. No, my brain went back to that old Spanish guitar solo I'd learned for a recital.

The music danced around us. I kept my cheek pressed to Layla's, not needing to look to the strings. Instead, I felt through her, not only the rhythm of the song, but the pounding of her heart matching the beat. "You're enjoying this," I whispered.

She bit her lip and let me keep playing.

"Are you picturing me on stage? Tattered vest, mohawk, singing my heart out to a captive audience?"

The last performance of my life, I'd managed such a sick solo, I leaped into the crowd. They'd cried for more, lighters high, heads banging. We did four encores.

Then Brian had killed me.

My finger slipped and the music sputtered to an end. I clung to the body of the guitar, not feeling like the rock god who'd dazzled on stage. I was ten in a choking bowtie, playing at the temple for all my parent's friends. They'd said my music skills would look good on a resume. Not that I'd find freedom and release in the music my parents feared.

I strummed the strings once more, prepared to launch into a lick that'd make my father pray for me.

"Layla? Since when can you play a guitar?"

What? I stared down at my hands, except the fingers were thinner and darker with long nails. *They're not mine. I'm in Layla's...* I fumbled back, nearly falling on my ass.

"Oh, ya know." With control returned, Layla passed the guitar on to Garavel. "Long time ago. Guess it's like riding a bike. Which I also haven't done in years."

"That was amazing," Fariah continued.

"You should do another performance," her girlfriend added.

Layla paled and laughed. "Sorry, that's..." She looked over her shoulder at me staring agape at my fingers. "That's the only song I know. Maybe we should get back to work? Gary?" Garavel stopped rubbing his palm over the strings like a cheese grater and looked up. "Can you help me move a heavy thing?"

"Gladly," he said, leaving the guitar on the ground. Like a lost puppy, he followed after Layla, walking close to protect her. Everyone else filtered out, Cal and Ink returning to their firewood chopping. The two girls left hand in hand and Dante shook his head before standing to leave.

Only I remained. Forgotten, lost—a soul without the body, a mind without the tongue, a heart without the fingers. The music wouldn't leave me, but without Layla, I had no way to create it. Without her, it remained dead inside of me.

I reached for the abandoned guitar. My finger sailed past the string, the note silent. Concentrating, I pictured myself on that old stool in the basement, struggling to read the tabs. Another miss.

No. I imagined Layla sitting alone in the audience. How her eyes would light up and she'd smile bright as I approached the mike and played. Resistance caught and a note rang through the air.

Chapter Eighteen

Layla

"I'm taking the boat!"

The bickering, the glares, the unmistakable threats to start wailing on each other... All froze. Whatever was bugging Cal couldn't get resolved with Garavel right there talking about wanting to eradicate all werewolf kind. And Ink had been no help, smirking and pushing the buttons of both of them like an evil shoulder devil. I wanted to scream without anywhere safe to do it.

Before they could all start in, I dashed for the only means of escape. I hopped into the sagging boat, a small puddle of water running down the middle spine. *I'm sure that's fine.*

"Do you want some company?" Cal asked.

"No." I waved to them with my back turned, all my attention on the motor. It took a few yanks of the cord before it started up.

"Are you well equipped for a sea voyage?" Garavel asked.

"I'm fine." I tugged the rope from the dock and shoved off. The boat creaked on the lake, slowly twisting to the left, but not doing much else. I sat on the back seat, one foot in the well, and cranked the throttle. It was supposed to keep going left, but the boat surged to the right and I stared into the concerned faces of three men. Well, two were concerned, and one found it all hilarious.

"Layla?" Cal asked.

"Leave her be." Ink collapsed an arm around his shoulder and waved me off. "Bon voyage, my bond!" he called, a white handkerchief wafting from his hand.

I finally got control and turned the boat around, puttering into the open lake.

"I give it two-to-one odds we'll be rescuing her before the night arrives," Ink said loud enough I'd hear.

Shaking it off, I cranked on the motor. The boat shot forward, nearly sending me toppling out the back. With no one in the front, the bow slammed into the minor waves, wrenching my stomach and slamming my feet to the metal ground. But it was far better than having to listen to another round of arguing that went nowhere.

How in the hell am I going to make this work?

There's my mother who tried to banish my incubus...who I said I loved to his face. Cal's up to god knows what. Again. Garavel is in deep denial about the part he played and seems to be taking all that self-hatred out on our only werewolf. Ink is...being weirdly helpful and I don't know why. There's a murdering sociopath who calls himself Conquest that wants to crash all the realms together and start Armageddon. Witch hunters who probably want to see my head on a pike after I slipped their clutches.

And Daniel... What am I gonna do about Daniel?

"Layla?"

"Holy...!" I yanked the motor in shock and fell off the bench. It sent the boat spinning and I could hear Ink's jaded laughter in my head. Reaching up, I stopped the aquatic dance and rose to find Daniel sitting in the prow. He smiled at me as I fought to get control of the boat.

"What are you doing here?" I asked, but Daniel cupped a hand to his ear.

I rather doubted he couldn't hear me, but I turned off the motor anyway. Ripples tossed the boat from the final waves before it and the air went silent. We bobbed on the vast blue-gray expanse.

"I came out here alone," I said, hoping he'd take the hint.

"I thought you called to me." He nodded to the necklace and I slapped my hand over it. I had to keep it safe—it held our connection. But it also reminded me that somewhere out in the forest lurked my mother, like an emotionally traumatic Bigfoot.

Daniel rubbed the back of his neck and stared across the water. "Do you want me to leave?"

My hand dropped and clung to the bench. "No. I just...I needed a minute to collect myself." Every time I tried to make it better, it kept getting worse.

"Maybe I can help." Daniel lit up, his dark eyes dancing with mischief. I only saw that when he had a good comeback against Ink. But he turned to reach behind him and...hefted the guitar from the front of the boat.

"How are you...?"

He placed the instrument on his knee and smiled. "Seems I can move this too." Then Daniel strummed his fingers down the strings and music rang out. Not very loudly—the birdsong from the pine tree island competed with it. But it was beyond impressive and confusing.

"I thought you could only move books." I abandoned the back of the boat and climbed closer, watching him run his hand up the neck and twist the little knobs on the side.

"So did I. Maybe I'm getting stronger, or maybe I always could. Either way..." Closing his eyes, he picked at the strings, drawing forth not the manic playing from the bonfire but a slower ballad.

I dropped to my butt, luckily hitting the bench across from him. Not that I'd have noticed if my ass landed in water. All my brain knew was the beautiful music coming from the painfully handsome man. With his hair tossed back, his body swaying and nimble fingers dancing, I'd never been so turned on and near tears at the same time.

Then Daniel started to sing. His voice was low and rough, but that only made it more heartfelt. "Never been awake, never seen the sun break, 'til the day you walked in. I'll never be the same again. You're like magic, one touch and I soar, you're like magic, one kiss and I'm yours."

His fingers stilled, the final notes drifting across the lake. I blinked, realizing tears had slipped down my cheeks. When I tried to wipe them away, Daniel laughed. "There's a reason they didn't let me sing except for backup screaming."

"No!" I reached over to catch his hand, and froze. "It was beautiful. You're beautiful. Your voice is. Okay, you've also got a face that's like painful to look at some days and I don't know why I'm babbling."

He dipped his head and smiled, then ran his fingers over the strings once more.

"I've don't think I've heard that song before," I said.

"You wouldn't." Daniel sat up. He shook his falling blue streak to the side and sighed. "I just wrote it, for you."

He did?

"It's why there's only the one verse. Sorry, I'd hoped to have more, but you...you looked like you needed something."

I held my hand out to him. Daniel stared a moment, then he shifted the guitar. First, he brushed his palm over the back of mine. I closed my eyes, willing myself to feel the touch of his skin, but only the chill chased goosebumps up my arm. He sank his hold in and reached back with my hand to caress my lips.

It was our kiss. Some days, I wanted it more than any other.

As he tenderly traced my mouth, I gazed into his eyes. In that moment, I'd have sucker-punched the devil if it meant I could touch the man who'd written me a love song. Then again...? "If you can touch the guitar...maybe you can touch more?"

Daniel drifted my hand lower, settling my fingers on the top of my chest. I felt my own palm there, not his. He could take control, but it was my skin that touched me. I'd accepted that limit, thought it enough, but what if...?

He raised his hand while keeping control of mine. Daniel breathed slowly, a steady sigh as he stared into my eyes. "Layla, my champion, my meadow flower."

Oh god, I couldn't stop blushing. Nervously, I clenched my thighs together and a tingle ran through me. Daniel darted his finger against my wayward hairs dancing in the breeze. Did he move them? I clung tighter to the bench, trying to keep from leaping for him as he guided a single finger closer.

His eyes closed in concentration. He reached over and opened his palm to caress my cheek. I couldn't take it any longer and leaned into him.

Cold. It cut to my quick, causing me to shiver in place. I kept fighting, willing myself to feel him even through the depths of winter, but...

I opened my eyes to watch Daniel sigh. "Nothing."

"Maybe over my clothing?" Jesus, I'd take some teenage backseat fondling at this point.

Daniel pulled back, removing himself from my hand as he fell to the bench across from me. Our knees would almost touch if he wasn't...dead. "I'm sorry." He sagged in his seat and glared at the guitar.

"It's my fault. I shouldn't have pushed like that. You can hold a guitar, that's amazing. That's worth—"

"Stop." He held up a hand but wouldn't look at me. "I can handle being worthless to them and to you, but I cannot stand the patronizing."

"You're not worthless. Not to me, anyway."

Daniel snorted and raised his head. The tears struck me, but the rising blood stain on his chest worried me more. "Yes, I know. I am the research guy. I do the long, painstaking work of collecting data that everyone else thinks about for a minute before moving on."

The research guy? What was he talking about? "You're not just here for research." I reached for his hand, but Daniel kept his firmly planted.

"Is that not what I do for you? For this coven?"

"You do a lot of amazing work that I can't, and…I wouldn't trust Ink to do. You've taught me so many spells I thought I could never learn."

Daniel glared as if that was no different. "I'm the professor in the tweed jacket who helps the attractive ingenue become her best."

"What?"

"We all have our roles to play. Cal is your provider, giving you a home, food, comfort and care when needed. Garavel the muscle. Ink is…frankly, aside from a splitting headache I don't know what he adds."

I winced, not understanding any of that. "This doesn't make any sense. Cal's…Cal. And Ink…can be a headache, but he's more than that. You're more than that thing you said. The professor in a tweed…" I stopped and stared at the punk hottie and tried to picture him in the bow tie and glasses get-up. It wasn't working.

With a great sigh, Daniel dropped his head. "I can't touch you. I can't pleasure you like the incubus. I can't protect you like the angel. I can't even make you a sandwich. All I'm good for is finding new ways that could get you killed."

"That is not true."

"Why keep me then? Why have me around?" He pointed to my locket and groaned. "Why carry a piece of my body around your neck if I'm not the researcher?"

"Because I love you!"

The guitar fell through Daniel's hands. It landed with a possibly broken twang, but he only stared at me and I flushed. "You're not the book guy. No one has a damn job title in this…very complicated relationship."

He closed his eyes and raised his hands into the air. The sunlight cut through the clouds, glancing across him, except it skipped past the ghost and lit up the bench instead. "How can you love a man who's dead?"

I fumbled for his palm and settled for holding my hand near his. "No one's shown me such patience, with my spells, my reading. I've never had anyone sing to me like that, quote poetry like you do." Made me feel like my brain wasn't broken and I could be special. "It's not what you do for me — it's that you care to. I don't know what I'd be if I hadn't met you, Daniel, but it wouldn't be pretty."

"Layla...sometimes I feel as if I've loved you before we even met. You were a piece I didn't realize was missing. And no matter what I do, I will never be enough for you. I can't pleasure you the way Ink can, I can't comfort you —"

I held a finger to his lips. A chill wafted down my skin but he stopped. "You can and do all of that, in your way. Daniel, I...I'm sorry if I made you think you had to prove yourself useful."

"It isn't you. I need to be. I need to have a reason to..." He clenched his hand and the waves rocked harder against the boat. I lashed to the sides to hang on and Daniel sighed. "You're my only hope, my only light in a dark, unending future." He placed his palm to my cheek and I held my hand behind his, imagining what it would feel like.

"We're going to bring you back," I swore to myself. For the others, it was to find a way to stop Conquest. For me, for us... "And once I can touch you, I'm going to lick every divot of your body."

Daniel shivered, a smirk rising. "You'll have to wait until I've finished touching, sucking and rubbing you first."

I laughed to try to shake away the rising tension that wouldn't get any release until we found demon blood. "What was that you said about hell? That you found a way to open a portal to it?"

His tantalizing smile dropped. "It's not the best solution."

"But you can? I can rip open hell and get a demon's blood?"

He fully turned, staring out across the lake.

"What is it? What do I need? What do I have to do? Can we get the ingredients together soon? Daniel?"

"I shouldn't have told you," he whispered.

"If this is about your mom, your family, we can cross that bridge once you're back. Breathing. Living." I stood up, prepared to sit beside him so he'd talk to me.

Daniel raised his hands and stared at them as if he expected to find a stain. "It isn't that."

"Then what is it?" Why wasn't he excited about this? We could finally be together beyond steamy text messages and dildos.

Slowly, Daniel turned to me stupidly standing in the boat. He pulled in a slow breath and stared up. "Layla, in order to do this, you'd —"

The boat shook. I lashed a hand out to try to catch the sides, when it rocked even harder. My legs wobbled under me and I stared around the still lake. "What in the —?"

A long dark line rose from the depths and smashed straight into the hull. I pinwheeled my arms, fighting to keep in the boat, but whatever it was struck one last time. My legs gave out and I crashed backward into the water.

"Layla!" Daniel shouted just before I went under.

Gray-green lake water gushed into my nose and open mouth. I sputtered in shock, fighting to get to the surface. I couldn't see anything in the clouds of silt blooming across the water. Paddling, I broke to guzzle in air.

The boat was a good three yards away. *How did I fall so far?*

"Are you okay?" Daniel asked.

"Yeah. Feeling really stupid, but otherwise..." The lake cooled below my paddling feet. Goosebumps rose across my flesh and I stared down. The darkness came closer.

"Oh, shit. Shit, shit, shit!" I paddled for the boat, Daniel asking me what it was. I didn't have the wherewithal to explain, my brain screaming two words—lake monster. He hunched down and held his hand out. I swam faster, the water rippling the wrong way behind me.

It was getting closer. The cold cut through me like a knife.

"Come on. I've got you." Daniel reached for me. "Layla, hurry!"

A sound like a yawning tornado broke from behind. I didn't turn to look and leaped out of the water. With my hand extended, I reached for Daniel's...and my palm fell straight through. Tightness clamped to my leg and yanked me back.

"Layla!" Daniel screamed, flailing for me, but he couldn't reach. Even if he could, he couldn't save me. The monster's grip was unshakable, and it was starting to dive.

"Get..." I tried to call for help, but green lake water gurgled into my mouth. Shaking my head, I took one last breath, and plunged into the darkness.

I gave up fighting to swim away, and tried to kick the creature. Every thud of my foot against its head did nothing. The skin felt rubbery and sank in with each thrash. It kept swimming backward, dragging me down into its watery lair. It didn't matter if it was going to eat me. I'd be dead before it got the chance.

There was a spell, a breathing spell. But I only knew the wards and I sure as shit couldn't draw it while drowning. *Think.*

Ink? He could pull me out of this and...

My ass broke through the surface. Cold raced up my bare skin and I gasped, shooting out the last of my oxygen before I guzzled it back in. The clamp around my leg didn't let up, dragging me across wet sand. It abraded my stomach and chest, cutting up under my shirt. I started to turn my free leg back for another thrashing, when the creature let go.

Holy fuck!

I stared up at a mouth the size of a bus. Lips of dark green as wide as Cal opened to reveal teeth taller than Garavel. The skin reminded me of a whale's, but the longer I stared, the more I noticed what looked like small razor blade edges to every inch. I couldn't fight this thing. I could stroll down to its tonsils and it wouldn't even notice.

Scrambling to my feet, I turned to run. Didn't matter where. There was rock overhead, and a sign of light to the left. That would work. I got a foot under me, then I took a step with the one that'd been in the monster's mouth. It hit the sand and pain seared apart my calf. I lashed out to grab the rock and propel myself forward.

The creature hadn't noticed its prey was running. I didn't have time to heal. Fighting through the pain, I dove for the light.

The trees moved.

No, something that'd been hiding in the trees stepped in the way. As it stared at me, its scales shivered, shaking away the camouflage until a man with purple and green skin stared down at me.

"Hello, witch."

Chapter Nineteen

Ink

The boat carrying my bond roared farther away, much to the consternation of the two men left standing adrift on the shore. I draped one arm around Calvin, then another across Garavel.

"Well...orgy then?"

Calvin had the decency to scowl at me before he focused most of his ire on the angel. Garavel returned it, showing even the Celestial-born could embrace belligerency. With a great heave, the wolf threw me off of him and stomped to the long-abandoned grass clippers.

"We have the perfect opportunity to explore each other and discover hidden aspects of our sexuality never before realized."

"Not in the mood, Ink," the wolf shouted back before he hefted up a pair of scissors the size of his head and attacked an innocent bush.

"Shall I explain to you the techniques for erotic touch from the eyebrows down?"

The angel sighed and picked my hand off of him. "I should return to Dante. He said we'd be adding gas to the fire box today." As Garavel strolled off, he smiled at his kitten, then glared at the mutt. Calvin returned it tenfold, their ire reaching near-boiling. It was only a matter of time until blows were exchanged. *I should stock up on bouillon cubes for the show.*

The wind shifted and Layla's heartbeat picked up. Curious…ah, the ghost was there. No doubt he'd keep her distracted and bothered for an hour or two.

"How is she?" Calvin asked.

I blinked and stared askance at him. He chopped off a dead branch and sponged the sweat from his glistening forehead. His pecs remained un-dried.

"She is being visited by the specter. Who is no doubt attempting his pathetic pantomime of wooing."

"Well, that's…something." He didn't wince, but his stance shifted slightly at the mention of the cursed ghost. Was he feeling a twinge of jealousy at last? Or had more been growing in the dark?

"I am most curious, if you'll indulge me."

Calvin tossed the decapitated branches out of the way and stared at me. "Can I stop you?"

"Doubtful." He struck a strange figure with his chest exposed to the uncaring sun but thick gloves of workman's leather upon his hands. It wasn't unappealing, though the low-slung denim could use better tailoring. Without a care, I stepped in beside him as he resumed his menial labor.

"She has three of us at her beck and call."

"What about Daniel?"

"Three and a sneeze. You are content with this fact, yes?"

It wasn't a question, but Calvin nodded as if he'd made it fact ages ago.

"Yet what would happen if you took up rutting in the woods with another female of whichever species caught your fancy?"

The clippers plummeted, the blades digging into the soft ground. Calvin dropped his shoulders and groaned. "Nothing, cause it won't happen."

"It hardly seems fair for her to have—"

"Knock it off." He waggled a finger in my face, the stench of wolf musk and sawdust thick on the tip. "It doesn't matter what's considered fair. I don't want anyone else. Simple."

"But in the future…"

"Why are you doing this?" Calvin glared at me, a hint of the growl rippling in his words. "In the future, who knows? It'll be the future. Right now, and pretty sure for a few years at least, all I want is Layla."

"Despite her having a stable of handsome gents at her ready?"

"Yes." He scissored the bottom of the wayward sapling in half, sending it toppling onto a pile of laid-out tile still in the packaging. Calvin cursed and hauled the tree away. "It's simple, okay. I've been with other girls, and…it wasn't like this. I love her."

Love—an inane concept to facilitate simple biology. Yet I couldn't stop wondering. The wolf had been able to toss aside Lust without breaking a sweat. That had to be a quantifiable power. I just needed to understand it. "How do you know?"

"Butterflies in the stomach. Dancing like an idiot to make her smile."

"That's lust, stupidity or a need to urinate. More than likely a combination of all three."

"Maybe that's it. There is no because, no knowing. I'm terrified that if I lose her, I'll lose whatever shred of humanity I have, but I don't know that. I want to believe nothing would make me happier than seeing her every morning, but it could change. Love's... I guess it's faith."

"Religion, delightful." The concept had never held my attention, though its cloisters and clergy had provided fertile hunting for all sins.

"Why do you care?"

I shrugged it off, but his sharp gaze cut through me. "Mere curiosity."

"Are you worried I'm gonna make her get rid of you?"

I scoffed at the toothless threat. "Hardly." But there had been talk of doing just that. It was an arrangement I'd readily agreed with, happy to return to my carefree wanderings once I was certain the witch hunters would not find me. Instead, I'd bound myself even tighter to her without thought to what that would mean should the winds shift.

"I won't do that," Calvin said as if he needed to reassure me. I stared at his offer of friendship and handshake. He dropped it and returned to his work.

Layla's heartbeat increased. No doubt she was in the throes of masturbation gussied up as sexual perversion at the hands of the ghost. He couldn't even pervert right.

"She's bound to you, right? That unshakable bond that tells you everything she desires and other crap you brag about."

I snickered. "It is hardly a brag if..."

"Yeah, yeah. So, if you can read all of her desires, then you must know how she feels about you."

Love was a lie. Any lips that proclaimed it of me were warped by the talents of my fingers and tongue. They could not love me, only lust—for it was what I was created for. "I know her desires, not her heart. They are not always of the same mind."

"So unbind from her. That'll tell you."

"She would never allow that. She believes she is saving lives by keeping me chained to her."

Silence fell and Calvin, annoyingly wise at the worse times, leaned closer. "Is she right?"

"I could kill, if I so choose," I said carefully, but he smiled, showing his fang. He knew the truth without me saying it. My choice to no longer kill had been a long contention between me and Lust, then others who subscribed to her hunting methods. I kept it quiet from Layla out of habit. No other reason whatsoever.

Exhausted with this conversation, I abandoned the werewolf's sweaty yardwork for the calm reflection of the lake.

"There's your test," he said before I could walk fully away. "Tell her the truth and see what happens."

"I..." *Have no intentions to discern the reasons why Layla keeps me bound to her. It is no concern of mine if a woman of her make would or could carry a meager sin in her heart.* She was better off with the ghost.

A flush carried across our tether, one I took for sexual release, until I spied the boat without Layla present. "Calvin!" I shouted for the wolf. He looked too, leaping to my side as we stared at the rocking vessel without a being inside. It floated sideways, careening across the lake sans a captain to steer it.

"Where the hell...?"

"Monster!"

The ghost appeared beside us, his eyes wide and much consternation on his brow. If he were alive, he'd have bent over to gather his breath. As he was stubbornly dead, he pointed to the drifting boat and gawped.

"Where's Layla?" Calvin asked.

Daniel shouted, "A lake monster got her."

"There is no such thing as..." A scream of terror jangled down my nerves. "Layla." I took a step forward.

"Ink, we need to —"

Calvin's diatribe to work together faded to nothing as I stepped into the in-between and ran. Time stilled in the realm. I could peter about and take hours while still appearing one millisecond after I stepped in. Yet, I ran with all the speed in my body. Our tether glowed an assuring white, guiding me to her hand. I clung to its electric zip, praying it would not fade until I reached the end.

Instead of patiently slipping to the side and appearing as a gentleman, I ripped through the realm and leaped to the air. My hand caught Layla's and I swung her up into my arms.

"Ink?" She gasped, no doubt in elation at my rescue.

I stared down her attacker, a man in a suit of varying colors with undulating scales across his face. "Let us leave before you suffer a fate worse than death," I ordered.

The stranger chuckled and his scales rotated, plucking his body from the visible spectrum. *Sorcery!* I clutched tighter to Layla, prepared to launch into the in-between and return her to safety when she placed a hand to my arm.

"It's okay. You can put me down."

"You were attacked?" I said slowly. I waited a moment, watching the camouflaged creature, before doing as she asked. "Or so the ghost declared."

"Yeah, it's... This is Torran. He's a—"

"I am an under-demon, keeper to Zaxigrath." The man of scales shifted back to visible. He extended his hand, that shivered to a purple and dark green hue. An under-demon? That meant he'd slipped through the bonds of hell as well. We had much in common.

Taking his hand, I inquired, "Who, pray tell, is Zaxigrath?"

"That," Layla said, jerking a thumb behind.

The wall I'd dismissed as simple rubbery foliage parted its gigantic mouth and smiled. "Ah, I see we've found the lake monster."

Layla smiled and reached a hand out. A gigantic wall of black flesh rolled out of the mouth and I nearly flung my bond aside. But Zaxigrath managed to winnow the tongue down until a simple tip touched her palm. She giggled at the gigantic demon licking her.

I tried to take no offense at another demon caressing her flesh with his tongue and focused on the scaled stranger. His eyes were duplicated, four giant sets of pitch-black orbs perched aside a nose the size and shape of a piece of string cheese.

"You were the one who spied us at the beach," I said.

"Yes," Torran responded. His scales shuddered, turning his face invisible.

"Well, if I knew another demon was in the area, I'd have invited you to join in."

"That's...not my thing," he said, returning back to visibility.

"What precisely is, beyond capturing women in boats?" Layla might be accepting of their kidnapping, but we'd been down this road too many times for me to let go so quickly.

She abandoned Zaxigrath's wily tongue. I hoped it was the demon's tongue, at least, or the wolf would have my head. Turning to me, she began to speak, when the air snapped and the ghost phased through.

"I'm here to...!" Daniel shouted, positively useless.

Because that wasn't enough, a flap of wings heralded the arrival of the angel. Garavel made certain to at least arrive with some dignity, his sword unsheathed and chest raised for the attack. No doubt the wolf was out there swimming this way to join in.

"Lady witch?" Garavel asked, staring from the shape-shifting demon to the gigantic blobby one.

Layla looked to Torran and sighed. "This is gonna take some time to explain."

Layla

Once I got over the initial shock of a lizard man who could vanish, Torran was a complete gentleman. He halted his explanation when Cal arrived, and politely dodged out of the way of his attack. After assurances from the others that there was no danger, all the men stood around like a class waiting to hear about recess.

"Forgive me for meeting like this. I'd intended to make less dramatic introductions."

Cal snickered. "Kidnapping is basically our hello."

All four of them looked to me standing beside Zaxigrath. He reminded me of a giant puppy with no fur, a massive whale-like head and skin of razor blades. Which might be a typical dog in hell, come to think of it.

"You've been observing us for some time," Ink declared, sounding uncertain about his fellow not-a-demon demon.

"He was who we saw at the beach," I said, before having the rest look to me. "After you left, long story."

"No," Ink interrupted. "I'd thought the scent of hell due to the charcoal briquets, and the eyes on my flesh from potential witch hunters. But it was you."

"Not always," Torran said. His scales shifted, morphing his appearance and clothing to various tourists who we could have run into anywhere. "I was hesitant to approach you even after observing your magic and demon heritage." For a moment, he snickered directly at me and I paled. Oh fuck, he'd seen me and Ink... Ha, well, at least it wasn't a hunter.

Ink seemed to find the whole situation hilarious as he sat up higher in pride.

"There are others lurking about. Men dressed in attire like this." Torran's scales shivered, flipping over to create a flat black suit.

We all went silent. Only witch hunters dressed like that.

"But those were real animal control guys," Cal said and I stared at him.

"What?"

"Garavel drew their attention but it was nothing more than a simple hate-based misunderstanding. Where did you see these men in black?" Ink skipped right on past whatever I'd missed, but I wasn't ready to move on.

"What did you do?" I asked the suddenly silent incubus.

Cal was the one to shrug. "He put on his demon act to scare them away."

"For fuck's... What if they'd told a real witch hunter?"

"No doubt they'd have taken them for imbecilic drunkards, as that was what they were. We have not seen hide nor hair of the real hunters, my bond. Which means they have yet to see us."

Except they could take the suits off. What if they'd been at the beach that day? Or had ridden past the resort in their boats? What if they had a way to detect demons, angels and werewolves?

I crossed my arms, trying to put my anger away for later. We had bigger fish to fry.

Torran waited until the conversation died down. His bottom eyes blinked, then vanished into his cheeks. He quickly shifted to a normal-looking human man, albeit a handsome one. "I have observed their tactics from afar in many disguises. Whatever they are doing here is beyond my understanding, but I feared it was to hurt Zaxigrath."

"Why would anyone want to harm this big lug?" I asked. Zaxigrath lashed his tongue out and drew it over my back. Where the wet flesh touched mine tingled with a thousand tiny zaps. Instead of hurting, it flooded me with energy.

"They're witch hunters. If they cannot understand it, they destroy it," Ink said.

"I'm sensing you've dealt with their kind before," Torran said.

"Often," Ink responded. "It surprises me you have not. Two demons residing amicably in a lake—the myths and legends from humans are certain to draw the bastards in."

"That's the issue that I need help with. Zaxigrath and I are not supposed to be here."

"Are any of us?" Daniel asked.

"A tear formed in the depths of hell's watery abyss. It pulled Zaxigrath in until he emerged, trapped in this warm water puddle."

"What about you?" Cal wondered.

"I dove in after, of course." Torran shifted his look again, banishing the human disguise for one more like Ink's demon skin. He did not wear the wings, and the four eyes blazed with fire, but the lava and black flesh was the same. "We need your help to get us back to hell."

Every man looked to me.

"Can we do that?" Cal asked Ink, then me. I in turn glanced to Daniel, who'd gone quiet as he took all of this in.

"I'd thought the witch would be necessary, but you have an angel at your call..." Torran waved to Garavel who jerked back.

"No." He shook his head, fighting off a shudder. "We don't."

The under-demon chuckled nervously. "But you are a demi-angel. You serve him, carry his sword."

Garavel picked up the blade he'd placed on the ground, staring at the edge that no longer glowed.

"Even if he is unavailable, you can channel his power—"

"We don't have an angel." To my shock, it was Cal who jumped in, cutting off the conversation. "So stop asking. Okay?" He glanced to Garavel, sheathing his sword inside his wings. For a moment, the demi-angel looked to him and nodded in gratitude.

"There is another way, right, Daniel?" I prompted.

I expected him to leap forward, proud of his discovery as he unveiled it to the masses. Instead, he shrank deeper into his shoulders and stared at me. Despair wallowed in his gaze.

"You told me you found a spell. A way to…to open a portal to hell. This is much easier. They've already agreed to give us a vial of Zaxigrath's blood in exchange."

"A minor compensation for us to break free of this prison and return to our paradise. But if you tried to take it without helping us…"

"We wouldn't," I assured him.

Ink hummed and tipped his head, making this worse.

"Daniel, please. With that blood…"

"I know. But am I worth it?"

Oh, no. I walked over to him, reaching a hand out to waft my palm near his cheek. He wouldn't look to me and I couldn't make him. All I could do was plead. "Of course you are. You know what you mean to…" Three demons, an angel and a werewolf all stared at me and I chickened out. "To us."

"Layla, you don't understand. The spell, it requires…"

"A human sacrifice."

We all turned to Ink calmly brushing sand out from under his nails. It was Daniel who shouted, "You knew?"

"Of course. I thought it common-enough knowledge, and the reason witch hunters rarely accomplished their goals. Few have the spine to slit enough throats to do the deed."

I had to kill someone. They expected me to… I clenched my hands, trying to not picture hot blood smeared across them. I couldn't. Daniel's life, stopping Conquest, keeping demons and their power out of witch hunter's hands. There were a thousand reasons why I had to, but I couldn't do it.

"Or, with enough magical power, you could force it open for a few moments," Ink said and he smiled.

Magic. I had that. *Do I have enough?*

"How much?"

He shrugged. "I'm no Celestial, but the rare time I have seen it work, there were five witches involved."

I was one. My body began to collapse, my wobbly knees heading for the cool sand. A hand scooped me up. I didn't know whose. I didn't even care. It could have been the whale demon's tongue. Find five witches before the hunters found them, or kill someone.

"Babe. Come on. Look at me. Please?" Cal drew a finger down my jaw and turned my chin. He then tapped my nose, causing my gaze to rise to his. "You are crazy powerful."

"Not powerful enough," I muttered.

"We've got some power among us too. Our own demons." Ink and Torran both rolled their eyes. "An angel." Garavel raised his chest and tucked back his wings. "A ghost who knows how to find even more."

I smiled at Cal, including Daniel, who was still clutching tight to his hands and looked like he wanted to run. Maybe we could. But what if it wasn't enough, even with everything at our disposal? I frowned, an idea growing cancerous in my heart.

"You are one of the mage creations, yes?" Torran asked.

Every person sucked in a breath. Cal clung tighter to me as he swirled his head to stare at him. "I'm a werewolf," he said with a locked jaw.

"The moon can amplify the power through him. And it is to be a full one on the morrow."

Cal snorted and shook his head. "So my evil heritage can be of use after all. Great. What do you think, Layla?"

I wasn't enough. Garavel was losing his power every day. Daniel could only read the spells, not cast them. Ink was of this realm, as much of hell as an ice cream cone. And Cal... I wanted to believe he'd give it his all, however werewolves amplified magic, but he ran from what he was as much as used it.

"We need more," I said, clenching my hands so tight, my nails dug into my skin.

"My bond?"

"Lady witch?"

I had to do it. I couldn't. I was so angry I wanted to spit fire, but what if I let everyone down because of my broken heart?

A cool hand broke through my fever. It touched to my cheek, then landed on my shoulder. I turned from Cal to look into Daniel's hopeful eyes. I had to try.

Placing my hand over his, I said, "My mother. She's the only hope we have."

"Are you certain that's wise?" Garavel asked.

"She did seem rather insistent on banishing Ink there," Cal continued.

I nodded to all their reasons. She'd lied to me, abandoned me, returned only to make demands of me. Yet I wanted to give her this chance.

"We don't have a choice," I said, trying to make it sound like a logical conclusion and not a little girl crying for her mommy. I took a step, my mind set, when I paused. "Er, how exactly do I find her?"

Chapter Twenty

Layla

I squeezed the tip of my finger until a drop of blood plummeted into the red plastic cup we'd found at the back of the kitchen. The cloudy white liquid didn't turn vibrant purple or begin bubbling. Trying to not think about what I'd just put in it, I tipped the potion back and swallowed.

"Can you see anything?" Daniel asked. He peered up from my book spread across his lap.

I shook my head. "No."

"The spell says a path should light the way to your intended target."

"So it's a nav point from a game?" Cal asked.

"Like the compass of discovery from Sheep Wars: Pirate Cove." Ink smiled at his reference while I wondered how much of my limited phone space was eaten up with his games. If I had any money, I'd get him his own.

Pain bit into my finger and I sucked on the poke still welling with blood. This was a stupid idea. I should be looking through my spell book to find other ways to open a portal to hell. Maybe another potion, or a...

"Whoa!" The lights dimmed. Not just the overhead bulb barely flickering its forty watts, but everything including the sun faded. In its place, a tiny blue dot twisted on the floor. I walked for it and another appeared ahead.

"I think I've found my path," I said.

"Excellent." Torran phased from the walls, shifting his camouflage to that of a brown-haired man of average-to-excellent build.

"Layla? You in here?" Fariah called.

I blinked at the lights. "I don't have time to distract her. This could fade at any minute."

With a great sigh, Ink stood. "Once again it is up to —" He snatched Cal's hand and pulled him forward. "Us. Good afternoon. What do you require?" Ink shouted to Fariah.

"Layla's taking a nap. She's still jittery after her fall from the boat. What can I help you with?" Cal asked.

We waited until they'd led Fariah away before I slipped out the cabin door and into the woods. Garavel stayed behind to guard the big demon while I took the other one. No doubt it was their way to make certain we didn't fuck them over, but I felt the same. It helped that Zaxigrath seemed as excited about the kitten as Garavel did showing her off.

Torran slipped in beside me. I tried to take the path slow, making certain I caught every blue flame. And it wasn't just because I was having second thoughts about this. Thoroughness, that was next to godliness, right?

"This realm has changed greatly in the eons since the Accord."

I focused on the lights, but asked him, "Were you here in the before times?"

He snickered. "Of course not. But my keeper was and he likes to tell tales of traversing the Earth's oceans before the worst began."

"You're so devoted to him. You must care a lot."

"Yes, I do much caring for him. It is why I exist."

I shook my head, guilt slogging me in the stomach. Garavel had been the same for Ramiel—devoted, unflinching—until I made him question everything just to stay alive. "I mean you care for Zaxigrath. You love him."

"Naturally." Torran bowed his head as if it was an obvious fact.

"Ink says that demons can't love. That they aren't built for it."

"He's wrong, no doubt due to not being a demon. We are all capable of bottomless, selfless love."

My lights traveled over a downed tree and I peered under it, trying to find a way past. Over was a challenge, but I had to try. I raised my leg and began to hop, when strong arms cinched around my waist. Torran lifted me into the air with ease, and placed me on the other side.

"Thank you," I said, trying to get my bearings. It'd be my luck for the lights to lure me into the middle of the forest, then abandon me. If I squinted, I could still see the roof of the office building poking through the trees. So far, so good.

We made it another fifty feet before my heart turned to jelly and I wanted to run back. I needed a distraction. "Can I ask you about hell?"

He nodded, seeming unconcerned with my thoughts.

"We all think of hell as fire, and torture, and screaming and giant bird creatures eating people."

Torran laughed so hard his scales shifted to a peacock blue. "Yes, I have seen that painting. Only such creative thoughts could come from a mage. Sorry, human. Hell is…is that really what you wonder about? Or is it demons themselves?"

"Yeah, we don't think too highly of them either." *Though everyone acts like angels are the shit and one tried to kill me.*

He snickered, showing no sign of offense. "Celestials harvest two sources of power. Creation magic formed the angels, which is why they in turned infused it into their protectors. Demons are made of destruction magic."

"Are you saying that angels can only create?"

"And demons can only destroy. I'd heard that witches were a class above other mortals, but you're sharper than I expected. I shall have to watch my words carefully around you."

All this time I'd thought Ramiel refused to be the one to kill me because he got some sick pleasure out of making Garavel do it. But he couldn't. He was bound by his magical programming.

Torran took my hand and helped me across a mere puddle. "It is why demons and angels rely on us underlings. The demi-angel like your dear Garavel can destroy."

"So you create?"

He smiled and plucked a leaf off the tree. After closing it in his fist, he opened his hand and a green butterfly flew into the air.

"Wow." I stared in awe at the new life gifted to the world.

"I do not often get to do my tricks outside of the court of Lucifer. Thank you for being impressed."

I didn't realize how close he was until his scales danced against my cheek and I shivered. Leaning to the side to try to tame my hair, I said, "I have a few questions about him too."

"Lucifer is not a demon. Not an angel, either. It is not really alive and yet is. I'm not certain if this is the best topic to discuss at the moment."

"But he…it leads hell?"

Torran laughed. "Hardly. That would be like putting your phone in charge of your empire."

I stared, waiting for more information, but Torran had moved on. "I do find myself curious why you are pursing destruction magic. Combining it with creation is a dangerous end."

I closed my eyes and locked my hand around the necklace. *Tread carefully.* If I said the wrong thing, he could call the whole deal off. "Because, I…"

The blue lights burst around me, circling the trees like a druid rave. I raised my hand to shield my eyes, when the entire thing went dark and my mother stepped out of the shadows.

"You could have just called."

I wanted to laugh, scream and turn around. But I clung tighter to my locket, willing myself to face this pain for Daniel. "Mom, I need your help."

"Of course you do." She turned away and walked into a camouflaged tent. I could make it out once she pulled up the flap, uncertain how I hadn't noticed it before. Holding her hand out, she raised up a book in blue leather. I wanted to ask what it was, when it hit me. That was her book, the book of spells from witches past that bound her to the magic leaking into this realm.

"Let's get started. Where's yours?"

"Uh… I left it back at the cabin." *With Daniel.*

"Layla!" she chastised.

"I didn't think I'd need it out here."

My mother snapped her book shut and strode closer. "You do not go anywhere without your spell book. It is your body bound in leather and parchment. Do you understand?"

I nodded, feeling like I was five and left my jacket on the bus. No. I had twenty years on that, fifteen of which were without her. "I'm not here for that."

"What?"

"You yelling at me, ordering me to be quiet and polite, and if I wasn't perfect at it, leaving me in the corner for hours."

I expected a sneer. Maybe even a grounding. But my mother sighing and dropping her head threw me for a loop.

"I did it for your protection."

"Right. That's been your excuse for everything so far."

"It's the truth!" she shouted so loud, the birdsong died. "Layla, I…I had to keep you alive. Even when we were being hunted. Even when the monsters you couldn't see prowled the streets outside our door."

"You could have told me. Instead, I had to find out from the sex demon that popped up in my living room."

My mom glanced to the other demon I'd brought into the woods and I waved it off. "Not him. He's a regular demon."

"Torran, if introductions are necessary."

"You give your name willingly?" she said with a surprise.

"Do I?" He smiled wide and I recognized the demonic way of lying without lying.

"Never believe a word out of a demon's mouth." My mother said like it was an aphorism to be found in curly script on the wall of a candle store.

"Yeah, well, angels can be dicks too."

She nodded instead of disagreeing with me. "If he is not another of your... Are you?"

I shook my head and Torran smirked.

Don't even think about it. We barely have enough beds as it is.

My mom stared as if she didn't trust him. "Then why is he here with you? Protection?"

"No, I need your help, like I said."

"To do what?"

I took in a deep breath and faced her. "To open a portal to hell."

Her mouth opened, no doubt to argue with me, but I was faster. "Torran here is the guardian of a demon, a real one. They both came through a tear from hell into our realm." I waited for the information to sink in. My mother stared at Torran who gazed back, neither giving anything away.

"There hasn't been a full demon on Earth in centuries," she said carefully as if this were some white lie I'd made up for attention. "You believe this to be the work of Conquest?"

"Who else could do it? He brought forth that deer thing, then murdered it for its blood. Creation magic. If he got Zaxigrath, then he'd have destruction magic too."

For a flicker, a smile of pride crossed my mother's face. She hardened her look and stared across the forest.

"I suspect far worse is at stake if White gets his hands on a demon."

"What do you mean?"

She didn't answer, her gaze a mile long while the breeze rustled through the trees. "I will help, but a portal to hell requires a lot of magic. Far more than two witches can possess."

I nodded and clasped my hand to my necklace. "We've got some ideas on how to make it work."

"We?"

The air snapped and warm fingers scooped mine up. I barely had to look before Ink placed my palm to his chest and strode forward. Daniel appeared on my left holding my spell book safe. He cast a look to Ink, then the new demon.

"For fuck's sake..." Branches snapped and shattered as Cal dashed into the clearing. "Would it kill you to not...? Oh. Hi." He haphazardly waved to my frowning mother who'd already cussed out his swearing once before. With a wince, Cal wrapped a hand over the back of my shoulders.

Taking a dramatic bow, Ink announced, "The coven is at your disposal. Oh, we have a demi-angel as well, but he's indisposed at the moment. Large fellow, big sword, tiny kitten. Can't miss him."

My mother's only response was to groan.

Chapter Twenty-One

Ink

"Raise your hand, split your fingers apart like this!" Isabel shouted unhelpful instructions at her daughter. Layla parted her fingers with the dexterity of a fishmonger who had caught his thumb on the hook. Even I winced at the strain shuddering down her spine. But she gritted her teeth and continued, her skin awash with an unnatural glow.

The elder witch paced about the circle, showing no sign of exhaustion, but my bond looked two moments from fainting. I could take no more.

"That is enough," I declared, striding across the runes with a fallen arch. My foot broke the spell, returning my bond from the micro tear in the realm. Her skin was cold, pocked with icicles and unnaturally pale. I reached to hold her, when the elder witch caught my hand and yanked it back.

I let her for Layla's sake, but glared at the woman. "Excessive pawing of my form requires permission of your daughter."

Alas, she did not even blink. "You're not touching her. He'll undo all of our hard work."

"No, he won't." Layla groaned. She reached a wobbly hand out, and Torran was kind enough to supply it with a jug of watered-down beer. The water to hydrate her and the alcohol to keep her from screaming out of the depths of her soul as she was subjected to the unending torment of the in-between.

After taking a long drink, Layla looked to me, still trapped under the talons of her mother. "He can control himself."

I shrugged off the grip of the elder Leeland and cupped my bond's cheek. With my thumb, I wiped away the drop of beer beside her lips. She radiated with energy, her hair nearly standing on end like a dandelion in season. One kiss and I could feed for a week.

"He's a sin. Their one trait is not having control."

I dipped back, allowing Layla to walk of her own volition to the stump where the ghost had taken up residence. She peered down at her book, reading through the spells her mother had been calling out. The ghost had cheered her on as he could do little else.

With a smug grin, I rolled my gaze back to Isabel. She glared longer at me then called to her daughter, "We can't wait too long. Every second out of the tear is power lost."

"How much more of this can she take?" Calvin inquired. He'd been the loyal but lost mutt, stuck at his mistress' feet while waiting for a pat as she worked herself to the bone. With her free, he caught her hand and pulled her closer for a kiss. "Babe?"

"I'm fine. See, still standing. Haven't caught anything on fire."

"Your eyes are glowing," he said.

Layla slapped a hand over her face as if to disguise the unnatural shine emanating from her eyeballs. All it did was amplify the light beneath her palm. She shook the concern away. "We've only got one day to get this to work. There isn't time to worry."

"Oh, I assure you, the wolf will find the time. See, he's already hewn an entire acre of forehead furrows." I pointed to the wrinkles etched into Calvin's brow. He shook me off, but kept staring in concern at Layla.

She blew him a kiss and returned to her runes. After she re-drew what I'd smudged, Layla's eyes rolled back until only the whites were visible and she moaned. Her mother resumed her pacing, instructing her on the best ways to siphon in the power that should come in drips, not rivers.

"I hate this." Calvin abandoned his post in order to whisper behind my ear. "She's not looking good."

"A most curious thing to say of your beloved. Shall you compare her to a winter's morn next? Your eyes, the pallor of a gray dawn, your skin as lifeless as the leaves beneath my tread…"

"You see it, too. You wouldn't dodge otherwise."

It unnerved me how easily the wolf could mine my internal thoughts. We'd spent far too much time together. I focused on that instead of the power spiraling from every pore in Layla's body. The realms were an eternal spring of magic, and witches the vessels to capture it. Some could only hold a thimble's worth, others an entire jug. Layla had already been pumped with a bathtub and was pulling in more.

I wanted to rip her away from this. Take her in my arms and flee to a secluded grotto in the islands where none would find us for days. She could release this magic in bursts from my touch and tongue without suffering any ill effects save a cramp or two.

The only problem was that was not what she desired. The ghost, the demon and her cursed heart all kept her locked in that cage, absorbing until she could take no more. I looked to the mutt who had the same desires as me. While it would be easy for me to set him rescuing her, I clasped a hand to his shoulder.

"I could say the same of you."

Calvin stared, his pale brow rising.

"You're looking ragged around the edges, werewolf."

He shook me off, proving I'd hit deep. All of his smiles and japes could not hide the veins throbbing in his eyes, the deep scratches of his nails digging across his arms or the flush of red that'd overtake his pale skin at any moment. Either the others were too polite to point it out, or he'd burned every bridge save mine.

"Why don't you care about Layla for once instead of getting under our skin?"

"There is none who can give better care than I to our beloved."

"Yeah? Told her about what happened in the woods yet?"

I frowned at his mentioning Lust. We'd had an agreement to keep her in the past. Yet he intended to use that as blackmail against me? How low the mutt had sunk. Shaking my head, I turned my back on him and caught the murderous eyes of the mother instead. Out of the iron maiden and onto the impaling stick.

She did not draw a finger across her neck, but the implication was there. For what reason was I subjecting myself to such idle threats, as if wolf or witch could harm me?

An answer called from the deep trenches of my mind, but I scoffed at it before it barely formed. "Under-demon?"

Torran turned away from Layla, who was beginning to pulse from the rise in magic.

"Walk with me to relieve the angel from his duties." I held my hand out, prepared to split into the realms. Due to the power coalescing in the air, it nearly broke with a thought. Torran nodded to the others and joined me.

"I would like to check in with Zaxigrath. I assume you have this under control?"

Layla gave a minor raise of her thumb while the mutt glared with hunched shoulders. Before another argument broke out, I stepped into the in-between, and Torran joined me. The skies melted to an eye-searing green. Trees that'd once impeded our movements vanished to pillars of salt with writhing hands of skeletal fingers. I paid it all no mind as I walked in the direction where we'd left Garavel.

He did not gawp at the treacherous turn of the scenery, drawing my curiosity. "If this is your first visit to Earth, how did you know to use this place?"

"Oh, we have the same in hell. It's not as finished, mind you. Mostly a blank canvas from one level to the other for demons to slip down."

I gritted my jaw. "Strange. I never found any."

"You've been? Did you meet with Gorgar the devourer? He's a cut-up at parties, I swear. Always pretending to eat the moon then dripping cheese from his eyes. Ah…"

"My time in hell was not so appreciable."

The plane we walked on shifted, rising to skim above the lake. If I closed my eyes, I could sense the plain water lapping above. If I looked, I saw the molten mercury boiling below us. The Celestials had dumped every remaining block here once they'd finished, like a trash heap outside the city walls. None but the unwanted were to venture in between realms.

"That's odd," Torran said.

I intended to point out how most liquids were some form of metal here, but he was staring at me.

"How did you wind up in hell?"

A shudder caught in my chest. I ignored it and soldiered on. "The men in the suits you saw. Though back then they preferred hosiery and buckles upon their shoes and hats for unfathomable reasons. They banished me, because one cannot kill a Sin."

Torran chuckled. "It is funny to meet you. Like discovering an unknown cousin from a lower level. You are more like me than I expected."

"Oh?"

"Born of destruction in order to create."

I hadn't considered it, but there was truth to his words. I was sundered from my creator, cast aside like the garbage around us. With my skills I created passion, lust, the trembling quakes in thighs and buttocks all for a sip of their enflamed desires.

"Though, unlike you, I don't have to drain someone to maintain my power."

"How do you then?" I took no offense to his fact, though I suspected my bond would have for me.

Torran smiled. "It comes from my creator."

He said the word the way a priest would his god, the way Garavel spoke of the murderous angel. My jaw clenched at the thought. "You speak of him as if you are devoted to Zaxigrath."

The plane dipped and we stepped off it. Instead of sinking into the mercury sea, we landed on a lower platform and continued toward said demon and demi-angel. Torran tipped his head back, his body's embedded camouflage shifting to a warm pink. "Who else would I be devoted to? Zaxigrath created me, gives me purpose, life. He is my beginning and my end."

"That sounds exhausting."

"I take it you do not share the same thoughts with your creator."

"He was a pathetic man who deluded himself with thoughts of grandeur and, once the world snapped back, turned his blame on me. The only thoughts I ever gave to him were pity."

"That's a shame."

"I never considered it a loss."

We approached the cave and I reached to split apart the air, when Torran extended an arm. He aimed all four of his eyes at me, the black orbs swirling to form a green and blue marble — much like the miserable planet to which he was exiled. "You can't know what it is to lose what you never had."

"Tell me then. What do you feel with Zaxigrath? What did Garavel feel for his angel?"

Torran scratched his sharp chin with a short nail. "I cannot speak for the angel and whatever occurred there."

He asked a question without speaking it, but I would not answer. If it was such a bone of contention, he could put it to Garavel instead.

"But Zaxigrath is…well, he is home. He is safety. I leave at his orders, and even at my whims, but every moment away is a minute of pain without him. He created me. He shapes me still in how I better myself, in how I can better him. Do you not feel this way about someone?"

Home. For thousands of years my life was leaving — towns, villages, cities, kingdoms. If I overstayed my welcome, questions rose and the hunters came. Safety? All I knew was the hunt, and with it came an unending source of contention and concern. At any moment, my prey could vanish, I could falter, fail and wither away to a pathetic scrap of a sin more worthless than the ghost.

What of now?

I snickered at the thought rolling in my mind. My fears were increased tenfold thanks to Layla's incessant need to help all who crossed our paths. Even if she was the first I'd ever known who risked her life for mine. Yes, she provided a place for me to return, a familiar lair of food and walls to contain me. But was that home?

What is home to a sin?

Bodies welcomed me, hearts beat for me, minds begged for me. What was one out of billions? What was she to me other than a source of desire?

"The way you talk sounds of love," I scoffed, distancing myself from the dark thoughts he dredged up. This was hardly the time or place to debate my standing in our relationship pantheon. Let the ghost be the god of love, the angel the god of protection, the wolf the god of devotion. I preferred being a free agent of chaos.

Torran tipped his head and smiled. "I suppose it is. A love only a demon can know."

I ripped through the realm and plummeted into the cave. The ground shifted, dropping me an inch from the in-between. At the sound of my feet hitting, Garavel glanced over his shoulder and smiled.

"Ink! And you brought the new demon, too. Hi, demon."

Torran returned his wave. "He is certainly enthusiastic."

"You should see him after cotton candy. How do you fare, Garavel?"

"Great. Watch…" He scooted back from the ground to reveal the tiny black kitten batting at a shell. Her paws slapped it back and forth at lightning speed before sending it skittering into the cave.

A massive guffaw broke from the giant mouth. The demon Zaxigrath was laughing at the antics of a kitten.

"We've been talking about the changes to Earth since the accords. Kittens, ice cream. He really wants to go roller skating."

I smiled and approached both the huge man and the gigantic demon. Garavel dipped his wings, allowing me to slip in beside him. "I'm afraid that might prove a challenge. Does Zaxigrath possess feet?"

"There are about two-dozen smaller ones beneath him," Torran said.

"Many skates will be required. Garavel?"

He turned, his eyes wide and smile infectious as he snuggled his kitten. It was obvious why my bond bore such affection for him. I feared her adoration transferred to me. Or perhaps it was because I too knew the confusion of waking in a world that'd moved on in four hundred years without thought to me. When I had first emerged from hell, I was trapped in awe for nearly ten minutes, which was terrifying.

The kitten mewled and Garavel plucked her up to his shoulders. She was quick to vanish into the feathers, forever playing with the interdimensional rift on his back.

"Why don't you take a break? Get out, stretch your wings, see the sun. You've been trapped under this rock for three hours."

"It's all right. I don't mind being here." He gazed around the cramped cave with the wonder of a first-time castle owner. "It's cozy."

Oh. He'd found familiarity here. The cave bore much in common with his previous lair, trapped underground with nary a hint of sunlight. And he was free to listen to a mighty being involved in the formation of creation itself.

His smile didn't dim, but I noticed the wear in his eyes and the chips of ebony tumbling from his skin. He looked liable to crack, and I knew only one solution to this.

Draping an arm around Garavel, I encouraged him to lean down to my level. "Layla has been preparing for this spell. It's dangerous and none of us have ever dealt with a witch filling herself with so much magic."

"She has to be careful or the magic could come spilling out!" Garavel's eyes widened in instant concern. "All the witches who did that before a battle required calm and meditation."

"Why don't you go tell her? She'd be extremely grateful."

He nodded, not realizing I was setting him up for another rendezvous with our witch. Showing care and concern for her wellbeing then tending to her needs was the quickest way for the two of them to finally make the winged beast of two backs. The sooner that tension snapped, the easier it would be for me to incorporate him into our ménage à cinq.

With his lady witch on his mind, Garavel said his formal goodbyes to the demons, then folded his wings back to fly.

"Offer her a massage. She quite loves having her shoulders and back rubbed."

He grinned and called to me from the sky. "I'm good at that."

Thank Satan for small miracles at least. With that romantic encounter sealed, I turned to Zaxigrath, who rumbled in a voice I almost understood.

Torran spoke for him. "He's inviting you to join us in hell."

"I thank you for the offer, but as I previously explained, my time in your domain was not so pleasant."

"He was cast there," Torran said.

The demon roared without sound again, and I looked to the translator. He nodded along, then his eyes widened. "Of course. You must have been mistaken for a mortal. We do our best, but the mortal-born of our kind can get mixed in with the chaff. I'm sorry. Trying to shape the aftercare to answer for the deserved desires of every mortal that falls our way is a strain."

"Desires?" I chortled at the idea. "Hardly. I was trapped in an eternal void only marked by broken and dead scraps from my life. It was nothing but nothing."

"That's odd." Torran looked to Zaxigrath, who must not have had much to say.

"I took it for what it was, a punishment."

"We don't torture. I know, mortals misunderstanding a glimpse through the realms. What else is new?"

"If it wasn't torture, what was that?" I'd only subsisted thanks the pity of a headless statue. I'd had none to speak to, nothing to experience, only the endless void of existence.

Torran nodded to his creator. "When mortal scraps plunge to our realm, we try to make them happy. We give them what they desire in the moment of their death."

I laughed at the idea. *Nothing. I desired absolutely nothing after my two thousand years on Earth. Me? A sin of lust and only desire.* It was a farce.

Torran stared at me, his four eyes focusing sharply. "What do you desire, Ink?"

I answer their desires. I feed them so they feed me. I move from town to town, hunting new prey, feeding and continuing the cycle until the world ends or I do.

What I desire is…

My smile slipped into place and I shrugged off Torran's concerns. "For this demon and hell business to be done with."

He nodded along, falling into a private conversation with Zaxigrath. I tried to listen, ignoring the small voice in my chest telling me exactly who it desired.

Chapter Twenty-Two

Layla

My body hummed with the vibrations of dawn's light. I knew every flap of an insect's wing, heard the fish deep at the bottom of the lake, tasted the sap pulsing in every tree.

"Try again."

It wasn't enough.

My mother looked worse for the wear. She'd never been the stylish *maman* in pressed designer suits that'd hustle away from us. But she hadn't been like the shoeless bohemian types who'd sometimes appear at our doors asking for help. Even when the world was falling down around our heads, my mother expected a certain level of decorum. Yet she'd let it fall completely by the wayside.

I raised my hand, and my mother lashed her arm out. Power sliced through me, twisted around my arm and embedded barbs under my skin. Each one wicked away the magic I'd spent the past twenty-four hours building. I opened myself back up.

It was the opposite of how I'd felt when the witch hunters had ripped my magic away. Instead of a looming hole, I feared if I opened my mouth, magic would tear through the entire forest and leave nothing but ashes behind. It was awe-inspiring and terrifying at the same go. The power rippled down my arms, tearing and rebuilding the flesh before I could feel it. I'd tried to not watch at first, but now I couldn't look away. There wasn't even a scar. It was as if magic kept pulling me apart just to put me back together.

I gripped back to the tether from my mother. Her eyes went wide, as if I shouldn't be able. Pinching my fingers to the pulse of magic, I stared at the flow and thought, *Why not reverse it?* My mother flew back, her hand snapping away like she'd shocked it on a broken outlet.

Wings opened, sundering the air. Garavel caught her before she fell. The way he held her as if she were a frail mortal stung deep. I'd only been curious, thought that it might do something interesting to reverse the spell. "I'm sorry, I didn't mean to…"

My mother pushed him away and swept back her hair. "It's fine. You're getting there."

"Can she take a damn break already?" Cal stomped forward. He was still in his pajama pants, his feet bare despite the forest floor of pine needles and burrs.

"No," my mom insisted.

He ignored her and looked to me. "Layla?" Worry wrinkled his forehead and overran his eyes. "You need to take a breather."

"It's okay. I've got it." I tried to smile when my jaw slipped and the force nearly sent a lightning bolt zipping through the trees. Instead, I settled for a thumb's up. That hadn't been too dangerous, yet.

Cal folded his arms and glared. He knew me too damn well. "Did you even sleep?"

If I closed my eyes, I could see the whole universe lit up like Vegas at Christmas. Rather than lie, I tipped my head so he could read whatever he wanted.

"The monster is...right." Garavel gritted his teeth and breathed deep while glaring in Cal's direction.

Fuck. I do not need them fighting now. If I tried to stop it, I might set all of Canada on fire.

To my surprise, Cal shrugged. "I don't care if he calls me a butt-sniffer as long as he gets you to take a break." He held out his hand and my certainty wavered. The protection bubble died and I took his fingers.

"Butt...? Do you do that?" Garavel asked him earnestly.

Cal shivered even as he pulled me closer for a hug. "Why do I give them ammo?"

"Because you're such a good sport?"

He held my chin and smiled, then began to pull me closer.

"Whoa!" I yanked back, accidentally sending my body speeding backward and leaving behind a puff of smoke from the burnt needles. Cal's smile dropped and pain stung his eyes. "I'm sorry, but I don't know if..."

"She's liable to take your head off in her state," my mother said. She wrung her shoulders out, then stepped into the ward. The protection bubble snapped in place, and my mother ripped apart the realms. A queasiness rumbled in my stomach and I slapped a hand over my mouth, trying to keep anything from shooting out.

"How long is she...are you going to be like this?"

My mother snorted. "Until we open the portal tonight. If you can't keep your hands to yourself until then, perhaps Layla should look into a shock collar."

Cal managed to keep his face stone while I fought against the blush literally burning up my skin. The fire stopped on my belly, which I'd had to leave exposed after two of my shirts went up in smoke. With great power came great flammability.

My mother caught me first slapping at the tiny flames, then using a dash of magic to quench it. "What?" she asked, her eyebrow perched and tongue ready for scolding.

"They have already opened dialogues into such a purchase." Ink sauntered back, having to get one deep dig in with a smirk. "I suggested including the barbed options to save on coin down the line."

Sparks trembled off my fingers. I flexed them at my sides while glaring at him. *Happy, calm, everything's just fine.* "How's Torran?"

"The demon of scales is prepared. Though he is hesitant about using the beach."

We'd been over it all night. The spell would require a lot of area to get Zaxigrath through, and somewhere malleable to draw on. Daniel had suggested we use the beach once the full moon rose and it seemed our only option.

"He fears that it may draw the attention of more than a handful of vacationing mortals."

"Tell him…" If White and the witch hunters didn't already know we were here, a whale-sized demon hanging out on the sand would. "Tell him that we have to risk it."

Ink shrugged. Then he placed a finger to my cheek. I walked closer, my lips parting. He twisted his finger, winding a spool of magic around it. With a smirk, he sucked on the tip, literally consuming the power. All the while, my mother watched with a snarl.

I couldn't let him take a kiss of magic from me for this to work. Leaning closer, I was about to tell Ink, when he whispered, "You were beginning to crack."

In shock, I slapped a hand to my cheek but felt only unbroken skin. Ink smiled. "Garavel? I believe she requires your skilled ministrations. Do be careful to control it."

"I've got this." I tried to assure myself because the incubus knew I was full of it.

"It's more your compassionate heart I'm concerned with." After whispering that to me, he stepped back. "I shall return to Zaxigrath with much haste and an armful of twinks." Ink bent over and snatched up an array of snack cakes from Cal's stash.

"Those are called..." Cal began, when Ink smiled.

"I know," he said with a wink and vanished.

"I'm gonna..." Cal looked to me, isolated from all of them for their safety. "...check on Daniel. Make sure he's got this spell right. Babe?" He reached over to take my hand, but froze. "You've got this."

Cal shot me two thumbs up before he wandered off to join Daniel back at the cabin. It was easier to hide the floating books from the others that way.

"Lady witch, would you care to sit?" Garavel asked. He dusted a leaf off the fallen tree. I nodded and tried to walk over without leaping twenty feet ahead. With each step, I heard the crackle of a thousand autumns and the screams that birthed the forest.

I perched on the edge of the bark and flexed my hands. If I didn't keep moving, my muscles seized up and the power built. Garavel placed the massive water jug in my hands, then he swept my hair back and pressed his palm to my shoulder.

"Drink deep. I can always find more for you."

Placing the rim to my lip, I girded myself to open my mouth when Garavel dug in. A gasp slipped free, almost hurling the bottle to the ground. I clung tighter with a force that could rival a hurricane and drank.

"The witches required as much hydration as possible before battle." He continued to knead across my shoulders, rubbing out knots on top of knots. With his wide hands, he worked the backs of my arms and biceps.

I hadn't realized how much tension had built up until Garavel undid it. Groaning, I closed my eyes. The universe's heart beat through me, but I forced myself to focus only on the man carefully working his way down my back.

"I'm not surprised. I feel like I've been fighting a fever for weeks, but also like I could punch a mountain."

He smiled and spread his thumbs over the small of my back. *Fuck, that feels so good. Just a bit lower and...* The heat caught in an instant. A muted flame that'd been carefully tended in a lantern erupted into a five-alarm forest fire as Garavel's innocent fingers drifted to the top of my ass. A million thoughts burst in my mind. *Biting his lip while I sit spread open on his thighs. Grinding back on his thumbs as he pulls my ass higher and dives in. Sitting on that rock-hard face and clinging to his bald head like a drum.*

"Layla...your buttocks are smoking."

I snickered at the compliment then smelled the charred tree. "Shit!" Leaping to my feet, I smacked at my ass that'd caught fire. It wasn't helping, only reminding me of the last time Cal and Ink had me spread out on the table.

Calm down. Keep control.

Clenching my hands, I willed the magic back. It fought being corralled, the power wanting to destroy or create, do anything but be kept waiting. Exhausted, I collapsed to my knees. "I hate this," I muttered to myself. All this power and I couldn't even walk without fearing I'd hurt someone.

Garavel pressed his hand to me. I almost jerked back, well aware how hot my skin was, but he kept his ebony palm to my cheek. Tenderly, he combed my hair I was lucky hadn't burned off yet. "If it helps, Zaxigrath is impressed at the lengths you're going to for him."

I smiled. "You two get on better than I'd have expected."

Garavel's gaze dropped and he stared to the burned tree while helping me up. He wrapped his arm around the back of my waist, keeping me pinned against him. "It is easy for me to fall back into my place."

Serving a Celestial being without question. I pursed my lips to keep from saying what would only hurt him. "You like him?"

He smiled. "He is quite funny, almost as humorous as Ink."

So the giant whale demon was telling a bunch of dick jokes. Great. "Do you... Garavel, do you want him to stay here?"

He closed his eyes and sighed. "Torran is his keeper, not I. And his being here is bad for us, for him, for the whole world."

"Except..."

"There is no except. He wishes to return home, it is best for all of us to make it happen. And you are pushing yourself to make it happen. It's amazing, and..." He glanced down, his brown eyes widening until the sunrise glinted off them. "You amaze me."

"You're pretty amazing too. I couldn't survive this without your help. The massages are wonderful. Did you do them a lot?"

"Only if the witch in our care requested it." His eyes dropped and his cheeks pinked.

"Which I bet they did outside of battle."

He swallowed deep and looked around as if expecting an inquisition. "That... Sometimes, marching could be... I just wanted to help."

I caught his panicking hand reaching back for his sword out of habit and held it tight. "I like them, a lot. Especially when we're not about to go to war."

"That is..." He guffawed sharply, then winced. With a deep breath, he traced his fingers across my collar, his wide hand stretching until the pinkie reached my biceps. "I like giving them."

Kiss him.

Do it now!

I started to pop up on my toes, when I froze. If I did and it sent shockwaves of energy through his body, he'd never want to kiss me again. Cooling my blood, I patted his hand instead, trying to not imagine what those carved tendons and knuckles would feel like roaming over my body.

Garavel turned from me, the moment gone in a second. This wasn't the time for me to figure out what, if anything, was going on between us. I had a demon to send to hell—which was a lot less cool than it sounded. Nobody was even in any leather.

"Babe?"

The sound of Cal jerked me in surprise. I thought he'd been going to check on Daniel. But he stood there, looking like nothing happened.

"Yes?"

"I'm gonna resupply at the store. You need anything?" He was smiling, which was good. But his shoulders were hunched inward, and he kept digging his toes into the ground. Maybe it was all of this demon stuff, or the angel and demon stuff. Yet Cal was trying to act like everything was normal. Once I fixed all of this, I'd talk to him about whatever was bothering him.

"I don't know." *When did I last eat?* I wasn't hungry. I couldn't imagine putting a crumb of food in my body — the magic crammed into every nook it could find.

"She requires more of the beer and freshly boiled water." Garavel stood taller, his form shadowing me from the sun.

Cal stared overlong, and Garavel shook out his wings. They cupped around both him and me, almost tugging me back into an embrace. Cal's lip rippled and I prepared to bolt to stop him when he smiled and pointed. "Got it. I'll pick up some more marshmallows, too. Just in case."

With a cheery wave, he said goodbye and turned to leave. I moved to talk to him, certain that for a second I saw the wolf in his eyes. But when I took a step, the ground sundered. Time peeled away not just the leaves, but the roots, the dirt, the very bedrock until only blood-red sand remained. I breathed and the vision vanished.

"Cal?" I called to him, my legs locked in place. "Are you...?"

He didn't walk closer, his chin quirked as he listened intently. But he kept clenching his fist tighter while staring past my shoulder to the angel behind. "Are you capable of getting some caramel too?" That made him tip his head in confusion. "You know...for later?"

Cal caught what I pretended to care about. "Ah. Got it. Maybe hot fudge too in case Ink wants to join in."

He walked away in his pajamas without any shoes on, to go to the store. I watched, aching to put out feelers to try to pick apart what was happening with him. But with each tremor, I tugged back, fighting to keep from trespassing in his memories.

A growl rumbled behind my ear. I flinched. Shit, did I steal one by mistake? Would I see what happened when Eric had caught and nearly beat him to death? That night almost killed all of us, if I had to relive it through his eyes... Oh, no, the growl came from Garavel, who stood taller while watching him leave. Whew.

Wait.

"Are you going to hate him forever?" I was tired of dancing around this. Of pretending that either of them could just play nice for a day. This Band-Aid was coming off.

Garavel raised his chin as if he could hold a grudge for a million years. Then his eyes dipped. "I don't know. When I see his snarl, the claws and fangs, all I can think of are my friends being set upon by the same. I existed to stop monsters like him."

"You know, he's doing the same."

That caught Garavel who stopped pulling out his sword and stared at me.

"He's fighting the same fight as you are now. I mean, for fuck's sake, he killed his father just like you did."

Garavel raised his chest. "His father was a flea-bitten werewolf. He deserved to die."

"And your creator wanted to kill the world."

He whipped around, his face scrunched up in pain. "Ramiel..." Garavel groaned at the name and fell silent for a while. When he spoke again, his voice echoed as if from deep inside a canyon. "We believed in the accords, angels and demons. Even still, hell honors them."

The sunlight caught on a diamond tear sliding down Garavel's cheek as he turned to me. "Even your werewolf does, yet my creator — the one who executed them — turned his back on everything they fought for, everything they died for. It makes no sense."

I reached out, holding my palm above his shoulder. Keeping control, I placed my hand to his skin. He could be so hard one minute, then soft as cotton fluff the next. I clung tighter, trying to keep him upright as the giant man sobbed.

"Sometimes…we don't know people like we think we do. Even if we spend our whole lives with them, even if…" I looked to my mother, her hair standing up as she ripped apart the fabric of the universe and filled herself with magic. "Even if they created us. We can't always fix them, we can't always change them. Sometimes we can't even save them."

I didn't hate her, not anymore. I didn't know if I'd ever hated her. For a long time I had hated myself, blamed myself for losing her. All that anger had to go somewhere, but I was tired of it. Maybe it was time to let go and try again.

My hand almost slipped off his shoulder as I prepared to return to the ward. Garavel caught it, pressing my palm to his skin. His head hung low and he whispered, "I did it for my friends. So all that they died for would still mean something."

Oh. I held his cheek, running my thumb under his eye to catch the tears.

"Even the cursed werewolf had the honor to kill to save you."

"Truth be told, I think that's what he tells himself." God, I'd never said this aloud. I'd always let the thought stew in the back of my mind. But as I held Garavel, rocking on my feet, I couldn't stop the confession. "In that moment, I think Cal did it to avenge his brother."

Garavel's eyes opened wide and he stared to where the whistling man of sunshine had been. "His brother?"

I couldn't deal with this anymore. Pulling my hand away, I joined my mother. Nightfall would arrive fast and I had to be ready. But before I returned into the bubble, I called to Garavel. "You two have more in common than you want to admit."

Chapter Twenty-Three

Layla

Everywhere I stepped, the sand burned and crystalized, forming bursts of molten glass. Yet I couldn't stop shifting, the power roiling inside of me. Daniel kept calling directions to my mother, who'd stop her drawing to glare at him. Garavel was more willing to listen, dragging a large branch through the wet sand out to Zaxigrath. The tension was rising fast along with the full moon.

"It's nearly at its zenith. Are we ready?" Torran asked.

I nodded and tiny sparks shot from my nose. Yelping, I placed a hand over it, then fought to pull in more magic to replace it. The demon caught me losing my fight and he winked his right eyes. "Where's Ink?"

"Finished." He waltzed over from the border, the summer wind pulling open his shirt. The torchlight lit up his chiseled pecs and abs. Instead of his pants, or even the tastefully tacky trunks, he had a skin-tight pair of briefs wrapped around his thick cock. Fire pulsed down my legs and I leaped into the air. Landing wouldn't help, my burning body certain to make more dangerous glass.

Arms caught me before I hit the sand. Ink held me tight. "My bond, you're positively atwitter with anticipation."

"It's your fault for wearing that. Why aren't you dressed?"

"I'm hopeful that once this business is concluded, we shall be free to celebrate." He leaned closer and breathed in my ear. "Whether the tail makes an appearance is in your hungry hands."

Flames shot down my legs and up his arms. As they went, Ink's human skin vanished, reminding me what was below. He didn't even flinch, only held me tighter as the others finished the preparation.

"Are we ready?" I asked. Ink eased me back to the sand. I tried to ignore him and how he kept teasingly pressing the edge of his cock against my hip.

Daniel pointed to the runes drawn across nearly the entire beach. "Should be, unless someone missed something." He looked to my mother.

"Laylee, please take your book back from the ghost before it goes insane and destroys it."

Ink snickered at my mother's cut while Daniel glared. I trusted him with my life, as I did all of my guys, but I walked over to him and took it back.

"Shall I take one last look at the perimeter?" Garavel asked.

"No, that's more likely to draw attention." I pressed my book to my chest, trying to calm the erratic thunder in my chest. Literal thunder. Lighting wouldn't stop striking in my lungs and it was starting to ache.

"We cannot wait to return home." Torran nodded to me, then my mother, before he breathed deep.

This was almost it. All we had to do was kill an hour, then send a demon to hell.

"The offer yet stands," Torran said to Ink.

"Offer?" I asked.

Ink parted his hands. "I'm content at the moment and shall have to pass."

The waves slopped against Zaxigrath's beached form, but couldn't wash away the runes Garavel had dug nearly into the bedrock. *What if this doesn't work? What if we fail?*

"Where is the wolf? He will be necessary for the moon's power."

I craned around. Cal had walked with us to the beach. He'd carried the cooler then... "Cal?"

"Layla?"

Oh no. It wasn't my furry boyfriend, but Fariah who answered back. And she'd brought Maram with her. She stared at the horde of us, some holding torches, all of us standing inside a ward, and her eyes went wide. Torran leaped in front of Zaxigrath, somehow blending the two in with the lake, but for a second, they were visible.

"What are you doing here? Are you okay, you look...?"

I ran over to her, or tried. The glass problem kept happening, so I had to kick it aside, embedding shards under my molten bare skin that shifted and spit it back out.

Fariah stared me up and down. "Your eyes are bleeding!"

I reared back to avoid her and laughed. "No, they're not." I focused, tamping back the fire by thinking of ice cream in a freezer...dripping down Ink's pecs. *Damn it.*

"You need to get out of here," I said.

"I haven't seen you in days. Cal keeps coming up with excuses, but they don't make any sense. Then you run off here in the night when the beach is closed. I'm...worried."

I shrugged, trying to think of any excuse in the book, when I noticed Maram. She tried to hide behind Fariah, but a light burned inside of her.

"Maybe we should leave. They've got something planned." Maram skittered farther away and I pursued, trying to find what she was hiding.

"Without us? Layla, what is going..." Fariah's voice stalled at the deep growl shattering the night air.

I clenched my fists, balls of lightning circling up my arms and splintering at my shoulders. Whatever it was, I was prepared.

The bushes shivered, something giant moving among them. Without thinking, I moved to join the others. Garavel unsheathed his sword. Ink stood taller, his shadow wings swooping back.

Witch hunters?

Mr. White?

Worse?

Torchlight glanced across the beach and struck pale skin—specifically a leg with dirty blond hair. "Oh." I shook my hands, feeling silly for leaping to the worst conclusions. "It's Cal. Sweetheart. We're almost ready."

His head jerked at my voice and I almost took a step back. Were his eyes black? He blinked, revealing blue.

"Good. Werewolf, you're needed to direct the moon, here," my mother ordered.

I stared at the two trespassers who held hands and refused to move. We needed to get them out of here before this started. And Cal... I took a step to try to chase Fariah away when a hand clamped to my shoulder. The shock sent the same racing back to whoever held me. Worried about hurting them, I looked to find sparks harmlessly grounding against Garavel's stone flesh.

"Something is wrong," he said, his glare narrowed on Cal.

He kept shaking his head and pacing in a circle, kicking sand up into the rising winds. "It's..." I tried to shrug off the angel, but without blowing his arm off there was no moving him. "It's the full moon. Right? Cal?"

Wild animal. The black eyes in the flashlight, the erratic steps pressing to the ground, the muscles locking back into place. This didn't make any sense. He had control. He always controlled it. Unless...

"Ink? When did he last shift?"

"Why do you think—"

I grabbed him by his dangling lapels and yanked him to my face. "Tell me Cal's shifted!"

The clouds parted. A ray of moonlight cut through the morbid sky and lanced across Cal. He snarled and threw his arms back. I hadn't paid attention. In a second, the once softer muscles hardened, his skin shrinking around them until he looked like a photoshopped body builder. Cal dropped a hand to the ground and fur erupted up his arm. The gray hair raced back, his bones popping and grinding, his muscles shifting, and the skin rippling to fit the growing wolf body.

He stared straight at us, his eyes burning, and lips rising.

"Cal?" I took a step closer, my hands lifted. He answered with a snarl, the torchlight catching on his fangs.

"Lady witch, this is unwise."

"I'm fine," I assured Garavel. But as I returned to my feral boyfriend, I caught the set in Ink's eyes. He wasn't so certain either. What if I failed? What if it'd been too long and he couldn't be…?

No. I was not even entertaining that thought.

"Sweetie. Listen to me. Okay?" I reached a hand out, willing it to not shake or catch on fire. But I couldn't entirely bury my fear, a chill racing up to my elbow. Cal growled a warning, his tail straight back.

There was a very good chance he might attack. Wouldn't be my first time. Closing my eyes to hide the tears, I bent lower until my knee hit the sand. "I love you."

A whimper struck the air. I looked to find his ears and tail drooping. He reached a paw closer, then skittered back. I moved my hand for him, nearly skimming his head. The gray fur tickled my palm and I began to smile.

"Is that Calvin?"

Fuck. The second Fariah shouted, he spun in the sand. The fur down the length of his spine stood straight up and he growled at the two vulnerable women. Fariah's eyes widened and Maram leaped in front of her, but neither could stop the startled wolf running at them.

"No!" I fought to control my power while also protecting them. Flames and sparks burst along my arms as I reached to catch Cal, but he was too quick. He leaped into the air, claws out and fangs exposed, when a force knocked him to the ground.

Garavel rose from his bullrush, his head scuffed but not bleeding. With a shake at the wolf scrambling for his feet, Garavel reached behind for his sword.

"Don't!" I shouted. The angel froze for a second, long enough for Cal to dash into the forest.

"He has escaped. He could hurt hundreds of —"

I ignored Garavel to turn to the rest. "Cal's not in his right mind."

"How is that giant wolf your boyfriend?" Fariah asked.

I didn't have time for her either. Luckily, Maram seemed to have the sense to pull her back.

"Mikki told me about this. If he doesn't shift he…" Why didn't I pay attention? I knew something was wrong, but I had kept putting it off. "We have to find him. If we can get to him, talk him down…"

"Layla." My mother pointed a finger to the moon rising to its crescendo. "We don't have much time."

I twisted my head, seeing, then unseeing Torran and Zaxigrath. Both waited patiently but the unease was growing. If we missed our window, then what? It'd be another twenty-eight days until we could try again.

A howl fractured the night sky and I turned to it. "We need him." *I can't lose him.* "For the spell to work." *For fuck's sake, I love him.*

Ink wrapped a hand around my stomach. I was about to elbow him to let me go, when he whispered in my ear. "We will find him."

And if we don't?

I couldn't say it. Instead, I clung to his protective arm and tried to breathe. The power surged and fire burst from my fingertips. Ink took it without complaint.

"This is foolhardy. He is a threat and has shown as such. Do you not care for your friends?"

"Layla's right. We need him or this won't work. The moon's part of the Celestial system. One of the gate keys, if you will," Daniel explained.

"Why in heaven's name would they give that power to a werewolf?" Garavel said, staring at Daniel clinging to the book, then Torran, who shrugged as if he had known all along.

"It explains why they let them live instead of wiping the whole species out after the war," Daniel said with such calm logic I wanted to throw up.

"None of this matters. We have to find Cal and we have to do it fast. Split up. Each of us take a different route into the woods. Ink?"

"Should I not remain by your side?" he asked while taking my hand.

I shook my head. If anyone could get to Cal first, it was him. He sighed and closed his eyes. "Very well. But if your dog tries to bite me, I may be forced to tie him down. Do with that what you will."

"Don't hurt him!" I called as Ink did his vanishing trick. He'd find Cal. He could do anything.

"And if the wolf has already eviscerated an innocent person?" Garavel thundered.

Tell him to stay here. Don't risk Cal.

But if other people are in danger and he can save them?

The angel read my silence like a Bible. He raised his head and shot up into the sky. For a brief second, his wings were outlined against the moon and I gulped.

"Mom...?" I turned around to tell her to try up the beach, but she was already gone. Maybe she had some magical tracking skills I didn't.

"What about me?" Daniel asked.

"Stay here. Keep them safe." I jerked my head to Fariah and Maram left alone.

"From your boyfriend or...?"

"Please?" was all I could say. He crumbled and nodded once. I closed my eyes and breathed deep.

Cal, I'm coming. Please be okay. Please be in there. Please let me help you.

Dipping into the well of power, I loaded my legs with strength and speed. Pushing back on the ball of my left foot, I put out my right, and launched off. The beach vanished into a sandy blur, then there were trees. At the last second I dodged around them, twigs and branches snapping at my skin. But the breaks only lasted for a millisecond, the magic healing them instantly.

The forest shifted. Once indigo, the sky became black as midnight while sounds echoed in colors and circling waves against the background. Tiny wafts of greens and pinks came from the insects and birds. All my focus was on the gold, sharp and panicky, dashing from the beach into the woods — Cal's howl.

It twisted around a corner, all of his energy put into his fleeing. Werewolves were fast, but I knew I was faster. I couldn't take too much — I needed this for the demon. Still, I slipped another jolt of magic into my legs and the trees vanished. The entire world flattened into a two-dimensional drawing.

The plane stretched out before me, a simple map with trees and rocks done in line doodlings and there, not too far from the high cliff, was a lone wolf mid-leap. Cal.

I took a massive step as far as I could stretch. Two more and I'd be by his side. Pulling in a breath, I took another, and my stomach twisted into a knot. Icy daggers stabbed me in the belly, gnarling my insides and sending my knee crashing to the ground.

When it hit, the world shivered. Green lightning crackled through the blood-red sky and a thousand eyes darted to me. *No. No, no, no!*

This was the in-between. I wasn't supposed to be here. If I stayed too long, I'd…

A slow clapping reverberated in the air. With each smack, a blade sliced just above my head. I tried to turn, but my body was frozen. The air hardened around my skin, trapping me. All I could do was pivot my head and eyes as a white light walked across the vast expanse of nothing.

"Good evening"—Conquest tipped his hat and smiled—"little witch."

Chapter Twenty-Four

Ink

The forest offered up no resistance as I pursued the wayward Cal. Foolish of him to put off his necessary wolfing for so long. *All I need do is stop him and bring him to Layla. No doubt she can look into his eyes, scratch his belly, and all will be right as rain.*

The in-between shuddered and before me rose a silhouette of a man and wolf howling as one. Ah, I'd found him.

Wrenching apart the realms, I stumbled into the cooling and dark forest eclipsed by trees. "Hello? Calvin? I have a doggie treat with your name on it."

The trees remained stubbornly uncooperative as I strode forward. Despite seeing him in the garbage chute, he was nowhere to be found. "This is hardly the time to be shy. You can feel shame and other pointless emotions after we—"

I swung my foot, as one must to propel forward, and it stuck. Blinking, I lowered my shoulders and prepared to slink away from this invisible wall, only for light to surge from beneath me. Runes burst from below placed leaves, revealing I'd once again walked into a demon trap.

"This is growing tiresome." I sighed. Clenching my fist, I reared back to punch the bubble apart. Just as my knuckles made contact, the opalescence shimmering in lovely confinement, a figure stepped out of the darkness.

I'd prepared to rip the witch hunters to shreds, but the woman in long and tasteful robes surprised me. She held her book out and wiggled her fingers above the pages, but her lips didn't move. It was all for show.

Approaching the demon wards, she tossed back the hood and stared me in the eye.

I crossed my arms. "Are you here to remove the ward or use it?"

Isabel smirked and I tossed my head back in exhaustion. She began to pace in a circle, chanting in old Celtic as she went.

I barely bothered to follow, only shifting my eyes before gazing to the forest. "I could point out that your daughter is potentially in danger."

She didn't answer.

"Also that you yourself acknowledge the time crunch."

Still no response.

"Is this how you intend to treat all of your daughter's suitors? You'll need a bigger ward."

Isabel slapped her book shut. She stopped before me, her legs wide in a power and or exhausted-rider stance. "I know what you are."

"Was that in question? I thought I made it rather clear. Incubus. Drainer of energy via sexual congress and the occasional back rub."

She snickered but not the way Layla would laugh at my *bon mot*. No, her face gnarled in a callow fashion I had never seen on my bond. Isabel snapped her fingers and a tiny flame leaped from them. It was aimed at me — not that I flinched in the face of a puny thing. But before striking the bubble, it swerved and dropped to a tiny candle outside. Then it carried to another, and another, lighting five in total in the form of a star.

My arms fell as I read the runes of an interrogation spell.

"You recognize it," she said.

I stared at the candle, but all five flames were going. It wasn't a question I had to answer. "Yes, your daughter used one against a Marid."

"Layla challenged a...?" The statement threw her, no doubt leaving her flustered that a damn sex demon knew more about her spawn than she.

"A rather loathsome fellow who intended to harm her. We stopped him and many others."

"You think you can bamboozle me, as if I haven't dealt with hundreds of creatures like you in my life."

I blinked in surprise. "A hundred sins taken to bed is no mere trifle. That is bragging rights indeed. I don't know why you don't put that on your business card."

Ah, the growl of anger was distinctly Layla's though. I let myself smirk instead of hiding it away.

"Are you going to ask your questions, or shall we while away the night together?"

It was clear she expected me to be panicking, perhaps even attacking. While I dreaded what the old witch could pull from me, I knew better than to let it show. And if I did fight to break out, it might harm Layla's mother. Better to wait and see.

Isabel raised her head as if she didn't come to my chest in her pocket-sized body. "You were in hell, then arrived in Layla's home the moment she became of age."

Still not a question, the flame burned bright.

"Tell me, demon, who broke you out?"

I smiled, a tingle running through my body. If this was all she intended to put to me, it would be an easy night. "No one."

The witch watched, waiting for me to fall in agony. I calmly inspected my nails and dusted a spiderweb off my shirt. She kept glaring at the candle, making certain her question was asked, though without my writhing she couldn't know if it was answered.

"Wait. Do you think I am in cahoots with our dear Horseman? Is that why you planned all of this to capture me for questioning?"

"I have to protect my daughter."

"Mm-hm, while she's out in the woods chasing a crazed werewolf, you concern yourself with me. Truly mother of the year. I do wonder how you had time to do this. You weren't the one to push our Calvin over the edge, were you? Your daughter will be quite cross. She rather likes that one."

She pursed her lips, telling me that she had played some small part in this chain of events. "I'd intended to question you since you whisked my daughter away. It was only a matter of timing."

"In the dark, mosquito-ridden forest. Excellent choice."

Isabel tapped her lips and stepped back, perhaps to keep from accidentally triggering the question mechanism. "If no one broke you out of hell, then you must have gotten here by some other means. The realms breaking down." Her eyes shone bright and she glared at me.

"I know you want to ask it. Go on. Did Conquest send me to seduce your daughter? Do the riders even know about sex?"

She glanced to the candles, realizing I knew the one flaw in this trap. They got five questions... After that I was free. And if she didn't think I wouldn't tell Layla every word from her mouth, she was in for a surprise.

Resuming her pacing, she traversed around the bubble, tapping her lips as she went. At the stump, she paused and raised her head. "Why bond yourself to my daughter?"

I jerked, not expecting that question. The tingle began again, a fiery sensation licking up my toes and calves. I'd known pain as a human, chased it to its near-end. This was completely different. It tore at my flesh, not the human illusion but the demonic skin, plunging icy cold into the gaps, then reversing the order.

"Tell me demon, why did you pop out of hell and bond yourself to Layla?"

My body teetered, but I refused to fall to my knees before her. "To protect myself."

"She was a new witch, unaware even of her powers."

"I didn't exactly know that at the time. I needed a witch to feed me until I made certain I could resume hunting properly without having to deal with a poker up my backside. Without consent, anyway."

Her eyes gleamed at me admitting I fed off of Layla, but it was no secret. She knew, she let me. "So you are here to drain her, to keep her weak."

I rolled my eyes to look. Three candles still lit. Damn it. "If I wanted her weak, she'd be laid up in bed for days. Which, come to think of it, does sound like a wonderful proposition."

"I know what you're up to. Dressed like that when she's full to bursting with magic. You must be salivating at the idea of draining her."

Placing a hand to my hip, I jutted it out in a pose and drew my fingers down my shirt. "I happen to enjoy my body and the stunning look it cuts in the proper ensemble. Forgive me for not feeling a debilitating ocean of shame for daring to possess genitals."

Isabel fumed at me and I snickered. "The demon, fresh from hell, sought out any witch to feed upon. From a fear that he refuses to confess to."

"You remind me of the witch hunters, leaping to conclusions without thought for reality. Come to think of it, you and your repression would have fit in wonderfully with old James."

"Hunters, of course, they'd pursue you as readily as they would any witch." She kept talking to herself, circling me like I was the prized pig.

"Course the daft fool had no idea he bedded a demon. Some witch hunter sent by g-d."

"You knew to go for a witch. You knew that her magic would sustain you for longer than one...night." For a brief moment the mother shivered at having to acknowledge her daughter's sex life. The maternal bond only lasted a second before she resumed her shrewd deliberation. "That means you've been with a witch before."

My face remained neutral, but my mind couldn't stop the face from rising out of my memories.

"The bond is a tether, meaning if you are banished, so is my daughter. And if my daughter is killed..."

Eartha's sharp scream ruptured my ears. I'd only heard the one before the ground opened up. It had rung clear across the village, reaching to the distant well as I sank into hell.

Isabel stopped and I knew a question was coming about the past I'd tried to forget. About the first woman to take years of life from me, then so much more.

"She was…" I began, but the woman asked over me.

"How did the first witch you were bound to die?"

What? The pain hit fast, snapping my ribs like kindling then jamming hot coals into my spine. I jerked back, fighting to keep my mouth closed even as my skin boiled away.

"A witch powerful enough to trap a demon, and a demon at her side, at her beck and call? She should not have easily fallen. How? Speak!"

"Speak, demon!" Eartha's voice commanded from beyond the grave.

"Witch hunters." The pain instantly stopped. I caught myself before I fell, my head tipping down to hide my conflicting emotions.

"Witch hunters are fools in most centuries, yet they killed one. They got to her and you did nothing to stop them."

Worse. I had found them and pointed them to her. She wasn't like Layla. An older established woman, she had found me enjoying my dinner rather vigorously with a holy man in the barn. Better than him lusting after his sheep. Bound to her, I became her servant, her pet. Silent save when ordered, tasked with the most demeaning of jobs. I thought seducing her would put an end to it, but even that couldn't free me.

The hunters were to be my freedom, but in my betrayal, I had doomed myself.

"You were the reason your last witch died. You will do the same to my daughter."

"Never!" I shouted. No more playing her games. I slammed my palm to the bubble. The magic snapped at me, trying to interfere. I clenched my claws, digging past the barrier while I glared at the woman torturing me.

"Because you know if she is hurt, you return to hell, a fate you seem to fear. And yet…"

I slammed my fist into the barrier. It jolted, momentarily parting. I couldn't get more than a fingernail through, but it was breaking down. Isabel's eyes widened and I tried again. The illusion vanished, my wings rising. Shadows dripped off them, casting me into darkness save the veins of lava and fire burning in my eyes.

No more. This game is over.

The witch darted back, her eyes on the two remaining candles.

I swung again, this time getting a whole claw out. If my arm punctured, I'd go for her throat. Not to kill her, but enough pressure to knock her unconscious and end the spell. It'd be easy. Layla would understand, and if not…

I can handle her hating me. I've done it before.

"Why…?"

The start of her question froze me. No, she wouldn't get another word out. I leaped for the barrier, prepared to bash it open with my skull.

"Why are you still bound to Layla?"

"Gah!" The pain slammed into my spine. I dug my claws into the barrier, but it fought back, breaking every bone up my arm and down my chest until it struck my heart. The foolish thing stopped for two seconds. Gray passed before my eyes, then it began again. An army of razor blades diced up my inner organs, and I fell to a knee.

"You do not need her any longer. She is only a detriment now, yet you are bound to her. Why?"

May your brain boil in the fat of a dead man's grave. May your throat fill with spider eggs. May you...

My hold slipped and I crumpled, my body kowtowing to the woman torturing me.

"Tell me, you stupid demon."

None of it mattered. Not Lust. Not Eartha. Not even this wretched witch tearing me asunder. I couldn't say it. There had to be another reason, a logical purpose to why—

Lightning whipped against my back, splitting the shirt apart so it could spread across every vertebrae. I began to shake, unable to stop as I clenched my hands tighter.

Layla wouldn't put up with this. She could barely stand doing it to the monster that tried to kill her. That damn tender heart would break to see me in this position.

"Because..." I shuddered, my ribs crushing around my heart like a bear trap. But even as it popped apart, it couldn't stop beating. "I don't want to lose her."

Everything flipped off at once. "Oh for g-d's sake," I groaned, the freedom from pain better than most mortal's orgasms. I tested my hands and lifted my head. The witch had taken a knee and placed her palm to the bubble.

I could reach out and smash the barrier. Snap her wrist, toss her in here and see how she liked this. It would kill any mortal.

"Demons don't care," Isabel said slowly. "Demons don't love."

That's what I keep telling myself. It's beginning to feel like a losing fight.

"There. You've objectively humiliated me, discovered I only have intentions to protect your daughter and have wasted all of our time." I tried to stand, but my legs were yet wobbly. I'd need a longer moment to compose myself. "Are we finished here?"

She looked properly cannon-shocked, as if her plan had been for me to confess to nefarious deeds, then she'd tear me into a thousand pieces. Isabel tapped her lips in thought, a move I was coming to despise. Her shrewd eyes darted to the last candle and I groaned.

"One more question, then you're free to go."

"How much more can you take from me?" I steadied myself and faced her for the worst.

Her lips lifted in a smirk. "What's your name?"

Chapter Twenty-Five

Garavel

At the apex of my flight, my little lieutenant emerged from her nap. The chillier winds of the night buffeted my feathers against Fiona's face, but she remained steadfast. Her claws dug into my skin as we both gazed down at the forest below. All looked quiet.

An unnatural darkness circled the brush near the place for storing vehicles. I jerked back at lights piercing the sky. Ah, it was magic. That must be the lady witch on her hunt.

Perhaps I should join her despite her orders. *For her protection, of course.*

Fiona meowed in my ear, and I sighed. "Yes, I know I have other reasons. But if I do not guard her then who...?"

A streak darted through the woods. Gray as the skin of a dead man, it dashed over the rocks and up to the cliff's edge. I'd found the wayward wolf.

Tucking my wings back, I dove. Fiona squeaked at the branches and attempted to battle them. I caught her before the momentum pulled her off and held tight to the kitten. "Best for you to return to your safe spot. Who knows what the werewolf will do?"

The monster dug his paws into the rocky terrain, his eyes trained on the long drop below. I unfurled my wings silently and dropped, but the wind must have caught my scent. He spun in place, the hair on his unnatural body standing on end. Digging his front paws into the moss, he began to snarl, drawing my attention to his large fangs.

"You cannot escape," I said. "Best to give up and return to the beach."

If the man she insisted on was in there, he'd understand the logic and join me.

The wolf took a step backward. His paw broke a piece of the mountain, sending a rock pinging down the drop. With another growl, he skittered away from his body falling in the same way. Which put him directly in my path.

"It's clear the beast is all that remains." I reached behind and plucked my sword free from the gap in realms on my back. Fiona leaped inside to safety as I dispensed with this danger.

Feral eyes incapable of thought darted up to me. I'd seen the same across countless battlefields. Vengeance, hunger, rage—they only knew how to hate. Never once, even when their fellow wolves were killed, did they show compassion, generosity, care.

There was one more emotion, however, and I would draw it from him—fear.

Brandishing my sword longer than his spine and twice as wide, I took a step closer. The wolf noted the giant blade prepared to cleave his head off. He calculated the chances of him making the leap to savage my face or neck, then took a step back. He was cleverer than most—I'd give him that.

"Do you have any idea how many of my friends creatures like you have killed?"

The monster tried to dart to the right, but I cut him off with a slice of my blade. It sent him scampering back toward the edge and the fall. An easy out for a creature created only for death.

"I know the brutality claws like yours inflict. I've seen the wounds from fangs that cut through to the spine. A werewolf is good for a rug and nothing more."

He lashed a paw out, aiming for my leg. I dodged it in time, but just barely. In doing so, the monster threw me off balance. He used that to leap into the air, claws extended to slash me to ribbons. I raced to meet him, my blade arm lagging, when a tiny mewl cut through the air.

Fiona poked her head out in excitement and was met with a giant wolf crashing for her tiny face. *No!* I tried to fall to protect her, but the wolf did the unexpected. Midair, he swerved, twisting his body so it tumbled to the ground. A yelp cut through the air. He tried to rise, but his front paw crumbled, sending him crashing to the rock.

The wolf was momentarily neutralized. Though if it was only a sprain, he'd be back into fighting form quickly. I reached behind and scratched the small black head. "Be careful," I scolded my kitten, trying to push her back in. A great purring rumbled up my arm as she nuzzled her cheek to my palm.

"You made a mistake," I said to the limping wolf. He couldn't beat me to escape, not with his paw injured. It left him trapped against the precipice with nowhere to go but down. "A foolish one."

The wolf raised his gaze. He stared not at me, but the kitten walking across my shoulders. Did he do it on purpose? Risk his own life for a baby animal that was not his master?

No. Of course not. He is only the beast. Fur, claws, fangs – there is no man left to reach under the rays of the moon.

We could have slaughtered them all in their sleep. Rows of helpless men slumbering under the sunlight without a care in the world. That day I chose mercy, and that night I watched three of my friends die to their claws.

I had sworn I would never make that mistake again.

"You're a threat. You've threatened everything the angels created! You serve nothing but greed!"

The wolf glanced down the fall, his tail drooping. He knew this was the end. There was no escape, no fleeing into the woods. There was only the fight, and I'd silenced over a thousand of his kind.

Quickly, he girded his body for the attack. His lips pulled up. Saliva dripped from his fangs as he snarled out his last threat. The claws dug into the dirt, all save the broken paw he kept gingerly placed to the ground. An easy weak point to exploit. Even if he was the best werewolf of the pack, he didn't stand a chance against me.

I raised my sword in preparation, but he didn't move. "If this is what took down an alpha, then your kind has fallen far," I taunted, then flexed. Still, the wolf remained in guard mode.

"Why did you do it? To protect your brother? How laughable."

There was the vengeance, his eyes blazing with rage. He jerked a shoulder forward and I too shifted, ready to cleave him out of the air. But he stopped and made no more moves.

"Werewolves are nothing but killing machines. All you were bred for. All you were made for. I know it. And you do too. It's why you run from her. Why you fled into the night." My arm drooped, nearly laying my blade against my shoulder. "To protect Layla."

A whimper. No growl, no snarl and gnash of teeth to tear me to pieces. All he gave was a whimper and cast his gaze away.

There is no man, there is only the beast.

If we question the person inside the fur, we leave ourselves open to them.

I do this to protect the angels.

I do this for her.

Extending my sword, I declared in the voice that commanded legions, "I will protect her now."

Calvin growled one final warning, then he leaped.

Chapter Twenty-Six

Layla

Thunder rolled beneath my feet, the lightning arcing up from the ground to splinter across the clouds. Conquest paused to watch, his desiccated lips perched in a near smile. "See that little burst of blue at the end? That's copper oxide drifting in the sky."

I clenched my hands tighter, the cold seeping up my feet and fingers. The last time I was trapped here, I'd nearly died. And when I'd been spat out, the horrors of what it had done to my body sent me into such a tailspin I almost didn't heal myself.

There had to be a way out. I swerved my gaze, staring down one unending plane. It was all straight lines like a sidewalk, but the same color and texture of the ground. Swiveling, I looked down the other direction and saw nothing. Last time I'd found a door with Ink on the other end.

I looked to my wrist, expecting to find the bond, but Mr. White chuckled.

"I'm afraid your lap dog will not be so easily summoned."

The shackle was on my wrist, but the line vanished two inches from the end. It was a trick. It had to be there. Gritting my teeth, I fought against the invisible shell collapsed against my body. It shifted, then snapped me back into place. All I could do was watch the Horseman circling me.

He stared me down, his face blank save the eyes. A darkness erupted inside the pale irises, smoke and fire churning from centuries of death. My eyes slammed shut at the millions of voices screaming in agony, and he laughed.

"Why am I here?" I asked, refusing to face him.

"Not an easily answered question. To the angels, you are here to do their bidding. To the hunters, you are here as a menace. To—"

"Here," I snarled, interrupted his game. "In this nothing space. Why am I here specifically!"

"I take it you're not much for philosophical debate."

"I'm not for anything when I'm pinned down and about to die." Cold seeped up my arms and I clenched my hands tighter. Fingers, bones, the full flesh scraped against my palm. They should be withered by now. I kept breathing, even though my chest couldn't rise against his trap. That was impossible. The diaphragm had to drop to create a vacuum to pull air into the lungs.

I risked a peek to find Conquest leaning on his cane, his hat perched to the side. Freezing pain struck my toes, shrinking them back before they popped out again. "Why ain't I dying?"

"You are. Second by second, day by day. The moment your cells sparked together, the clock began its unending countdown."

I snarled at his dodge and tried to move. The shell vibrated and it drew his attention. I stopped, but wondered if more magic would get it to shatter. *Could I tap this place?* Opening myself up, I willed the magic inside of me.

"What you're doing is wrong!" I shouted, trying to distract him. "Destroying the realms, all that was gained after a war, going against the Celestials…"

Conquest chuckled. "You know the truth? Few do any longer, even witches, even those once plucked from their paradises and banished to this dungeon. They forget because what else can they do? There is no escape from the prison. Or so they claim."

He tapped his cane and blood bubbled up from the ground. It washed across the plane, leeching through the shield and drenching my frozen feet. All I could do was watch while he stared in fascination.

"You'll kill billions."

"Far more have died in my name, little witch. You'd do well to remember that."

Sparks burst from my teeth, catching his interest. Damn it. I'd overdone it and needed a distraction. I directed the magic down my arms, keeping it sequestered in my constantly shriveling and unfurling fingers. "Is it smart of you to piss off the beings that created the realms? The Earth? That gave you life?"

Conquest slammed his cane down again. The blood crackled, drying to a crisp, then splintering to dust, and flew away. "Do you know who created me?"

"Humans." Our greed, our hatred, our wrath—it all boiled together to give life to the concept of conquering our neighbors.

He tipped his head as if annoyed he couldn't peacock more. Then he smiled. "Do you know who created Death?"

I opened my mouth to give the same answer then reared back. It couldn't have been us.

"They did." He jabbed his cane to the sky and leaned closer. "For the Celestials were so ridden with sloth, they created the angels to give life, and the demons to take it. Yet still their creations were not perfect, causing problems that could threaten even a god. Those beings you want to protect, you fight so vigilantly for, they created death, chaos, entropy, because they were too lazy to pick up their own toys."

Thunder rolled and the sky changed. Instead of the deathly crimson, the color drained from a small whirlpool where the moon should be. Pure white stretched above us and Conquest raised his hands. "We have been trapped here because of their ignorance. They set creation into motion, exhausted with having to do it themselves. Then, when their creations grew too numerous to tend to, they unleashed destruction. You feel it inside you, a war of two magics forever at odds, but both necessary in balance."

"This is some yin and yang shit?"

He tipped his head and smiled. "Why do you think humans yearn for a binary? Good, evil. Black, white. Living, dead. They set it, they decreed it and we have to suffer it for an eternity. No more. I will change that. I will free us from a prison enacted by our forebears long since dust."

"The last time all humans had access to magic..."

"They nearly usurped their gods." He leaned closer, almost brushing his lips to my ear. "Imagine the conquest from that war."

His entire face was warped with hunger, his lips salivating, his eyes glistening with greed. All he cared about was feeding and he would destroy everything to get this meal. I had to stop him.

White turned from me to stare at the grand expanse of nothing. He waved his cane, creating a horse in the void — except it was flayed, with only pulsing muscle and bones as it galloped. It screamed with every step. This was my chance.

Clenching every muscle in my body, I directed my magic. It sprang free and vibrated the shell. The mold-like squeeze began to bend like a plastic bag. I tipped myself back and forth, trying to rip apart a hole. One had to break, just a tiny thing, then...

"Be careful."

I froze at his words, but he didn't turn back.

He ran a hand under his jaw. "That massive influx of magic is the only thing keeping you alive. Spend too much and..." Conquest turned to me and raised his hand. A tiny butterfly took flight, but it didn't get more than inch before its delicate wings curled and cracked to dust.

"What do you want from me?" I shouted.

"For now, to speak. I must admit, your attempts to disguise yourself were quite entertaining. But you needn't have bothered." He twisted the cane in his hand, the horse statue on the end running in place as he did.

Because he could have found me at any time. I was never safe.

"Though overloading yourself with magic was a choice. I could have spotted you from across the world for how bright you glow. Let me guess — your mother's idea."

How did he know that? Had he been spying on us this whole time?

White plunged his cane to the ground, but nothing horrific appeared. Instead he leaned on it, looking like a frail man about to crack. But I knew better. "You are fascinating, little Leeland."

"My name is Layla!"

"And such a poorly trained witch to give that freely. Though I knew it already. Samuke is generous with his information."

"That fucking…" I dug my nails in, wishing it was the Marid's throat instead.

"You disobeyed me. Few do that. Even fewer live to see the next sunrise."

"I'm sorry I'm not a good little witch who'd lie down and die for you."

He laughed. "Oh, don't worry. You'll serve your purpose yet."

Purpose? What is he talking about?

"But I can't have you interfering with the demon. I require another touchstone and he'll do nicely."

What the shit was a touchstone? White turned away, finished with torturing me. His plan the whole time was to trap me, to let his minions steal away with Zaxigrath and Torran. The bellow from that poor deer monster as Conquest slit his throat echoed in my mind. I bit down, accidentally nicking my tongue. Blood welled up, then vanished, the wound instantly healed.

That was happening to my whole body. If I got away, even if I spent almost all of my magical stores,

I'd have some time to run. But where? Ink could be anywhere, and his bond was... I glanced to my wrist, the ephemeral tether loading my heart with dread.

Mr. White tapped his cane once more, then he began to walk away.

Of course! "You won't hurt him!" I shouted, pausing the Horseman. "I'll send him back to hell before you get a drop of his blood." Wrenching open the small gash in my palm, I drank deep of the magic pulsing around me. It shot through me, exploding out my back, but I didn't care. I had to get it all.

"I'll stop you tonight, then I'll stop your whole scheme." The shell began to vibrate, faster than before. I didn't fight against the bubble, but fought to lift my hand. My fingers were shriveling, pain sundering apart every nerve up to my elbow, and I kept going.

"Ask your mother what happens to those who stand against me. Ask her what happened to her coven."

"You took her from me!" I screamed, the pain needing an outlet and choosing rage. It was almost there. The shell was cracking and I reached not to Conquest, not to my wrist, but the locket on my neck.

"I've taken countless lives in name and deed. But your mother's..." He finally turned and found me eclipsed by light and shadow, both fighting to break apart his prison. I braced myself for another attack, but Mr. White laughed.

"I did it. I never thought it possible, but you are the perfect balance of creation and destruction."

I pressed the heart necklace so tight to my palm I could feel the bone inside. It radiated a warmth through the cold, beckoning me.

Conquest smiled. "I created you, Layla. You're going to serve me better than I could have ever anticipated."

The bubble shattered. I only had a second to dig in, the in-between racing to kill me. What did he mean he created me? *No. Oh, fuck no.* That didn't make any damn sense. Cold jabbed into my back between my ribs, then splintered, every jagged edge racing to regroup in my heart.

Daniel. I need Daniel. Take me to...

The world collapsed.

White inverted into dark and the once solid ground sank around me. I lashed out, trying to grab anything before I was pulled under...and my hand smacked into a table. My eyes burned like I'd been staring at the sun, but I forced them open to find a hint of a torchlight and the sound of lapping water.

"Layla?"

I'd wanted Daniel and it'd spat me out beside him. He stood next to my spell book, his eyes only on me as I struggled to take a breath and heard a creak. My body ached like it'd been run through that old-fashioned laundry press. But a little magic would...

I didn't realize how my skin had been radiating with power until it was sucked away. I hadn't lost everything, but almost all that work was gone just to break me free.

"You just left. How are you back here? I didn't see — "

"Daniel!" I reached over to grab him. My hands sank into his shoulders and I barely had a chance to feel stupid. "Conquest is here."

"What?"

"He wants... Zaxigrath? Torran?"

The lake shimmered and Torran walked forward. He waved his arm and the big demon appeared as well. "We are here, though you look worse for the wear."

"Listen, Conquest, the Horseman, Mr. White, whatever the shit we're calling him. He ambushed me in the forest. He's here to abduct Zaxigrath and…"

I gulped and stared past Daniel to find Fariah and Maram listening in.

"We need to get the demon out of here before this gets worse," Daniel fumed, already flipping through my book.

How much of that did they see? How much of this did they overhear?

"Layla?" Fariah said slowly. "I need you to explain this. One minute you're running into the woods, the next you appear and begin a one-sided conversation with the picnic table."

Technically the ghost beside it, but she couldn't see him.

"And what happened to Cal? How was there a wolf? What is happening?"

"I…" *Swamp gas. A dream. We're putting on an elaborate play.*

The branches parted and my mother strode out, her head high.

She'd lied to me my whole life in order to protect me. Hid who she was, what I'd become, just to let me live a normal life for a few years.

"Fariah, I…" I met her gaze and breathed deep. "I'm a witch."

My friend began to laugh, then stopped as I didn't.

"This is a ghost you can't see. Torran is a shape-shifting demon we're trying to get back to hell."

She went silent, her eyes widening.

"Ink's a demon too, well, an incubus. It's complicated." Hopefully he was with Cal.

"Gary?" was all Fariah said.

"Who? Oh, Garavel. Angel. Kinda. It's…"

"Complicated? Layla, if you expect me to believe—"

"I don't need you to believe. Magic isn't a religion, it just is, like cheese. I need you to get out of here. Run. Take Maram and get out of the forest as fast as possible."

I didn't realize I'd taken her hands until she pulled them back. Fariah squinted at me. "Why?"

"Because…" A Horseman of the apocalypse was coming to take the giant whale demon from us. "Because it's not safe."

"Then you need to leave too."

How I wish I could. Grab Daniel, Garavel, Cal and… "Ink?"

He strolled onto the beach, his arms empty, looking like he didn't have a care in the world. I abandoned Fariah and ran to him. "Ink!"

"Ah, my bond." He smiled brightly and my heart sank. The shirt he wore was torn to strips, the frayed ends flaring in the wind.

"Where's Cal? Did he…? Did he hurt you?"

Ink looked to the tears then shrugged. "I haven't the foggiest. I did not find him."

"Then what are you doing back here? We need him. I…" Without thought, I took a step to run back into the forest, when Ink clamped onto my arm. He held me tight, his gaze carrying over my head to something behind.

"You are drained. What happened to you in the woods?"

He didn't whisper in my ear or trace across my arm. He just kept holding me like I wasn't allowed to leave and stared past.

Was he upset that he wasn't there? Or that I'd burned through all that delicious magic? "It was Conquest."

Ink's mile-long stare shuddered and he looked to me. His hands fell from my arms and he cupped my cheeks. "My bond, are you...? You appear unharmed. But there could be sores hidden below your clothes. Take them off."

"Not now."

"You said it was Conquest." My mother's voice caused me to whip around to find she'd been the one lurking behind. She tipped her head. "How did you escape?"

"Luck. He pulled me into the in-between."

Ink's entire human form vanished, his demonic skin blazing like the fires of Mount Doom. He caught my hands and raised them to his eyes, looking for the damage I'd managed to shake off.

My mother had more pressing concerns. "That isn't possible."

"Well, that's what happened."

"Conquest is of mortal make. He cannot enter the in-between."

"Ink can. Other sins too." I faced her even as my incubus kept inspecting my fingers, then tenderly kissing them.

"They are also of hell. It is..." My mother groaned and cursed in Romanian. I hadn't heard that in a while. "What if he didn't pull you in there? What if you pulled him in instead?"

I sneered at the idea. It didn't make any sense. I hadn't done whatever Ink could do—I didn't know how. And if I did by mistake, when I was trying to find Cal and…?

"We have to get to Cal."

"In due time…"

"No! If you're all here, that means the only person out looking for him is—"

I heard the wings. Massive, pure-white feathers cutting apart the air with a *woomph*. Dread plummeted in my stomach as Garavel dropped to the sand. Clutched in his arms was a massive form wrapped up in a cloak of pristine white.

Just like a shroud.

"No," I moaned, shoving away Ink and my mother. Garavel didn't flinch, holding the still body. I ran over, failing to keep the tears at bay. All my mind could do was scream. Pale moonlight struck a tuft of gray fur until it glowed.

Trembling, I reached a hand for him, knowing it'd be a cold body. "Cal…"

Chapter Twenty-Seven

Layla

The coarse gray hair skimmed across my fingertips. I used to run my palms over it whenever he'd rested in my lap. Now, it lay as still as the body. I wanted to run. Right back into the forest, let Conquest kill me so I wouldn't have to face the pain of...

It's warm!

I dug in, sinking deeper into the heat from his still beating heart. "Thank god!" I shouted and buried my face into his fur. Stroking up his silent jowls, I fought to keep from screaming in fear and joy and only held him.

"His right leg is broken," Garavel said matter-of-factly, lifting the gigantic wolf in his arms to show me.

"Why is he unconscious?" I asked even while tenderly holding the paw. When I touched it, Cal whimpered and I died inside. "I'm sorry, sweetie, I have to heal it." I whispered the spell, not caring how little magic I had left. I'd drain it all for him.

Garavel shifted and looked around. "He did not want to come willingly."

As the magic knit together his bones, I placed my forehead to his. "Cal. Come on. I love you. Whatever happened, we can fix it. Okay?"

"He may not rise for some time," Garavel said.

"Layla." I ignored the concern, all my focus on my comatose boyfriend. Was it a concussion? We needed to get him up and moving if that was it.

I tried for another healing spell when a solid hand landed on my shoulder. "We have company," my mother said sternly.

Flashlights blazed in the dark forest, the mass of them marching for the beach. I staggered to my feet, my body exhausted, but I couldn't stop. "We need to get them to hell, now."

"You're drained. They can return to their island for the next…"

"Mom, Conquest is coming for him. That's a fucking werewolf army out there. If we don't get them out now, they'll track them down." I felt like a nine-year-old begging to stay at my first slumber party.

She was unbending, her word law, but as she stared into the darkness, my mother nodded. "Very well. But we need the wolf. Put him near the water."

Garavel looked to me before walking Cal closer to the lake. I chased after, trying to wipe away my tears. Ink stood by my side and took my arm as if he feared I might fall. "But he's unconscious. How can he help?"

"We need what he is, not what he can do." My mother didn't explain. "Even still…" She glared at me. "I don't know if we have enough."

I shouldn't have healed him. It was a waste of resources when both magic and time were at a premium. I clutched tight around my locket, my heart sinking at how I let everyone down. Fingers brushed back my destroyed hair. "You are stronger than any here."

I turned to find Ink gazing at me with such assurance, I almost believed him. "Stronger still for doing what you believe in." He caressed a claw across my cheek and I reached for him.

"Do not let the demon drain you further," my mother scolded.

I scoffed at her. "He's not a demon. They are."

Torran nodded at my mention. "Where do you need me?"

"Protect Zaxigrath. Hide him until we can get this set up."

There was no telling if his illusion would work on werewolves, but we had to try. Garavel placed Cal's limp but breathing body near the water. The waves brushed up against him and his tail started to thump. With his job done, the angel pulled his sword from his back and met my gaze.

"I shall hold the line," he said and flew to the edge of the beach where the trees began to break.

Ink released my hand. "I believe I will join him. That red wolf requires a demonic neutering." He grinned as if enjoying this, but I couldn't escape the dread.

We had to get everything perfect, or they'd rip us to pieces. My mother dropped her spell book at her feet and raised both her hands. The wards lit, the entire beach glowing first a harmonizing blue, then shifting to a demonic red. I walked to her side, ready to join in the magic dump.

The guys had it. They'd distract the wolves long enough. We could do this.

"Uh, Layla?" Daniel's voice drew me back and my heart sank. He jabbed a finger to Fariah and Maram holding hands and staring at the impromptu light show. Damn it. They didn't have a chance to run, and now... "What do we do with them?"

"Protect—" I said, when a shot shattered the air.

My first thought was to look for fireworks, because the idea of a gun at the beach was ludicrous. Garavel grunted and I whipped back to find the angel waving his sword around trying to swat bullets out of the air. Most were hitting him dead mass, thankfully doing little while Ink took a few of his own.

I raised my hand, the shield spell twisting on my tongue. My mother slapped at my forearm, but I kept it high. "What are you doing? We need all the magic."

"If we get shot, it won't matter." I winced, watching Garavel twitch as more of the bullets chipped off his body. My mother understood protecting us, but I knew why I did it. Closing my eyes, I willed another chunk of my magic forward and a great barrier erupted off the ground. Invisible save the occasional glimmer, it instantly stopped every bullet.

"Excellent work," Ink cheered.

"How's Garavel?" I shouted. My mother yanked me back and gripped onto my hand. She began to tug the magic from me, siphoning it into the wards at our feet. The circle of lights shifted faster, going from red to blue so quick it became a blur of purple.

"The angel will require minor buffing and sanding, but is otherwise unharmed. I do have another concern, however..."

"What?" Exhaustion pounded at the back of my skull and a painfully familiar emptiness opened in my gut. I focused on the portal, willing it to open.

"They're not werewolves."

"What?" I spun back to look over my shoulder as the advancing guard broke through the trees. Instead of a snarling line of fur and teeth, ten people in black suits holding an array of guns stepped forward. "Fuck, it's witch hunters!"

"Focus," my mother snapped, but she was too ensnared redirecting the magic to pull me away.

The last time I'd faced so many, they'd nearly killed me. Whatever they'd do to Zaxigrath would be ten times worse than Conquest. At least he'd kill the demon quickly. "Torran! Hide him," I shouted over the rising winds circling from inside our ward.

Torran raised his hand so both he and Zaxigrath vanished just as the hunters advanced. I couldn't keep my back to them, and spun away helpless as Garavel and Ink both retreated closer. Bullets pounded into the barrier, weakening not only with each one, but from my vanishing magic. It wouldn't be long before they breached it.

"Mom? How much longer?"

"It'd be less if you paid attention. Leave them to fight it. Your job is here." With a glare, she looked at Cal and the ward shifted. The lights froze, reached up to the sky, then bent inward. When they struck, the ground began to part. Sand dumped into the eternal darkness, only a pinprick but growing larger.

"Keep it up. This is working," my mother ordered before she took my hand and pulled more from me. I grew weak at the knees, but couldn't falter. She clung with all her might, somehow propping me up like a blood bag on an IV stand.

"My bond?" I jerked at the touch of Ink's hand on my shoulder. He pointed past Garavel standing in preparation, to the hunters marching closer. "They're coming through."

One jammed a cattle prod into my barrier and the pain snapped back through me. I clenched, fighting to keep it in place, but the second attack drained me. The barrier fell.

The hunters took no time to line up their guns and aim. Ink stood before me, Garavel at the ready. I closed my eyes, waiting for the bullet with my name on it.

"Give us the demon, and you won't get hurt."

My mother laughed at the decree. "Right, a witch hunter let two witches go. That'll happen."

"This is your only warning."

Ignore them. Trust in Ink, trust in Garavel. Get the portal open then…

"Fire!"

Garavel screamed in earth-quaking rage. He ran at the hunters, sword swinging. They fired, automatic rounds striking his ebony skin and the blade, but with each hit, a powerful force rang out. It struck back, shuddering their weapons and throwing off their aim. Ink nodded to me, then vanished. He appeared behind one of the hunters and…

I looked away just as he reached for the back. But the sound of the body was enough to tell me what he'd done.

"Layla!" Daniel shouted. He stood vigilant over Maram and Fariah who were both trying to hide under the table. But the hunters saw them, and were out for any blood.

Two directed their laser sights, pinging one off Maram and another on Fariah's back. She'd turned to shield her girlfriend and rage shook through me. I dipped into my wells, willing fire to burst free and burn them to ash. But as I extended my hand, only a pathetic poof of smoke erupted. I was drained. I couldn't do anything.

"Mom?"

She shook me off, focusing on the now dinner-plate-sized hole to hell. We'd have to force it all the way to get Zaxigrath through. I couldn't do anything, only siphon magic into her. Helpless, I cried out to anyone listening.

"Cal? Please. You have to get up. I don't know what he did, but..."

A glass spike burst out of the sand and impaled straight through the hunter's chest. His last sight slipped but he squeezed off a round, shooting at a branch above my friend. It cracked, then shattered, falling to the picnic table. At the last second, something stopped it, then hurled the massive branch back at the second hunter. She fell to the ground with a great whoomph, the gun scattering from her fingers.

"How...?"

"You're welcome," my mother said. "Now keep going. We've almost got this."

A low growl struck my heart. *No. Not them too.*

I turned to find a werewolf standing guard, fangs and claws at the ready, but this one was on our side. "Cal!" I shouted, tears trying to come despite my body on the verge of collapse.

He looked back to me for a moment, then leaped. A hunter took aim, but Ink took his arm instead. Garavel held off the main horde, unable to get close enough to stop them, but keeping it to a standstill. Cal bit into a shoulder, blood spilling down his white chest.

"It's working, it's..."

The magic shifted. Like the air just before a tornado, the pressure dropped. Winds whipped not inside our ward but outside. They increased, yanking Cal off his feet, then Ink. A hunter took aim not with his gun, but a scythe. It sliced into Garavel's wing, shattering the bones. The crunch sickened me and I wanted to puke. He cried out and fell to a knee.

No. I wouldn't let this happen. Strength returned. I dug a foot into the sand and began to raise my hand.

Ink caught Cal, the two tumbling to the ground near Fariah's table. Daniel clung tight to my book, keeping it safe while Garavel limped to join them. The hunters walked, the man with the scythe in the lead. He grinned, a terrifying red glow rising off the blade. They were pinned down. If one blow could cripple Garavel, what would it do to Cal? To Ink?

The hunter raised back his weapon, prepared to swing.

"Stop!" The ground sundered, tossing the hunters. They fought to roll with it to keep their balance. The man with the scythe stayed up and swung. I ripped apart the earth. A massive void opened, draining the beach and racing for them. The hunters leaped back, running from the earthquake. But scythe man wouldn't give up. He jumped closer, weapon at the ready to cleave through Garavel's neck.

A whirlwind splattered into his chest, hurling him twenty feet back and into a tree.

My mother panted and lowered her arm. Her skin was turning gray and she struggled to breathe. "I hope that was worth it, because…"

The lighting began to fade and the gap to hell shrunk. It quickly closed in on itself, the two-foot hole a pinprick, then nothing.

"No!"

"Witch. Do you think you can win?" a hunter shouted.

Not anymore. We'd wasted everything on this, and I'd abandoned it the second my men were in trouble. "Torran. Torran, you have to run. Take Zaxigrath and get out of here. We'll find another way."

I couldn't see him. No one could. But I had to trust he'd heard me, that he was fleeing and we'd find each other again once we escaped. Breaking the seal with my mother, I turned to face the hunters as one stepped up with a piece of paper in hand. She raised it high and read aloud.

Every illusion on the beach vanished. Ink's demonic skin crackled, his wings snapping back. No! I raced to try to hide the giant demon with my body, but it was too late. Zaxigrath was revealed and Torran could do nothing to hide him again.

"Get the demon. Kill any who interfere!" the hunters shouted. Their team guzzled down healing draughts and other potions they'd forced their captive witches to make. We were bruised and exhausted. My body ached, but I split open and reached for the magic, siphoning as much in as I could. The hunters who'd been savaged by the demon and angel ran for them, weapons I could barely see swinging.

I fought to raise the barrier, to give them a fighting chance, but the magic was too low. All I could do was watch as the hunters descended upon them.

Fire burst through the air.

Not from the witch hunters, not from the witches.

A great wall of flame rose between the hunters and my guys. Numb, I looked to my mother, who was too drained to do anything. The picnic table burst into ash and a woman of fire stood up. Maram screamed and the entire beach went up in flames.

Chapter Twenty-Eight

Layla

Flames shot up through pockets of sand, bursting in the faces of the hunters and cutting them off from my men. Cal planted his feet and snarled, protecting Fariah, who looked as shocked as I was. Ink helped Garavel up and guided the wounded angel closer to me.

"Did you know she was an ifrit?" Ink asked as I caught Garavel's giant arm and tried to fit it over my shoulder.

"A what?"

"Ah, so that would be a no. Seems they were ill-prepared as well." Ink folded his arms and laughed at the panicking hunters, who were now partially burned and on fire.

I held on to Garavel and began to recite my healing spell, when he caught my cheek. His thumb reached from my jaw up to my cheekbone and he smiled sadly. "That won't work on me."

"Then what will?"

"Yes! Excellent play. Oh, one is trying to escape." Ink's shouted commentary either reached Maram or she had already noticed the hunter making for the forest.

Garavel brushed his fingers behind the nape of my neck and he pulled me in. When our lips touched, I realized it was a kiss. Strange time for it. We'd have plenty of time after to...no. I shoved myself away from him.

"Don't even think about it. You are not final-standing here."

"I am injured. We are bogged down. What other option is there?"

We were all together, and now we had that thing Ink said on our side. That could be enough to send Zaxigrath home. "We're opening a portal to hell."

"And leaping inside?" Garavel asked uncertainly.

"Mom? Do you think...?"

She stared at Maram and frowned. "If it agrees."

"She." I glanced at Fariah, her hands clutched together in fear. This wasn't using my friend for leverage—it was laying out the options.

"Maram! We need to talk."

The fire creature stared back at me. Her eyes were pure white while the rest of her crackled in the ever-shifting flames. Raising a hand, she pointed to Fariah. I nodded at Cal, who dashed under our friend. Fariah cried out as the giant wolf lifted her off the ground. She dug into his fur, trying to keep her legs crossed even while they clung to him.

I reached out to take Fariah's hand as she kept babbling, "Why did you...? Layla, I am so sorry. I didn't mean to, I never expected to..."

"It's okay. Cal does this all the time."

Ink laid an arm across my shoulder and smirked. "You should rent the man out for rides more often."

I didn't have time for him, and held Fariah while staring up at Maram. She gave one last lash of her hand, erupting ten-foot-tall fires from the ground and hedging in the hunters. Quickly, she descended to the sand before us. Each footstep crunched with glass as she walked closer.

"You weren't supposed to see this."

I knew she wasn't talking to me, but she didn't look to her girlfriend. The once meek voice boomed with authority, her words crackling to make the smoke.

"Will you help us get Zaxigrath back to hell?" We didn't have time to dance around the subject. Everyone knew what was at stake.

"They will not stop until they have him," she said, staring up at Zaxigrath. The giant demon opened his mouth and bellowed. It was deeper than the deer, but the sound cut me to the core. I'd failed once—I wasn't going to again.

Slowly, her gaze dropped to Fariah, who was clinging to my arm, and Maram nodded. "What do you need of me?"

"Power. Magic. Anything you have."

"Where?"

I glanced to my mother, and she tipped her head back to restart the runes. The beach glowed blue and Maram's eyes widened. "Understood. But...there might be singeing. Be careful." With that, she flew into the air and directed both hands at the ground. Blue fire burst free, firing into the sand like a flamethrower. The sand began to smoke, then the runes shifted color. A red deeper than blood radiated from the ground.

"Garavel? Can you protect Fariah?" He took her out of the ward just as the wind picked up. I held my head back, urging the magic to pipe from me into the portal. My brain ached like I'd been pulling all-nighters for a week, but I couldn't stop.

"The flames are lowering," Ink said. Sure enough, the walls of fire that'd kept the hunters at bay were dropping. We had to do this fast.

I clenched my toes in the sand and dipped into the last of my wells. The dreaded emptiness billowed in my stomach. I wanted to vomit, my heart racing and legs shaking. It was just like when the witch hunters had kidnapped me. If I did this too long, I would die.

"Calvin?" Ink held his hand out to the werewolf. "Shall we?"

Cal leaped up beside him, his paws dug in for an attack. But he looked back once and I mouthed 'stay alive.' He couldn't answer, and only gave a small nod just as the hunters jumped across the dying flames. Ink was first, rocketing behind, though they'd anticipated it this time. Cal went for the ankles, yanking a hunter off their feet when they'd turned to fight Ink.

I needed to be by them. I needed to help... I couldn't move.

"Remain here," Torran said. I risked a peek to find him giving a pat to Zaxigrath before walking out of the runes.

"You'll miss the portal," I shouted.

He winked at me and raised his arms. "I can always catch the next one." With a quick jerk, massive spikes sprang from his elbows. Each ball joint looked like a mace, except the ends were two feet long. Torran reared back and swung, impaling then knocking a hunter into the next, which let Cal slash at his back.

The portal was opening, the sand sinking to hell.

"Layla!" my mother shouted. "It's not enough."

Even as I watched it barely move an inch, I said, "We have to keep going."

"This is suicide!"

"Is it your first time?" Ink asked. "I daresay it isn't a holiday without one of you nearly dying in some horrific fashion save the final miracle."

"Does he ever silence his tongue?" Maram asked. Her body was darkening, the flames shrinking as she began to droop. But when Ink stuck out said tongue, her fires burst a moment and the power surged.

"The hunters!" Garavel shouted.

"Thanks, big guy, but we noticed them," Ink said before digging his nails into the head of one and hurling the whole person back into the woods over his shoulder.

"No! They are amassing to fire at the witches!"

Shit. I looked up into the barrel of a massive gun. One man held the butt while another had it balanced on his shoulder. Sure enough, they were aiming it at me and my mom. Garavel noticed because he was used to protecting witches, but no one was close enough to stop them.

I began to throw up a shield, when the muzzle flashed. No time. I moved to shove my mother aside and take the hit. The air wobbled and I jerked, expecting to find a hole through my chest. Scales flipped up, hiding away the gawking hunters and murderous gun. In their place stood Torran, who breathed a deep sigh and glanced over his shoulder to smile at me.

"We are claiming this one," Ink shouted. "He's in the coven now."

I'd like to think I had a say in that.

Torran winked and I giggled. He took another deep breath, then a step for me. I reached out to pull him into the ward before it sealed off. Just as my hand was about to take his, he fell.

"Torran?"

"Do not stop your power," my mother chided, but I was too busy falling to the sand with the demon that took a bullet for me.

"What is it?"

"I think…" He gulped and black ichor dripped from his lips. It began to drip and leech out of every scale, drenching his body. "They have killed me."

"How? Demons can't die."

Torran raised a hand and placed it to my cheek. Instead of the raging inferno, he felt cold as winter. I began my healing spell, but what could I do? If it didn't work on Garavel, then… "Torran's dying!"

"That's impossible," Ink scoffed even as my hands stained with his blood.

"Hey. Come on, stay with me. We're going to send you home. Remember?"

He smiled and his head lolled to the side. I shook him, trying to keep him awake even as his scales turned gray. After the third jiggle, he jerked up. Torran clenched his hand to my shoulder. "Send him home. Save him. Please."

"Torran…? Torran!"

His head tumbled down and all four eyes stared vacantly at nothing. Zaxigrath screeched, his cry bursting through the air, sending everyone to their knees except for me, who was already there. I kept mopping up the ichor, trying to push it back in. That had to work, right? Demons didn't die.

They can't die.

They killed him.

The hunters can kill demons. They could kill any of us.

"Those fools," my mother snarled. She guided Torran's slack body off of mine. I tumbled back, somehow numbly rising to my feet along with the rest. I couldn't stand to look as my mother swept a hand over Torran's eyes to...

Not to close them. No, she collected his spilt ichor, then clenched her fist. Magic gushed into my body and straight into the portal. It split apart, rushing for the edges of our gigantic ward.

"With this sacrifice, we can finish this, Layla." My mom nodded as if that'd been my plan all along. She held her bloodstained hand out to me.

His dying wish was to save his creator, his friend, his father. Fighting off my revulsion, I clasped my mother's hand and my legs locked in place. There was no stopping now. The power looped through us, running like a circuit. If anyone tried to break it, we'd all get burned.

Which was when the hunters lined up a second shot. I held my breath and blinked. Tattered crimson danced in the wind. *What the...?* Ink stood before me, his hands wide like he was hung on the cross.

"What are you doing?"

"Protecting you."

"That thing kills demons. It will kill you!" I screeched, tears bubbling up. "Ink. Please. Get out of the way. Don't you do this." Why was he doing this?

He only cared about himself. He only protected me to save himself. If he died...

He glanced over his shoulder, ignoring the hunters about to pull the trigger. Instead, his eyes were only on me. "My bond, I l—"

"Ahhhh!" The air split and Daniel leaped in front of the gun.

"He's going to give himself a hernia impotently screaming like that," Ink said.

The moment distracted the hunters, but they rebounded and aimed through him. Which was when Daniel clenched his hands together and raised them. The two hunters shot up off the ground, their legs dangling in the air.

"You deserve worse than death," he snarled and bashed them into each other head first.

"Oh dear, he's gone full poltergeist."

"Layla, the portal is nearly open," my mother said. We had to jump fast, but I was enthralled and a bit terrified by Daniel's rampage. He hurled one of the hunters at a tree, slamming him face first. The other he hefted up, and turned around.

Zaxigrath opened his mouth, razor teeth glinting in the moonlight.

"Have a nice...trip!" Daniel shouted, hurling the hunter straight into Zaxigrath's massive maw. The hunter tried to fight back, but all he had to cling to were rows of knives. Zaxigrath slammed his mouth shut, scissoring off the arm and swallowing the hunter whole. That was going to be in my nightmares for a while.

"I've got another one for you," Daniel kept on.

"Layla. Now."

What? But the... Oh no. The sand shifted under my feet. I tried to run, but there was nothing to grip to. I stumbled, almost falling to my knees, when my mother shoved me. My body rolled clean out of the ward and she vanished. I blinked and turned, shouting for her.

Zaxigrath bellowed, whether celebrating his meal or in anger I couldn't say. He thrashed his tails, slapping the lake as the water and everything around it tumbled into the portal. Ink took me in his arms.

"Wait. Where's my mom? Mom?"

I tried to fight him off, but he carried me away to join Garavel and Fariah. Cal too limped beside me. I clung to his head and watched as the massive Zaxigrath dipped down to tenderly scoop Torran's body in his mouth. He gave one last look to us before diving down the hole.

"After it!" a hunter shouted. Then the damnable fools broke into a run, each one breaking across the ward's barrier.

"What are you doing?" I called. "There's no getting out once you —"

"Let them go, lady witch," Garavel said.

Ink smirked. "They deserve worse than a lifetime in hell."

As they crossed the ward's unbreakable line, the portal clenched at their bodies and hurled them down without a care. I clung to my guys, bruised and broken, but alive. The beach kept falling, wiping away every hunter who thought they could beat hell. The purple light broke into undulating blues and reds before both magics faded and the portal to hell closed forever.

"Is that it?" Ink asked.

We won. Except, we had also lost. Maram dropped to the ground. She shook her head back and the fires vanished, to be replaced by the meek woman. Torran's blood stained my hands and chest. Garavel's wing was shattered. Cal was in agony. And my mom...

I'd just gotten her back and they'd taken her again.

"Laylee?"

"Mom?" I cried and turned just as warm, tender arms crushed me in a hug.

Chapter Twenty-Nine

Layla

We did it.

Instead of joy or even relief from pulling off the impossible, my skin prickled at the death burned into the beach. Blood was splattered from one end to the other, pieces of witch hunters left behind. I looked to where Torran's body had been. The ichor stain had dumped into hell along with Zaxigrath, but I could still see him. His eyes were rolling back, his muscles collapsing and his scales fading to a deathly gray.

"Well, who's up for the orgy?"

I glanced to my demon who had nearly met the same damn fate.

He looked no different than when we had first met a lifetime ago. Ink raised a hand to Garavel and smirked. "Angel? Why not leap into the deep end on your first go? Ghost? You already know how to watch.

Calvin? Ah, the fur's been dispensed, on to the debauchery."

I whipped around to find Cal hunched over. He held his hand tight to his chest as he sat slumped in the sand. Zaxigrath might have gone, but our demons hadn't gone anywhere.

"What of you two?" Ink pressed to Fariah and...

Okay. That problem somehow seemed the easiest. I walked over, keeping abreast of Maram, who had tugged her sleeves down over her hands and turtled into her neckline. "Fariah, are you... Did you get hurt?"

"No. My..." She gulped and cast a glance to Maram. "She protected me, and the...angel?"

I nodded.

"He did too. Great job, all around. Thank you." Fariah nodded to everyone as if that'd bring her sense. As she did so, her scarf began to tug back. It was a wonder it hadn't been wrenched off by the winds of hell.

"You're, uh..." I pointed, but it was Maram who reached over and tucked it tight, framing Fariah's skin. Slowly, Fariah looked to her. Maram gulped and moved to pull her hands away when Fariah caught them and pressed them tight.

Maram whispered something super-fast in Arabic. For a beat, Fariah nodded along, smiling, but she didn't know. She couldn't understand.

"Are you safe?"

Breaking from Fariah, she stared me up and down. "I could ask the same of you, witch."

"You're an ifrit. That's like a djinn. Right?"

Her face crumpled and she banged her knuckles together. She risked a glance at Fariah before dropping her head. "You have the right of it."

"What were you going to do to her?" I pressed.

To my shock, the fire genie blushed. She gulped and her eyes widened as sweat rose on her brow. "Um, I'd... I mean, I wanted to. We, it was, uh..."

Samuke had posed as a cop and created an elaborate web of henchmen and powerful people that owed him favors. Whatever Maram was up to could be even worse. I had to get to the bottom of this fast. "Why are you pretending to be Fariah's girl...?"

A hand landed on my arm. I jerked in shock, not expecting my quiet and patient friend to do it, much less interrupt me. "She is not pretending."

Maram gulped and raised her head while I gawped at Fariah. "But she's been lying..."

"She isn't the only one. How long have you been a...witch?"

"Technically, my whole life, but I didn't know until this last Halloween."

Fariah bowed her head in thought. She was the calm one in our group, the level-headed member of our trio. But she'd nearly come undone in the midst of that chaos, and I wouldn't be surprised if she refused to speak to me ever again.

"That explains Tattoo, the...?"

"Incubus."

She swallowed and blinked. "Yes. That in your life. No wonder you've been so distracted lately. I guess every time you were late, you were off saving the world."

"Eh, some of those were just exhaustion."

"I imagine keeping an incubus fed is a drain," Maram said and I wanted to die.

"Fariah, I'm sorry I didn't tell you. I didn't know how. I guess I wanted to..." I gulped and stared over my shoulder to the woman incinerating the blood on the beach. "I thought I was protecting you."

"By keeping the truth from me."

"It's a pretty stupid excuse, now that I think about it."

Fariah chuckled. "Indeed."

"I should have told you. I wanted to. About Ink, and Cal and Daniel."

"Who?"

The invisible ghost was hovering over my book and staring down at it. Whatever force had given him the power to hurl grown men through the air was long gone. "Never mind. I'm sorry."

"You're forgiven. Though I'm not certain how Dana will react when she hears the news."

Oh shit. "We, uh…we're gonna tell her?"

Fariah nodded then reached over and took Maram's hand. The fire djinn blushed and gazed down at the touch.

"What about her? Why did you lie to Fariah?"

"Because I saw this beautiful, gamine woman striding with confidence across the road and I feared her fearing me."

Fariah brushed back Maram's hair and smiled. She said something in Arabic, then glanced to me. "Never you mind, Layla."

"But… Djinn. I've fought a Marid before —"

"This isn't about you. We'll figure it out ourselves."

I stumbled back, my mind boiling over with information on the water djinn that'd tried to kill me. But…Samuke wasn't Maram. And she was right. This wasn't about me.

My legs began to move, pulling me away even as I watched the two women lean closer for a private conversation. I wanted to fix Fariah's relationship because...it was so much easier than dealing with all of mine. Cal sat alone, clutching at the sand. Ink, in his unexplainable tattered clothing, stood where he'd nearly died for me. Daniel hovered, but when a leaf blew on the wind, it landed on his shoulder. Poor Garavel was clutching his broken wing and gazing out across the horizon.

"Mom?"

She paused in setting a forearm on fire and looked to me.

"We need to talk. About everything."

We didn't walk far. I couldn't let them out of my sight and I got the feeling she didn't want to either. Down the beach, the lake crashed into the rocks, dampening our conversation. The moon fell into clouds and my mother opened her hand. Light beamed into the sky and she held it under her face like she was about to tell me a scary story.

"Conquest is out there," I said.

"You removed a piece of his puzzle. That will smart for a long time. We may even have weeks before he tries again."

"He trapped me, was going to kill me in the in-between."

Her wincing I expected, but a moment of guilt flashed across her face.

"He said things."

"About his plan?" My mother touched my hand, not to pull magic from me or yank me along. It was a tender touch of comfort that I hadn't felt in fifteen years. Tears bubbled in my exhausted eyes and I nodded.

"A classic villain monologue. Delightful." Ink popped in behind my shoulder. I didn't even flinch, only reached behind to hold him. He returned the touch, shielding my hand in his.

My mother glared at the interloper, then looked to me. "What did he reveal? Dates? Location?"

"Sadly, he wasn't in the day-planner mood, nor did he bring a secretary with him." I pulled in a breath and my ribs creaked just as they had in the bubble. "He knew how to find me...because of your plan."

She opened her mouth, no doubt to explain, but I was too tired for this fight.

"You can't hide this shit from me, not anymore. I'm not nine. My head's on the chopping block too."

"Laylee, my little lamb, I never meant to..." She stopped from reaching out to hug me and sighed. "This all went wrong. I did what I had to for the sanctity of the line."

The what?

"I thought it was the right move, to draw his attention from you if he believed I was dead. I never thought he'd..." She closed her eyes and moaned. "Poor Didi."

"How long has Conquest chased us?"

"Your whole life. Why do you think we kept moving?"

It was what I had known. I'd thought my mom was chasing opportunities, clients, living with friends. It was normal. How many nights when the power was out and we'd sit in my bedroom together hiding under a blanket were those to escape the ever-present eyes of a Horseman?

"I can't ask you to forgive me, but I need you to understand. This war has been building since I was a child. I'd hoped it wouldn't be you caught up in it, but it seems he's finally playing his cards." My mom toyed with my hair as if she wanted to pull it straight. When she let go, the twist hung lower than the others and I frowned.

I wasn't ready to let her into my life. Not as a mother. But I needed another witch because there was too much I didn't understand.

"He said that he was going to use me as his touchstone."

Ink was the one to whistle. "That...actually that makes sense."

"What is a touchstone?"

"Mostly it's an elf thing. They leave a piece of themselves on a different world and use that to..." He rolled his hand like a wave. "Zip between realms."

That sounded bad. I curled my hand to my chest, my palm cupping the locket out of habit. Was that why I could already fall into and out of the in-between? How much longer until I was falling into different realms?

"Laylee, why did you want the demon blood?"

"Fuck!" I clenched my hand around the locket and stared across the beach. "I forgot the blood! Why didn't I ask before? I should goddamn learn—get the blood, then fight. Every fucking time it all..."

My mother caught me by the shoulders, holding me in place even as I curse-screamed at myself. "I need it to bring Daniel back."

"That's the only reason?"

"She's rather single-minded when it comes to the soul goo. I think it's the cheekbones."

I glared at Ink and he shrugged. It wasn't the only reason. It wasn't even in the top ten.

My mother stared across the beach to the man I'd failed. He had no idea, already back to research minutes after we almost died. "He moved men. And he uprooted the trees."

"I know. If it weren't for that I'd be..." I was impressed, but the dour look on my mother's face stalled me. "What?"

"He's becoming a poltergeist."

"You said the same thing." I jerked a thumb to Ink who suddenly didn't want to be a part of this. He held his hands out, then vanished. Coward. "How is his being able to move things bad? He can help, he can finally fight. He's almost..."

"Alive? A ghost that is cognizant of their limitations, that knows they are a ghost, is stable. A ghost who shrieks and wails, who uses their immense spectral power to hurl objects around, is not."

"What are you saying?"

"His grip on reality is shattering. It's like ghost dementia. They forget they are dead, pitch a fit and burn out. Soon it will all go and then...so too will he."

Daniel? "No. I need another demon. We can open a portal and..." Except all that power would draw Conquest and the hunters right to me. "Maybe he's already pulled out another demon and we can make the same deal. I have to..."

My mother shifted and held out a finger-long vial of black-red liquid. She gave it a shake, and the inner core lit up white and pulsing before fading away.

"Is that —?"

"The blood of a full demon. It is a power unlike anything I've held before." She shook it again, the black-red blood eclipsing the blue of her eyes.

"Mom?"

She jerked and held out her hand. "Take it. Protect it."

I scooped the blood up and the hair on the nape of my neck stood on end. She was right. The feathers were light and inviting. This felt like holding on to a downed wire and surviving—pure destruction. I could do anything with this.

"Guard it carefully." My mother cupped my hands around the vial and pressed it to my chest. "Every bastard on this planet will try to steal it away." She stared first at Maram, then glared across the beach at everyone. "Keep it to yourself, just in case."

"Mom?" I had to tell them. We had to plan how to... The way she stared cut through me and I nodded. One day, once I was certain we were ready.

She cupped my jaw and brushed her thumb against my cheek. "You've grown up so much. I can't believe it."

I tugged my face away and stared across the beach. "I'm not ready for that, Mom. I'm still mad."

"Okay." She took a step back, then another.

"But I need you. To train me. To figure out how we can stop Conquest once and for all."

She nodded and smiled. "Of course. Little Laylee. I'll leave you to your friends and the rest, then find you later."

"Sounds good...Mom." Would I ever get used to saying that word again?

My mom kept walking back. Her eyes drifted down to my necklace and she grinned. "You wear your father's locket well."

My what? I cupped the gold heart and Conquest's words snapped back at me. "*I made you.*" What did he mean by that? "Mom, who is...?" When I looked up, she was gone.

All I had were a thousand questions and two thousand problems. It'd be nice for an answer and solution to drop on my head, just once. Instead, I gritted my teeth and walked toward Cal. Only the dewy air of pre-dawn ruffled his hair. The rest of him remained stagnant.

"Hey." Glancing my finger across his naked shoulders, I tried to lean down, only for my weary legs to give up. I plummeted beside him, kicking sand up into every scratch and gouge in my skin. The irritation made me groan and I reached to wipe it away when arms caught me.

Cal crushed me to his bare chest, his cheek on mine as he began to rock the both of us. Slowly, I held him back, swaying together as the loons cried out from the lightening sky.

What happened?
Why didn't you shift?
Was it me?

Every time I tried to voice one question, Cal would gulp and I'd feel another tear sliding down my cheek. I couldn't guess how long I held him, listening to his ragged breathing as the sky shifted from impenetrable indigo to dawn's pink.

"Control." The first word from Cal didn't make any sense. Was I controlling him? Was he worried about Conquest? About the witch hunters?

I risked leaning back to try to read his expressions, but the moment I did, he dropped his gaze. God, his lips were cracked and his skin dry as kindling. I wrapped my palms around his jaw and brushed my thumbs over the damage.

Cal leaned forward, placing his forehead to mine. He wouldn't open his eyes, keeping them locked away as he spoke. "Every day growing up, I had no idea when they'd start. I could be beaten for talking too loud, for not answering loud enough, for running the wrong way. There was no escape...except when I shifted."

I wrapped my hands around the nape of his neck, holding him to me. Cal fought to breathe, his past crushing him. He began to shiver, goosebumps rising across his already battered flesh. I tried to rub warmth into him when terrycloth landed on my fingers. Glancing past him, I watched Ink give a quick smile, then walk away, leaving me to drape the beach towel across Cal's shoulders. He huddled deeper into it.

"Every night, we were supposed to shift. To run through the woods, howling at the moon and following *him*. I couldn't do it. To turn into *him*, over and over, and I stopped. I'd go for days without. It was the one thing, the one moon-damn thing, he couldn't control. The only thing I could."

Cal gulped and looked at me. His eyes were red as fire and he cupped his palms to my face. "I could have hurt you. Fuck, why do I do this?"

The same reason I ran into fires without looking back. "It's how you cope."

"It's not good for me. I've pushed it before. Always right up until the full moon. Nearly an entire month and no problem. This time..." Cal groaned as if he'd let all of us down. "You must hate me."

"Never. You had me worried, but I knew you were hurting, that you needed help. You do. Sweetheart..." I pushed back his hair, running my fingers through the white-blond until they snagged on crusted blood.

"I can't stop him. I can't even fight him when he's human, never mind as a… How do I protect you? How do I…?"

He meant Eric, his eldest brother. I caught Cal's palm and pressed it to my lips. He winced and tried to look away, but I wouldn't let him. "We're here. We're all here. He can't get you. He won't get to you, or me."

Cal gulped and nodded, but his eyes were hooded, the truth a hard pill to swallow.

"You can't do this alone," I said. "You shouldn't have to hide in the basement to shift. It's not shameful, it's necessary. It keeps you…safe. You."

He leaned against my palm cradling his head, but a shudder climbed up his chest.

"Let me help. I'll sit with you, make sure that you…that you shift. To keep yourself healthy."

"Layla." Cal raised his eyes and dread lurked deep in his ocean blues. "I can't… I don't want you to…"

"I will sit with him."

Cal's eyes opened wide and he turned in my hold to stare back at Garavel. The angel stood framed by dawn's rays, his bald head glowing as he held his sword tight to his chest. Fiona meowed from the handle's end and he scritched her head.

"Every night, I will sit with the wolf and make certain he completes his transformation."

I reached a hand out to thank Garavel, but Cal stared harder. "Why?"

Hearing that he was a potential threat wouldn't help him. I tried to talk over Garavel, but the angel was too quick.

"Because it's what you need. And if we don't help our brothers and sisters, we won't stand a chance against the enemy."

"Thank you, for not killing me." Cal held out a hand.

Garavel stared at it a moment and didn't stop petting his kitten.

"I know you did it for Layla's sake, and it means the world to me that she doesn't have to suffer for my —"

"That isn't why," Garavel interrupted.

We both jerked in shock. Cal nearly spun around to face him as Garavel dropped his hand from the kitten and stared off into the distance. After a minute, he said, "You didn't hurt Fiona," and walked away.

"That's it? He didn't kill me because I like cats?" Cal gaped in confusion.

But as I watched the soldier turned peacekeeper tenderly rub down his kitten's back, I understood. He had gotten through the war believing werewolves to be mindless and deserving of slaughter. Knowing one as intelligent, as caring of tiny, helpless creatures, upended everything in his past and present. Garavel was in more pain than he could admit, much like my poor werewolf. I cinched tighter to Cal, pulling myself against him as he ruffled my hair.

"My bond? While I hate to disrupt your communal sob, I believe it's in our best interests to retreat to a safe haven."

Even though we'd stopped them, the hunters, the werewolves and Conquest were all still out there. We couldn't stay any longer. Cal stood first, scooping me off the ground. I didn't realize how exhausted my legs were until I tried to stand on my own.

"Take her, Ink," Cal said, passing me off. Before he did, he gave one tight squeeze and whispered, "I love you so damn much."

"I love..." The 'you' vanished on the wind as my incubus transported us back to the cabins.

Chapter Thirty

Ink

"What about the others?" Layla put to me.

"I believe they all possess the necessary limbs to ambulate on their own," I said with a smile. Her crumbling lip caught me and I took her hands. "I will go and fetch them. Who would you like first — the dog or the angel?"

"Cal's in a bad state, but Garavel's hurt and I don't know if I can even heal him. I—"

Taking her hand, I raised it to my lips and kissed her palm. "I will pick for you. Flip of the ghost."

Layla forced on a smile and took a step closer. Her body bowed, exhaustion rampant in her waning form. Cupping her waist, I hefted her into my arms.

"You require rest," I declared, as if she'd show me a moment's consideration. No doubt she'd be sitting up, waiting for the werewolf and angel to return for more tending by her ever-caring hands. I expected an argument, but she nuzzled her cheek to my chest. An unnatural prickle washed over my skin at her touch. Not hunger, not even delight in teasing out a desire. This almost felt like...calm in the eye of a raging inferno.

Shaking it off, I bundled her into her bed. She tumbled to her side and reached a hand over to the other mattress pushed next to hers. "He will be fine, in time," I said while unearthing her blanket from the edge of the bed and raising it over her body. "Mortals are surprisingly malleable. I suppose you have to be to handle the concept of death without going mad."

"Ink. You almost died tonight."

Did I? Torran had succumbed to the cruel tactics of the hunters, yes, but I'd been... An endless void opened in my brain. I tried to peel back whatever was blocking my memory, but a pain shocked through me. With an easy smile, I tucked the edge of the blanket against Layla's chin. "Almost is a mere trifle, as ephemeral as a soap bubble."

Her hand shot out, clamping to the back of my neck. I anticipated a kiss, but she pulled me to her forehead. This was a position for her and her wolf, not one of libidinous debauchery, but tenderness. Instinctively, I tried to rear back, but she held me tighter and looked up.

The fear in her eyes trapped me in a swirling panic to end whatever was terrorizing her. "Don't do it again, okay? I need you here."

"For shuttle service."

Layla smiled weakly. "For lots of things." She kissed me gently on my lips. A tendril of desire floated through her, the magic already returning to her void. I left the power inside of her. She needed it to heal herself far more than I did.

Stepping back, I began to slit apart the space, when my bond called out, "I'm sorry that you didn't get your feast."

Did she think I only agreed to help with this madness because I could eat after? *I am a creature of a sin, born from lust, destined to devour. There is nothing but the hunger.*

With a smirk, I bowed. "There is always next time." And I bounded into the nothing. When I emerged at the beach, the wolf had at least found his pants, not that I'd have much cared.

He was first to catch sight of me and call out, "Layla?"

Always on his mind. Even deep into the monster lurking inside his body, she never left him. "She is sleeping in the cabin safe and sound."

"It is Layla we're talking about. There's a ten-percent chance aliens have invaded right this second," the ghost said with a weary sigh. If I closed one eye, his form from the waist down faded to nothing—a most unappetizing thought for the lady of the hour.

"I should get back to her," Calvin declared, then he glanced to the angel among the demons. "Er, unless you want to…"

Garavel didn't answer him, but gave a quick shake. That was good enough for me. I held a hand out to the shirtless man. "Come, I will leave you to watch over her as she slumbers. Don't act as if you don't do that from time to time."

"The only way you'd know is if you were doing the same," he countered, a nugget of logic I had to tip my head to.

I took his arm and prepared to rip apart the in-between when he stared at the others paying him no heed. Calvin whispered near my ear, "You were right."

"Of course I was. About what precisely?"

"I knew Layla was special, different from any other girl."

"Yes, tell her exactly that. Perhaps mention in minute detail all the previous women you've bedded."

He frowned at me. "Nothing got through the wolf, nothing got it to give up except for her."

As I'd already surmised. "Huzzah and whatnot. Why are you droning on at me?"

Calvin darted his gaze once more and lowered his voice. "Don't tell the others yet, but... I think I'm gonna make it official."

"You will register yourself with the city pound?"

"Funny," he said, staring at me, then he clasped two fingers around his ring finger and smiled.

Marriage, as I'd been growing to suspect for some time. A curse of monogamy, of long days in the solarium arguing over the price of tulips and deciding how best to fatten up the children.

"What do you think?" he inquired.

It would make Layla very happy and render me obsolete.

I smirked. "That you leave much to be desired in woo." As Calvin's excited smile dimmed, I whisked him off and left him with Layla. I could not guess if she was already asleep, or if he'd curl up next to her and whisper the question in her ear. Either way, it had nothing to do with me.

When I emerged once more on the beach, the angel was walking back in the direction of the campgrounds. "I may whisk you away, Garavel," I called.

He raised a hand and waved. "No, thank you. Dawn's the best time for walking."

Layla would have my head if I let him traverse the entire way back. But the final member of our coven drew my attention. "What of you, ghost?"

"I can transport myself, thanks." He had her book in his hands. How she trusted him to tend to it was beyond me.

"You do realize the danger you are."

Daniel tossed his head back and scoffed to the heavens. "I get it, because I—the feckless one—saved your life, you're pissed."

"Incubi do not urinate."

"That's…" He shook his head and turned away. "Nope. I'm not doing this with you." Without a thought, Daniel tucked the book under his arm. He took a step, no doubt intending to use Layla's locket to beam in on her.

Imagine his chagrin if he appeared mid-proposal. I almost wanted to let him go for that outcome. But my concerns grew as he leaned down and a twig cracked from the pressure of a dead man's foot.

"You're forgetting yourself, aren't you?"

Freezing, Daniel refused to turn to me. He raised his head and called over his shoulder, "What?"

"That you are dead slips from your mind. You will do actions a living man would without thought, then laugh it off when caught."

His form jerked and the spell book tumbled through his arms. "No!" he declared while bending over to pick up the book.

"You are dead. You were pierced through the heart and your body rests six feet below the ground in the earth and worms."

Daniel's spirit fingers passed through the spell book thrice before he growled at me. "Thank you for the reminder."

"You'd do well to keep it in mind."

"Why are you being such a dick?"

Because if you fall to the state of a pure poltergeist and are lost before she can pull off a miracle, it will shatter her heart.

I leaned through him, my arm and face plunging out of his chest in order to pick up Layla's wayward spell book. Daniel jerked and leaped to the side where he partially sank into the ground. Holding the book lightly to my chest, I smiled. "Why not?"

He gave one final snarl to remind me his face was far too fair for such a poisonous attitude, then he vanished. I stood alone on the sands, watching my solitary shadow waver at my feet. For thousands of years, I'd walked with only it for company. For thousands of years, I'd thought it enough.

A slow clapping echoed off the dawn's light. Sashaying through the sand in her ten-inch heels, Lust gave one final slap of her palms before she came to a stop. "That was quite the spectacle, Eros."

"Of course." I shook my head, smiling at the fool I'd been. "Tell me, Lust. Who was it?"

"Hm?" She twisted back her hair, forever the spider even when there was no fly to be had.

"Were you offering your ample services to the werewolves? Are you foolish enough to join with a Horseman himself?"

Lust giggled, each breath armed with a dagger. "What are you telling yourself, Eros?"

I blinked and sighed. "Do not tell me you are working for the witch hunters."

"I don't work for anyone," she snarled. The mask fully slipped, her green and black face prodding from below the fair skin. But with a toss of her shoulders, the carefree woman returned. "My dear, my heart, you had me worried. I was only looking out for you."

"From a safe vantage point."

Lust shrugged as if she would do no less. She was not the kind of woman to stand by anyone's side beyond her own. "Do you realize what danger you face if you continue this charade?"

"I'm sorry that we thwarted your employer's plans, but it seems from where I'm standing that I was on the winning team."

"Oh, Eros." She reached out and took my cheek in her hand. Lust swept her thumb against my lips while she spoke. "You always were so foolhardy." Her nail dug in deeper, past the soft, pliable skin, to the tissue then the muscle. "I'm concerned for you. The hunters, did you not see what they did to that under-demon?"

Of course I had. It had been impossible to escape the panic on Torran's face as his body had bled from the inside out. "How can they kill a demon?" I whispered to myself.

Lust pulled back on her attack, leaving my lips bruised. She darted her thumb into my mouth, unable to get past my locked teeth.

"Who knows? Could be the work of technology, or witches." Her eyes gleamed as if she'd known about the witches the hunters had enslaved.

Digging her fingers into the hollow of my cheek, Lust pulled my face closer to hers. "And you are bound to one of those creatures the hunters are looking for. Eros, what if they catch you instead?"

I laughed at the idea. They'd had ample opportunity and failed every time.

"What if they kill you?"

A flash punctured my memory of me standing in front of the weapon, arms out, waiting for it to end me. *No! I would never do such a thing.* Sacrifice was not programmed into a creature of devouring.

I shook my head hard and took a step back. "They can certainly try," I declared to her. "If you will excuse me. I have to return this book." I patted Layla's lost tome and took a step. The in-between had never felt so welcoming as I ran from Lust's glare.

Before I could vanish she snickered. "What if she does as you once did, and your witch turns you in to the hunters?"

I ran, never once looking back to Lust and her web of manipulation. But the idea she birthed lingered. *What if...*

Chapter Thirty-One

Garavel

The tiny kitten leaped, her paws cupped before her face in anticipation of pinning her prey. But in her landing, she knocked the ball of various strings under the bed. Without pause, Fiona scampered after, her little legs slipping as she went.

I watched from the floor, my back pressed to the cool wall while sunshine stretched across the dusty air. A strange sense of pride filled my heart at how my kitten refused to back down in her play.

"Oh good."

The familiar twang of a spring pulled to its reach, then the slamming door caused me to look up into her watchful but excited eyes.

Layla smiled at me stretched out across the small cabin. "I hoped you'd be in here." She unhooked a bag of canvas from her shoulders. Without pause, she laid out bottles and boxes no doubt full of potions and other various witchcraft oddities. I picked up a white box so light it was nearly weightless and opened it. An array of small rectangles and tubes sat inside.

Magic had evolved much since my days.

"You, um…" The lady witch brushed her fingers over my arm, trailing the minor divots from the attacks. With each one, her eyes drooped and she swallowed. "I wanted to do this earlier, but breakfast was… awkward."

Soldiers camped around the first meal post-battle, struggling to understand what the new normal was after facing such carnage was a feeling I knew well. The others seemed to have more of a challenge with it. "I felt bad for Dante. Should we have told him what happened?"

Layla winced and took a roll of linen from my box. "No. Better to keep the mortals as much out of this as possible." She paused in laying out her weapons and stared into the distance.

"You are worried about your friend."

She bit her lip and darted her eyes to the side. Pink rose on her cheeks and my hand reached for it. Warmth tingled up my skin and I brushed my thumb across the dip of her smile line. It'd been struggling often as of late.

"I'm worried about you too. Your wing?" Layla pointed to above my shoulder. With a slight groan, I hefted my wings from where I'd painfully stored them. The right fluttered with no problems, while the left dangled precipitously where it'd cracked.

Rising on her tiptoes, Layla reached a hand against the bent bone and I jerked back. She placed her palm to my chest and stared up into my eyes. "I'll be gentle, I promise."

Nodding, I took a knee, bringing my wing to her. Bent to the ground, I was a little shorter than her, letting me gaze up into her patient and caring face as she brushed her fingers up my wing.

"Your magic won't work, I'm afraid. Witches used to try. They'd do anything to help us."

"What would you do after battles?" She reached the area of the break and I gasped. More than the pain, a fear clenched my heart that the whole wing could shatter with a touch. Then where would I be?

"We…" I struggled to focus. "We would take all that we could, then return to our creators to be forged anew."

She placed the edge of the linen wrap to my wing and began to wind it. "That sounds hard."

Some had never made it back, splintering to shards before they could be saved. Some were too far gone even if we'd saved them, the creators deciding they'd be better off making new. I'd never questioned the design. It was from the angels—it had to be perfect. But while mages could heal and fight again the next eve, we were left in pieces that might never become whole.

"You're quiet." She laid a pair of heavy sticks against my wing and resumed her wrapping.

"I'm thinking about how clouds taste."

Layla giggled and leaned back to stare at me. "Clouds have flavor?"

"Oh, yes. At dawn, when they're fluffy and delicate, they taste of strawberries and cream."

Her cheeks pinked again and she reached up with another roll of linen. This required more concentration on the tips of her toes, and she pressed her body closer to mine. I tried to bend lower, which nearly placed her ample bosom in my face. Layla teetered and I placed a hand to her hips, holding her safe while I did my best to not stare at the tempting breasts practically against my nose.

"The circular clouds, they taste of fresh mineral water with a dash of lemon."

She'd abandoned her starchy work clothes and wore a loose white shirt above the thin swimming attire the demon had chosen. The black called from below the thin cotton, the nubs on her breasts lengthening. I gulped, wondering what they'd feel like on my tongue. My hand slipped, fingers spreading across the inviting curve of her backside and my thumb slipping down around the bone of her hip. It was an accident, nothing more.

"What about storm clouds?" Layla asked. She stuck her back out, pulling her breasts from my vision, but placing more of her buttocks in my hands. As she stared down at me, her eyes glimmered. "What do those taste like?"

You. A zap of magic that tingles through the whole body and makes me feel more alive than I thought possible. "I, uh...I forget." My face burning and stomach flipping, I stared down. There would be no more cloud tastings for me. With my wing in disrepair, I could not risk using them. With the last angel taken from this world, I could never heal them.

"How's that feel?" Layla asked. She staggered back and stared not at my face, but my wings. I stared in confusion and, out of habit, dipped my wing.

A twinge of pain shuddered through my back, but nowhere near as deep as once before. "What did you...?" In shock, I ran my fingers across my feathers and found a large band of pink and green gauze wrapped around the break. She'd wisely added supports, keeping the wing up instead of hanging down.

"It may not be magic, but it should heal now. Hopefully right. I asked Daniel to get me a book on veterinary medicine. The principle's the same, and I didn't have to worry about you pecking my eyes —"

I wrapped her tight in my arms, crushing her to my chest. She went quiet and tenderly cupped her hands behind my head. "Your kindness, your heart, it knows no bounds." I'd never thought to try the simple art of medicine, but she'd put her all into it without pause.

"I should have done it last night, to give it time to set properly." Her eyes were pinched with worry, her teeth nipping into her lip. Despite all she did, it was not enough. I knew that feeling far too well and wished I could take it from her.

Curling my hands around her cheeks, I held Layla safe and gazed into her face. "How can this world of chaos create a witch of such kindness and beauty? It doesn't seem possible."

She swallowed deep and her lashes lowered before she stared up at me.

I pulled her to me, guiding her lips to press to mine. The zap of lightning coursed down my spine, but with each passing second, her taste shifted. From flying at the height of the sky on a sunny day, to plunging in a dive into a turquoise pool, and finally…

My head turned, breaking the kiss, and I fought for air. As it filled my lungs, panic set in. I hadn't done anything Ink told me to. Where was the cleft? And I needed a chicken. I nearly leaped away, prepared to fly off until I was ready, when a warm hand slipped under my baggy tunic and caressed up my back.

The touch soothed me in a way I'd never known. It was more than an accidental brush or a friendly pat in excitement. Layla pressed her fingers in and I ached to feel her hands across every inch of my skin. I kissed her, gently holding her cheeks while my body flushed from a heat boiling inside out. My legs began to shake as she drew her hands across my waist and placed them to my hips.

I wanted to take her hand. To place it on my loins. To feel her gasp in delight. To let her touch what none but me had.

Layla parted her mouth and I did the same, trying to match her. She giggled against my lips then abandoned my waist to run her fingers across my naked scalp. Each nail brushed over my skin, sending a shiver in its wake.

"Your touch is…" I gulped, realizing I didn't have the words. Her delicate fingers paused and I caught both her hands, clasping them together. "I don't know how to do this right. The incubus tried to teach me, but…"

"Forget whatever Ink said." Layla turned her hands and I let them go. Both her palms pressed to my chest and I breathed deep. "Be you, Garavel, the sweet, excitable angel."

Me? The fool who'd run from her with every chance? That couldn't be what she wanted.

"What—" Layla swept her hands across my pecs, the tunic interfering with the full sensation. As she caressed lower, reaching my stomach, she stared up at me. "—do you want?"

"To kiss you," I declared without thought. She laughed and puckered up. I held her cheeks, entranced by the smoothness of her skin, the taste of her lips. She parted them again and this time, her tongue stuck out. Not in a jape, but to lick over mine. She plied at my mouth and I opened it.

Sweet lord! The tingle amplified tenfold as I tasted her pliant tongue. Heat drenched down my throat and I clung tighter to her. My unused gift hardened, pressing from inside my trousers to her curvy belly. She'd notice. She'd fear it and…

Layla took my hands from her face. Slowly, she guided them down her shoulders. My heart fluttered as my palm traipsed over the tiny black string keeping her top up.

"What are you thinking?" she whispered, the breath in her voice causing me to pant.

"This is amazing," I gasped in awe.

She chuckled once, then guided my palms over her bosom. I squeezed, not expecting the give to excite me to my core. Layla winced and pulled back on my fingers. "Little less pressure."

"Sorry." I went slack, terrified that a single touch could hurt her.

She took control again, guiding my fingers under her breasts. They bounced in my hands and I raised one, only for it to rebound defiantly. There was far more to this than a simple answer to feeding infants. I caressed my hands below and around the sides, pausing the second her skin pressed too tight. Every time my fingers dared to caress higher and brush over the growing nubs, Layla would toss her head back and moan.

"Try this." Without pause, she took my hand and guided the fingers over the nubs. They prodded out further, tugging the thin fabric free of her breasts. I wasn't certain what they were, but the spiritual cries from Layla's lips made me love them. I toyed with them, then her breasts, careful to not press too tight. She left me in control and clung to my waist while I kissed her lips.

When I tugged on her nub, she gasped in my mouth, causing my loins to burn with holy fire. I tried to slip my tongue into her mouth, but misjudged and accidentally knocked a tooth into her lip. She squealed in a way I recognized as enjoyment and not pain.

Nudging her head to the side, I kissed the side of her neck. Layla wrapped a hand around my head, holding tight to me as I traversed lower. Slender but strong, her muscles had fascinated me and the freckles down her skin. Each one I kissed to her collarbone, Layla arching her back to encourage me. The shirt's fabric roughed across my tongue and I kept going, eager for a taste of her.

"Hang on." Layla didn't push me off, but I rose, fearing I'd done something wrong.

She caught the bottom of her tunic and, with crossed arms, raised it over her head. *Holy creators and their scepters of enchantment!* Her body glowed, skin of lightest earth, fertile for new life. I stared at her stomach, entranced by the soft curve poking over the sides of her pants. I wished to suck upon her breasts, to grip to them and run my hands down her back.

Risking it all, I placed my palm's heel to her waist, watching her belly quiver. Layla reached up and paused. "Shall I?" she asked, her fingers around the knot at the back of her neck. "Or do you want to do the honors?"

Did I? I wanted to tear her clothing off, to bask in the golden glory of her skin, to caress and lick from her toes to her earlobes. But I didn't know how to begin.

She tugged the end of the string thrice and waggled her eyebrows. That was how. Smiling, I took the string in my fingers and began to pull. It came easily, the bow falling apart. I wasn't certain what would happen next. But the tiny material falling from her chest to reveal a mystery I didn't even know existed was far from it.

Layla placed a hand to her hip and smiled. My eyes only darted to her face for a moment as my entire being was wrapped up in the naked breasts before me. The nubs were larger than I ever imagined, and a thrilling dark color that made me want to lick them all the more.

"These are...perfect."

"I bet you say that to all the half-naked witches." Layla laughed.

"No. Never. I've...I've never seen more beauty in all my days."

"Wait." Layla took my hand. "There's even better." With a smile, she guided my fingers to her breast and I lost all control.

Layla

The air turned gold and Garavel's eyes glittered like a black diamond. His wings extended higher to cup around his head like a medieval painting. All of that came from touching my boob. He was careful, almost too tender, but after last night, gentle was a balm to my soul. I leaned back, savoring in the swoop of his fingers over all of my breasts, but the nips.

Did he forget?

I opened my mouth to remind him when Garavel circled his arms around my waist and plucked me off the ground. Giggling, I tried to tell him to put me down—he was injured. Then his hot, trembling lips sucked on my nipple.

"Oh, fuck!" Pleasure shivered through me and I wrapped around his head to keep him in place. Garavel was a lazy Sunday at the beach to Ink's rapid fire and I loved it. He kissed and licked across the whole of my breasts, between the cleavage then to the other nipple.

I wiggled my legs, not fighting him, but trying to push myself closer. My hands slipped and I lashed out, clenching my nails into the back of his shirt. It began to rise as I shivered back and forth trying to clench my thighs for that just-right friction. Before I fell, I dug in, my fingers pressed to rock-hard muscle.

"I'm so goddamn wet," I groaned.

Garavel broke off and stared at me in confusion.

Panting, I tried to laugh. "That's a good thing. A very good thing. Why don't I...?"

He opened his hands, letting me slide back to my feet. But as I went, I tugged his shirt with me. I couldn't understand how his clothing never snagged on the wings, but the tee slipped straight off, leaving me gazing up at the impenetrable muscles of the cuddly angel. If it weren't for his body being strong as ebony, he'd be a big old teddy bear. The round belly looked perfect for bouncing off rockets and cuddling. His arms were bigger than my thighs and the cut was deep. No veins were evident, but each muscle stood out before feeding into an even larger one.

With a shy gulp, Garavel bounced on his legs and he blushed. "You're incredible," I said, holding his cheek. He smiled and bent lower to kiss me when I gripped his jeans and pulled him closer.

"Are you ready for more?" I asked, trying to sound playful.

He nodded, then winced. "I didn't find a chicken."

"Okay? That's a... We can look later. I think." That had to be some weird angel code. I popped open the button on his jeans, then the zipper, before pausing. This didn't seem fair.

Taking his hands, I guided the gentle giant to my pants. "I do you, you do me?" I said.

His smile rose and he nodded. Fuck, his fingers were so big, he could barely pinch the zipper pull. But pull it he did. I wiggled my hips, trying to encourage my tight pants off. Garavel grinned and he tugged off not only the jeans but the purple bikini bottoms. A breeze struck against my drenched vulva and I gasped.

Before he could panic, I tugged off his pants and led him for the bed, kissing him as we went. The springs squealed from my ass, then the entire mattress nearly sank to the floor as Gravel climbed up with me. "Here…" I took his hand, guided it down my belly and placed it against my thighs.

He clenched, worrying my muscles before his eyes opened wide.

"Don't worry, those can take the squeeze."

"They're so soft, I want to eat them."

Oh, he was going to kill me. The innocent way he said dirty things made me gush.

"Do you want to do more?"

Garavel kept massaging my thighs, each time dipping his fingers further in between them. But he looked to me and nodded.

I parted my legs and guided him to my soaking vulva. His eyes went wide as he glanced his finger over the tender skin. I cried out and curled my toes. He almost shrank back, but I clung tighter and kept teaching him. "This is sensitive and loves the gentle graze of a finger or tongue." I swirled him all over my labia, his giant fingers making short work.

His once whisper-quiet breathing began to deepen, then turn into a low groan as he watched with rapt attention. "I've never felt like this," he said.

"Here's the real secret." Cupping my hand around his index finger, I led the single tip to my clit. Garavel gave me full control as I swerved it up the hood and down, slow at first, then picking up the speed I'd need. All the while, he toyed with my hair and bent over to kiss my breasts before gazing down at his hand between my legs.

A hand clamped to my wrist and pulled me off of him. I stared up, fearing it'd be from Ink or even Cal. But the skin was ebony and Garavel smiled down at me as he extended my arms higher over my head. "I understand," he said. Using his knee, he pressed my thighs farther apart. One leg fell off bed and the other he guided around his waist.

With unbending focus, he gazed down at me spread-eagled, and began to finger me on his own. I didn't realize how close I'd been until the sensation shifted, almost draining away. But Garavel was patient, watching my eyes roll back, listening to me moan when he pushed just right, and increasing speed with every squirm of my thighs. The once-quick orgasm took its time ramping up, the heat steaming up to my throat and down to my toes.

Tell him to go faster.

End this.

But it feels so fucking good.

Just another eon or two.

"May I kiss it?"

The question shocked me awake. I blinked, my vision swimming with spots, and I focused on Garavel. He shyly raised a shoulder, then glanced down to me.

"You want to…?" *Talk about leaping into the deep end.* "Okay. Yeah, that's…that's a good thing." Jesus, I sounded pathetic, but as he guided my legs around his waist and bent over, I didn't care. Last thing I'd expected was to be eaten out by an angel.

Warm, tingling lips pressed to me with nothing but sweetness. I groaned and reached for his head, aching to feel his kiss higher on my clit. Before I could even tug on his ears, Garavel rolled out his tongue and I lost it. That tingle zipped across the whole of my vulva, gaining steam as it circled me before plunging to my clit.

I gasped, all the air sucked from my lungs. My body crumpled inward, then exploded like the birth of a star. Energy, pleasure… I couldn't even guess what raced from every fingertip and toe, from my lips and my vagina. I was flying.

I could see everything at once, feel the orgasm in every cell of my body. I was a god.

"Holy…" The star collapsed, leaving me whimpering even as the final trembles of pleasure shook my body. My world shifted and I reached out, fearing to find a mountain collapsing, but it was the bed. "Garavel?"

He gazed down at me, a golden halo rising off his bare skin. I pulled him close. He puckered up, but I kept yanking until I could whisper in his ear. "I want you, now. Without question. Do you…?"

There was a good possibility of a no. It'd been a lot. We'd leaped from first to third base like a gunshot. Fourth could wait until…

"With all my heart," he said, slipping in between my legs. I kissed him, massaged his back, ran my calves up his ass. He deserved to feel as comfortable as possible, and it wasn't until he was panting that I brushed my hand up his inner thigh. At the ballsack, Garavel gulped, his bottom lip trembling.

I sucked on it and reached higher.

Oh, thank god.

I'd been fretting he was somehow bigger than Cal, but his cock was just right. A bit shorter and thinner than Ink's, it was perfect for a romp in the cabin.

"Layla... This is—"

"Going to get so much better," I said, guiding him to me.

"Are you...?"

"I'll be gentle." I placed the tip inside of me, then wrapped my hands around his shoulders. He opened his eyes and gazed at me, his face full of wonder. "I promise."

Garavel thrust, instinct taking over. He grunted and did it again, the heat of his body inflaming mine. I pressed against his forehead and he kissed me deeply. "My lady, my witch...this is. I've never. I want to...Ah!"

Tossing his head back, he shouted to the skies as he bucked wildly, then went still. Much like with Ink, I didn't feel any signs of semen pumping into me, but Garavel shivered with an orgasm. Seemed not-demons and angels had a lot in common. I ran my hands across his back as he buried his face against my shoulder.

Slowly, he lowered to the bed, crushing me tight in a hug. I held back as he began to rock, no doubt falling to that dreaded orgasm sob.

Garavel suddenly sat up with a huge grin on his face. "That was the best thing ever," he shouted with a great laugh. Holding me, he flipped both of us so I landed on his body while he lay on the bed. He kissed my lips, then down my arm and my hands, repeating his thanks and gratitude.

"You're making me blush," I said, fearing my ego getting out of control.

"If I'd known, if I'd thought to…" He shook his head, then leaned back against the pillow.

How many years had he been denied a simple touch because his creator didn't see the point? I nestled my cheek against his chest, hearing not a heart, but a faint ringing of bells. Tender fingers brushed against my cheek. "It was worth the wait."

"If someone said I had to live for thousands of years before my first orgasm—"

"Hundreds of thousands."

God, that made it so much worse. "I'd be pretty damn pissed."

"But it got to be with you, and I can't imagine anyone else being so kind and gentle with me."

I could picture hundreds of women, witches even, more than happy to throw themselves on that soul-shaking orgasm grenade. Garavel swept his hands over me, holding me close, and I shook off my doubts. *There's enough bad in this world. Just enjoy a minute of good. Okay, more like an hour of fantastic.*

"I was going to leap into the abyss after I killed Conquest."

What? Garavel's revelation caused me to jerk up, but he pressed me tighter. "It's what is expected of a demi-angel who's broken his oath to his creator."

"Garavel, please, there's so much to…"

"I have lived a thousand lives, in a way. I've helped to create this world."

Tears burned in my eyes and I tried to shake them away before he saw. "Why are you telling me this?"

Was that on his damn bucket list? Lose virginity. Save the universe. Then die? No!

He pulled in a breath and brushed his finger against my cheek. I raised my eyes to look at him. "Because —"

Ten pounds of black fur leaped from the floor and onto his chest. Garavel chuckled as Fiona kneaded her biscuits on him before curling up to sleep. With one finger scratching her slumbering form and his other hand holding me, he whispered, "Because I was wrong. My duty, my oath is to you. Layla, will you…?"

"Yes! Whatever it is, yes!" I leaped up and kissed him, trying to silence the foolish thoughts of honor in his head. It wasn't until I had lain back down and was nearing the edge of sleep that I wondered. *What did I just agree to?*

Chapter Thirty-Two

Layla

Daniel sat next to my spell book, his fingers acting like the wind to turn a page. No one else paid him any attention as they gathered around the grill. Leaving behind the last of my coleslaw, I joined him.

"Did you find anything?"

He jerked, nearly springing into the air before placing a hand to his chest. I glared at the jacket above his heart, but no blood seeped out. Even so, I had to do everything I could to keep him from thinking he was alive. A slow smile wound up his lips and he swept back his hair.

"Perhaps. No other way to break into hell, I'm afraid. I guess we're stuck waiting until the first Horseman plucks another demon out to get the blood."

I frowned and clenched the vial hidden in my pocket tighter. I wasn't going to keep it from him, only wait until we were safely behind reinforced walls.

"But look at this." Daniel pointed to an excerpt in the book.

I had to step around the giant log to peer down. He stood behind, the crispness of his form fighting off the sear of the nearly-June sun. It took me blinking a few times to get the words right.

He beat me to it. "Demon's blood combined with an angel's feather can create almost limitless options."

"Such as?"

"I mean, this reads more like a witch's speculation but she seemed to think that one could close the realms off entirely."

No more dangerous creatures leaking through. No more spending all my waning free time risking near death to stop them. Would that also mean no more magic?

"Though, I suppose if one can close a door, it's just as easy to open it."

White. Was that what he wanted? Were the touchstones a backup? Or did he have even greater plans for the demon?

I clenched my hand tighter around the vial—a mother viper guarding her nest. He'd take it, along with the feathers, if he knew we had them. I couldn't tell anyone. I...

Daniel's winsome gaze drifted from my spell book to the guitar. "I can't move it anymore. Not even a string."

That's good. The less he could manipulate, the longer he'd remain whole and with me.

"I'm sorry." He blinked, his deep eyes glistening with unshed tears. "Your song will have to wait a bit longer to finish."

"Use me," I said, holding out my hands.

"To write your own song? That will ruin the surprise."

"Not... I mean, when you want to play. To do something. I shouldn't be so stingy. You're a piece of my life, too, Daniel. As vital as everyone else."

He gazed at the others, Ink gossiping with Garavel, Cal awkwardly standing next to Fariah and Maram. A soft sigh escaped him and I leaned forward. There was no resistance, but a chill shivered against my forehead and I closed my eyes. "I have the blood."

"What? How—?"

"Eyes, ears..." I looked up and watched realization dawn. He closed his mouth and nodded.

"This. Layla, we could do so much with..."

"We can bring you back. It's all we want. Everything else, there's another way."

Daniel snickered and nodded, his ghostly forehead slipping through mine. Reaching out, he took control of my hands. I turned with him, both of us bending over to pick up the guitar. The scrape of my thumb over the strings stung deeper than before and I winced.

"How long does it take to grow a callus?"

"With luck, before I can play for you." He nuzzled against the back of my neck, only the chill of his body caressing me. I leaned back, giving in to the song. The sound drew the others over to investigate.

Cal popped a leg up on the log and shouted, "Do you take requests?"

Ink slapped him on the back, causing his mountain of hot dogs to go rolling. "The eternal silence of the grave?"

"Layla, you're sounding..." Fariah began to compliment me, when her flame genie girlfriend leaned over and whispered. "Oh. Um, it's lovely."

Daniel finished the song and, together, we returned the guitar to the ground. Once I got home, I'd find him one, anything to give him a taste of hope before we finished the spell. He began to slip from my hands, his cool touch traversing out of my fingers and up my arms. Before he went, he whispered in my ear, "Until I can strum you myself."

Oh, boy. I dipped my head down, trying to hide the blush, and when I raised it back up, it was directly into Ink's smirk. "Why are you so happy?"

"There are free libations," he said, raising up the cheap beer. "A warmth upon my taut flesh." For that he placed a hand to his stomach, the buttons parted to draw all the eyes to a new tattoo that pointed directly to his favorite feature. "And you've clipped the angel's wings."

I frowned in confusion.

"Polished his halo? Mounted his miter? I had more, but thought the wing one the best."

I clamped onto his arm and pulled him closer. "How do you know that? Did he...?" Those two were thick as thieves — it shouldn't surprise me.

Ink glanced over to Garavel, who was holding a hot dog bun full of whipped cream — one of Ink's creations — and laughed. "My bond, give me some credit. Your desires are positively pulsing."

"And yours are as plain as the horns on your head." I snickered, reaching up to flick the empty air where they should be.

"Do I wish to debase you in a den of sin, then watch the angel purify you in his muscular arms? What demon wouldn't?" He laughed as if all his dreams had come true, but we hadn't talked about what came next.

"Ink, when I... After we'd, I'd used the l-word —"

"My bond, cease your concerns. I am as committed to you as the shackles upon my wrist require."

"Then you...?"

"Are not as flighty as the common man who'd flee into the night upon hearing such devotions."

He wouldn't say it. He'd never say it because, as Ink kept insisting, demons didn't do love. Though sometimes they sacrificed themselves for a person they were devoted to.

"Babe!" Cal called, partly fleeing from Fariah no doubt peppering him with a thousand werewolf questions. He wrapped a hand around my arm, pretending to be out of breath before popping up to kiss me. "While it's been...an exhausting vacation, I can't wait to get back home."

His going-along shields were up, but I didn't play. I wrapped my arms around him and held him tight. For a moment, he hung there, as if wanting to fall back to what protected him. Slowly, he lowered his arms, clenching me safe in his embrace.

"I'm never letting you go," I promised.

"Me either, except for class...and work."

Shit. My arms went slack and I tried to look away, but Cal locked his hold in. "I mean, maybe in class if the professors don't care. Clinicals could be hard. I have no idea how—"

"I quit."

"What?"

"Bellpeppers. I asked for the week off, they wouldn't give it to me and I...I quit on the spot. Without a damn thought to what I'd do for money. I don't know why. I just, every little thing kept building and I knew that—"

Cal pressed his forehead to mine, silencing my babble. "Babe. It's okay. Whatever you need, I'm here.

We all are. Right, guys?" He raised his hands up for the others.

Ink was first to swoop in, nuzzling his cheek to mine as his hand swept…straight to my ass! I almost leaped in place when a cooler touch slipped through him. Ink shifted his hand higher but grumbled about the dead chaperone. I peered to the side for Garavel. He stood the odd man out, staring warily at Cal before looking to me.

Tossing his plate away, Garavel swooped in, locking off the giant hug with me in the middle of all of them. A blush burned across my cheeks and I tried to hold them back. "I love you," I whispered, meaning it for all.

"You guys did a good job. This place's all ready to open, and…what's with the huddle?" Dante jerked a thumb to us, breaking up the momentary love-fest.

We broke apart as if it hadn't happened, Garavel and Cal distancing themselves, Ink laying claim to my hips and Daniel moodily drifting back. But for a minute we were all on the same page.

"Nothing. What were you saying?" Fariah prompted, barely hiding her smile.

Ink kept tugging on me, guiding me to sit on his thighs while he plunged to the trunk. Cal popped up a leg on his left, then Garavel hurried to the right. Daniel drifted behind as we all turned to Dante.

He stopped wiping off his hands and shrugged. "Just that, it's done. Camp's ready to go. So you've got the last two days to kick back. Why don't we spend it at the beach?"

"No!" everyone shouted at once.

"Uh…" Dante blinked and nodded at the massive force of seven traumatized people. "There's go-carts up the road instead?"

Laughing, we all agreed to a couple of rounds of racing then mini golf. For the next two days, we could all pretend we were in love and the world wasn't about to end. It'd be paradise.

Epilogue

His chest ached after lying on it for five hours, but Stone caught a flash in the distance. That was either the signal or another seagull had stolen a bag of chips. Sliding closer to the scope, he pressed his eye to it and gently turned the lens.

It was impossible to miss the man in white even at five hundred yards. He glowed against the marina's turquoise waves, yachts of unsavory types bobbing behind. The twins he talked to were known, a pair of rich idiots with more money than brains. No, what surprised Detective Stone was the door to the boat opening and a woman in a long red dress stepping out.

A giant crimson hat hid her face, only showing a tumble of long blonde hair resting on her shoulder. "Come on." She took the hat off just as the yacht bobbed, yanking them out of focus.

Stone struggled to adjust the lens in time. White stepped in front, disguising her, but he'd been trailing

Conquest since New York and wasn't about to let up now.

One of the idiots cracked a joke, no doubt at the lady's expense. He laughed uproariously. His twin started to join in when the woman's hand lashed out. She clenched his throat and, as the sun glinted, her skin peeled back to reveal the unmistakable flesh of an incubus.

Lilith is working with Conquest, as feared.

Stone's cell rang. He shifted at the noise, setting the scope off course. After re-aligning it, he caught the rich idiot's body tumbling overboard and the two moving the meeting inside. He'd have to reposition to catch their return.

"Yes?" he said the second he answered the call.

"Detective Stone," dispatch's detached voice said.

"Do you require my passcode or can I keep doing my job?"

"You asking that's enough. Check your phone. You've been sent images of a suspected witch, powerful and dangerous."

He pulled the phone from his ear and scrolled to find a candid image of a woman in a bikini lying on the beach. "Dispatch, there's some mistake. I got a vacation..." His mouth dried as he zoomed in on the face, her eyes hidden behind the sunglasses. But he knew they were a deep brown. Stone saw them every night on the edge of sleep.

"Name?" he asked.

"Unknown. Find and contain her."

He pursed his lips and tried to focus on the picture. As he zoomed in, his finger trembled and he accidentally caressed her face.

"Understood," Stone said and killed the call. After dropping the phone to his stakeout towel, he reached into his bag. Clenched in his palm was a small keychain of a black kitten in a witch's hat.

"Well, Leeland. I guess it's finally time we meet...again."

Want to see more from this author? Here's a taster for you to enjoy!

Coven of Desire: Thorns
Ellen Mint

Coming August 2023

Excerpt

Stone

None of this is right.

No matter how hard I stared at the data, none of it made sense. Conquest arriving here was an ill omen, but unsurprising. He'd been assumed to resume his activities to a world-encompassing crescendo thirty years prior. What had me snapping pencils at my desk were the known accomplices. He'd only worked with humans before. Now there were demons, werewolves and sins approaching his known residence at all hours.

Why?

"You're gonna give yourself eye cancer."

I didn't jerk at Detective River's booming shout.

"That's a myth," I said, sitting back in the office's ergonomic chair and closing my pile of notes.

River picked up one of my pens and gnawed on the end. "Maybe that's just what they want you to think."

We'd worked together for nearly ten years, and I had yet to learn his first name. It was easier that way.

Besides, I didn't need a name to know the make of a man. He was infuriating with his conspiracy theories, but solid in the field. I could deal with a laugh about the earth being pomegranate-shaped as long as he had my back.

"Wha' ya working on?" he asked, his drawl slipping out. Those years of training to suppress any hint of our individual history had never seemed to take with him. "Conquest? Really?"

"He is a being of unimaginable power. I am keeping tabs," I said, locking down my computer to the best of my ability while being aware of the IT djinn that watched over everything.

"And Zimmerman told you to cut it out."

Even if other agents were trailing Mr. White, there was no reason to not have all hands on deck. Besides, the distraction kept me too busy to deal with other matters. As I gathered up the broken pencil bits, I noticed the middle folder in my stack. In the day's shuffling, a bikini picture had fallen out.

"Who's this?" A hand lashed out from behind and snatched up the image. I spun in my chair to find Drake leering at the image of a potential witch in a very form-fitting bathing suit.

On the back of the cheap printing was an old form for a ghost exorcism. We tried to recycle even while keeping everything as physical as possible. I focused on the line about telling the home owner to leave a salt circle outside the door instead of Drake's sharpening eyes. "They let you keep naughty pictures around, Stone? That's not fair."

"It is not—" I ripped the image from his hand, tearing it at her neck in the process. "It's for the job." Returning it to the pile, I slammed the folder to the back of my in-pile, which I should have done earlier.

"You telling me that's a green skin?"

"Potential," I said.

He whistled without a care, setting off the werewolves in the maul tank. "If she turns out to be a wicked witch, I call dibs."

My hand found its way into my pocket. I didn't realize until my palm clenched around the familiar curves of the scuffed-up keychain. No one else remembered her. Perhaps an occasional flash of familiarity would appear in their eyes, but no one knew her name. No one knew she'd escaped from our labyrinthian jail and fled into the night. No one but me.

"You can't call dibs," River argued back.

Drake glared at him. "What? You think you got a shot? She looked pretty young. Gonna need someone to fill her up soon."

"You cannot stake a claim when the Council will decide where to use her." River set down the chewed-up pen and turned from Drake.

Drake pried at my folders hunting for the photo. "I wouldn't need long to get the job done."

He jerked when I slapped my hand down on his. "That's a boast certain to send all the girls running," I countered. "If you will excuse me, I have work to get to."

River nodded, then told me that, should we need to head out, he'd be ready. Drake pouted. "We need to fill you with tequila and set you loose. Work that two-by-four out of your ass."

Pinche mamón.

As I turned my back on the idiot, both he and River stood at attention.

"Gentlemen."

The voice caused me to leap to my feet without question, slamming the pull-out keyboard into my thigh. I ignored the pain with a smile and faced Director Zimmerman as he hustled through the open office. An unknown woman in the same black suit and skinny tie walked just behind him. He slapped Drake on the back and pointed a finger to his office suite. "We've got a meeting. Spur of the moment. Just bring your ass...and a pen."

Drake nodded, took the director's hand in his and shook it. Zimmerman stared with a laugh perched on his lips. He didn't let it go, but he looked over the brown-nosing man to me. "Stone? You made any progress on that witch?"

"Ah...not yet, sir."

"It's been a month."

I frowned deeper. This farce couldn't go on much longer. I'd either have to pull her in for a second time, and do an encore to our song and dance, or dispose of her on my own. "I'd prefer to be thorough and slow, than quick and fail," I said.

Zimmerman smiled and slapped me on the back. "Good man. Come on. We've got a lot to talk about."

As I tugged open my drawer for my notebook, my gun rattled to the front. For a brief flash, I almost reached for it. My heart pounded in my ears as I stared at the cold steel, but I wouldn't need a gun for a meeting. We were Animal Control, not the NRA. Closing the drawer and leaving my piece behind, I followed Drake and River into the chief's office.

The last time I'd been here, we were fighting off a complete containment disaster. One we still hadn't determined the cause of. My gaze darted to the secret escape hatch behind the director's desk when the mystery woman stepped in front of it. She folded her arms and tipped her head low enough the plain sunglasses slid down her nose. Eyes of purple burned at me.

Strange. Not without precedent for the AC to work with creatures in disguise. But it was also highly rare.

"A-hem," Zimmer coughed. The woman shoved her glasses up with her middle finger and fell back into place.

"Please, take a seat," the director said, waving a hand to the two chairs. There were three of us, but River slipped in beside the woman without pause. Almost as if he knew this meeting was going to happen.

And he didn't think to tell me? Rude.

"Sir, if this is about the incident in the break room, I can assure you that Rusalka came on—"

Zimmerman raised a hand to silence Drake. "This is a matter of utmost secrecy. What I am about to reveal cannot leave this room. Understand?"

I flipped to the level-five-clearance pages of my notebook. They were charmed so only my eyes could read it. Jerking my head, I held my pen poised above the pages. "Ready, sir."

He did not launch into his laundry list of requests. Instead, he gazed down at me with an expression I'd never seen on his weathered face. For as long as I'd known him, he'd had enough wrinkles to put a bulldog to shame. But they always lifted with a warmth and lightness, reminding me more of a grandfather than my *abuelo* did.

"Stone? Catch this."

I barely had a chance to drop my pen before he flipped a flat coin my way. It landed in the middle of my palm and a flush of pain burst up my arm. I kept my face neutral, using every second of training to hide the agony. Revealing the pain was an opening for most monsters, and some grew stronger from it.

"Sir?" I asked, my voice level even as my skin began to blister. Whatever charm this was, it was powerful.

Zimmerman reached over and plucked the coin from my palm. On instinct, I slammed it shut, but not before we both caught the oblong redness burned into my skin. He stared into my eyes and sighed. For a flash, his lips opened as if to speak, but the director pulled it back and pocketed the coin. He looked to the woman, who nodded.

I prepared myself to learn what was so dire. No doubt this had to do with Conquest and whatever he was planning. I held my pen above my notebook, ready for the answers.

In one fluid motion, Zimmerman extracted a silenced gun, held it to Drake's head and pulled the trigger.

"What!" I jumped, uncertain who to protect in that moment. Drake's brains splattered against River's suit, the man staring down at the gray matter staining his shirt. Before I could even pivot out of the chair, the muzzle turned on me.

It took all my focus to look up from the deadly metal pressed against my heart and into the eyes of the man holding it. "I'm sorry," Zimmerman said. The pressure struck first, then the sound. I collapsed backward, my body and the chair slamming to the carpeted floor. Pain spidered across my chest, my lungs filling with my blood.

No! Drake dead. River... Numbness leadened my limbs, but I could still dig my fingers into the ground. Tugging, I tried to pull myself as if I could protect him.

My partner of ten years wiped off the brains of one of our fellow agents and nodded. The director, the man that'd saved me from murderous creatures in my youth, pocketed his gun as if nothing happened. Cold seeped into my chest, the pain unbearable. I'd faced down the worst monsters the realms could throw at us, but I'd never known this agony that was ripping my lungs to wet tissue. Each breath filled them with more of my blood. And with every heartbeat, a small slug pressed tighter and tighter against the only organ keeping me alive.

Zimmerman scooped up my notebook stained with my blood and Drake's brains. He flipped through it before pocketing it. With a jerk of his head, he led the only two remaining people out the door. Before walking away, he said, "Tell Mr. White," and slammed the locked door.

No one would come in, not even if I screamed, but my voice was drowning in blood. I reached into my pocket, trying to find any salve to slap on the gunshot wound in my chest. My numb finger snagged on a ring, and I wrenched out that cat keychain. It flew out and landed in a puddle of my blood.

About the Author

Ellen Mint adores the adorkable heroes who charm with their shy smiles and heroines that pack a punch. She has a needy black lab named after Granny Weatherwax from Discworld. Sadly, her dog is more of a Magrat.

When she's not writing imposing incubi or saucy aliens, she does silly things like make a tiny library full of her books. Her background is in genetics and she married a food scientist so the two of them nerd out over things like gut bacteria. She also loves gaming, particularly some of the bigger RPG titles. If you want to get her talking for hours, just bring up Dragon Age.

Ellen loves to hear from readers. You can find her contact information, website details and author profile page at https://www.totallybound.com

Home of Erotic Romance

Sign up for our newsletter and find out about all our romance book releases, eBook sales and promotions, sneak peeks and FREE romance books!